FORGO  S0-BCL-954

Ed Greenwood

The Sword
The Knights of Myth Drannor Book III
Never Sleeps

The Knights of Myth Drannor, Book III

THE SWORD NEVER SLEEPS

©2008, 2009 Wizards of the Coast LLC

Published by Wizards of the Coast LLC. Forgotten Realms, Wizards of the Coast, and their respective logos are trademarks of Wizards of the Coast LLC in the U.S.A. and other countries.

Printed in the U.S.A.

Cover art by Matt Stewart
Map by Todd Gamble
Original Hardcover First Printing: November 2008
First Paperback Printing: May 2009

9 8 7 6 5 4 3 2 1

ISBN: 978-0-7869-5015-7
620- 21897740-001-EN

U.S., CANADA,
ASIA, PACIFIC, & LATIN AMERICA
Wizards of the Coast LLC
P.O. Box 707
Renton, WA 98057-0707
+1-800-324-6496

EUROPEAN HEADQUARTERS
Hasbro UK Ltd
Caswell Way
Newport, Gwent NP9 0YH
GREAT BRITAIN
Save this address for your records.

Visit our web site at www.wizards.com

FORGOTTEN REALMS

Ed Greenwood

tempore felici multi numerantur amici

To my loving lady, Jenny, who puts up with so much from me.

From The Knights Who Came To Shadowdale
by Ornstel Maurimm of Selgaunt:

Although they had beyond dispute saved the life of the wizard Vangerdahast, many lives, the loyalty of the Wizards of War, and the peace and stability of fair Cormyr, Vangerdahast's reward to these brave six was a hasty expulsion from the realm, for the Royal Magician suffered Cormyr to be beholden to none but himself.

Forth then they rode for Shadowdale once more, these six Knights of Myth Drannor.

They were led by Florin Falconhand, a handsome ranger, famed for saving the life of King Azoun Obarskyr. Noble and kingly of spirit was Florin, but as yet young and unsure.

The strongest blade among the Knights was swung by Islif Lurelake, a sturdy fighting lass of Espar, who like many a farm girl was quiet, level headed, unlovely, and large.

Among these adventuring companions, the Art was wielded by sleek Jhessail Silvertree, the smallest of the Knights, flame haired and beautiful.

The quieter of the two holy Knights was Doust Sulwood, priest of Tymora, destined to become Lord of Shadowdale. Like many wise holy ones, he watched and pondered more than he spoke.

The other holy Knight wielded a swifter, sharper tongue and was hight Semoor Wolftooth. As was customary among priests of Lathander, he would later take another name, Jelde Asturien, as he rose in service to the Morninglord.

The most lawless and experienced of the Knights was the only one among them who had not been reared in Espar: the shapely, sharp-eyed, and sharper-tongued thief who preferred to be known only as Pennae. Her wits delivered her younger companions from trouble almost as often as her shady deeds plunged them into it.

Six bumbling adventurers, notorious in Cormyr but unknown outside it—and heading out of the Realm of the Purple Dragon as fast as Vangerdahast could urge them along.

MAP OF CORMYR

Prologue

I t all began with the gruesome murder of Ondel the Archwizard, whose various pieces were found on many stoops, porches, and thresholds up and down Shadowdale.

Or perhaps it began with the finding of the legendary, long-hidden hoard of Sundraer the She-dragon.

Or then again, mayhap it started the night Indarr Andemar's barn exploded in stabbing lightnings and balls of green flame that soared up to try to touch the stars.

Or the morning the best woodcarver in Shadowdale, Craunor Askelo, discovered his wife was not his wife and that for years he'd been sleeping with something that had scales and claws when it wanted to.

Or a handful of days after Vangerdahast, the Royal Magician of Cormyr, had stood inside a dank stone castle sally chamber, seen the Knights of Myth Drannor provided with new mounts, armor, weapons, and much spending-coin by his command, gestured in the direction of the rising portcullis, and given them a firm order of his own: "Tarry within Cormyr no longer!"

Days that had been spent riding and discovering just how hard new saddles can be—and, despite what they looked like on maps, how astonishingly *large* the wilderlands of northeastern Cormyr were.

Not for the first time, Semoor rolled his eyes and asked, "Gods, will these trees never *end?*"

"Picture each of them as a willing wench, arms and lips opening to welcome you," Islif told him, her saddle creaking under her as she turned to smile. "And the ride will seem less endless."

Semoor closed his eyes, growled appreciatively a time or two, then opened them again to favor her with a sour look. He shook his head. "My aching shanks remind me that this is not the sort of ride I'd prefer to be endless."

"You fail to surprise me," Jhessail said in acid-laced tones of mock disapproval, running fingers through her red hair to rid it of some of the clinging road dust. A small cloud obligingly swirled away in her wake, causing Doust—who was riding there—to wince even more than she did.

Islif shrugged. Dirt had been their constant companion growing up in Espar—dust when dry, and mud when wet. Grime bothered her not at all. Little crawling insects, now, itching in intimate places . . .

Under the hooves of their patient mounts, the Moonsea Ride ran tirelessly on northeast, rising and then falling away again over gentle hill after gentle hill. Around it, as they rode, steadings grew fewer and fewer, and the scrub of abandoned fields and forests ravaged by woodcutters gave way to darker, deeper woods. Cormyr this might still be on maps, but much of it seemed unbroken wilderland, the road spawning small campsites at every trickling stream, but the trees otherwise standing dark and unbroken.

Pennae and Florin rode at the head of their band of six, peering watchfully into the forest shadows on either side. Florin's searching gazes were almost hungry.

Yet Vangerdahast's order had been both curt and clear. "Tarry within Cormyr no longer!" The Royal Magician wanted them gone out of the realm before anything *else* befell them and hurled trouble across Cormyr—or as Pennae had put it, "Gave us a chance to save the Forest Kingdom from itself, while nobles and war wizards dither, *again.*"

That sentiment had earned her one of the wizard's coldest, darkest looks and a slowly rising, menacingly silent finger pointing at the doorway beneath the risen portcullis—not to mention Purple Dragon patrols following them along the road, so far back as to be just clearly visible, for the first few days.

"Subtle, isn't he?" Semoor had asked everyone then. Several aching days in the saddle later, he stirred himself to ask, "So, are we fated to spend the rest of our lives riding out of fair Cormyr and not making it?"

"Avoid all inns," Doust said darkly, in the same grand portentous tones favored by priests of Tempus and of Torm, who often visited Espar.

Islif gave that feeble jest the sour smile it deserved, then turned and asked Semoor, "If I answer you, will you say nothing more about our journeying and progress until the morrow?"

The priest of Lathander winced. "Well," he said carefully, "I'll certainly try."

Pennae turned in her saddle to fling a single word back at him: "Harder."

That smoothly twisting motion made the arrow that sped suddenly out of the trees burn past her cheek without striking anyone.

The second arrow, however, hissed to catch her squarely in the ribs. Sinking in deep, it smashed her, sobbing, right out of her saddle.

Chapter 1
FOR THE GOOD OF CORMYR

Why, down the passing years, have so many
Purple Dragons died?

Why, every day, do courtiers in Suzail lie so
energetically?

And why have war wizards and Highknights alike
Slain so many, stolen so much, and destroyed so
much more?

Why, for the good of Cormyr, of course.

The character Ornbriar the Old Merchant
In the play Karnoth's Homecoming
by Chanathra Jestryl, Lady Bard of Yhaunn
First performed in the Year of the Bloodbird

Wizard of War Lorbryn Deltalon sat alone in the small, windowless stone room, staring silently at the carefully written notes spread out on the desk before him. He was no longer seeing what he'd penned these last few months. He was staring past his neat jottings and beholding memories.

Recent memories. A succession of pain-wracked, sweating faces belonging to a lot of tormented nobles. Every one of them staring back at him in wild, mouth-quivering terror.

All too often, the sharp-eyed, faintly smiling visage of the Royal Magician of Cormyr loomed up amongst them. Looking back at him mockingly, Vangerdahast's unreadable gaze seemed a silent challenge. No frightened nobleman, he.

Deltalon sighed and shook his head, seeking to banish the piercing stare of the great mage he served. Yet the weight of Vangerdahast's menacing regard refused to fade.

The veteran war wizard sighed again, passed a hand over his eyes, and tried to stare at the all-too-familiar curves and swashes of his writing. He did a lot of silent staring these days.

Ever since Vangey had set him this task. The slow and distasteful work of spell-slaying all the mindworms Narantha Crownsilver had put into the minds of nobles. Hopefully without killing said nobles or leaving them more furious foes of the war wizards than they were already.

Work that, time and again, left him sitting alone, brooding.

He had now only two nobles left to cleanse: Malasko Erdusking and Ardoon Creth. Young, handsome fools both, who would be improved by a little healthy fear.

Yet Deltalon had something else, now, too: grave misgivings about the whole matter.

At first, Vangerdahast had commanded several senior war wizards to visit the nobles the ill-fated Lady Narantha had infected and to use magic to slay the mindworms. When some nobles had been left witless or damaged in their wits and bitterly aware of it and one young lord had died along with the mindworm riding him, the Royal Magician had ordered the work to cease.

Yet that hadn't meant dealing with the mindworms was abandoned or unfinished. Rather, Vangerdahast himself had without warning taken over the task of "fixing nobles," abruptly and imperiously whisking himself to mansions and country castles all over the realm.

Vangey's visitations had gone on for most of a month before he'd just as abruptly summoned Lorbryn Deltalon and ordered him to use "all slow, deft care possible" to kill the mindworms still in the heads of a handful of remaining nobles.

Lorbryn Deltalon was a careful, loyal Wizard of War, and several other things besides, but he had never been a fool.

Vangerdahast, he strongly suspected, hadn't killed a single worm. Instead, the Royal Magician had altered their spell-bindings to make them obey him rather than the fell and vanished wizard who'd compelled Narantha to spread the little horrors. And, no doubt, he had commanded them not to gnaw away any more of the brains in which they dwelt.

In other words, Vangey had spent a little less than three tendays crafting a small army of nobles whose minds he could control whenever he desired—for the good of the realm, of course.

The few nobles he'd deemed the least useful—or perhaps judged any meddling with them would be suspected and sought after by wizards hired by their noble kin—he'd assigned to Lorbryn Deltalon for curing.

Deltalon knew he should be flattered. The Royal Magician absolutely trusted the loyalty of rather less than a handful of his Wizards of War—or anyone else. Laspeera, yes, and . . . well, perhaps no one else but Lorbryn Deltalon.

Yet therein lay the problem. For some time Deltalon had harbored growing misgivings about Vangerdahast's mental stability and loyalties.

The Royal Magician grew ever more glib and self-satisfied as bodies fell and rotted, years passed, and the realm endured.

A realm shaped more and more to Vangerdahast's liking. In the humble opinion of Lorbryn Deltalon—an opinion held only within the deep mind-shielding spell he'd found in a tomb all those years ago and ever since had kept secret from the Royal Magician and everyone else—Vangerdahast was increasingly likely to convince himself that only he was capable of ruling Cormyr for the good of all.

He might already have reached that conclusion. Wherefore Lorbryn Deltalon watched the royal family of Cormyr *very* carefully.

Sooner or later, if Vangerdahast was so deeply corrupted, he would work spells to make the Obarskyrs mere puppets, or have them eliminated—by "enemies of the realm" of course—so he could "reluctantly" take the throne.

Others held similar suspicions. Several of the elder nobles did so openly, daring Vangerdahast to confront them. The Wizards of War watched and listened to such nobles even more attentively than they spied on the other highborn of the realm—wherefore Deltalon and most other war wizards knew that many who suspected Vangerdahast of seeking the throne had found reassurance in the rebelliousness of the young Princess Alusair and Vangey's seeming tolerance for her willful nature.

Privately, Deltalon held a much darker view. In his opinion, Vangey was encouraging the tantrums and defiant escapades of the younger princess—and thereby happily allowing his grounds for a future argument (that the Obarskyrs had become unfit to continue ruling) to grow ever stronger.

"For the good of Cormyr," Deltalon murmured, staring unseeingly through the notes on the table before him.

He didn't want to think such thoughts.

He didn't want to *do* this.

Yet, for the good of Cormyr . . .

His lips twisted at that irony, but he found himself nodding and bringing one of his hands, clenched into a fist, down—slowly and softly—to strike the table. Deep reluctance would claw him with tireless talons, but he could stride on.

He, Lorbryn Deltalon, must make these last two nobles his own mind-slaves. Just in case. And he must do it deftly enough that Vangerdahast must not suspect the worms were in stasis rather than dead, and the nobles would have no inkling of what he'd done. Until the day came—and by the Dragon Throne, let it never come!— when he found it needful to awaken the worms and enthrall the two. Just two, not the dozen-some the Royal Magician commanded.

Of course. Hadn't Vangerdahast had years upon years longer than he to become truly evil and self-serving? Able villainy takes practice. . . .

He was strong enough to do this now. For the good of Cormyr.

No longer would he have to trust in a deep shielding spell that faded over time and needed to be cast anew. Now, he had the elfstone.

Small, pale, egg-smooth, and far more ancient than Cormyr. Deltalon had found the gem hidden beneath stones under poor old Ondel's rain barrel, when sent to investigate that archwizard's murder.

Deltalon had carefully neglected to mention it in his report to Vangerdahast, and he'd swallowed it that same night. It remained safely inside him, magically nudged out of his stomach into adjacent tissue, to lodge there behind rehealed skin, hopefully forever.

Ondel had almost certainly recovered it from the hoard of Sundraer the She-dragon—whom he had loved and been loved by, when she took human form—after her death.

Elves had fashioned and enspelled the stone long, long ago. Just which elves, where, and how, he would probably never know. It was enough to know this much: Lorbryn Deltalon could now cloak his innermost thoughts and memories from any mind-probe, spinning false memories at will to deceive Vangey's mind readings.

So if he was careful enough, deep shielding or no deep shielding, Vangey would never know what Deltalon thought of him—or what his oh-so-loyal Wizard of War was up to.

Hmph. Those secrets would be among the very few things afoot in the realm that Vangerdahast did *not* know all about.

Yes. It was high time the Forest Kingdom was protected against its sworn, too-powerful, far-too-tyrannical protector. A check on Vangerdahast's might; a first small step toward finding a balance.

Smiling ever so faintly, Lorbryn Deltalon gathered his notes together, rose, and headed for the door on the other side of which Malasko Erdusking waited fearfully.

One more scared noble, who'd forgotten what nobles must never be allowed to forget: For the good of Cormyr, we must all sacrifice a little.

"More wine," Rhallogant murmured to himself. "That's what I need, just now."

Yet he put off seeking it to continue pondering, not wanting to lose his quickening path of thought.

The Obarskyrs and their bootlicking Wizards of War worked tirelessly to rein in and frustrate the powers of all nobles. Everyone knew that.

Most nobles considered that reason enough to justify any amount of treason against the Dragon Throne, and Rhallogant Caladanter was proud to count himself among their number.

Getting caught meant an unpleasant death. Short of such capture, anything done to frustrate the decadent royals and the lawlessly skulking mages who served the tyrant Vangerdahast—the *true* ruler of Cormyr—could only be a service to the realm and all Cormyreans henceforth.

Long after Vangerdahast had been shamed and executed, the philandering King Azoun and his icy queen swept into "accidental" graves, and their two wayward daughters married off to nobles fit to lead the Forest Kingdom, Rhallogant Caladanter had every intention of happily standing among those "all Cormyreans henceforth." With gold coins bulging in his coffers and the good regard of fair ladies all across Suzail.

A little treason was a small price to pay for such a bright life in a brighter realm.

Few even among the nobility knew who he was, yet. The son of a minor upland noble, Rhallogant was young and only recently ascended to his title—and hadn't intended to be anything more than a wild young blade, enjoying the amusements of Sembia and perhaps Westgate or even fabled Waterdeep, for years yet. His father's trusty Firelord had changed all that early one morning; the war-horse had thrown Lord Caladanter and then had fallen and rolled on his longtime master.

Rhallogant intended to be a trifle more subtle than Firelord had been. For a long time he'd idly contemplated treason against the Dragon Throne—but like most young highborn schemers, he had done nothing but contemplate and talk over his contemplations with other nobles of like age and opinions, over copious fine wine.

Such indiscretions, albeit trifling, made Rhallogant wince now. Just how well did the war wizards know him?

He was far from the only noble thoroughly frightened by the fates of the Lords Eldroon and Yellander—vanished and widely rumored to have died under prolonged magical torment at the hands of the Royal Magician—and of Lord Maniol Crownsilver, also now gone from public view and said to have become a suicidal, empty husk of a man under the constant care of ever-vigilant priests and war wizards. Yet Vangey's skulkers would doubtless deal with more important nobles first, leaving the "young puppies" (as he'd heard a scowling senior war wizard refer to a rather noisy hall full of young nobles deep in revelry, which had included one Rhallogant Caladanter) until later. They might be moving down their rolls of the doomed toward his name even now.

Two of the nobles who'd so excitedly put their heads together with him over steaming larrack wine in that upstairs club in Saerloon were dead already, in a trade dispute in Westgate that Rhallogant didn't *think* had anything at all to do with a few whispers of treason. The knives that had killed them, wielded by professionals of Westgate, had been poisoned, and Lord Eldarton Feathergate had happened to be aboard a ship just gliding into Westgate harbor when those knives had struck. He'd found the bodies and had disposed of them, before any war wizards could poke and pry them with spells and uncover things they shouldn't.

Which left, aside from Rhallogant himself, just one other conspirator in this particular sordid little conspiracy: Eldarton Feathergate.

Dearest Feathergate. Useful, efficient Feathergate. Feathergate who knew far too much about Rhallogant's ambitions and current business. Tall, as swift-witted as a viper, and the sole son and heir of a highborn family just as minor—but far wealthier—than Rhallogant's own. Neither a fool nor an easy target, he.

Which is why only Rhallogant's most trusted bodyguard was good enough to kill Feathergate.

The bodyguard Rhallogant had just summoned with a firm, decisive tug on his private, personal bell pull. Boarblade would arrive in three breaths or less, as quiet and as impassive as always.

Not that it had been a bad plot, if he did say so himself. Frame Baron Thomdor Obarskyr, Warden of the Eastern Marches, as a traitor to the throne, portraying him as a jealous lout aided, goaded, and controlled by Vangerdahast. Set swords to swinging and nobles, Obarskyrs, and commoners alike to raging, with the intent of getting rid of Vangey and as many war wizards as possible. Many of those hated wizard spies would be butchered by common folk across Cormyr, led by one loyally outraged Rhallogant Caladanter, enthusiastically commanding his bodyguards to use their swords on these "traitors to the realm." He'd had those speeches written for *months*.

The third arrow glanced off Florin's shoulder as he was clawing at his shield buckles. It smashed the wind out of him and spun him around sideways, all in one whirling instant.

He reeled in his saddle, fighting to find breath enough to shout hoarsely, "Spread out, ride hard, and *get down!*"

Around him the Knights' horses were snorting and bucking, Pennae a gasping heap in the road dust under their dancing hooves.

The volley of a dozen or more arrows sleeted out of the trees, sending two of the horses down to join Pennae. Another bolted with Doust shouting and tugging vainly at it to stop—until he fell off. The rest reared, spilling their riders, and fled.

The Knights found themselves wallowing in the dust of the Moonsea Ride in the company of two very large and pain-wracked horses, who were wildly rolling, writhing, and kicking.

"Holy naed!" Semoor swore, skidding his chin along rather stony mud as an iron-shod hoof lashed the air just above his head. "Down on my tluining face eating dirt with some tluiner trying to kill me *again!*"

"You sound surprised," Islif grunted, rolling hard away from the horses in the opposite direction from where the arrows had come. "Really, holynose, you should be getting used to it by now!"

Florin staggered to his feet, clutching at the arrow standing out of his shoulder. His arm felt on fire, and he couldn't feel the hand at the end of it at all, even when he clenched his fingers into a fist. The shaft had struck his chest and glanced along the armor over his heart to go in under the edge of his shoulder plates. The fire seemed to grow hotter. He winced. At least it wasn't his sword arm.

Taking a few steps, as if he could walk away from the pain, he snarled defiance at the trees, hoping the sudden lack of arrows meant that the unseen archers had run out of them.

It seemed he was right, judging by the armed men who answered his snarl by bursting out of the trees with swords and daggers drawn and nary a bow in sight. Much good that it would do him.

"Up!" Florin barked to his fellow Knights. "Up and together!" He spared not a glance for them, his eyes never leaving the grim faces of the men charging at him. They were all in well-worn fighting leathers adorned with no hint of badges or house colors. Outlaws—or men trying to seem outlaws.

Movement to right and left; the ranger shot swift glances in both directions and saw Islif clambering to her feet, her sword singing out, and Doust limping back to rejoin the Knights, mace in hand.

From her knees, Jhessail snapped out a battlestrike, sending magical missiles streaking at the ambushers in a hungry swarm of glowing blue darts. Men stiffened and cursed as they were struck—Cormyreans, by their accents—but none fell or fled. There were more than twelve of them . . . a score or so.

Florin wrestled with the arrow in his shoulder, trying to snap off its shaft before an outlaw could reach him and grab hold of it, but—

He was out of time. Swords came swinging at him in a steely rain.

He ducked away, parrying furiously, and heard ringing steel and Islif grunting as she did when putting real might behind a slash. More clanging and clashing of swords, then a shout of pain—an outlaw—and Jhessail unleashing another battlestrike. Semoor was casting something, too, calling on Lathander for aid in smiting.

Smiting was something Florin had to take care of himself. His blade bit deep into the side of a screaming outlaw's face, lodging in bone, and he couldn't—couldn't—

The swords that thrust into him then, under the edges of armor plates low on his side and high on his neck, burned like fire and chilled like a deluge of icy water.

Florin staggered back, dragging the man he'd slain with him—but the weight of that toppling body snatched his sword from his hand, leaving him with nothing to parry a grinning outlaw's wicked roundhouse slash.

"Die!" another outlaw shouted, hacking with the dagger Florin was trying to snatch out of his fingers. "For Cormyr and Yellander! *Die!*"

Those words echoed strangely around a rising, pounding dark flood that seemed to race through his ears, wash through his head, and back out to blind him as grinning men closed in, and fire and ice lashed Florin again . . . and again . . .

Not far away, Jhessail screamed as a hurled sword spun at her face. She ducked, and it tumbled through her hair, slicing open her cheek and catching fast in the tree behind her, still tangled in her hair.

Clawing at the enemy steel to get it away from her eyes, she saw Islif beset by six outlaws. One staggered and went down, sobbing and spraying blood—but was followed by several of Islif's armor plates that went flying aside as she reeled and then toppled, two swords buried in her.

Islif down, a bare breath after Florin's fall . . .

Muttering words that sounded more like curses than prayers, Doust clawed aside a sword and bounced his mace off the face of the outlaw wielding it, hard.

That face exploded into a burst of teeth and gore. Doust slammed his mace into the throat beneath it before whirling to meet a one-eyed outlaw who'd come leaping from the fallen Islif to hunt red-haired spellhurlers.

Almost casually the outlaw hacked Doust aside, her lifelong friend crumpling and spitting blood, and came right for Jhessail, swinging back his sword to chop—

Nothing at all, as Semoor swung away from busily battering an outlaw to the ground to bash in one side of the one-eyed outlaw's head. The man crashed to the ground, dashed senseless, his arms and legs jerking like fish flapping when pulled out of a river.

"Over here!" Semoor panted at Doust, who was still doubled up, one bloody hand clutching his stomach. "Over to Jhess, here, to stand over her, so she can either rescue us all with some bright spell or other . . . or we can at least die together. *Tluining* Vangerdahast! I'll bet he's behind this! Where's that Dragon patrol that was riding at our heels? *Hey?*"

Doust nodded but managed only a groan by way of reply, as Jhessail grimly clutched the sword that had arrived in her hair. She had no spell left that could deliver them from so many foes. Dark and dripping blood, her two friends loomed above her as they came together, back to back.

They were standing guard over her, for the last few breaths any of them were likely to take. Around them, on the dusty Moonsea Ride, their ambushers closed in.

Not hurrying now, the outlaws—or whoever they were—formed an unbroken ring around the last three Knights before slowly, in unison, striding closer.

White-faced, Jhessail stared at them. They looked back at her, showing their teeth in grim, unfriendly smiles.

Then with slow care, they closed in, cruel grins widening.

"Know any holy spells that'd be really useful about now?" Semoor shouted desperately over his shoulder.

"No!" Doust shouted back. "Do you?"

They stepped apart long enough to turn and stare at each other, as if some divine deliverance might be found written across the face of one of them for the other to discover.

Jhessail looked helplessly up at them, clutching the heavy and unfamiliar sword she so hoped she'd not have to try to use. They were going to die. Here, a few breaths from now. This wasn't some bardic ballad, where an improbable rescue would burst upon them all.

She could see that same realization in the faces of her two friends, as they peered at each other, found no up-any-sleeve escape . . . and let all hope drain out of their eyes.

"*Tluin!*" they snarled, in emphatic unison, and spun around to slam shoulders against each other once more. Waving their maces and staring at the battle around with empty, despairing faces, they prepared to die.

Telgarth Boarblade slipped through the study door, glided to a halt in front of his employer, and bowed, saying nothing. Aside from his eyes, asking an eager, wordless question as to how he could tender service, his face was an impassive mask. Rhallogant Caladanter might be an unobservant fool, but from time to time rather more sharp-witted folk had been known to visit him.

Boarblade already knew why he had been summoned and Caladanter's intentions regarding him, but he let nothing of that show in his expression or manner. Letting one's guard drop or getting careless had meant death long before he'd ever come to Cormyr and let the foolish young Caladanter heir "discover" him.

Caladanter was reclining in his favorite chair, one glossy-booted leg up on a footstool carved into quite a good likeness of a snarling panther. The decanter beside it was already almost empty, and the ring-dripping hand that waved that huge goblet so jauntily trembled visibly. Drunken sot.

"Boarblade," Rhallogant greeted him almost jovially, leaning forward like a bad actor broadly overplaying a sly conspirator. "I've a task for you. A dangerous task. A *secret* task."

"Lord?" Boarblade murmured, taking a step closer to signify that he heeded his employer's lust for secrecy, and bending forward to show how eager he was to hear the great secret that might be imparted.

"I need you to kill a man."

Chapter 2
WHAT TRAITORS ARE UP TO

. . . And if it should come to pass, between dragonslayings
Or late nights of downing fiery oceans of strong drink
In the hungrily enfolding arms of too-willing wenches,
That we for once have time to stop and use our wits,
Let there then be no shortage of matters to ponder.
In Cormyr, there never is; two things, at least,
They never tire of considering:
Whose bed lusty King Azoun will conquer next
And what these traitors, or those,
Are up to since this morn.

Sharanralee of Everlund
My Years With Blade And Harp
Published in the Year of the Lion

Kill a man, indeed.

If Caladanter had meant those words to shock his most trusted bodyguard, they failed to do so. Little wonder. This was not the first time he had ordered such a deed. Boarblade merely nodded and waited.

"You are familiar with Lord Eldarton Feathergate. His usefulness to me is ended. Go to Feathergate, slay him in a way that will *not* lead all the Wizards of War in the realm right back here, get away unseen, and return here promptly. The customary reward will be waiting for you."

Telgarth Boarblade had been able to control every muscle of his face for years. It was no work at all to keep the sneer off it now.

Customary reward, indeed.

Telgarth Boarblade knew the reward Caladanter intended him to receive upon his return wasn't the usual satchel of gold coins but a hail of arrows from a dozen waiting archers, whose work would leave no one alive who knew of Rhallogant Caladanter's treasonous intentions but Caladanter himself.

"And you would trust such a fool as yourself?" Boarblade murmured, in mild rebuke. "The rest of us are not the gaps in your armor, Lord."

Rhallogant Caladanter blinked at his bodyguard in disbelief. "Hey? Quoth you—?"

"Lord Caladanter," Boarblade said firmly, "the time has come for you to know one of *my* secrets."

The young nobleman was staring at him as if he had several heads, and he was going pale. Good.

"I am a wizard," the Zhent announced in a low voice, taking a step closer to Caladanter—who flinched as if his bodyguard had drawn a sword with a menacing flourish, instead of spreading his empty hands reassuringly, "but *not* a war wizard. Rather, I spy on the Wizards of War for the royal family. I serve the Obarskyrs."

Boarblade held up one hand in a "bide easy" gesture and added, "Yet the king does *not* hold your little plot against you. Rather, he sees it as your love of our fair land and anger at what is being done to it goading you into trying to do *something* to aid Cormyr. The king is saddened that like so many highborn of your age, you have been so misled by the villainous Vangerdahast as to think the royal family of Cormyr your foe. Not at all! The Obarskyrs consider themselves the prisoners of the Royal Magician and his sinister Wizards of War and want to make common cause with dissatisfied nobles against the scheming mages who have ruled the Forest Kingdom for far too long. The king has need of you, Lord Rhallogant Caladanter, and intends you for high rank at Court and much wealth and power, when the fell power of Vangerdahast is broken!"

Rhallogant Caladanter responded with impressive alacrity. Unfortunately, the only action he took was to drop his mouth open and gulp several times, like a hungry bullfrog too clumsy to catch flies buzzing around his tongue.

When it became obvious the now white-faced noble was unable to find anything intelligible to say, Boarblade continued.

"For years, I have been spying on the war wizards for the royal family. I *know* they are the true traitors in Cormyr, who have oppressed all highborn in the realm, letting the Obarskyrs take the blame—and goading angry lords into treason that Vangerdahast then uses as pretexts for further hampering the rights of all highborn. You know this too, if you think about it. Have the war wizards not recently suffered scandal after scandal, all involving self-interested traitors in their ranks?"

Boarblade paused to let Caladanter nod. The frightened young noble managed to do so. Eagerly and repeatedly he nodded, like some sort of string-pull toy, excited hope now joining the terror that had shone so starkly in his eyes.

By Bane and the deft hand of Manshoon, this weakling couldn't be trusted to aid the Brotherhood, even out of abject fear! So no hint of the Zhentarim must ever enter his head.

Boarblade pressed on. "Saying or doing anything against the Obarskyrs will only get you dead—unpleasantly, painfully, and *shamefully* so. And consider: Why have you contemplated disloyalty to the Dragon Throne? Not out of personal hatred for a royal family you have barely met, surely. No, you schemed purely to avenge slights done to the highborn of our Forest Kingdom and to wrest what power has been taken from nobles back into noble hands. Yes?"

Caladanter found his voice at last. "Y-yes!" he almost shouted, and then clapped a hand over his mouth in fresh fear, looking beseechingly at his bodyguard for acceptance.

Boarblade gave it to him, smiling the warm smile of an admiring friend. Young Lord Caladanter actually sighed in relief—as the lying Zhentarim thrust the collar that would enthrall him around the foolish lordling's neck and tightened it, hard and fast.

"So instead of marching yourself straight to a needless execution that will end the Caladanter line in disgrace, why not win back power for nobles and the Dragon Throne for the Obarskyrs and us all by working with me in *my* little scheme? A plot that has King Azoun's personal approval? I intend to eliminate a poisonous few Wizards of War, discredit the lot of them, and weaken their stranglehold on the throat of fair Cormyr. When King Azoun can truly rule from the Dragon Throne once more, he will need loyal officers and courtiers—and he knows he can find none better than the nobles of Cormyr. Not those with the longest, proudest lineages, nor yet those with the most coin to flash. Rather, he will look to those who aided him in the dangerous times when the shadow of Vangerdahast loomed over the land. To them he will grant power and high station and confirm the high regard all Cormyreans will hold for such brave men. *You*, Lord Rhallogant Caladanter, can be such a one."

His master blinked at him, downed most of his oversized goblet in one great gulp that left him reeling and blinking away tears, and gasped, "M-me?"

Boarblade nodded. "I have seen it in you, these seasons we've spent together. I *know* you can be among the foremost lords of Cormyr." He leaned closer to Caladanter and made his voice fierce with belief. "I know you deserve it!"

"I-I do?"

"You do," Boarblade decreed firmly, "and the time has come to prove it. Not to me, Lord; I already know your true worth. To the king, whose hopes rest in you, and who so long ago sent me here in hopes you would take me into your service, and so set you on the path that has led you here, this day."

Was it Oghma he should pray to for forgiveness, for wallowing so grandly in every last cliché? Or Deneir? Both, Boarblade decided, and for that matter Milil and a few more gods; they must all be snorting at this tripe he was talking.

But hold, the young lordling was finding his feet at last. Rather unsteadily. "C-command me," he gasped, eyes shining. "How can I best serve Cormyr?"

"Spare Feathergate and keep me close at hand henceforth. Take to bed and get some sleep; if you're too excited for slumber to come easily, have a drink or two. You must be alert and rested three mornings hence, when King Azoun's next orders will come to me."

"Done," Caladanter agreed, waving his goblet with a wild flourish that almost overbalanced him into a stumbling run into the nearest study wall.

Recovering, he gave Boarblade a wide smile, strode to the door that led into his bedchamber, and more or less fell through the opening, sketching a fanciful salute.

Idiot noble.

Boarblade watched the door slam and then listened to a faint series of crashes that marked the drunken lordling's progress toward his distant and grandiose four-poster.

"That went rather well," he told the snarling panther and settled himself into his master's favorite chair.

He cast another of the mind-prying spells the Lord Manshoon had taught him, which he used so often to spy on Caladanter's thoughts—shallow, boastful, and self-serving, most of them—to make sure his inspired young master wasn't hurrying to arrange the slaying of his hired assassin or to contact a Wizard of War.

Then he relaxed, allowing himself a sigh of his own. Young Rhallogant wasn't—instead, as expected, he was hurrying to drink himself into a stupor.

"Stout fellow," Boarblade murmured aloud, glancing idly around the study as he wondered what mischief he could most profitably pursue once his master was blind drunk and snoring. The rushing thoughts he was spying on grew both wilder and more confused as all that wine took hold.

Boarblade's gaze settled on a magnificent gilded map of Cormyr that he'd admired before. Grant young Rhallogant one thing: he had an impeccable taste in maps.

Boarblade clasped his hands together and stroked his chin with them. If he could just keep this now-leashed lordling from doing something so stone cold *stupid* as to draw Vangerdahast's attention to him, he could do a lot of damage to the Wizards of War.

And hasten the day when he could cast the spell that would bring him, in the depths of his own mind, face-to-face with the coldly approving smile of Lord Manshoon as he reported, "I have done it, Lord. The wizards of Cormyr are subverted, and their realm awaits your covert rule."

Not that he—unlike some nobles he could name, this one and others far older, who should know much, much better—was impatient fool enough to expect that day to come soon. No. Patience and slow, deft deeds and more patience. Step by careful step, until the destination becomes inevitable. Those who boldly leap tend to topple, hard and fast and fatally.

Lost in such thoughts, with the blurred glories of Azoun ushering dozens of bared, beautiful, and adoringly eager noblewomen of the realm into the waiting and deserving arms of Lord Rhallogant Caladanter, Telgarth Boarblade of the Zhentarim failed to notice something silent and stealthy rippling its way across the room behind him.

Something mottled and shifting in its shape. It looked like an old scrap of tanned boarhide that was somehow alive and able to grow its own tentacle-like arms that flowed continually into new shapes, yet tugged the shapeless thing along with menacing purposefulness.

Ghoruld Applethorn, had he still been alive, would have known it for what it was and would have been eager to learn just why the hargaunt, after keeping company with him in such evident satisfaction, had so abruptly left him somewhere in the Royal Palace of Suzail.

Yet a plot had failed, and Applethorn was dead, so there was no one to identify the hargaunt as it moved purposefully across Caladanter's study, unnoticed by Telgarth Boarblade. Gloating does take some concentration.

Silently the strange shapeshifting thing flowed up an ornately carved chairback, reared up to deftly shape a long, narrow tentacle—and thrust it, ever so delicately, into one of Boarblade's ears.

The Zhent stiffened and shivered, just once. Then, as the tentacle reached his brain, Boarblade's face went from astonished horror at being invaded to a calmer expression of interest, an expression that drifted into sharper, stronger interest—and then into a pleased exclamation: "Ho! *Well,* now!"

Then, slowly, Telgarth Boarblade smiled an evil smile.

Dark and scowling Brorn had been one of Lord Yellander's two best house swords, and tall, scarred Steldurth had been the other. A dozen armsmen each they'd commanded in Yellander colors.

"My bullyblades," Lord Yellander had called them all proudly, and he entrusted them with all his "dark work." Slayings aplenty they had done for him and had fetched drugs and poisons by the caravan-load out of Sembia to enrich him. Thefts, too, and spyings. There were the Dragon Throne's laws, and there were the handful of those laws that the Lord Yellander cared to respect.

The gap between had been the business of his bullyblades.

Until their lord's disappearance. Purple Dragons had come to the Yellander lands then, six or seven for every bullyblade, and Wizards of War had ridden with them. They had taken firm possession of Yellander's properties and wealth, notably barn after barn full of the unlawful drugs thaelur, laskran, blackmask, and behelshrabba—to say nothing of several coffers of poisons. Those barns, packed to the rafters, had been guarded by Yellander's bullyblades.

Not even an upland idiot farmer would believe their claims to have loyally served the Lord Yellander yet known nothing of what was in the barns.

Wherefore Brorn, Steldurth, and the rest of the bullyblades had found themselves out of work, unpaid, and under suspicion. Still angrily proclaiming their innocence, they had been exiled from the realm for six summers each—and marched to the Sembian border under watchful eyes.

It was Brorn who rallied them in a stable in Daerlun and slew the Cormyrean spy who tried to eavesdrop on their moot. It was Steldurth who emptied his own boots of coins to buy out the guards of a Suzail-bound caravan nighting over in Daerlun. It was Brorn, again, who found a few merchants in Suzail who wanted goods rushed north to Arabel and got a smaller caravan on the road again before any Wizard of War had time to grow suspicious. Whereupon it was Steldurth who sold the wagons and the plodding draft horses in Arabel, bought hardy remounts, and had the lordless bullyblades heading along the Moonsea Ride before a Dragon commander thought he recognized Brorn's face.

By the time that officer recalled a name to go with that face, the bullyblades were gone into the trees, and a higher-ranking Purple

Dragon was shrugging and telling the officer who'd confided in him that the bullyblades had probably stolen back into the kingdom just long enough to snatch one of Yellander's coin-hoards, ere heading for the Moonsea where they could be as lawless as their dark-booted little hearts desired.

That option always awaited, but Brorn and Steldurth loved Cormyr a little more than that. And hated the Knights of Myth Drannor a little more, too.

In their busy day in Suzail, they'd learned from a surviving Yellander spy at Court of the Knights' coming ride and the wealth the Royal Magician was about to hand them.

Brorn and Steldurth reacted to that news in the same manner, and together concluded it would be fitting revenge to slay the Knights, redeem themselves as loyal to the realm by claiming the Knights were butchering innocent upland farmers and merchants—murders they would do themselves, to gain coin, food, and goods—and relieve the Knights of all those coins, too.

So here they were, with only a handful of their foes still standing.

Brorn smiled. The revenge was going well. He threw up his hand to signal the ring of men should stop, closing no further.

"Spellhurlers, all of these," he said curtly to the best bowmen among the bullyblades, indicating the last three Knights. "Turn them into pincushions."

"You miss her, don't you?" Torsard Spurbright murmured, refilling his father's goblet.

Two summers ago he would have uttered those words in a fury, enraged that his sire's dalliance with the lady envoy of Silverymoon—and the old, old friendship they so obviously shared—amounted to an insulting spurning of his mother, the Lady Delandra Spurbright.

But then, two summers ago *everything* Lord Elvarr Spurbright said and did had infuriated or at least embarrassed Torsard. Now, he understood his father—and the ways of the world, or at least

Cormyr—rather better.

Now, he would have given almost anything to have an old friend he could trust as much as Lord Spurbright and the Lady Aerilee Summerwood trusted each other. And if that old friend could also be a lover . . .

And if he could have her—gods, if it was *he,* Torsard, the beyond-beautiful lady envoy wrapped her welcoming arms around and melted against! O, Sune and Tymora both, I would heap gold on your altars!—and still love and be loved by an unresenting wife . . .

Well, either women were far greater fools than he'd ever thought in all his green years up until now, or Lord Elvarr Spurbright was someone . . . remarkable.

He'd never thought past the resentment before, to try to really *see* his father as others might. Now that he was doing so, much as he hated to admit it, his father was, he supposed, rather remarkable.

Which made his son, Torsard Spurbright, that much more important. And more obviously the green fool, too.

"I do," his father replied, meeting his eyes with a level gray gaze that startled Torsard with its honesty. His father, speaking to him as an equal? Well, now . . .

Lord Elvarr Spurbright had always loomed large, dark, and a little terrible in his son's mind. The Great Forbidder who decreed this or that limitation on Torsard's behavior, yet was also the person whose approval the heir of the Spurbrights most craved. And found hardest to earn.

To step around that great darkness and look at the older man across the table as a . . . a fellow Spurbright, perhaps even a friend . . .

He found himself blinking at someone familiar, who at the same time looked utterly different.

For one thing, he'd never seen his father this melancholy before. Grim, yes, and snappingly angry many a time . . . but not this weary sadness that rode atop remembered joy.

He wanted the angry Lord Elvarr Spurbright back.

With that sire, at least, he knew where he stood. Cowering and disapproved of, but that was, at least, a familiar cloak.

Wherefore he tried again to lift his father's melancholy mood. The cause lay like a great silence between them, obvious to the entire household in the wake of Lady Summerwood's departure for Silverymoon.

Gods, his mother must love this gray-eyed man across the table so much to smile and embrace him so earnestly and often, last night and this day!

Yet she did, and he so obviously loved her, too, kissing her more fervently than Torsard could remember him doing for years. It was as if the lady envoy was a fire that warmed and then ignited those she touched, kindling them into little flames of their own in her wake.

Torsard shuddered in remembered lust, seeing Aerilee Summerwood again, sleek and beautiful, all catlike swirling grace as she turned her head, laughing.

He'd stood watching, shaking with longing but not daring to speak or step closer. His father had met his gaze and had seen the longing in his eyes, and he had done nothing but nod in silent understanding. Not condemning or mocking, imparting no hint of anger, just . . . understanding.

They were two men smitten by the same laughing arrow.

That smiling, dancing-eyed face, the lush, flawless body below it . . . Torsard swallowed hard and had to clear his throat twice before he managed to ask, "Will we . . . ever see her again?"

Again the level, direct look. "King Azoun," his father said carefully, "has promised to send me to Silverymoon as Cormyr's envoy to the Gem of the North, but 'twould not be seemly to do so before next spring."

"Send you," Torsard echoed, not knowing quite what he dared to ask.

"I will go nowhere without your mother by my side," Lord Spurbright said firmly. "Neither I nor she wishes to be sundered from each other, and the Lady Summerwood wants to see us both."

Torsard blinked, trying to imagine his mother abed with the Silvaeren lady envoy—and then trying hard *not* to imagine it.

"I'm sorry, Son," his father murmured. "You must keep the family banners high while we are away from home. However, envoys are housed differently in Silverymoon than here; visitors choose where in the city they wish to dwell, and the High Lady's purse pays for it."

Torsard frowned. "I—I don't follow you."

"Aerilee promised to help her dear friends the arriving Spurbrights find suitable lodgings," Lord Spurbright said gently. "If I were to send you to Silverymoon some months ahead of us . . . well, you *are* Lord Spurbright, too. You saw how approvingly she measured you."

"M-me?" Torsard knew he was blushing hotly and didn't care. Had she really?

His father nodded, ever so slightly, and smiled in a way that made Torsard suddenly grin and feel very warm indeed and want to be in Silverymoon right now. He settled for bringing his fist down on the table—gently, not with a crash—and asking, "You'll do that, Father? You promise?"

"On one condition. Having tasted of the lovely Aerilee, you return here at an agreed-upon time and start to become truly *Lord* Spurbright. My successor and head of our house. The gods, after all, might decide I'll die in Silverymoon, yes?"

"If you do," Torsard dared to say or rather said before he could stop himself, "I can guess how!"

Then he stopped, staring into his father's eyes, suddenly afraid—until the sudden, boyish grin that appeared flashingly beneath them swept away all fear.

"There are worse ways to die," Lord Elvarr Spurbright observed, apparently addressing the rim of his goblet. He went on staring at it for a long, long breath as his grin faded, and then shook himself and fixed Torsard with that steady gray look.

"However," he said, "let us be serious with each other now. You will be in charge of the affairs of House Spurbright in our absence. I want you fully mindful of what that *means*. Oh, the freedom to get drunk and spend imprudent coins on toss-skirts on more than one night, yes, but Torsard, heed me. It's time. You must now learn to be careful."

Torsard found himself a little nettled. His father seemed to be treating him as a sullen boy in need of reprovement again. "Careful, Father?"

"Watch out for Vangerdahast's plots. He'll be seeking to press the advantage he holds over us in the eyes of the common folk, that he does what is distasteful for the good of the realm, because we nobles shirk our duty. And why? Because all nobles are rich, sneering traitors who should be reined in, hard!"

Torsard spread his hands, feeling real exasperation. "And just how am I supposed to even *know* what old Thunderspells is up to? He works behind closed doors, and anyone who tries to peek past them, even with magic, gets their brains fried!"

His father nodded and replied calmly, "Watch where Purple Dragons are sent around the realm, and watch the Knights of Myth Drannor."

"The *Knights?* Exiled *adventurers?*"

"Son, son, hearken: They are the queen's pets, so Vangerdahast regards them as expendable weapons the realm is better off without. He may well succumb to the temptation to wield and even expend them. Moreover, the Knights are sought after because—as all the realm knows by now—they bear the Pendant of Ashaba. If they are slaughtered and the Pendant taken, it entitles the bearer to the lordship of Shadowdale."

Torsard sneered. "A northern dale? A few farms in the forest? Who—"

"And Shadowdale," his father interrupted, favoring his son with a tongue-stilling glare, "is a place Zhentil Keep has wanted to own for quite some time now. Establishing an open presence there will provoke our armies to march and Zhent-hunting Harpers to spring out from behind every tree, to say nothing of marauding elves and opportunistic Sembians and perhaps even a few fools from Hillsfar."

Torsard's answering shrug was smaller than usual. Though his father's face could be hard to read, he'd had a lot of practice in doing so and could tell he'd won some small measure of Lord Spurbright's approval. Just why, he wasn't sure. He knew he was now wearing the frown that always stole onto his face when he was thinking hard; perhaps that was why. "And so?" he asked, making that question far less of an insolent challenge than was his wont.

"And so when we all converge on the tranquil farms of Shadowdale, the beholders and mightiest mages of the Zhentarim, standing a safe distance from what they hold dear in Zhentil Keep, will take great delight in slaughtering us all and using our aggression as a pretext for all sorts of things."

"What 'sorts of things?' " Torsard could not quite keep the scorn out of his voice.

"Alliances with Westgate and Sembian interests to invade and conquer Cormyr," Lord Spurbright replied firmly. "*Those* sorts of things."

Chapter 3
Arrows and Tapestries

So is it to be arrows in my face?
Or daggers thrusting through
Tapestries into my back?
Always 'tis arrows and tapestries
As my blood spills, and I struggle
To go on serving the realm.

The character Graerus the Purple Dragon
in the play Land of Dragons
by Aunthus Durl of Westgate
first performed in the Year of the Spur

The bowmen among the bullyblades nodded to Brorn, plucked up arrows, and raised their bows. The ring of warriors around the Knights watched the archers and waited to stand aside to make way for their arrows.

Around the three Knights the air suddenly shimmered—seeming to surprise the Knights as much as the bullyblades—and a distant thundering rumble arose back west, along the road.

Brorn flung up one hand to prevent any arrows being wasted, and with his other hand he pointed west along the Ride. Steldurth was already striding in that direction, frowning and peering.

For a long way hereabouts the Moonsea Ride seemed both straight and level, but in truth it rose and fell as it mounted a succession of hills, sacrificing the wandering ways and gentler grades of many local lanes for a straighter, steeper route.

Up over the nearest of these now rose a line of Purple Dragons in full armor, visors down, riding their horses hard—straight at the bullyblades and Knights in the road.

"Glorking *war wizards!*" Steldurth spat, whirling around and waving his arms in alarm.

"Into the trees!"Brorn bellowed. "If you've a bow, scatter and hide—and loose at any war wizards you see! Everyone else, to horse! Mount and swords out, or they'll ride us down! Forget the Knights! *Move,* hrast you!"

The bullyblades moved. As Jhessail, Doust, and Semoor watched, not daring to abandon the little cloud of air that tingled and shimmered around them, their attackers scrambled for saddles or raced into the shadows under the trees.

The Purple Dragons came on, riding hard, the thunder of churning hooves growing. The Knights stared silently at that magnificent charge, until Jhessail cursed and tried to slither out from between the boots of the two priests.

"Stand fast," Doust snapped. "I have a spell that should turn aside the horses, if it looks like they'll ride right over us. Gods, look at them come!"

It was a scene right out of a fireside tale. Three ranks or more of mounted armsmen were all galloping shoulder to shoulder, armor gleaming and swords out. Two bore banners on long lances—and as they drew nearer, the bullyblades wildly shouting and hauling on reins as they tried to wrestle their own mounts out into the road, those lances lowered to menace the road before them with long, glittering tips.

Brorn took one look at those sharp points and the number of grim Dragons riding hard behind them, and he bellowed something the Knights didn't quite understand.

The bullyblades did, though. In the space of a swift breath they were galloping, too, fleeing east along the road with Brorn at their head and leaving the Knights—and their own bowmen, one of whom burst out of the trees to try to run after them ere he realized his peril and ducked out of sight again—behind, abandoned in swirling road dust.

Steldurth was at the rear of the bullyblades, spitting a steady stream of curses. He gave the Knights a glare as he spurred past, but—perhaps deterred by Semoor's ready mace and eager grin—didn't lean out from his saddle to try to carve anyone with his sword.

The Knights watched the hooves of Steldurth's mount rising and falling in the dust, as he and the rest of the bullyblades dwindled eastward.

Then the Dragons were upon them and thundering past in a racing horde of hooves, streaming manes and tails, and flashing armor.

There were six ranks of them—more than thirty riders, in all, with uncomfortable-looking war wizards bouncing on saddles in their midst—and the later ranks started to slow as they swept past the Knights, descending from gallop to canter and then to a trot, ere they started to circle back. Several Dragons sprang from their saddles, hefted their swords, and plunged into the trees, obviously seeking the bowmen. One of the war wizards, his reins held by Purple Dragons riding on either side of him, cast some sort of spell that made lights flare brightly amid the trees. Those lights moved swiftly and stumbled and cursed, running blindly into trees or branches until the Dragons reached them—and their running and cursing swiftly ceased.

The last light was dragged out onto the road. It proved to be a disheveled bullyblade, arms held out from his body and his head obscured by a blinding whorl of light.

"No strangle-binding," a thick-necked Purple Dragon lionar ordered curtly, "and no 'accidents.' This one is to be kept *alive* for questioning."

Then he turned to peer at Doust, Semoor, and Jhessail. He waved his hand imperiously at the young war wizard riding beside him, who nodded and murmured something.

The shimmering shield around the three Knights faded, leaving the Knights staring into eyes that were as steel gray as the lionar's sparse hair—and held just a hint of weary amusement.

"Is fair upland Cormyr so devoid of interest," he asked almost tauntingly, "that you must swing swords for entertainment in the middle of the King's High Road? Or does being an adventurer demand your participation in a certain count of hopeless battles each month?"

Jhessail, who had risen to stand between the two priests behind Semoor, promptly bit Semoor's ear, and as he flinched in startlement said into it, "Whatever cleverness you're thinking of uttering in reply, don't. Nor yet the second witty thing that rises to mind. In fact, just leave the talking to me."

Not waiting for a reply, she grounded her sword, met the lionar's eyes, and told him, "We *personally* receive our orders from the Dragon Queen and are knights of the realm. As well as entertainment-starved adventurers."

The amusement in those gray eyes grew stronger. "Ah. That must be why we were given orders to see you *safely* out of the realm. Are any of you three hurt? Or can our healers get straight to work on the others?"

War wizards were busily vanishing through the row of tapestries at the back of the Griffonguard Room when the princess entered. They were hurrying under the lash of the Royal Magician's tongue, and he was spitting orders in a tone and at a rate that made it clear he was *not* in a good mood.

Alusair wondered briefly what had gone wrong in the realm now, and then decided she really didn't care one whit. She saw Vangerdahast start to turn in her direction, and she swiftly drove an imperious finger into the ribs of the Palace herald.

Who announced hastily yet grandly: "The Princess Alusair Nacacia Obarskyr!"

No one reacted in the slightest, but Alusair had expected that. She had also expected that Vangey wouldn't bother to hide his annoyance at her appearance in his ready chamber. He didn't.

"Princess," he greeted her with a curt nod, "to what do I owe the pleasure of your—?"

He didn't even bother to finish the sentence but devoted himself to glaring at the herald until that courtier bowed hastily and withdrew—as far as the spot where Alusair's hand clamped fiercely down on his forearm. "Attend *us*, herald," she said loudly and merrily. "By our royal command, we require your presence with us a breath or two longer, to bear witness to what follows."

Vangey had still not even bothered to meet her gaze. He

transferred his glare from the herald's back to the war wizard shadowing Alusair. He was one of an endless succession of silently polite escorts that Vangerdahast had assigned, seemingly to her elbow, to attend her every waking moment and report back to him everything she did. Every careless word, break of wind, and nose-picking moment. *Gods*, she hated wizards. This glaring one in front of her right now in particular.

"Royal Magician," she said, before he could speak again and so control the converse, "we have personally come to return this Wizard of War who hath so ably and attentively attended us. He is polite and capable and hath offended us not at all, but his presence at our side every waking moment is no longer required. Cormyr needs his services—and those of *all* the war wizard escorts you so kindly have seen fit to provide us with, these days past, *far* more than we do. Now that we have our own personal champion, approved of by both our royal father, the king, and our royal mother, the queen, to protect our person and attend our every need."

Alusair delivered one of her sweetest smiles to the glowering Vangerdahast. She had determined beforehand that no matter what befell, she would remain oh-so-sweet during this confrontation, because if she lost her temper she lost everything in the fires of Vangerdahast's sneering satisfaction at her—what had he called them? Oh, yes—"immature inadequacies."

Vangerdahast slowly raised an eyebrow in the manner of a man condescending to humor a young fool. "Your Highness, this welcome news puzzles me, in that I am utterly unfamiliar with anyone suitable for such an important office, who is not already fully engaged in tasks vital to the realm. As Court Wizard it is imperative I know the identity of such a personage, to prevent loyal war wizards from destroying him—or her, I suppose—in their zeal to defend your person. So this, ah, champion of yours would be—?"

Oh, but the man was a right *bastard*. Alusair clawed at her rising temper with both hands. Seeing by his smirk that her color must already have heightened, she said, "Ornrion Taltar Dahauntul, better known to all as 'Dauntless,' has been named our personal champion. Ably protected by him, we shall no longer have any need of war wizards, to say nothing of their heavy-handed authority—or yours."

Her words fell into a sudden icy silence.

Two war wizards who'd just shouldered into view through separate tapestries froze, staring at the princess. The herald trembled beside her, and the tingling of the ring-shielding that Alusair had awakened as she swept through the Palace told her the war wizard escort had stepped behind her—no doubt to hide himself from Vangey's fury—and was shaking, too, probably with mirth.

Then, with a shivery little thrill of fear, Alusair realized she had succeeded in enraging the Royal Magician.

"No, Princess, your conclusion is unacceptable," he said. "Dispense empty titles if you feel the need, but your doing so can *not* affect my deployment of our loyal Wizards of War. Your survival is vital to Cormyr, wherefore your escort must remain on duty by your side. May I remind you that ruling is not a *game?* As your longtime tutor, I urge you to reconsider your behavior, and as Royal Magician of Cormyr, I order you—for the good of our Forest Kingdom—to return to your senses."

Alusair stared at him, fighting not to cower before the anger now bright and clear in his eyes. She forced herself to take a slow, leisurely step toward him.

"Tell me, mage," she said, abandoning formal pronouns because they were unfamiliar fripperies her tongue could all too easily stumble over, and she *had* to do this right. "Which of us in this room has royal blood in her veins and therefore a *right* to order the realm and so give orders to citizens of it—and which of us is an overbearing tyrant of an old man who wields just as much authority as we Obarskyrs let him have? Royal Magicians outlive their time and overreach their rightful authority, just as the gods tempt us all to do—and wizard, you long since ran out of yours, on both counts!"

Without waiting for a reply, proud that her voice had sharpened but neither risen into a shout nor ascended into querulous tones while speaking her last few words, Alusair turned away—and so of course found herself facing the white-faced herald and the open-mouthed and staring war wizard escort. "So *this* little matter has been decided," she told them and treated them to a brief, bright smile. "Well and good."

She swept out, leaving a trembling-with-rage Vangerdahast staring after her.

He did not have to say a word to make the herald and the war wizard escort both bolt after the princess. They almost collided in the doorway in their haste to be out of the room. Tapestries roiled and billowed as the other two war wizards plunged back through them, leaving the Royal Magician alone in the room, glowering at an open doorway.

He was not alone for long. Laspeera emerged from behind one of those busy tapestries so promptly it was obvious she had been eavesdropping. "She's right, you know," she murmured, taking care not to smile.

The look Vangerdahast favored her with was as sharp as a dagger, but Laspeera stood her ground, uncowed.

"In one thing, Vangey," she added. "You *are* getting old. Years back, you'd never have let any Obarskyr's behavior get you this angry."

"Angry, lass?" Vangerdahast snapped. "You misunderstand me. I'm just enjoying getting my blood up. Our Alusair at last is growing a backbone and turning into someone it's going to be *fun* crossing swords with—just as the realm needs her to be! *That* is my life's work, forget not!"

He started to pace. "First, this Dauntless—this conspirator for a young princess to work her mischief with! We must remove him far from her feckless royal grasp, faster than immediately. A good long mission elsewhere, of course . . . and as it happens, I have just such a task going begging. Bring him here."

Laspeera nodded. "By your command," she murmured sardonically, as she slipped back through the tapestries.

Her tone made Vangey flush—but he found himself glaring around an empty room.

"Overbearing old tyrant, am I?" he said, striding across the floor. A wall loomed up before him, and he spun around abruptly and marched back, pausing mid-stride to twist a ring on one of his fingers and announce to the empty air, "Tathanter Doarmund, make ready both the Halfhap portals and six horses—the latter with full field provisions, tents and all. You'll be escorting the six riders from the east doors of the Griffonguard Room to the portals, so after you've seen to those matters, I'll want you waiting outside those doors just as fast as you can get there."

Wizard of War Tathanter Doarmund's reply was inaudible from halfway across the Palace, but Vangerdahast heard it and turned again, nodding ever so slightly. *Some* folk in the realm still obeyed him with alacrity, it seemed.

It seemed doubly so, a moment later, when the open doorway showed him a sternly expressionless Ornrion Taltar Dahauntul marching toward him, with Laspeera striding along a pace behind.

Vangerdahast took a stance before the tapestries, matching the soldier's expressionless look, and waited. As Dauntless strode into the room, Laspeera softly closed the doors behind him, shutting herself out.

When the ornrion halted before him, Vangerdahast tendered a bright smile and said, "A mission has arisen that requires your amply demonstrated capabilities, Ornrion Dahauntul. You are to shadow the Knights of Myth Drannor, see that they truly leave Cormyr, find out where they go, and report back their location, wherever in Faerûn they may be, when they show signs of settling down somewhere. If they split up or get involved in potential treason against the realm, you are to send some of the loyal Purple Dragons who will be accompanying you back to tell us, and redeploy your forces so as to lose track of not a single Knight. No Wizards of War shall be riding with you."

Dauntless frowned. "Lord Vang—"

"Neither of us has time for needless questions, Ornrion,"

Vangerdahast snapped. "You are to depart the Palace *immediately,* speaking to *no one* but the five men under your command—not even personages of the Blood Royal—about this task. You will find mounts and provisions ready, and these men will be riding with you—"

The tapestries behind the Royal Magician were drawn apart then by unseen hands to reveal five Purple Dragons who were all too familiar to Dauntless: First Sword Aubrus Norlen, Telsword Ebren Grathus, Blade Teln Orbrar, Blade Hanstel Harrow, and Blade Albaert Morkoun. Dauntless managed not to groan, but it was a struggle.

"—to make sure that you don't try to speak with, say, a princess before you depart."

"Uh . . . *yes,* Lord," Dauntless said, watching the five veteran Dragons—lazy dolts all and notorious even as far afield as Arabel for being so—march stiffly around the Royal Magician to form a careful row behind him.

"You are all dismissed," Vangerdahast said. "Get going."

With a curt bow of his head, the ornrion grimly led the march, following the wizard's pointing arm. Vangerdahast was indicating the doors he'd come in by; rather sourly Dauntless flung them wide and strode out.

He was unsurprised to find a war wizard waiting in the passage outside. It was Tathanter Doarmund, whom he'd worked alongside a time or two before. Doarmund gave him a careful nod and gestured to Dauntless and the other Dragons that they should all follow him. Dauntless fell into step behind him, his five unwanted dolts at his heels.

His thoughts, as he went, were furious shouts in the burning silence of his mind.

One day, Royal Magician Vangerdahast, you will take a step too far, just one, and someone, someone, will pay you back in full for all your highhandedness, believe you me . . . and I will give much to be there and watch every bloody, broken moment of your fall. I and the jostling host of thousands who share the same hunger . . .

In the room behind the furious ornrion, the man he was silently cursing smiled at the marching men dwindling away down the passage.

A tapestry whispered aside, and a women stepped out from behind it, her stride as fluid as any dancer's. She was all sleek curves covered by supple oiled black leathers and crisscrossing weapon belts. There was a black metal gorget at her throat, and the black hilts of daggers bristled all over her body. Even above that gorget she looked dangerous; menace was awake and hungry in her large and dark eyes. Her sharp-featured face was bone white but framed with helm-bobbed hair of glossy jet black, and her smile was like the tip of a gently brandished sword blade.

Cormyr mustered few Highknights, and only a handful of them were women. The Lady Targrael was by far the most infamous of these, and for good reasons.

Gliding to a stop by Vangerdahast's shoulder, she said, "Shall I tarry to defend you, when little Princess Alusair hears of this and storms in here to break things over your head?"

"Your offer tempts me," Vangey said, "but no. I can't trust yon six departing Dragons to use *chamber pots* without guidance and instructions. See that the Knights get out of Cormyr—in particular, that none of our over-clever nobles manage to speak with any of them and arrange anything. Once they're off our soil, I care not what happens to them. So long as I am not implicated."

Targrael smiled coldly, dark eyes glittering. "I am not that careless. I have my own score to settle."

Vangerdahast returned her less-than-lovely smile. "Precisely why I need to know your orders, in every detail, have been clearly understood."

"They are. In every detail." She strode past him. "I assume some of my garb has been enspelled so you can listen?"

"Of course. Yet it would be unwise to discard it, Ismra."

"I try to keep my unwise moments to a minimum, and I rarely work bare-skinned. You'll see that Baerem—?"

"He will be looked after more than properly. Cormyr neither

forgets nor abandons those who have served her faithfully."

"So much, I know well," the Highknight replied as she went out, very carefully keeping her voice utterly neutral.

There was a hard, cross-ribbed cot under Florin. By the smell around him, he was in a cool, damp room of stone walls. Still in his armor but without the weight of his sword and daggers, he was lying sprawled on his back, as the probing hands of an experienced healer squeezed and gently moved his limbs, seeking breaks.

Florin felt no wrenching pain, just the many strong, surging aches of remembered agony. Echoes of pain, rippling through him. So he'd been healed already.

Florin kept his eyes closed, feigning senselessness. The voices above him had been saying something interesting—and folk who spoke so had a habit of abruptly ending such converse when an interested audience became evident.

". . . no longer our problem. Once they depart here, Dauntless will be waiting in the eastern gate towers to take over their shadowing and see them clear of the realm."

The other, higher-voiced man chuckled. "Dauntless who loves them so. Heh, they've probably seen more of scenic Halfhap, these Knights, to suit them all their lives!"

"Which may soon be ended, if they keep on like this," the first and deeper voice responded. "We can't go galloping along behind them, healing them wherever they wander in Faerûn. Priest, are you about done? I'll lay odds this one lying here is awake and listening to us, right now."

A gentle boot kicked one leg of Florin's cot, and he judged it the right time to groan and stir and seem to slowly come awake.

"You're fooling no one," the deep-voiced man said from somewhere close above him.

Florin opened one bleary eye and mumbled, "Wha—?" with a clumsiness he did not have to feign. His mouth and throat felt like someone had stuffed a dusty rag down them and left it there, and his aches were growing stronger. His *fingertips* ached.

A lantern was moved closer, to shed light on his face. The ranger Knight blinked, his eyes suddenly watering, and tried to stare past its glare at the dark stone vault of the ceiling. He could see at least four faces looking down at him, all belonging to men who looked like soldiers. "What," he asked them slowly, "is this place?"

"One of the two western gate towers of Halfhap, gateway to everywhere," the deep-voiced man said, a distinct touch of cynical amusement in his voice. Florin's answering groan required no acting, either. "We Purple Dragons are trying to make sure you manage to travel on east from here, this time, and actually reach Shadowdale."

"On the road," Florin mumbled, trying to sound more dazed than he really was. "Outlaws. Lots of them. Took an arrow. The others, my companions. How fared they?"

"They'll all live, thanks to our priests—and the queen's commands. Try *not* to play arrow-catchers, next time. It is fortunate that you entertained unfriendly archers right on the royal high road just as our largest patrol of the day came riding along. We routed those darkswords and brought you all back here."

"All? We numbered—"

"All. Or so your sharp-tongued little flamehair affirms. She doesn't much like being questioned."

"Aye," Florin agreed. "That's . . . her."

Above him, Purple Dragon officers chuckled in unison.

"Fortunate we were," he added slowly, try to play innocent but fishing for a truth he already suspected, "that you happened along then. 'Twas almost as if you were sent to follow the Knights of Myth Drannor and see them safely through your patrol area."

The Dragons didn't disappoint him. "We were assigned just that task," the deep-voiced commander told him. "If you know the truth, perhaps you'll succeed in swaying your companions—the ones called Pennae and Semoor in particular—to behave themselves."

"Your candor," Florin told the officer—an ornrion, balding and with what little hair he had left gray-white at his temples—"is appreciated."

"I'll bet." The ornrion did not quite smile. "The Royal Magician ordered us to send out patrols and shepherd you out of Cormyr, trailing behind you unseen until needed. We were to make very sure you didn't turn aside into hiding to try to stay in Cormyr or get caught up in troubles along the way."

"As we did," Florin said, a little wearily. "We seem to be good at getting caught up in trouble."

"A judgment I share," the ornrion agreed, wearing a smile at last. "You owe your lives to the diligence of Lionar Threave, as it happens. It was he who insisted on doubling up two of our usual patrols and bringing along Wizard of War Rathanna"—a homely, unsmiling woman in dark robes stepped into view from behind the ornrion's shoulder and gave Florin a nod—"and our priest, Maereld, Able Hand of Torm. With their aid, you Knights were healed and brought here to Halfhap. You'll night over here in the gate-tower, and we'll see you all fed in the morning, given what remounts you need, and attended by holycoats to lead you in prayers. Then we'll let you forth—to go *around* Halfhap, mind, and ride on."

Florin sighed. "You'll not be escorting us, just to be sure?"

The ornrion half-smiled. "Oh, someone will. If Tymora smiles, you'll not meet with them. They're led by someone who's fast becoming an old friend of yours."

Florin sighed again. Dauntless, for all the coins in his purse.

He politely didn't ask the ornrion for confirmation. He was beginning to be able to read the manner shared by many Purple Dragon officers, and that particular half-smile meant "expect to receive no answers."

"Thanks for my life," he said instead. It seemed the polite thing to do.

Chapter 4
JUST SUCH A TASK

The realm needs saving again?
No need have ye to even ask
Every Purple Dragon we train
Works daily at just such a task

(Anonymous)
from the ballad "Dragon High, Forever"
first heard circa the Year of the Adder

The tapestry had barely fallen back into place behind the departing Lady Targrael when Laspeera slipped into the room from behind another one. "That one is on the proverbial sword edge," she said.

Vangerdahast shrugged. "Send one problem after another. If they destroy each other, that's two fewer we must deal with."

"*If,*" Laspeera said doubtfully. "No Wizard of War riding with Dauntless, hey? So is it to be the belt-buckle method?"

The Royal Magician shook his head. "Rumors about that are finally beginning to drift from Dragon to Dragon. No, I want the spells cast on items no Purple Dragon will leave behind: his codpiece and boots. Belts they can—and will—contrive to change, so cast something swift and worthless over those, to fool them. Their cods, and *both* boots, mind, are to be enchanted so that I—and you and Tathanter—can listen through them at will. See to it."

Laspeera nodded. "Wouldn't it be easier to just—?"

"Send a Wizard of War riding along with them? And have Dauntless blind and foil us at a time of his choosing by arranging matters so 'something happens' to our mage? I think not. Our loyal ornrion is proving to have . . . surprising depths."

Laspeera nodded again and smiled. "I'll see to it." Bowing her head, she turned and departed the way she'd come, the tapestry swirling gently in her wake.

She was careful not to sigh until she was no less than three closed panels away from her irascible superior.

Like almost every mage of the Brotherhood, Mauliykhus of the Zhentarim was ambitious. Wherefore he was going to dare this casting, risky though it was.

He had locked and barred two sets of iron-bound doors between himself and the common passage in Zhentil Keep, and there was nothing suspicious in that.

He had his orders from Lord Manshoon, spell-workings that were both dangerous and would yield results that should be kept secret from stray eyes. Wherefore the shielding scepter was resting in its holder, in the heart of the flickering yellow-green flame of the brazier to which he'd so carefully added powders, and no one but the most powerful archmage should be able to spy on what he did next.

Which was a good thing, because he intended to disobey both the leader of the Zhentarim and one of its most powerful and mysterious mages.

Manshoon had given him a working to perform—just such a task as he needed for an excuse to raise a shielding—and Mauliykhus was going to do something else instead.

And that "something else" was a casting that Hesperdan had just specifically ordered him not, under any circumstances, to attempt.

No fell creature of the Abyss was to be contacted, for any reason, until he received explicit orders otherwise from either Hesperdan or Manshoon himself.

Mauliykhus had no idea if Hesperdan suspected what he planned and was trying to prevent him—or goad him into doing it in all haste, for that matter—by forbidding him to seek out a demon . . . or if all Zhentarim were forbidden from demonic contact, forthwith. It *sounded* like the latter, but Hesperdan was very good at imparting impressions without actually saying what you *thought* he'd said. Hrast him.

Mauliykhus smiled, shrugged, raised both hands dramatically
above the black table upon which he'd arranged everything he
would need—and began the incantation. *Sealing One's Own Doom,*
some of the older grimoires tauntingly entitled the words he was
now reading.

It took only half a dozen of the deep, harsh-sounding words for
the room to darken, all of the braziers flickering at once, and chill
shadows to start to glide and swoop out of the darkness.

He spoke on. The dark, cruising wisps seemed sentient, yet he'd
been told many a time they weren't. They merely sought life and
light and warmth, stuff of what made up worlds and that which lay
between worlds.

A way started to open between his locked and barred stone chamber in Zhentil Keep and somewhere in the Abyss.

Mauliykhus brought his hands down, watched fire that was
not fire form between them and circle from thumb to thumb and
smallest finger to smallest finger to shape a silent *hole* in the air . . .

The way began to open, and he was through and doomed.

Darker shadows of malicious—and gleeful—awareness streaked
into him out of the yawning, howling darkness. Into his ears they
plunged, before he could say a word to stop them, lashing into his
mind like burning ice.

Fury drove them, fury and exultation. Harsh, ruthless, and insane
they were, and they knew themselves as Old Ghost and Horaundoon
as they reveled in ravaging his mind.

What had been Mauliykhus quailed and cowered, unable to
even mew in his terror; one of the terrible spirits in his head had
already slashed control of his mouth and hands. They leered into
his silently shrieking self, leaned in, and *took big, greedy bites* . . . and
Mauliykhus knew no more.

The body of the ambitious Zhentarim wizard stumbled around
the locked room, toppling a brazier onto the stones, its coals spilling
harmlessly amid hissing smoke. His head sank in slightly, literally
beginning to melt from within as both angry wraiths, snarling their
Abyssal madness at each other, roiled around behind his eyes.

Mauliykhus lurched upright and staggered to tug at the bars of the innermost iron-bound doors. Mad Old Ghost and Horaundoon might be, but their cunning was stronger than their raving, and they knew very well what they both most wanted.

Mauliykhus of the Zhentarim clawed the doors open and hastened to the next set of doors.

Vangerdahast favored the tapestry that had fallen back into place behind his loyal Laspeera with a faint smile. He knew very well she'd be sighing and rolling her eyes about now.

"Such a task will nettle you as it always does," he said, "but you'll do it, darling Lasp, as you always do." Then the Royal Magician sighed and turned away. "If you knew just a little less about what I've had to do . . . and I were a whole lot younger . . ."

He sighed again, went to one of the magnificently paneled walls of the ready chamber—the only one where tapestries and broad doors were both lacking—and put a finger onto a particular piece of carved trim on the glossy dark phandar wood. It obediently swiveled into the wall, undoing an unseen catch, and the ornate panel just below it smoothly folded down from the wall to become a seat, revealing a shallow drawer set into the wall behind it.

Vangerdahast sat on the seat and pulled open the drawer to reveal a dressed leather desk surface complete with quills, an inkwell, and a small heap of parchments. He plucked up the topmost, set it aside with a snort, took up the one that had been beneath it, nodded, stroked his chin, and settled down to read and hopefully—if the scribes hadn't been *too* creative—sign this heap of decrees he'd ordered drafted earlier.

There was always much to be done and never enough time to do it.

When, some six parchments later, the faint but approaching din of a raging princess fell upon his ears, echoing down passages and rooms and through several closed doors, he allowed himself the faintest of smiles.

Royal Magician of Suzail was an office that afforded him so little real entertainment, but he was going to enjoy some now.

"Farewell, Halfhap," Semoor said mockingly. "Deathtrap inns, dragonfire swords, and all. I wonder where our faithful Purple Dragon shadows are, this time."

Florin shrugged. "Using a war wizard to scry us so they can stay out of sight, but I'll wager Dauntless is leading them and that they came from yon gate towers on this side of Halfhap. So they got a good look at us when we rode around Halfhap and past them. They'll be somewhere behind us all the way to wherever along the Ride they usually turn back."

"I'm not complaining," Pennae said. "I can *still* feel that arrow." She shuddered, shook her head, and then asked, "They're still out there, aren't they? The ones who attacked us, I mean."

"Yes," Doust said quietly. "Six at least got away. I heard the Dragons talking. They took one alive and questioned him. Our foes were—are—Lord Yellander's bullyblades."

Pennae cursed and added, "That's not good."

No one argued with her.

"I'd rather talk about Shadowdale," Doust said. "I've heard 'tis all trees and farms, with the Old Skull landmark along the Ride in its midst. Oh, and the beautiful lady bard Storm Silverhand that they tell so many tales about dwells there. Yet what's befalling there *now*, that the queen wants us there with such urgency?"

Semoor snorted. "The urgency is to get us out of Cormyr, out of the royal hair—"

"*Vangerdahast's* hair!" Pennae corrected sharply.

"—not any urgency in and about sleepy Shadowdale, I'll wager."

"Vangerdahast paid us to get out of the realm, that's what he did," Jhessail said darkly.

"And this *bothers* you?" Semoor gave her an incredulous look. "More coin each than we'd probably have made in a summer of hard work, if all of us had been striving together?"

The stare the fire-haired mage gave him back was grim. "And what if we don't live to reach the border? Vangerdahast is a powerful *wizard,* remember? Who rules an army of wizards who can watch every step we take and whisk themselves to stand in our path with blasting wands ready, whenever they choose. I suspect Old Thunderspells has every intention of retrieving these gold coins from what's left of us— when we're well away from where the citizens of Suzail can see our smoking bones and mutter unpleasant comments about what happens to heroes of the realm when Vangey gets his hands on them."

Doust held up a hand and then waved at the trees along the road, beside them and ahead of them as far as the eye could see. "We're well away from where the citizens of Suzail can see anything *now.*"

"But not yet where the traders in Halfhap and travelers between Halfhap and Tilver's Gap can't see what happens to us," Islif said.

"And you think Vangey—or the nearest Purple Dragon or anyone else in all the fair Forest Kingdom, for that matter, gives an altar-warming damn about our fates?" Jhessail's voice was bitter. "Other than how entertaining the tale of our fall is when told at taverns? Or reassurance that one more dangerous irritant has been removed from their lives?"

"Our little lady hath found armor at last," Doust murmured. "Stout, strong, gleaming—and very properly called cynicism."

Jhessail shot him a searing look, then accompanied it with a certain gesture.

Florin raised his eyebrows at the sight of that rude signal. Semoor and Islif chuckled.

Pennae murmured, "Teeth at last. I knew she had some . . ."

"Are you going to be this gloomy all the way to Shadowdale?" Semoor asked Jhessail, his innocent manner a blatant fraud.

"Not much to look forward to, is it?" Pennae teased.

"Neither is my blade up your backside," Islif said. "Which is what certain folk riding here are risking by goading our Jhess."

"Oooh, the threat direct!" Pennae gave Islif a rather disapproving look. "Haven't learned much subtlety yet, have you, Longface?"

"I have not," Islif replied flatly. "Slyhips."

"Ah," Semoor told the sky loudly, dusting his hands in evident glee. "*This* should be good."

"*Enough*," Florin said heavily. "Semoor, stop goading—hrast it, that goes for all of us. We'll *all* die if more outlaws attack us and we're busy tongue-lashing each other and scheming to do worse. We're supposed to be one—a fellowship, a shieldwall!"

Slowing her mount to a walk, Pennae turned in her saddle to fix him with a level look. "Agreed. Yet when you say that, you really mean, 'All of you must do as I say, for I stand here, and the shieldwall must form to me, thus.' So I then have a question for you, tall and handsome ranger: Are we always fated to be your slaves? When will the shieldwall form where and when *I* say?"

Florin frowned in a sudden tense silence. Everyone had slowed their horses. "I never asked to lead this company," he said, "and am less than experienced, but—"

"But someone has to? So I ask again: Why you? I've *years* of adventuring under my belt, and—"

"And you're a thief," Jhessail said, "and known for it. Riding under your command would make us targets for all, where otherwise our knighthoods might see us past *some* folk without bloodshed. And we all know each other from growing up together in Espar, and we look to Florin. *We* chose him; he didn't name himself. He won the charter, yes, but once we're in our saddles and out from under the noses of everyone—except the war wizard spies who are undoubtedly listening to every word of this now and having a good grin—only we know who truly leads. And I like to be led by a man who is my trusted friend and who doesn't *want* to lead or think himself good at it. Overconfident and glib 'I can handle this' sorts are buffoons. *Dangerous* buffoons."

"Hearken for Pennae's answer," Semoor told Doust lightly. "Will she admit to being a dangerous buffoon?"

Pennae turned again to Florin and asked calmly, "Commander, have I your permission to smite yon priest?"

"Only gently. And using nothing that is edged or pointed. Or poisoned."

"Except your tongue," Semoor added brightly. "I'd rather enjoy—"

"I'm death-steel certain you would," Pennae told him sweetly, bringing her horse no closer to him. "So, Sir Florin, if you govern how fast we go and how we conduct ourselves along the way, what are your orders? Ride fast and steady, and get ourselves out of Cormyr as fast as we can?"

Florin shrugged. "I know not. Steady, yes. No thieving or acting like lawless adventurers. No raiding anyone who looks villainous and threatening, just because we happen to see them. No pilfering from orchards."

"No thieving? After the way we've been treated by Vangerdahast, why not?"

Several of the Knights tried to answer her at once, all of them sternly, but it was Jhessail's voice that overrode those of her companions: "Because he can turn us into toads or blast us to dust, along with whatever mountain we're hiding behind, that's why!"

Pennae sighed in mock dismay. "Oh, dear. Too late."

"Oh? What does *that* mean?" Islif snarled. "What clever theft have you managed now? Does it involve the Royal Magician of Cormyr directly?"

Pennae shrugged. "Once, there was a thief who was also a Knight of Myth Drannor. Let's call her 'Pennae.' And being a woman and therefore vain about her appearance, she owned a mirror. A little oval of bright-burnished metal. Now, not being quite that vain after all, there were days on end during which she never took up or even looked at the mirror. Yet she knew its heft and looks and tiny nicks and scratches well enough—and one night, in the Royal Palace of Suzail, this particular wench got a little surprise. Her carefully packed mirror was gone, and *another*, very similar—but lighter and with different scratches and nicks—mirror was just as carefully packed in its place."

"War wizards," Semoor murmured. "Vangerdahast."

Pennae inclined her head in firm agreement. "Indeed. Some war wizard stole my mirror and introduced a substitute. Obviously on

Vangerdahast's orders, and almost certainly so he could spy on us all and trace me with ease. *Such* trust abounds in fair Cormyr."

Islif frowned. "So because of this you intend to steal—"

Pennae threw up a hand sharply to indicate she wasn't done. "So I dropped that new mirror down the guard tower garderobe last night. However, I considered Vangey's little ploy ample justification for a theft of my own."

Islif sighed. "Of course."

Pennae shrugged. "If wolves force me to run with them, may I not take an occasional bite, too?"

"A moral stance that gets debated often by we who serve Tymora," Doust said, "and—"

"Holynose," Islif said pleasantly, "shut up."

Pennae nodded thanks at the Lady Knight, inspected the back of her left hand, and told it, "The Palace is a large and fascinating place, just made for wandering. It's astonishing what one can overhear from time to time on such meanderings, if one escapes notice. Among many other fascinating things—remind me to relate some amusing details of the sexual preferences of some high ladies of the Court, should we ever need, say, a tenday of verbal diversions—I overheard one Wizard of War proudly explaining the powers of a row of gems he'd just finished crafting for the use of Vangey's little army of spell-hurlers, on the Royal Magician's orders, of course. Tracer-gems, they are, and I have one of them with me now."

"Tracer gems? As in, you're making it easier for the war wizards to trace us right now?"

Pennae shook her head, did something to her leathers on the inside of her left elbow, and held up what she'd slid out of them: a small, dull, almond-shaped stone. "This works for just two beings, possibly only humans. *If* you can get blood, tears, or spittle from them to smear on it, one person per side of the gem."

"Works how, exactly?" Florin asked, glancing alertly at the trees and hills around them, as if he expected arrow-loosing armies to rise up out of concealment at any moment and charge down on the Knights.

"There's a word graven around the edge, here. When it's spoken, the side of the gem that's uncovered or uppermost is the side that works, telling the bearer the direction and distance away the one it can trace is at that moment."

"So use it," Semoor urged—and then frowned. "Wait! Who are the two people?"

Pennae gave him a tight smile. "Well, I managed to get some of Vangerdahast's spittle when he was snarling at us."

Florin rolled his eyes. "And the other?"

"Dauntless," Pennae told him. "Gained the same way, at rather closer range."

"Use it," Semoor repeated.

Pennae raised her palm out before her and set the gem into it, pinning it in place with her forefinger. "Who first?"

"Can you use it whenever you want?" Doust asked. "Seeking one person doesn't delay you in looking for the other?"

"Yes. And no, it doesn't."

"Vangerdahast," Florin and Islif said in unison.

Pennae shrugged, murmured a word the other Knights couldn't catch, closed her eyes briefly, and then announced, "Back in Suzail, so far as I can tell."

"Dauntless?"

Pennae turned the gem over, pronounced the word, and promptly acquired a wry smile. "Right behind us."

"So Vangey wants us safely out of the realm—just a stride or two will do—where the laws of Cormyr won't apply," Semoor said, "before his personal band of oh-so-loyal Dragons sink their swords into our backs. And those bastards'll do it, too!"

"They're not *butchers*, man!" Islif snapped, as Pennae put the gem away. "They're good and loyal folk; stalwarts doing the best they can, following the orders of the king and laws of the country, just trying to get by."

Semoor matched her glare with one of his own. "Aye. And so are all the good folk they kill, too."

"Before we really get going at snarling at each other," Pennae interrupted, "I suggest we settle one thing in our minds: Whether or not Dauntless really is following us—and it certainly looks that way, doesn't it?—or by a very long and supple arm of coincidence, is merely following orders that have nothing to do with us at all, that just happen to take him along the same road."

Doust's smile was as wryly crooked as it was sudden. "And we're going to establish the truth with certainty on this matter *how,* exactly? Turn around and ask him? When his reply may well be arrows or spears down our throats?"

Pennae gave him a mocking smile and waggled all the curled fingers of her left hand, back outermost, in Doust's direction, in the latest fashionable rude gesture that meant, to state its message most politely, "Right back at you, stonehead!"

"It may astonish you to learn, Holiest Ornament of Tymora," she replied, "that one or perhaps two personages of Faerûn have, in the days before this one, given some thought to situations similar to this one. It may even stagger you to learn that some of them have proposed solutions—and bids fair to stun you into mutely blinking insensibility to grasp that I have heard of, and myself understood, their proposals. To whit: I hereby suggest that all of us turn north off the Ride, the moment we're not seeing thick forest beside us, into the wild countryside."

Semoor frowned. "Right into the jaws of the waiting wolves, outlaws—or worse."

Pennae arched a brow in his direction. "I thought we were adventurers," she said, in a precise imitation of his voice at its most mocking.

"He's the priest of Tymora, not me!" Semoor snapped, jerking a thumb at Doust.

"Enough," Islif said. "Florin?"

The ranger stared back at his fellow Knights thoughtfully. Then his eyes flashed in a decision made, and he nodded at the trees flanking the north side of the Ride.

"Pennae's right," he said. "We look for the first way into the wilds that won't lame our horses, and take it. Seeking a place where we can hide and watch the road. I'd like a word or three with Ornrion Dahauntul, with whatever magic we can mount that tells us when he's speaking truth and when he's not. I think we need to know why we're being followed."

"Who's using us this time, and why?" Pennae murmured.

Florin's answering word and nod were equally grim. "Precisely."

"I believe that's a break in the trees, ahead there," Semoor said, pointing.

"So who's waiting there to feather us with arrows, d'you think?" Doust asked, crouching a little lower in his saddle.

Islif shook her head. "There may be archers hereabouts, but not there. I've been watching birds fly in and out of it. Unconcernedly lighting on a branch, soft-calling their kind, then hopping to the next."

Pennae, in the lead, nodded agreement. "Yon's an old road, by the looks of it. Overgrown but wide enough for wagons, for all the tall weeds, and—"

She held up a hand to signal a halt, swung down from her saddle as smoothly and swiftly as any stream eel ever eluded a snatching hand, and stalked forward, crouching low.

Florin pointed at Jhessail and then at Pennae, indicating she should watch over the thief's advance. Islif was already waving at the priests to keep eyes out east and south, as she swung around to peer back along the Ride behind them.

Pennae turned and came back to them. "A very old road but used recently by lots of horses, some oxen, and wagons. Mules, before that. Doust, get down off that beast, and come with me."

The quietest of the Knights blinked at her and then looked at Florin, who nodded.

Doust sighed. "Tymora be with me," he muttered and swung himself awkwardly down, almost falling from his horse.

Wincing at the stiffness riding had given his thighs, he stumbled after Pennae, who shot out a hand to catch hold of his nearest elbow, dragged him to a halt, and with a glare and some wordless miming, indicated he should *try* to move as stealthily as she was.

Doust rolled his eyes, kissed the holy symbol of Tymora he wore around his neck, grinned at her, and attempted stealth. The result made Pennae roll *her* eyes.

"Follow about a dozen strides behind me," she whispered. "Quiet is better than haste, but keep me in sight. If I'm attacked, yell for everyone to come running."

Without another word or looking for his nod, she turned away, sank down into a wary crouch, and set off through the tall grass with no more sound than faint whispers.

Doust watched her go, thinking she looked remarkably like just another tree-shadow. She very soon became hard to see, blending into the dark trunks of stunted trees and the gloomy shadows under leafy boughs. Without thinking overmuch, just trying to keep the curvaceous thief in sight, he followed her.

Grass and dead, brittle-dry shrub branches crackled under his boots, and he was startled by something dark rising up right beside his face.

Before Doust could turn his head, whatever it was bit the lobe of his ear gently—and then caught hold of his wrist when he instinctively flung up his hand to strike whatever was biting him away.

"Stay right here," Pennae breathed into the ear she'd nipped. "Don't move at all. Not at *all*. Until I come back for you."

Eyes fixed on his, she sank down to her knees, vanishing into the tall grass as if the ground were swallowing her, and . . . was gone. The priest of Tymora stood alone, staring around uncertainly, with the faintest of breezes ghosting past his throbbing ear.

Until Pennae rose up out of the grass again right in front of him, looming up dark and sinuous and sending him stumbling back on his heels with a startled *"Eeep!"* that made her grin like a satisfied vixen.

Without a word she stepped around Doust and back out into the road to rejoin the rest of the Knights, leaving the priest to scramble after her.

He did so, murmuring a heartfelt prayer to Tymora to keep all of their skins intact in the days ahead. Ears included.

Chapter 5
HIDING BEHIND OUR LADY

For in every blood fray we fight
And every exploit shady
We're nay so bad as priests so bright
Who daily hide behind "Our Lady"

The character Selgur the Savage
In the play Karnoth's Homecoming
by Chanathra Jestryl, Lady Bard of Yhaunn
First performed in the Year of the Bloodbird

The road leads to a hollow much used as a caravan camp, if I'm not mistaken," Pennae told her fellow Knights. "Old fire rings, stumps of trees that have been felled, dried, and burned as firewood, and a little creek that's been churned into mud by the hooves of horses and draft oxen. Out the back of the camp glade, the trail goes on, deeper into the forest, but it's really overgrown. No one has used it for a *very* long time."

"So this is our way off the Ride?" Florin asked quietly. At Pennae's nod he swung down from his saddle, waved to the rest of the Knights to follow, and started to lead his horse into the trees. Everyone followed, Pennae quickly capturing the reins of Doust's mount with her own.

By the time the Ornament of Tymora reached the hollow, Jhessail and Florin were heading back past him, out to the Ride to watch for Dauntless. At the sight of Pennae and Doust, Semoor beckoned and called, "Help me hobble our—"

Pennae let go of her fistful of reins, sprinted to him almost as fast as a speeding arrow, and caught hold of his chin.

"Idiot of Lathander," she hissed into his face, "shut *up*. Shouts and raised voices carry far. We're none of us deaf. *Yet*. Dauntless could be just the other side of yon duskwood, hmm? Stop trying to be a grand-voiced priest bellowing to impress folk in the next kingdom, and start being an adventurer. Talk only when you must, say as few words as possible, and say them *quietly*. Dolt."

"I love you, too," Semoor muttered as she let go of his jaw and strode past him. "Hey, don't you hobble horses?"

"I've work yet to do," she hissed, swiveling at the hips to answer him without slowing, then turning smoothly back to face forward again as she plunged into the deep woods at the back of the clearing. Once more she sank into a crouch and became a silent, flitting shadow, scouting along the overgrown continuation of the trail.

Doust and Semoor exchanged looks and shrugs and then bent in unison to see to hobbling the horses.

Not that there was much to do. Islif had already set to work, clamping her large hands around bits and rings to quell janglings. The two priests joined her. They were just finishing when Florin and Jhessail burst back into the hollow.

"Dauntless!" the lady wizard snapped, "and five Dragons with him! Mounted and heading right here as if they use this camp all the time!"

The two priests stared at her helplessly.

"Where'll we—? The horses!" Doust said.

"There's no place to go!" Semoor added.

"Get into the trees," Florin and Jhessail commanded in unison.

Jhessail promptly plunged past Doust and Semoor, doing just that, as the ranger snapped, "Leave the horses! We make poorer targets if we spread out. Keep low and work magic from behind trees where the likes of Dauntless can't get good swings at us! *Go!*"

The priests went.

Islif beckoned Florin as she headed across the hollow back behind the Knights' hobbled horses. It was the only way to have any hope of intercepting Pennae when she inevitably tired of poking around in the forest and came back.

"Someone's been through here," a man said, his voice coming from the direction of the Ride. "Can't still be here now, though. There's not an outlaw or a sneak-thief in the kingdom as can escape *my* scrutiny, know you."

The speaker pushed through the tall grass, on foot and leading his horse. Seeing the hobbled horses ahead, he stopped midword, jaw dropping in astonishment.

"Well, Morkoun?" someone jeered from behind him. "I s'pose ye'll now try to tell us yon horses are neither outlaws nor sneak-thieves and so managed to sneak past thy eagle-keen—"

"Will you dolts *shut up?"* Ornrion Taltar Dahauntul snarled. "Horses mean either horse thieves have left these nags—and 'tis an addled-fool place to leave them, now, isn't it?—or more likely, their riders have gone into hiding in the trees all around us here, just a breath or two ago! Why, they could be the Knights themselves! If you shattered-helm-brains hadn't been so cursed *talkative,* a-chattering through your unthinking, worthless lives, we might be staring at *people* now, not just their happily grazing horses!"

He urged his horse forward, pointing impatiently with his sword. *"Look!* Saddles still on them, and saddlebags, too! Why, I'll wager the Knights of Myth Drannor are watching and listening to us right now! Not that they'll dare to show their faces with all of us—"

A man with a sword in his hand and a half-smile on his face stepped into view around one side of the clustered horses, in perfect unison with the appearance of a tall, burly woman in armor around their other side.

"—here," Dauntless added, voice faltering.

"Falconhand!" one of his men snarled, drawing his sword.

"Aye," another snapped, amid a chorus of Purple Dragon curses. "The woman's one of the Knights, too! She was the one who—"

"Scatter!" Dauntless roared from his saddle, waving one arm wildly at his men as he pointed into the trees with the sword in his other hand. " 'Ware *spells,* curse you!"

His sword point indicated two small, faint glows that were growing stronger by the moment, outlining the slender hands in their midst. Above those glows, Jhessail Silvertree smiled coldly.

"There'll be priests somewhere around here, too!" Dauntless shouted, backing his mount away. "Best we get clear of this, and—"

A scream that was as shrill as it was high drowned him out and sent most of the Dragons wincing and stumbling backward.

It rose higher and turned raw as it came, approaching swiftly out of the forest behind the camp glade, becoming a series of pain-wracked shrieks rather than sounds of terror.

The Purple Dragons started to obey Dauntless, scattering in grunting haste and waving their swords. The horses under them snorted and stumbled as their riders lurched in their saddles, trying to watch not where they were going but the trees where those screams were coming from.

Trees that promptly vomited forth a screaming, sprinting woman in leathers, whose racing limbs were rippling with fire!

"That'll be them," Highknight Targrael said, an unlovely smile rising to her lips as they listened to the screams. "You know what to do."

Telsword Bareskar of the Palace Guard nodded, fitted his windlass to his crossbow, and set it to whirring.

A certain laundry chute had left him with a score he dearly wanted to settle. Even his growing fear of the dark Highknight hadn't made him regret the eagerness with which he'd obeyed her command to depart his post and accompany her in a little Knight hunting.

The head of a chartered adventurer or two wasn't the sort of trophy he'd expected to mount on the wall of the guard room, but he was warming to the notion.

Especially if it was the head of a certain half-naked lass he'd chased through half his floor of the Palace cellars . . .

Crossbow ready, he took a quarrel into his hand and dared to give Highknight Targrael a grin.

The cold grin she gave him back as she beckoned him on through the treegloom sent a chill through him, even before he heard her soft whisper.

"As do I."

The castle had seen better days. Roofless and forgotten, with old and towering trees thrusting up through its stones like so many dark spears and shrouding its crumbling walls beneath heavy boughs full of leaves, it stood in deep wilderlands, far from roads now in use and folk who might be ruled by a lord who dwelt in such a stronghold. Its dungeons and lower floors were prowled by dark, tentacled things, which had kept smaller, furrier forest creatures from lairing over-much in its riven upper rooms. Birds, though, hadn't the wits to care about tentacled things, dark or otherwise. Their nests and voidings covered the floors thickly.

Except in one corner of a small, high room that retained not only its roof but a stone table flanked by two stone benches. A large arched window overlooked the table. The window lacked all trace of shutters, framing, or anything that might have filled that frame.

Through that spacious hole flew a large, untidy black bird that might have been a hawk—if hawks grew as large as horses.

The hawk landed heavily and awkwardly, glared around at the gloomy emptiness of the deserted room with its fierce gold-rimmed eyes, and then shook itself—and in a moment of unpleasant shiftings became a broad-shouldered man in black robes with a pepper-and-salt beard and tufted eyebrows to match. His eyes were every bit as fierce as the hawk's.

Massive gold rings on his fingers winked and glowed briefly, then went dark. "Good," the man announced, seeming to relax. He strode to the nearest bench and sat, slamming his forearms down on the table. "I've arrived first. For once."

"If it pleases ye to think so," part of the roof replied as it leisurely peeled away from the rest and dropped down into the room, leaving a gaping hole behind. What landed feather-light on the floor was a white-bearded man in torn and patched gray robes and battered brown boots. He looked older than the hawk-mage and held a curved pipe in his hand. His blue-gray eyes were fierce and bright. "Myself, I can't think why it matters. D'ye *still* measure thyself against others? Truly?"

Khelben Arunsun was too disgusted—and astonished—to rise to

this bait. "But the rings showed no—"

"Haven't ye learned how to defeat such detections yet? Bend the Weave around them, man! Bend the Weave around them!"

As he delivered this vigorous advice, Elminster sat down across from Khelben and puffed his hitherto dark and empty pipe into spark-swirling life. "Yet before ye master such trifles, suppose ye tell me what's struck ye as so important that ye needed to mindcall me hither—*without* telling me why. What's afoot?"

"Trouble." Khelben glowered.

The pipe floated out of Elminster's mouth to hang hovering beside his lips. "Trouble is always afoot," he said. "Could ye be a bit more specific?"

"These Knights of Myth Drannor," the Blackstaff said. "Or to be *more* specific, the two self-made Zhentarim ghosts clinging to them."

"Horaundoon and the one who calls himself Old Ghost," Elminster said. "The elements that—aside from your connection to these adventurers and therefore Vangerdahast's desire to be rid of them in somewhat indecent haste—make the Knights of more interest to the Realms than any other band of bumbling novice adventurers."

"Ah . . . *precisely.*"

Elminster smiled, nodded, and acquainted himself with his pipe again. Waiting patiently.

Khelben glared across the old stone table into those mocking blue-gray eyes, started to speak—and paused to tap the table with a forefinger. He looked up from that finger like a lion lunging forward with a roar and said, "What do you know of these two Zhents?"

"They are, or were, Zhentarim mages of some accomplishment. Now able to pass into and possess the living, otherwise very much like wraiths, they're in hiding, pursuing unknown aims. Formerly at odds, they now seem to be working together. They've established links of some sort with the Knights and seem able to appear at will wherever those adventurers may be. Ye know more?"

"No," Khelben admitted, still glowering.

"So are we met, here and now, so ye can argue with me how to handle the Knights and these two Zhent wraiths?"

"Well, no, no . . . *Yes.*"

Elminster sat back and sighed. "Progress," he told his pipe as it floated out of his mouth once more. Then he locked gazes with Khelben again and said, "Suppose ye say what it is ye want to do—and want *me* to do and not to do—so we can get on to the shouting and blustering without further delay, hmm?"

"Elminster Aumar," Khelben asked, "can't you take *one* Lady-damned thing seriously?"

The Old Mage acquired a look of amazed horror. "What? After all these years? With all the sanity *that* would require?"

"Indeed," Khelben agreed heavily. "And as I know you're the sanest of us all and that there are just the two of us here, can you *please* drop the capering clowning long enough to discuss this properly? For once?"

"Well," Elminster said quietly, "so long as 'tis just this once . . ."

"*Thank* you." The Blackstaff seemed to gather both breath and thoughts for a moment, then said, "I believe these two Zhents are far more than just mere nuisance wizards. Each of them—Old Ghost in particular—poses a great and steadily growing threat. They must be destroyed, whatever the cost." The Blackstaff cleared his throat. "I can see to that, but I need something from you: Your commitment to stand back from the Knights, whatever happens, so I can have a free hand in dealing with Horaundoon and Old Ghost. If it costs the lives of these young adventurers, then so be it. I need you out of Shadowdale and not meddling in the doings of the Knights until those two wraiths—and I believe they're far more than that, now— are dealt with. Then, if some Knights have survived, by all means rush in and seek to salvage them."

Khelben stopped talking, and silence fell.

"So," he asked, after staring across the table at his fellow Chosen for some time, "have we agreement on this?"

"No," Elminster said cheerfully.

Silence fell again.

The Blackstaff sighed. "Care to be, in your words, more specific?"

The Old Mage nodded and said quietly, "Thy first two sentences regarding the nature and potential of the two Zhents—or former Zhents—I agree with. As usual, however, we disagree entirely on what to do and how to proceed."

"So your preference in this matter would be . . . ?"

Elminster's smoking pipe drifted to his mouth, but he waved it away. "I prefer to continue as I have been: I will watch over the Knights myself and as much as possible leave Horaundoon and Old Ghost alone for now, to see what they do. For one thing, after a brief disappearance during which I could find no trace of them, they seem to be slaughtering Zhentarim as fast as they can, without resorting to an open assault on the entire Brotherhood, or darting about hunting down lesser, far-flung Zhent agents. And anything that reaps Zhents so energetically is something I don't want to hamper. Nor have I any desire to stand back from the Knights."

"So you cleave to your whimsical meddling," the Blackstaff snapped, "because it's the style you prefer. Leaving threats that could and should be dealt with *now*, before they can do more damage to the reputation of all who work with the Art—and before they can claim more lives of mages, however evil and selfish the motives and aims of such victims. In other words, you stray from the very tasks Our Lady has set for us and defy Her will."

"I do nothing of the sort," Elminster replied mildly. "Ye prefer one style, and I another. Ye seek to cloak thy preferred style in the mantle of 'right' and 'holy to Mystra,' and deem mine to be disobedient straying. I reject thy judgment—and have my own good reasons for doing so." A faint smile rose to his lips. "Ye'll have to do better, Lord Mage of Waterdeep. Try again."

Khelben rose, tall and black and terrible, and stood glowering across the table. "This is not a *game*, Elminster. This is the future of the very world around us. I believe these two wraith-spirits to be that powerful or that they'll soon become so. I did not come here to fence clever words with you. That game you can always best me at, as I seek to cling to truths and consequences, and you ever seek to redefine and mock and introduce irrelevancies." The Blackstaff leaned forward. "So let us do this differently. For once. If I agree to let Horaundoon and Old Ghost continue to exist for now, so we can witness more of their villainies and hopefully learn something, you depart from Shadowdale and your oversight of the Knights. Leaving them to flourish or perish on their own, without meddling from any of us. And if needs be they serve as lures for the two wraith-spirits and suffer the consequences, so be it." He let silence return and after it had deepened asked, "So, can we find agreement on *that?*"

"No," Elminster said quietly, "I'm afraid not."

"Afraid? Afraid of what?"

"Afraid my refusal to agree to thy terms will widen the rift between us and weaken our shared service to Mystra. I feel no animosity toward ye, Arunsun. I hope ye can hold none for me, despite the irritation my manner awakens in ye, and thy great flaw."

"My great flaw," Khelben repeated flatly.

"Indeed. Thy habit of mistaking thy decisions and preferences for the 'right' ones, and anyone who disagrees with ye as a foe."

Khelben regarded his fellow Chosen in expressionless silence for a moment and then said heavily, "So when these Knights reach Shadowdale—and they *will* reach Shadowdale, under your vigilant guardianship—they'll find you there waiting for them."

"I fear so, though I promise ye I'll do my level best to hide from them."

"Why? *What* is so important about staying in that small, dust-filled dump of a tower in Shadowdale?"

"Mystra's will," Elminster said. "It brought me there, and it compels me to remain."

"Why?"

"Ask Her, son of Arielimnda. On this matter, I will say no more."

"Oh?" Khelben's eyes flashed fire, and he turned and strode across the chamber, black robes swirling. "So now you presume to decide what I am to be told and *not* told? As if I am your lackey?"

"It is the same presumption you make, Blackstaff," Elminster said, "when dealing with your fellow Harpers."

"But they *are* lackeys," Khelben told the wall, then turned back to meet Elminster's gaze and added gruffly, "That was a jest, mind. I—"

"We all presume to share and withhold news and lore, as we see fit," the Old Mage interrupted. " 'Tis something Chosen *do*. Yet misunderstand me not, Khel. Mystra hath *ordered* my silence on this. If it gnaws at ye not to know, yet ye prefer not to ask her, then take solace in the lesser reasons: I, Syluné, and Storm are a small cluster of rocks 'gainst the waves of Zhent expansion, and my tower is where it is to be adjacent to a divine breach in the Weave that can be hedged about with items of power I store and guard there. Moreover, it stands close to a way through which the dark elves can at any time surge up into the surface lands."

"Aye, aye, *aye*," Khelben replied testily, waving Elminster's words away. "Yet I wasn't speaking of you abandoning your tower! I seek your absence from the lives and doings of the Knights, so they can stand or fall on their own—and the two wraiths won't conceal or lessen their deeds and schemings for fear of you. So I can seize the best opportunity to destroy them both at once and *not* manage to fell only one and leave the other, warned but fled, to lurk and become twice or thrice the nuisance to hunt down."

Elminster nodded. "Thy tactics, I'm content with. Both at once is indeed wisest, *if* ye can bring it off. I find matters are seldom so tidy. Yet again I must say thee nay, Blackstaff. I must be *seen* to be in Shadowdale, free to wander elsewhere but appearing when great foes or matters of import—and ye'll grant these wraiths are both, just as ye paint them—unfold there. I have my orders, as ye have yours."

The black-robed figure across the room let out something that was almost a roar and came striding toward Elminster raging like a black flame. For an instant the form almost seemed gaunt-thin with large, snapping-with-anger dark eyes and pointed ears . . . and then it was the Blackstaff again, Khelben Arunsun as large as ever, towering across the table with both knuckles planted on its old stone surface, fists clenched white with anger.

"Secrets," he said, "may be the stock in trade of every Chosen, but it is folly and corruption when Chosen keep secrets from each other. I more than mistrust these 'orders' you speak so glibly of. They are far too handy an excuse for doing just what you want to do. Let me tell you straight, Elminster Aumar: I suspect you of deceiving me, of hiding behind Our Lady."

Elminster rose slowly from his bench, planted his own fists on the table, and leaned forward in exact mimicry of the Blackstaff's pose, until their noses were almost touching.

"You," he replied, imitating Khelben's voice precisely, "suspect far too much, Khelben Arunsun. Nasty, suspicious minds may be useful for wizards in keeping themselves alive, but no one should ever forget that they *are* nasty, suspicious minds." He sat down again, swung booted feet up onto the table, and puffed at the pipe that came swooping back to him. "I stay and do what I do," he said, in his own voice. "Have ye anything else ye'd like to try to bully me about? Or—ahem—discuss?"

Khelben stepped back from the table, glowering. "Again you take it upon yourself to decide what will be and what will not be. I will *not* back down on this, El."

"Well," a pleasant contralto voice observed from the long-empty-of-door archway behind them both, "it's nice to know that the Blackstaff remains as hog-headed as ever. And everyone's favorite Old Mage just as merrily, provokingly irritating. Haven't you two given the slightest thought to the notion that one day, in some small way, it might be nicer for everyone—yourselves, your fellow Chosen, the rest of the Realms—if you undertook to *grow up?*"

Khelben winced, eyes closing for a moment as he muttered an extremely creative curse under his breath. Then he turned and said politely, "Well met as always, Dove. What brings you to this rather *remote* place? A very long arm of coincidence, or have you been lurking at Elminster's beck and call until the so-called 'right moment?' "

"My," Dove said, striding into the room and stripping off her long leather gloves, "you *do* have a nasty, suspicious mind, don't you?" She undid two buckles, swung two crossed and linked scabbards off her back, and set her swords on the table. "You'll achieve more in life, Lord Mage of Waterdeep, if you're nice to people more often and bully, bluster, and snap commands at them rather less. Just some friendly advice."

She half-sat on one end of the table and announced, "I was sent here by Mystra, as it happens, who has shared with me your amicable discussions thus far. She'd like me to state the view of the Harpers of the Dales—*and* those of us based in Cormyr, too. We believe it will do much harm to the stability of those lands if the Knights are left undefended for any lowly Zhent to slaughter and Elminster vanishes from his visible guardianship. Even if *another* wizard—that'd be you, Blackstaff, but your face is less known hereabouts, and the Zhents are *very* good at spreading false rumors, to say nothing of wild-tongued Dalefolk and bored citizens of Cormyr—then shows up and engages in a spectacular spell-battle with some fell and scary wraith-things, the Zhents will rub their hands and probably start marching their warriors the next day, to 'protect' everyone in sight. By conquering them, of course."

She rose and strolled in Khelben's direction, wagging a reproving finger. "I hardly need to tell either of you *gentle* mages that Harpers disagree among themselves over all sorts of things. Yet on this, all local Harpers are agreed: Zhentil Keep must *not* be given any excuse to send forth the armies they're itching to use, nor emboldened in any way. Starting to think Elminster isn't sitting in Shadowdale watching their every move is a golden pretext in itself. Khelben, don't be stupid. For once."

"Now who's being rather less than nice?" the Blackstaff retorted, striding slowly to meet her. "And while I'd like to have leisure time enough to debate tactics with every Harper 'twixt here and the more distant isles of Anchorôme, in this particular matter—one Chosen keeping secrets from another—the views of non-Chosen are imma-terial. Consider them dismissed."

The sigh that resounded through the room was so deep and strong that it numbed their very bones and set the stone table to thrumming eerily. Khelben spun to seek its source—and found himself regarding two huge, long-lashed eyes that had opened in the old stones of the wall. Human eyes, by their appearance, but each as large across as he stood tall, and they moved over the surface of the stone and left it unaffected.

Blue fire surged through the veins of all the Chosen, nigh choking them. Mystra was not amused.

"Lady," Khelben said gravely, bowing his head, "how—"

Khelben mine, the goddess said, her voice thunder in all their heads, *hear and heed my commands, as Elminster has already done. You are to stand back from the Knights and Shadowdale and those known as Horaundoon and Old Ghost. You and all Chosen are merely to watch what befalls, meddling not at all. If one snatches tools out of every forge fire, they can never be tempered at all.*

"Your will commands us all, Lady," Khelben spluttered, "but— but doing nothing, if you'll forgive me for saying so, seems to render all Chosen unnecessary."

You are "doing nothing," as you term it, in this one matter. Let this be one tale you stay out of, all of you. It is needful. Remember also this, Khelben Arunsun: This world is large and full of striving life. You are not the only one playing a long game.

"That's so," Storm agreed, her face bathed in the light of the bright scrying sphere floating in the air above her kitchen table. "Even my patience is growing a trifle frayed just keeping these dolts Torm and Rathan *alive* so that they can join the Knights."

That thought prompted the Bard of Shadowdale to whirl away from one scrying sphere to another, to peer at whatever Torm was up to at that moment somewhere in the Realms.

The sphere brightened obediently. Storm peered into it, rolled her eyes at what she saw, and murmured, "Young Master Slyboots, you'll be the death of yourself yet!"

Chapter 6
GREAT MURDERING BATTLE

For all that of love our bards do prattle
And sages opine as they're derided
'Tis always in great murdering battle
That things get—in truth—decided.

The character Selgur the Savage
In the play Karnoth's Homecoming
by Chanathra Jestryl, Lady Bard of Yhaunn
First performed in the Year of the Bloodbird

The horse under Dauntless had tasted battle before, but that didn't mean it had any particular liking for fire that came racing right at it, shrieking.

It bucked, heaving and plunging under the ornrion in its haste to be elsewhere, away from those rushing flames, back out of these trees onto the open road, where—

Arrows came hissing out of the trees to thud hard and deep into the horse's haunches, causing it to scream in pain, rear, and dance sideways so wildly that Taltar Dahauntul decided being spilled out of his saddle was wiser than staying in it.

He crashed down hard onto his shoulders and rolled hastily away—or tried to. Pain stabbed across his neck and shoulders as the breath slammed out of him. He groaned, and the plunging hooves of another horse came crashing down all around him.

And were gone, leaving in their wake a cursing Purple Dragon who thundered to earth through a rather fragile thornbush, shouting out his own curses.

That straining, sputtering voice belonged to Telsword Grathus. Dauntless saw more arrows hiss past overhead and heard Grathus gulp suddenly, choke, and stop spitting out curses forever.

" 'Tis a *monster!*" First Sword Aubrus Norlen cried. "A monster,

75

to be sure! Hew it down! Dragons, to me now! Slay this beast that all Cormyr be delivered from its grave peril!"

Panting, he hacked at the lithe, dark, flaming thing that was rolling in the stream at his feet. A hissing cloud of smoke was billowing up from it. He could hardly see his foe. Yet he swung lustily, and his steel bit into something solid. That brought a shriek of pain from the thing, and it clawed at his ankles. He stumbled hastily back.

"Dragons!" he shouted again. "To me now! Aid, for the love of Cormyr! Aid, for the love of—"

"—a little piece and quiet!" Blade Orbrar snapped, coming up beside him and slashing at whatever was thrashing and rolling in the stream beneath the drifting smoke. "Norlen, will you belt *up?*"

"Whaaat? I am your *superior,* Teln Orbrar!" First Sword Norlen bellowed. "Obey me and address me with the proper respect and defer—*uhhh!*"

First Sword Aubrus Norlen's gasp was as loud as everything else that had been coming out of his mouth. It hung in the air as he staggered backward and sat down, hard.

The Purple Dragon Blade turned to see why Norlen was retreating so precipitously. He was astonished to see an arrow had appeared, sprouting as if by magic, low on his front. It was sunk deep in a gap in the First Sword's too-small armor, between two plates that had quite failed to grow and cover his expanding belly over these last few months. The arrow was quivering, and so was Norlen. He stared up at Teln Orbrar in disbelieving horror, spitting up dark blood, as the light behind his eyes went out.

Orbrar was neither a stupid man nor a slow-witted one. He flung himself flat on the ground right beside the First Sword even before Norlen toppled sideways. The arrow that had been meant for him whistled harmlessly past and was lost amid brief cracklings in dark undergrowth.

"Naed," Orbrar gasped, rolling frantically over and down into a little hollow in the ground, almost cutting himself on his sword doing so. "Gods-cursed stlarning *naed!* Oh, tluin, tluin, *tluin!*"

"Not now," a voice that was tight with pain hissed in his ear, an instant before a very, very cold knife entered his throat. "I'm too busy being wounded right now. Later, perhaps—you murdering Purple Dragon *bastard*."

Choking around the icy metal that had so suddenly somehow appeared in his gullet, Blade Teln Orbrar found himself unable to reply.

"Not—" he struggled to say, staring into two eyes that wept tears and blazed with pain and fury.

"Not a bastard," he managed to choke out as Faerûn went dim around him. "Not. Decent, really. I . . ."

Night fell. Forever, he knew. Forever.

"That's the last tluining arrow!" Halmur snapped, tossing his bow down and reaching for his sword.

Steldurth nodded, raised his own blade, and gave the sardonic, dusky-skinned Turmishan an approving smile. "You feathered Dragons enough for us. No one left to get in the way of us killing the Knights *this* time!"

"Kill?" Kraskus growled, bending down to thrust his red-bearded, brutish face close. "Time to kill?"

"Time to kill, Kraskus," Brorn said firmly from behind them all. "To avenge Lord Yellander!"

"Yellander," the bullyblades snarled in unison, hefting their swords, and rushed out of the concealing trees.

"I don't want to kill you!" Florin said, striking a Dragon's thrusting sword aside, then slashing in the other direction in time to parry a second Dragon's attack. "Stop this!"

"Stop this? Man, *we* are the law here!" Blade Hanstel Harrow snapped back at the ranger. "Lay down your sword, and we'll—"

"You'll kill us where we stand," Semoor Wolftooth said, retreating and vainly trying to wipe his forehead clean of blood from a gash made when the very tip of one of the Dragons' swords had *just* caught him a lunge or two earlier. His streaming gore was almost blinding him. "Those're your orders, aren't they? Well?"

Neither Dragon answered with more than wordless growls of exasperation and effort, as they went right on hacking at Florin as hard and fast as they knew how.

"Stop this!" Semoor spat through the blood dripping from his nose and chin. "Stop or someone's going to get *killed!*"

Raging, Dauntless came to his feet. Their horses were dead or fled, the last one lashing out with its steel-shod hooves at one of the priest Knights—Doust Sulwood, wasn't it?—as it reared one last time before racing back toward the road.

Grathus was dead at his feet, and their saucy wench of a thief was just rising from beside Orbrar, his life-blood all over the knife in her hand.

With a roar the ornrion launched himself into a run across the uneven, trampled ground, swinging his sword up and back for a great cleaving stroke that should end her sly evil forever.

She was reeling, wet with blood and with half her hair and leathers burnt off her, but her eyes glittered with a fury to match his own as she raised arms that trailed wisps of smoke, bloody knife coming up to greet him.

Dauntless slowed not a whit. That fang could do nothing against his armor for the moment he needed to hack her down—and then she'd not be using it on anyone, ever again.

"Die, outlaw *bitch!*" he bellowed, bringing his sword down. *"Die!"*

Florin sprang aside again. He didn't *want* to kill these Purple Dragons, didn't want their blood on his—

The snarling face of the nearest Dragon changed, fear falling across it ere its owner backed away. He was gazing past Florin, and so was the other Dragon, whose outflanking rush had faltered.

Florin kept moving, aside and back, but turned his head to see what they were both staring at.

A swarm of men with swords raced toward them, the foremost almost close enough to touch, clenched teeth opening to bellow, "*Yellander!*"

"Oh, *tluin,*" Florin said and set his feet to meet the nearest of Yellander's bullyblades blade-to-blade. Just in time.

Jhessail rose out of her crouch, daring to breathe again, as Doust said, "Guard yourself!" and erupted out of the little hollow where they'd crouched together. Mace in hand, he charged into the fray.

Standing—these outlaws must have run out of arrows, hence their charge out into the open—the spellhurler drew the dagger from her belt.

It seemed so *puny*, against all these hulking men in armor and their swords. Yet her battle spells were all gone now, most spent on half-seen archers in the trees. So she could run away, sprint after Doust, and do what little she could, or she could stand here and watch.

Which really bid fair to mean stand and watch her friends die.

Dauntless brought his blade down so hard, it couldn't help but break the dagger raised against it and both the wench's slender wrists gripping that knife, too. If she managed to parry at all.

Only to find himself stumbling awkwardly forward, almost impaling himself on his own pommel, as his sword bit deep into forest leaf mold. Somehow the thief had ducked or twisted away, and—*where was she?*

He spun, fearing being hamstrung.

Damn all if he didn't find himself looking into her defiant grin! Pennae was reeling, teeth clenched in pain and fighting to keep standing. Blood was running in a dark wet flood down the arm that held out her dagger to menace him, and that arm was wavering. She *had* been trying to hamstring him, gods take her. Only the weakness of her wounds had kept her from doing it before he could get his sword unstuck and whirl to face her.

"Curse you, wench!" he spat, stepping back from her to give himself space enough to swing his blade back up to his shoulder.

She fought to keep standing, lurching forward to try to stay close to him, too close for his seeking steel—but Dauntless turned with her, took another step back, and then leaned forward and put all the strength in his shoulders behind a woodcutter's chop, bringing his sword down in a cleaving that—

—missed the staggering thief entirely as something slammed hard into the ornrion's knees from one side, snatching his hacking sword away from his intended victim.

It was his turn to stagger, as his sword bit into turf again and plunged him into a fight to keep from falling. He managed amid all the awkward hopping to turn his head enough to look down his struck leg and see that his assailant was—

That weakling of a Tymoran priest among the Knights!

Sulwood, Doust Sulwood. That was his name.

And this Doust Sulwood was glaring up at Dauntless right now, gasping for breath with his hands still clawing at the knee-plates of the ornrion's armor.

Dauntless jerked back with a snarl and kicked his way clear of the sprawling priest.

"Deal with you *later*, holynose," he growled, swinging his sword aloft again.

Then he let out a roar that rang with the rage rising in him, and charged the thief again. If he did *nothing else* this day, felling this little bitch and delivering Cormyr from her tireless thievery should—

She was stumbling back, gasping, staring at him almost beseechingly through her hair. Defenseless and reeling, on the brink of begging for mercy.

"Not *this* time, wench," Dauntless said. "Not this time!"

He drew his blade back for a killing blow, bounded forward, and brought it down.

In midair it struck a bright blade that seemed to thrust out of nowhere, a sword as hard and unmoving as an iron bar.

The impact struck sparks past his nose, nigh deafened him with its clang, and numbed his sword arm right up into his shoulder. Dauntless roared in startled pain and hastily stepped back. The bright blade followed, thrusting at him.

"Well met, ornrion," said a cold, sarcastic voice, and Dauntless found himself blinking into a wintry gaze he recognized. "Islif Lurelake, at your service."

Onrushing bullyblades washed over Florin Falconhand in a tide of pounding boots and thrusting swords. He parried, danced aside, and slashed like a madwits, running another few strides toward the Ride whenever he could snatch an instant amid the frantic swordplay.

After those brief skirmishes, most of the bullyblades swept past him and across the clearing, seeking easier prey. Of the few who tarried, Florin sent one man staggering away clutching a slashed face, plunged his sword into the shouting mouth of a second to silence him forever, and drove a third to his knees, gurgling and feebly trying to hold his head on an almost-severed neck.

Not that there seemed to be any great shortage of arriving bullyblades. Whirling and panting in the heart of a ring of steel, the ranger fought on, wondering how soon it would be before it was his turn to be one of the dying.

Morkoun was doomed, as good as dead, and Hanstel would be too, if he didn't stir his boots and get *gone!*

Blade of the Dragons Hanstel Harrow ducked aside from an outlaw sword, tripped the man, then whirled and *ran*.

Head down, sprinting like a youngling in a race, he fled across the clearing, heading for the open road. If he could—

He tripped on one of the bodies he'd been trying hard not to look down at, and he went sprawling. Rolling to his feet and wincing, he looked back at what had tripped him.

It was the body of First Sword Aubrus Norlen, huddled dead on the ground with flies already buzzing around staring eyes and open mouth. Out of which hung that runaway tongue, now forever stilled. Well, at least he wouldn't have to listen to *that* particular flood of utter nonsense, ever ag—*hold!*

Norlen had been carrying something deadly, a "battle blast" or some such, for hurling at foes when a fray was going poorly. And if this wasn't going poorly, he didn't know what would be.

The weapon would be at his belt.

Hanstel found his feet and darted forward cautiously, half-expecting some deadly magic—or worse still, the corpse of the First Sword, stiff in fresh undeath—to lash out at him. There! That must be it, that hand-sized, unfamiliar thing tied at Norlen's hip. Gingerly Hanstel bent, plucked it, tugged hard, and dashed away, feeling the body stirring under his hands for one horrible instant before the thong broke and the carrion slumped back, leaving him the new owner of . . . of whatever it was, round and dark in his palm. It was starting to glow now.

Glow. Magic. It was going to do whatever deadly thing it was intended to do, very soon. The glow was spreading across it with frightening speed!

Something flashed in the air before him. Hanstel looked up.

He saw the dagger that had flashed as it came whirling end over end toward him. It arced down, falling short and thunking deep into the dirt right in front of him.

Beyond it, back across the clearing, was the one who'd thrown it. He'd seen her once, back in the Royal Palace when the reception for the envoy of Silverymoon had been so dramatically disrupted. It was the little flame-haired Knight of Myth Drannor, the one who could hurl spells like a novice war wizard. Quite a looker, he'd thought, and still did. A lass he'd not mind a kiss and cuddle with. Who'd just tried to kill him.

Their eyes met.

With a certain wild glee—he had the means to kill a *mage!* A Mystra-loving she-wizard!—Hanstel Harrow hurled the deadly glowing thing in his hand right at her.

At this range, he could hardly miss.

Bullyblades were everywhere, and he was meat for their blades, holy symbol of Lathander and all.

Semoor Wolftooth scrambled wildly across the clearing, fleeing he knew not where, still half-blind behind his mask of blood. His own blood, still streaming down his face, getting in his *eyes* with every step, stlarn it, keeping him from seeing—

He tripped over something, probably a body, and crashed to the ground like a felled tree, driving all the wind out of his lungs and shaking every bone in his body. Dazed and trying to groan, he rocked back and forth in agony.

Something slammed into his ribs, hard—something that cursed and thudded hard to the ground right beside him, a sword cartwheeling past his blurred gaze. It seemed he'd tripped a bullyblade who'd been rushing up to gut him.

He had to move fast, to get at the man before a knife came out or that sword got snatched up again, and "dicing-handy-Lathanderite-holy-man time" arrived. He had to—

Something slammed hard into his ears and heaved the ground under him in the same explosive instant. A blast hurled men off their feet all over the clearing, and the bullyblade's fallen sword spun up into the air again. Semoor's face met the trampled weeds of the ground, his ears ringing, and a sudden wet rain thumped and pattered to the ground all around him, like mud hurled in the wake of speeding hooves.

Wiping and blinking furiously so he could see what was going on, he caught sight of the bullyblade just beyond him, who'd struggled up to a sitting position and was now reeling dazedly. The man was drenched in gore—and more than gore: large wet things that were now sliding off him.

As the bullyblade groaned and tried to gather his legs under him, Semoor spotted a staring eyeball in the midst of one large and hairy chunk. His stomach lurched.

He knew what he was staring at.

He'd not have to turn around to see what wouldn't be standing there, back across the clearing.

The Knights' hobbled horses.

He swallowed, trying hard not to be sick. Well, at least there hadn't been any Knights of Myth Drannor slaughtered along with them.

Had there?

Desperately, Dauntless parried again. Steel shrieked, spitting sparks as it was driven back almost to his nose.

He gave ground, panting, as the sword came at him again. This farm wench wasn't giving him time to set himself, *time* to fight her off! He was—

He lurched aside, twisting so the thrust that had been reaching for his codpiece sang off his armored thigh. Bitch! Murderous *bitch!*

"I am an ornrion of the Purple Dragons of Cormyr," he shouted, retreating again, "and my words and my sword are the *law* of Cormyr! I command you to—"

"Surrender so you can butcher us?" Islif snapped back at him. "I wondered how soon you'd start to trumpet your legal right to butcher us on sight! The law, indeed! Vangerdahast's secret orders, more like—and your own gleeful desires!"

Dauntless was forced to parry again. She was driving him back, besting him in both strength and swordwork.

"Well, *I* have gleeful desires, too!" she told him, eyes blazing. "I desire to stay alive and ride Cormyr freely, so I can obey the *royal* orders given to me! Or do you and the Royal Magician of Cormyr now presume to ignore the words of their king and queen, in favor of what you would prefer to do? Hey? *Hey?*"

Her latest roundhouse slash almost struck his sword from his numbed hands; parrying it sent him slipping backward on some-thing wet.

He was afraid now, more afraid than he'd been in a long time. This hairy-armed farm girl could match him and more, toe-to-toe in a sword fray, and—

Dauntless backed right into someone, in a collision that startled them both and left him hopping awkwardly aside, his flank and face undefended against the Lady Knight's seeking blade.

She came not after him, though. Instead, she slashed at the man who'd blundered against Dauntless, laying open the side of the man's head and sending him spinning and squalling to the ground. Dauntless knew that face. It was one of the Lord Yellander's bullyblades, a man who'd once—

Someone screamed, right behind Dauntless, and it was a voice he knew, too.

The shriek died into a rattling gurgle before he could hurl him-self around to see its source: Blade of the Purple Dragons Albaert Morkoun, dying with two bullyblade swords in his neck.

As Morkoun staggered and fell, Dauntless hacked at the face of one of his slayers in a fury, then plunged past to get behind the man, to make him a shield against Islif Lurelake.

He needn't have bothered. The Lady Knight seemed to have forgotten him for the moment. She was hewing her way through bullyblades like a drunken reaper at harvest-tide, and wounded men reeled and fled in all directions. One tripped over the thief Knight and went boots-in-the-air, crashing down on his face and coming up reeling worse than she'd ever been. Another flinched back from Sulwood as if the priest had been some sort of roaring clawed mon-ster, and sprinted away across the dark, spattered gore that blast had left strewn everywhere.

Dauntless felt like running after him. They were between him and the Ride, all of them, these Knights, and everything had gone horribly wrong.

Whenever he had dealings with the Knights of Myth Drannor, everything *always* went horribly wrong.

Another bullyblade fell, this one merely grunting as he staggered forward and then went down, face first into the trampled turf. Florin barely had time to notice. He was still running and fighting, frantically fencing and thrusting and then rushing on to run and fight some more, trying above all to keep from being surrounded by bullyblades and cut down by blades he couldn't hope to parry. He was leaving a trail of slain or sorely wounded bullyblades in his wake, yes, but how many of them were left?

Florin sidestepped a man wielding a pair of swords who greeted him with a defiant yell and two vicious thrusts. He whipped his own blade across the man's throat and ran on.

Hadn't Yellander quietly assembled something like a private army? Not that he was the only oh-so-loyal noble the Knights had taken a hand—however clumsy or unwitting—in bringing down. They *all* had private armies, didn't they?

The bullyblade's eyes widened as he made it up to his knees, coming face to belt with Semoor Wolftooth. Instead of shoving himself to his feet, the bullyblade grabbed for a dagger at his belt.

Whereupon the Pride of Lathander swung the large and bloody warhammer he'd found lying nearby just as hard as he could in a roundhouse swing at the side of the man's head.

That swinging cost him his balance and all sight of his foe, but the hammer hit *something* solidly enough to rattle Semoor's teeth before whatever it was sagged a bit and then fell away. Letting go of the hammer and rolling hastily over and away, Semoor peered back at the man he'd struck, as swiftly as he could.

All he could see was knees, thrust upward at awkward angles and not moving. Little wonder, he discovered a few moments later; there wasn't much left of one side of the man's head. It looked as if some unskilled idiot had driven a warhammer just as hard as he could into the bullyblade's head.

Semoor started to chuckle, but it turned into choking, and he found himself spewing up his stomach all over the man's knees.

Which promptly vanished again behind a wet, red curtain of blood. Starfall, he had to stop this bleeding!

The dead bullyblade was wearing a broad leather sword belt over his breeches-belt, its sword sleeve and dagger sheath already empty. Semoor fought with the buckle only briefly, managed to drag it out from under the man, and wound it twice around his own forehead before buckling it up again.

It was tight—throbbingly tight—but at least his own blood wasn't sheeting down into his eyes any longer. One last swipe with the back of his own gore-sticky hand, and he could see again.

Really see. Which meant, as the belt's empty dagger sheath dangled into his eyes, bumping against his nose, Semoor could clearly behold four—no, five!—bullyblades now bearing down on him, running hard.

With a yell, he grabbed at the warhammer and rose to meet them.

Hoping, as he struggled to lift the heavy weapon, that Lathander wouldn't be overly offended at what he was bellowing.

"Beard of Omthas, you *useless* Star of the Morning! *Protect* me, damn you! How can I spread the stlarning holy word of stlarning Lathander if I'm *dead?* Hey?"

Doust Sulwood was hopping and whirling among enemy blades to parry and lash out with his mace this way and then that, not daring to stand still for a moment.

He hoped—oh, how he hoped—Holy Tymora would stand with him when he most needed her. Right now, for instance.

Semoor's shout brought a grin to his lips. Well, at least he wasn't the only priest fighting to stay alive. And being as he wasn't the one cursing Lathander, perhaps the Morninglord would aid *him* rather than Semoor. As long as that aid didn't offend Tymora, of course.

A sword missed him entirely, and Doust reached over it and

leaned into his swing. His mace crashed home above a bullyblade ear, and that foe dropped like a full potato sack. Ah, but he was lucky these murderers weren't wearing armor!

Oh. Aha. Tymora had seen to that, of course!

"Ah, but I'm lucky to so bask in the bright favor of Lady Luck!" he said as he spun to face a new foe.

And promptly slipped and fell.

Chapter 7
WHIRLWINDS COME A-REAPING

Though brave words ring out strong
Setting every bold heart to leaping
There'll be lessons hard and lessons long
When the whirlwinds come a-reaping.

The character Selgur the Savage
In the play Karnoth's Homecoming
by Chanathra Jestryl, Lady Bard of Yhaunn
First performed in the Year of the Bloodbird

Jhessail backed away, breathing hard. Her dagger was gone, hurled at the thing the Purple Dragon had thrown at her. It had stuck into that missile and had probably been blasted to dust in the explosion that had followed after the thing had skipped aloft, spinning end over end to crash down among the horses.

Her ears were ringing, and she was drenched in horse gore. More of it was splattered everywhere around her, leaving her slipping and sliding at every step as she retreated, trembling. She circled to the right as she went, not wanting to go into unknown forest where she might well get tangled among trees and trapped with no way to flee.

Wearing the grim beginnings of a sly and cruel smile, the bully-blade leader stalked after her, drawn sword in hand.

"Don't make me use my spells," she warned, raising a hand.

The man sneered. "A little cantrip that will make the end of your nose glow, perhaps? Or banish the rust from my dagger? Or perhaps you'd like me to stop and watch you light a candle with your fingertip?"

"Oh, I can light more than candles," Jhessail told him, smiling with a confidence she was very far from feeling. They were back amid the fighting now, curling around behind bodies and frays still raging.

"Then why don't you, Lady Silvertree? Mage so mighty of the Knights of Myth Drannor? Little lying slut."

"Oh," Jhessail said, still backing away. "Is there something wrong with your sword? Is that why you're trying to insult me to death?"

The man stalked forward. "Lady, I am Eerikarr Steldurth. I served a great and noble lord of Cormyr long and well. I feel no need to insult a landless, lowborn, backcountry hedge mage. I can merely say 'lawbreaker' or 'murderer of lords.' When I speak thus of you, I utter truths, not insults."

Then he was upon her, dropping into a lunge that brought his blade thrusting in so close to Jhessail that it whispered between her right arm and her body, slicing garment and skin alike.

She gave a little shriek, flung up her arm, and ducked away to the left as he rose back into balance and slashed at her, backhanded.

He was an instant too late. She was *just* out of reach and bounding back to the right as his blade swept by. Steldurth sprang after her, hacking, and caught one of his own men in the shoulder as that bullyblade hastily backed away from Florin's flashing sword.

The man yelled, lashed out blindly, and kept on turning and retreating, blindly jostling Jhessail and sending her staggering.

Steldurth sidestepped the bullyblade's wild slash then ran right at Jhessail. She ducked away, diving between two bullyblades, and then dodged around a third—and almost into the waiting arms of Steldurth, who'd guessed her tactic correctly.

She spun away, leaving a great torn-out handful of her hair in his hand, and plunged past a bullyblade. Or tried to.

That outlaw was in full retreat from Florin, and she tripped over one of his swiftly moving boots. Jhessail sprawled, clawing at the ground to try to get up and run. She almost made it, rising but being turned over in midair by a boot deftly hooked around her ankle.

She fell again, face up this time, and found that it had been Eerikarr Steldurth who'd tripped her. Looming over her, he grinned—and drew his sword back to plunge down into her breast.

A slender arm clad in dark leathers and fresh blood rose up under his sword arm, blocking his thrust. Pennae's head came into view over Steldurth's shoulder as she finished swarming up him from behind. Grinning through teeth clenched in pain, she plunged the dagger in her other hand into Steldurth's throat.

Blade Hanstel Harrow was a fairly skilled warrior, but there were five bullyblades around him. Five cruel swords sliding in at his face and hands and every seam and chink of his armor, darting past his parries to spread ice in their wake, ice and the sticky wetness of his spilling blood. He was going to die here.

He threw all caution to the winds and hurled himself wildly at one foe and then another, taking foolish chances as he lunged, slashed, charged forward where no sensible swordsman would dare—and managed to slay an astonished bullyblade.

He didn't get even a moment to exult at his daring before the rest cut him down, slashing at the backs of his knees and leaving him crumpled at their feet ere their blades came plunging at him.

Harrow died with one last name on his lips, but cold steel had pinned his tongue to the back of his mouth and was keeping his teeth apart. He gurgled helplessly, face twisting in disappointment.

The grinning faces above him did not look one little bit like the faraway lasses he was remembering.

Harrow was down. Dead. Dauntless didn't waste any breath cursing. Dahauntul was the last Dragon left, and there weren't all that many of Yellander's rabble, either. He had to get away.

Vangerdahast had been quite clear on that. He must survive to watch over these accursed Knights of Myth Drannor and make quite sure they departed the realm. He was to report back everything they did and said and everyone they met with, to the Royal Magician. While somehow letting Old Thunderspells know that silencing a certain ornrion forever was neither desirable nor prudent.

He wasn't sure how he was going to manage that last bit.

On the other hand, he hadn't accomplished the first part—the surviving—yet, either.

Parrying a bullyblade sword hard enough to send its wielder staggering back with a startled curse, Ornrion Taltar Dahauntul spun around and sprinted for the trees, aiming for a spot where they stood thinly, in hopes he'd be able to see a way through them and back out to the Ride.

He was more than tired of this particular battle.

On the other hand, the five Dragons who'd ridden in here with him were beyond being tired of anything.

Brorn Hallomond stopped and lowered his sword. Beside him, the tall, red-bearded pillar that was Kraskus noticed and stopped too, turning to look at Brorn and awaiting orders.

After Lord Yellander's most trusted bodyguard stopped and looked around, there were always orders.

Brorn watched the last Purple Dragon—the ornrion—sprint into the trees. Scratching his chin thoughtfully, Brorn peered here and there around the clearing, noticing Steldurth's body with its slit throat and still-spreading blood. The battles were very much going against his side.

He looked up at his bodyguard, Kraskus, and then pointed across the clearing at where the last few bullyblades were busy dying, and at the adventurers causing those deaths. "Kraskus, I need you to kill all the Knights for me. I'm afraid I can't be with you while you do it. There's something I must go and do. Something *very* important."

Without another word he turned and hastened off into the trees on the other side of the clearing from where the ornrion had disappeared.

For a long time Kraskus frowned and stared at Brorn's dwindling back.

Then the big man shrugged, turned, and launched himself into a charge across the corpse-strewn clearing, heading for those last few battles.

"Kill all the Knights," he growled, to make sure he kept it straight. "Kill all the Knights."

He was almost within reach of them now. With a roar, he waved his sword over his head and plunged into the nearest fray. "Kill the Knights!"

Then he corrected himself. *"All* the Knights." He repeated those words several times more as he thrust out with his sword and was parried. This was important, and he didn't want to forget it.

"And you attacked us *why?*" Islif snapped, smashing aside Halmur's sword as if the arm that held it were a mere twig.

Bones splintered, and the Turmishan screamed and staggered back, eyes wide with astonishment..

She strode after him. "I really want to know."

The dusky-skinned bullyblade dodged aside from her sword. He hissed in pain and, clutching his stricken arm, gave her a glare. "You really *are* a farm lass, aren't you?"

Islif nodded. "Yes. One who wants to know why you set upon us. We had our swords out and were disputing with Purple Dragons! Surely outlaws can be patient or sensible enough to seek easier prey than that!"

"We're not outlaws," Halmur snarled, his useless arm dangling in his wake as he hurried to a fallen fellow. The sprawled body— Yarlen, who still owed him three lions from their last dice game, curse it all—wore two sheathed daggers he could use about now. "Or weren't. Until you Knights slew Lord Yellander and lost us our livelihoods! We weren't here after 'easier prey,' you stone-witted slut! We were after *you!*"

"And now?" Islif asked, still striding after him.

"And *now,*" the Turmishan snapped triumphantly, ducking down, snatching out a dagger, and whirling to fling it in her face, "we still are!"

He was whirling back to the body to pluck up the second dagger and spring at her with it when the first one, in the wake of a ringing clang, came spinning past his head to bounce to a stop amid the crushed remnants of a shrub.

Halmur sprang forward after it, seeking to get away from the sword he knew would already be thrusting at his backside.

Islif sighed and slashed instead at his hindmost ankle, lifting her blade and tripping the fleeing bullyblade into a crashing fall into another nearby bush. He rolled amid crackling branches and found his feet—more agile eel than the wallowing warrior she'd expected him to be—to stand panting at her.

"Think you're clever," he gasped, "don't you? Playthings of Queen Filfaeril, above us all, daring to cross Vangerdahast himself!" He spat at her. "Tymora-kissed bitch! How sheer blind luck has kept you alive thus far, I don't—*urrrk!*"

The hurled warhammer crushed Halmur's throat and bounced away from him, leaving the stricken bullyblade to clutch his neck, stare wild-eyed at Islif, and topple.

Semoor strolled forward, dusting his hands in evident satisfaction. "See that? One throat, dead-on! Not many priests of Lathander could land that, I tell you! And the result? One *far* too sardonic Turmishan, silenced forever!"

Islif regarded her fellow Knight with something approaching contempt. "Does Lathander approve of his holynoses crowing about a slaying they've done?"

"Certainly hope so." Semoor grinned at her, chastened not in the slightest. "Because, look you, that's my fifth in a row! Four just back there—one got away, and I let him go because one *must* be merciful from time to time, just to allow some sort of balance to prevail in the world—and now this little dancing toad. I'd not waste tears on him, were I you. He was the only one of them I've heard about, in all our visits to revels and Court functions. Seems he liked treating ladies rather cruelly. I can provide details if you'd like."

"Spare me," Islif said. "And what're you wearing that sword belt for? That sheath makes you look ridiculous. Like a—a—" She blushed, unexpectedly, and turned her head away.

"An extra nightblade sticking out of my forehead?" Semoor asked cheerfully. "Hadn't thought of that, but I quite like the notion."

He struck a pose and strutted a few steps, making the empty dagger sheath bounce off his nose, before glancing idly across the clearing, stopping in mid-bounce, and adding, "Huh. Looks like we're done. Florin's just felled that great red-bearded brute. So unless there're still some arrows about to come whistling out at us—"

"Stoop," Doust growled as he came up to them, bedraggled and bleeding, "I *wish* you hadn't said that."

Semoor shrugged. "I believe I'm safe enough in doing so. I don't think there's anyone left in hiding who could take it as a cue. What happened to you?"

"Imminent death, deliverance from same by Florin," Doust said grimly. "I don't think Tymora intended me to wage war."

"I *know* Lathander didn't want me to," Semoor said brightly. "He meant me to intone soft prayers and bathe in the offering coins gently bestowed upon me by an adoring populace, and I've been practicing my intonings, too, but people who want to kill us keep *interrupting*, by—"

"Perhaps they're critics," Florin said in a dry voice, joining them with Jhessail at his side. "Where's Pennae?"

All of the Knights peered across the clearing, looking this way and that, afraid they'd catch a glimpse of Pennae's dark leathers among the sprawled fallen. It was Semoor who saw her first.

"There," he said, pointing.

Something that had been feebly rolling in the creek rose up rather wearily and gave them all a bleak look.

It was Pennae, looking rather the worse for wear. She had been wounded in several places, caked in foul-smelling mud, and most of her hair was gone, her scalp blackened and scorched. Doust and Jhessail both looked at the threads of blood curling lazily in the slow waters of the stream sliding past their boots, and then back along that winding water to the thief.

"She's hurt," Doust announced to no one in particular, and he started across the clearing.

"*Doust!*" Islif snapped, hastening to catch up with him. "There could be a score of foes in these trees!"

Doust shrugged. "Tymora, remember? The bolder I dare, the safer I'll be."

Islif frowned. "I'm not sure that's quite how the luckpriests put it."

He waved her words away, still hastening on to where Pennae was now standing, wincing a little as she settled herself into a pose against a handy tree trunk.

"Hail, fellow conquering heroes," she greeted them as they came up to her. Her face—even her lips—were pale, but her grin was as sardonic as ever.

"You're hurt," Doust said without greeting. "Sit down."

"No, you can paw me just as well if I stay right where I am," Pennae replied a little wearily. "Sit down would probably turn into fall down, and I've bled quite enough already."

Doust shook his head, threw up a hand to his fellow Knights to keep clear, and started to murmur a healing prayer.

"Heed me," Pennae told the rest of the Knights, over his shoulder. "Up this hill behind me, in the trees, there's a little hollow, and it's full of what's left of an old stone mansion. Ruined, overgrown—trees right up through it—but someone's still—"

She gasped as Doust's glowing fingertips touched the worst of her cuts. She closed her eyes and trembled for a moment as he moved his hands gingerly over her, and then she opened them, smiled, and said, "I *do* so love a man's hands on me. When he's doing me good, at least."

Semoor rolled his eyes. "You were saying? Someone's still . . ."

"Using it for something," Pennae said. "I got caught in a spell that had been cast across its doorway. Some sort of fire trap."

Semoor rubbed his hands and grinned. "Treasure!"

"Is that *all* you think of?" Florin and Islif asked disapprovingly, in almost perfect unison.

"No, but it'll do to think about until more important things arise," Semoor said. "Such as matters of the Morninglord, and . . . well, more matters of the Morninglord!"

"Indeed," Islif said. "This ruined mansion will be a good place to get well away from."

As if her words had been a cue, a crossbow quarrel came humming out of the woods and smashed her off her feet.

"Down!" Florin roared, flinging Jhessail to the turf as he spun down into a crouch to reach out a hand to Islif.

Who was clutching her ribs and groaning, her armor dented deeply on one flank.

"Are you—?" he snapped.

"Alive? Aye," she gasped. "More than that, I'm not willing to venture."

"Come *on,*" Semoor snarled at them all. "Stone walls are about all I know that can stop arrows!"

Pennae had already dropped from leaning against the tree to crouching in its lee, beckoning them.

The Knights scrambled after her. "I *told* you not to mention arrows," Doust told Semoor, "and *now* look—"

"Luckiest of Holynoses," Pennae said over her shoulder, "please accept my thanks for healing me, and forthwith *shut up.* Are you unaware that a bowman can loose at where he hears our voices coming from?"

Doust shut up.

Pennae beckoned them again, crouching low. Bent over and scuttling through the underbrush, she led them up through thickly standing trees, in more branch-snapping haste than stealth, and into the hollow.

The mansion loomed before them, low and dark in the gloomy shade of the trees that had grown up through it and flung out boughs to overhang it. Its scorched and empty doorway yawned like an open, waiting mouth, the air still sharp with the smell of the fire that had recently raged in it, but Pennae hurried past, keeping low. Ducking around a corner, she plunged without pause through a dark, gaping opening that had once held a window.

The other Knights hesitated, listening. All of them half-expected flames to roar up or to be near-deafened by the sudden snarl of some fearsome beast, followed by Pennae's raw scream.

They heard only silence. They had all traded doubtful glances.

Florin shrugged, put his hands in the exact same places on the lip of the window opening that Pennae had touched, and vaulted through it into unknown darkness. They heard the light thumps of his boots landing on what sounded like wood.

A moment later, he reappeared at the window, a warning finger to his lips. He beckoned them, wordlessly gesturing that they should each move to one side once they landed inside the window.

Jhessail stepped forward, waving at Doust to give her a boost, and went over and in—unexpectedly aided by Semoor's uninvited hand under her trim behind.

One by one, the other Knights followed to find themselves standing in near darkness, the only light filtering in through the shadowed window.

They could hear each other breathing but nothing more. Until one of them took a cautious stride forward.

As if that had been a signal, they heard a sudden roar and crackle of flame in the distance, from the far end of the mansion—a roar that was promptly joined by a scream.

An unknown someone had triggered *another* fire trap.

"Pennae?" Florin whispered. "You're still here, right?"

"Idiot," she replied, even more quietly. *"Now* you've done it."

And it seemed he had.

They heard the sound of a rope groaning as it stretched, then a squealing of wood sliding on wood—and the floor fell away under the boots of Doust and Semoor as if it were a door swinging open, pitching them down into unseen depths.

They landed hard on smooth, flat stone, yells dying as they clashed teeth, bit their tongues—and were driven flat and breathless under the sudden weights of their fellow Knights tumbling down on top of them.

Small squeaking things fled in all directions, Florin rolled off a squirming Semoor, and Jhessail muttered, "Well, at least the cellar wasn't too far down."

"Jhess?" Islif called softly from above them. "Is everyone—?"

"We're fine," Semoor said sourly. "Just fine. *Flatter* than we were a moment ago, mind you, but—hold! Where are you?"

"Up here. I'm holding onto the window, inside the house. My boots dangling into nothing."

"I'm getting out of the way," Semoor told her, rolling and groaning as he did so. "Just give me a moment!"

The hum of something approaching very swiftly filled the air. Before Islif recognized it for what it was, a crossbow quarrel came scudding through the trees straight into her arm, punching through armor and hurling her away from the window to crash down atop someone.

"Sorry," she gasped, and then she sobbed at the sickening pain her movements dealt to her arm.

"Islif?" Florin said nearby, concern in his voice. "Are you hurt?"

"Am I ever anything else?" she asked wearily, rolling off the unseen body and hearing it groan. Her landing bumped the end of the quarrel on the floor, leaving her gasping and shuddering in pain. "Gods!" she hissed. "Where are you, priests?"

"I'm over here," Semoor told her, from her left. "Trying to remember a prayer for calling up some holy light. As for Doust, you're probably sitting on him. Or whatever's left of him."

"Doust?" Islif asked doubtfully, before she lowered her voice and muttered a few more curses to herself.

The reply was some panting, and then the weak words, "Pray to . . . Tymora for me . . . someone? No breath to do it . . . m'self."

"I can still manage a glow," Jhessail said. "I think."

"Don't think," Semoor told her. "We're adventurers. Things always get worse when we think."

Someone snorted, not all that far away.

"Florin?" Jhessail asked. "Is that you?"

"Does anyone know what this place is?" Doust asked, his voice a little stronger.

"Yes," a cold voice answered out of the darkness.

"Hoy," one door guard whispered. "Whirlwind, come a-reaping!"

He and his fellow guard snapped to rigid attention. Old Myarlin Handaerback, the grandly uniformed doorjack standing between them, stepped smartly away from the door and then spun to open it for the swift-striding younger Princess of Cormyr. He stood ready to announce her.

Princess Alusair darted at that doorjack so swiftly that one guard snatched at his sword out of sheer habit. The princess took a firm hold of the elbow of Myarlin's gaudily trimmed jacket and dragged him bodily back from the door to stagger awkwardly to a halt beside her simmering gaze.

"Thank you," she told Myarlin, "but I do *not* wish to be announced. Bide you here, saer. Close the door behind me, and kindly refrain from trying to listen through the keyhole. For once."

Myarlin blinked and then bowed in acknowledgment. The other door guard snorted, but he was a veteran—as were all the sentinels in the royal wing of the Palace—and managed to keep his face as straight as that of the nearest statue.

The young princess gave him a warning look, opened the door, and slipped inside.

There were fresh furs down on the floor of the Helmed Lady's Room, and someone had cast rose petals into the lamp sconces to pleasantly scent the dimly lit chamber. From around the polished black bulk of the Helmed Lady statue that shielded Alusair's view of much of the chamber came a familiar voice. It made Alusair check her furious stride for a moment—and then shrug and hasten on.

Tana or no haughty Tana, this could not wait.

Chapter 8
DOORS, DISPUTES, AND SUDDEN DOWNFALLS

I do my work and preen my pretty head
Caring nothing for curses and catcalls
But listen right well for, and deeply dread,
Doors, disputes, and sudden downfalls.

*The character Charanna
the Chambermaid*
In the play Karnoth's Homecoming
by Chanathra Jestryl, Lady Bard of Yhaunn
First performed in the Year of the Bloodbird

So you see, Royal Mother," Tanalasta was saying smoothly, "I find the time I spend seeking to master the lute to be largely wasted, and I would prefer to—"

"Sire!" Alusair burst out, rounding the statue and looking to her father. "Pray pardon for the interruption, but I—"

"Luse, darling," Queen Filfaeril said firmly, "you are 'storming angrily.' Again. Is the realm being invaded?"

"No, but—" Alusair looked helplessly at her father, but he merely gestured that she should attend her mother.

"Is the palace on fire?"

"*No,* Mother, but—"

"If, as I suspect, your concern is primarily with a slight done to you," the Dragon Queen said calmly, "then you need not interrupt our private converse with Tanalasta *quite* so precipitously."

"Mother, I can speak with you later," Crown Princess Tanalasta put in smoothly, giving her younger sister a look of cold scorn. "*I* have learned a little patience."

"Stay," the queen said softly, bending her gaze to meet Alusair's blazing eyes. "Your matter is not trivial. Perhaps what Alusair is bursting to tell us is not, either. Daughter?"

This last word was clearly addressed to Alusair, who bit her lips to quell the curse that sprang to mind, and forced herself to ask quietly, "Royal Mother, have I leave to speak?"

Queen Filfaeril nodded. "Please do. Better to spew than explode."

The king smiled slightly.

Alusair sighed, threw back her head, and announced, "I have just learned that Royal Magician Vangerdahast sent my personal champion off to the northeasternmost corner of the realm on a mission that bids fair to get him killed and forbade him to inform me that he was going! I want—"

"Luse," her father broke in calmly, "hold hard a moment. I didn't know you *had* a personal champion. Who is this paragon, and how came you to have him?"

Alusair sighed, closed her eyes, opened them again, and said, "Earlier this day, I named Ornrion Taltar Dahauntul of the Purple Dragons my personal champion. To Vangey's *face* I proclaimed him thus and told our *good* Royal Magician that as I now had a champion to protect me, the war wizards he was assigning to spy upon my every last nose-picking and chamber pot-filling moment—"

"Ohh!" Tanalasta exclaimed in disgust. "Must you mention such things? *Really!*"

"I can well believe that *you* no longer use chamber pots," Alusair snapped at her sister. "In fact, that explains some things."

She turned her glare back to her parents before anyone could admonish her and added crisply, "Yet I digress. As I was saying, I informed him that his *spies* were no longer needed to be nannies and sneaks and jailers upon me—all three at once and every moment of my *life*, waking and otherwise. The Royal Magician openly sneered at me and said he took no orders from me, so I set him straight on *that*—and departed his company. Only to learn that the moment he'd seen my back, he summoned the ornrion and sent him off to be killed, doing this wholly to flout my will and hurl his disobedience into my very *teeth!*"

"And so?" the king asked gently.

"And so I want him disciplined—for once!—and Dauntless brought back to me."

"Disciplined?" the queen asked. "Disciplined how, exactly?"

Tanalasta rolled her eyes. "She's going to say 'horsewhipped,' Mother!"

Alusair gave her sister a look that had drawn daggers in it, and then turned back to the Queen of Cormyr and snapped defiantly, "*Publicly* horsewhipped. For a start."

Her father made a sound that might have been a suppressed snort of amusement—but when all three Obarskyr females looked sharply at him, they found his face stern and wearing the beginnings of a real frown.

"Alusair Nacacia Obarskyr," Queen Filfaeril began, almost sweetly, and both of her daughters stiffened. The use of a full formal name meant trouble.

"I should leave," Tanalasta announced quickly, ducking her head and starting for the nearest door. Only to discover a slender arm had somehow become hooked around hers and had become as unmoving as an iron window bar. The Queen of Cormyr was stronger than she looked.

"Stay and attend, Crown Princess," her mother said softly in an order as absolute as if she'd thundered it. "You are to heed and remember our words now, just as surely as your sister must."

Azoun cleared his throat. Again all three of his kin shot looks his way, but he merely held out his hand toward his wife, indicating that she was to proceed.

The Queen of Cormyr lifted her jaw just as Alusair had done earlier, drew in an unhurried breath, and said, "A time will come when you two princesses may freely give royal commands to the wizard Vangerdahast and will see good need to do so. That time may well, however, be years hence. For now, you are to obey him utterly, unless his orders contradict those of myself or your father—and even then, hear and consider his will."

The king nodded.

Filfaeril raised one finger to indicate him and slowed her speech to give each of her words weight, to impress their gravity on the two listening princesses.

"Your sire sits upon the Dragon Throne, but Vangerdahast *is* the

Dragon Throne. We cannot rule the nearest chamber pot, full or empty, without him, and if he should fall dead in our moment of need, so too will Cormyr fall. Whereas if I fall, or your father does, Vangerdahast will see to it that the realm survives. If he demands you appear before him naked, thrice a day and before all the Court, you will do it. Or that horsewhip shall see use—and not upon him."

Both of her daughters stared at her, suddenly needing to swallow and barely remembering how to do it.

Their mother leaned forward a little. "As one who has gone before you, and as a woman, I quite understand the irritation and embarrassment—nay, shame is not too strong a word—that the ever-present spying of our Wizards of War visits upon you. As one who has been the age you are now, daughter Alusair, I know how much this must chafe and set you afire, when you see your every whim prevented, your wanderings curtailed, the adventures we all must have alone ended abruptly or soured, time and again. Believe me, I *know* how you feel." She raised an admonishing finger. "Yet you are not any young backcountry farm lass. You are the future of the realm, an Obarskyr. You *cannot* have a carefree youth, and Vangerdahast's high-handed meddlings have ensured—thus far—that you have lived to enjoy a youth at all. He has personally prevented at least thirty-four attempts on your life that he has told me about—"

"Sixty-three," Azoun interrupted. "As of yestereve."

Filfaeril turned to give her husband a long look, then returned her attention to Alusair. "And as you see, the Royal Magician chooses to keep secrets from me, just as he does from you. I *hate* it, make no mistake—and yet, exasperating as he can be, I trust him."

She spread her hands in a gesture of helpless resignation. "I must trust him. We all must. For he could betray and destroy us all with the snap of a finger, but he does not. Time and again he has proven deeply worthy of our trust. No, he is not the most polite man in Faerûn, nor yet Cormyr, but never forget he is a wizard." She sat back again and sighed. "Strange folk, wizards. All that magic *does* things to their minds and tempers. The temptation must gnaw at them their every waking moment; they have such power and could just lash out at anything that angers them. Yet if they had—just a few of them, a time or two too often in the past—wizards would now be hidden, hunted things, with all the rest of us so fearful of magic that we'd bury our blades in anyone we merely suspected of being able to murmur a spell. And is that the way of the world? No. Wherefore, look you, even mages who are evil tyrants tend to hurl spells only when they deem it needful. And our Vangerdahast is not an evil tyrant. He's a tyrant, I'll grant, but Cormyr needs its tyrant. *I* dread the day when he is no longer with us. Who will keep us safe— if irritated—then?"

She stopped speaking and let silence fall. It was a long time before Alusair dared to stir and look to her father.

"Sire," she whispered, "is this also your view?"

Her father nodded. "Every word of it. Daughter Alusair, Vangerdahast is too useful—too *vital*—to the realm for you to defy or annoy. So you will cease doing both of those things, right now. And show him how polite and respectful and genuinely *thankful* a true Obarskyr princess can be. Or I may go looking for a horsewhip myself. Or tell Vangey to wield it for me."

Tanalasta's mouth dropped open, but her father merely turned to her and reminded her gravely, "Control."

Both princesses nodded soberly. The need for them to control their faces, words, and voices at all times had been seared into them so often in their lives thus far that they had long since lost track of how many times they had been lectured on the matter. They had even lost count of all the folk who had delivered those stern teachings.

"Sire, Royal Mother," Alusair whispered then, head bowed, "I hear and heed. Have I your leave to withdraw?"

"You do," King Azoun said gravely.

The princess bowed as deeply as any courtier who wasn't going to his knees, turned, and said to Tanalasta in an almost inaudible voice, "Pray forgiveness, Royal Sister, for my interruption."

Before Tanalasta could reply, Alusair glided away, back around the Helmed Lady, and was gone.

Seething, she traversed the rest of the chamber like a storm wind and thrust the door open, uncaring of whether or not the doorjack might be standing in its way. The door swung open freely, though she barely noticed, and the younger Princess of Cormyr bent one shoulder low like a running warrior so as to turn the corner faster, clenched her hands into claws, and—

Slammed right into a man who'd stepped from behind the door and must have been standing right outside it, listening!

A more-than-familiar man. The Royal Magician of Cormyr staggered back a step or two from their bruising meeting to regard her with a raised eyebrow and eyes that held . . . sardonic amusement?

In wordless rage Alusair launched herself at him, punching and kicking with a vicious disregard for his gender. She promptly and painfully discovered that he wore an armored codpiece under his robes—and that even Royal Magicians can be toppled by an angry youngling.

As they rolled together on the passage floor, Alusair was only barely aware that in the dimness around her there was no sign of the door guards or doorjacks who were supposed to be guarding the door.

She clawed, punched, and drove in her knees, spitting out curses in a raging stream that sounded incoherent even to her. The Royal Magician did not even try to defend himself beyond throwing his arms up to shield his face and throat. He grunted with pain, again and again, and tried to twist out from under her. When he thrust up his legs to try to spill her off, Alusair snatched out her little belt dagger.

"Too far," she heard him grunt, then murmur something so brief that she couldn't catch it. A moment later, magic burned her fingers and hurled her dagger away. She heard it sing off the wall some distance behind her.

"Not so easily done, sirrah." She brought one leg around until she could reach her boot and thrust her fingers into it to snatch out a little knife.

Her ankle-fang flashed out, she growled in triumph and found that the wrist of that hand had been caught in an iron-firm grip.

A face was looking down at her from beyond that grip—an all-too-familiar face that was icily beautiful and calm, yet whose eyes held a scowl to match Alusair's own fury.

"Royal command time," Queen Filfaeril said in a calm, level voice. "Remove yourself from the personage beneath you, and come with me."

Alusair barely had time to swing her other leg off the wizard before the Dragon Queen hauled her to her feet and started marching her back down the passage.

"Mother," Alusair said, "where are we—?"

"Yonder maid's closet. Or the one beyond. I don't share your preference for horsewhips, Daughter. The flat of my hand will serve quite well."

"You—me, a princess—a *spanking?*"

"Not quite the eloquence I expect in a Princess of Cormyr *I* had any hand in rearing," Filfaeril replied, "but you seem to have grasped the main points. *In here,* miss!"

A door banged.

Vangerdahast had sat up to watch and listen to the princess being dragged away. Now he slowly rolled over to his knees, wincing, used both hands to thrust himself to his feet, and staggered off down the passage.

He did not look back and so never saw the man standing unmoving against the passage wall in the dark lee of a tapestry.

King Azoun IV of Cormyr was standing ready to break Vangerdahast's jaw and knock him cold, if he could. Though he'd not have tried to punch the Royal Magician at all if the wizard had not dared to tarry and watch Alusair's punishment, for his own enjoyment.

A little relieved that none of that had been necessary, he smiled at the wizard's distant, dwindling figure.

"Those who deal in pain are fated to entertain it in turn," he murmured. "It's merely a matter of when. So reap this whirlwind, Vangey. It's puny, compared to most of your others."

"Who's there?" Aumrune of the Zhentarim asked sharply. He'd taken care that few of the Brotherhood knew where he liked to experiment with magic. It cut down on . . . the over-ambitious aiding "accidents."

The robed and hooded figure slowly spread empty hands in a "look, I bear nothing" gesture, and then reached up and put back his cowl to reveal a familiar face.

"Mauliykhus," the approaching wizard identified himself. "My deepest apologies for disturbing your work. There is urgent news. I thought you would want to hear it without delay."

Aumrune set his wand on the table, cast the cloak he'd brought to conceal from all eyes the array of clamps and stands and what they held, and strode to meet Mauliykhus. He awakened several of the rings he wore to glowing life.

Most Zhentarim harbored thoughts of doom befalling their superiors, and he supposed Mauliykhus was no different. "Supposed" because he'd never found the slightest whisper of a hint that the lesser mage was actually *doing* anything to bring such a doom down on Aumrune—and because his own deepening judgment of the character of Mauliykhus Oenren led him to believe that the man would never dare try anything beyond, perhaps, a sudden wild snatch at a bright opportunity.

And if there was one thing Aumrune Trantor was careful never to offer any potential foe—which meant everyone else in all Faerûn—it was a bright opportunity.

Wherefore he came to a careful stop two paces away from Mauliykhus and held up a hand, the rings on it glowing in warning. "What news?"

"Lord Manshoon," Mauliykhus said, lowering his head and edging forward. He stopped, appearing not to see Aumrune's stern "keep back" gesture as he looked back over his shoulder. "Best whisper this," he breathed quietly, edging still closer.

Aumrune took a step back. "Is it choosing a new foremost

henchwizard from among us all, again? I have an ever-decreasing appetite for idle gossip, and—"

Mauliykhus shook his head and looked nervously behind him again. "It's not that."

"If anyone's listening to us," Aumrune said, "they'll be using magic and keeping themselves safely far away from here, not tiptoeing along behind you." One of the rings blossomed from its glow into a faint singing in the air all around the two wizards.

"There," he announced. "No one can scry us now without overwhelming that. And if it collapses, we'll know, won't we? Now—"

He stiffened, then, as Mauliykhus put a hand on his arm.

The lesser wizard did rather more than stiffen. He staggered back a step—and then collapsed to the floor like a falling blanket.

Aumrune looked down at the fallen wizard, watching thin threads of smoke drift up from the burnt-out holes that had held eyes a moment or two ago. Dead as last year's moths and about as useful.

Aumrune Trantor stepped around him, reeling a little as the two entities still settling into his head fumbled for precise control of their new host body's limbs, and strode away, leaving cloak, wand, and all forgotten on the table behind him.

He no longer had need of such trifles.

+ + ✳ + +

"Lady Ironchylde!"

The whisper was urgent—and loud almost enough to echo the entire length of this obscure, out-of-the-way, upper passage of the vast and sprawling Royal Court.

Wizard of War Tsantress Ironchylde calmly finished locking the door of her chambers ere turning to look at whoever had hailed her. She was young and capable—and much of her effectiveness thus far, she knew well, was due to her ability to remain calm.

"I am not," she said pleasantly, "a 'Lady.' I am a war wizard, of low birth, as it happens. And you are . . . ?"

The man who'd hailed her was the only other person in the passage. Lean and lithe, he was wearing glossy black boots, black hose of the most expensive make, a black codpiece that might have made a jester snicker, and a black cloak that entirely hid his doublet and most of his face, too. He stopped every few feet to cast exaggerated looks up and down the passage.

"Are we," he whispered tersely, "alone?"

Tsantress quelled a sudden urge to giggle and assured him that they were. As she did so, she put one of her hands behind her, out of his sight, and awakened one of the rings upon it. Just in case.

"I *dare* not speak to you," the mysterious figure whispered, scuttling nearer, "out here."

"And yet you *are* speaking to me," Tsantress said. "Though you have as of yet failed to answer my question."

"So I have!" the man in black agreed, ducking his head and sidling still nearer, almost turning his back on her in his eagerness to look behind him—and then whirling around and leaning over to peer past her. "Madam mage, I am a Lord of Cormyr!"

"Whose name is . . . ?" Tsantress.

"Not out here, I pray you, madam! Not out here!"

Tsantress activated a second ring. If she was going to enter her chambers alone with an unidentified man, she was going to furnish *no* possibility of his successfully attacking her or snatching any of the unfinished—albeit cryptic—work she had spread out on her bed and tables.

"Very well," she said, and she unlocked her door with the deftness of long practice, keeping herself facing him all the while. "Pray enter, Unknown Lord."

The man in black winced. "I would not have you think poorly of me! I mean you no harm nor dishonor. Believe me! I desire but to aid Cormyr on a matter of utmost delicacy! *Please* believe me!"

"In here." Tsantress beckoned.

Her guest cast two last exaggerated looks up and down the hallway and then ducked inside, swirling his cloak away from his face with a flourish as she swung the door shut behind him.

Tsantress regarded him calmly. His face was quite handsome, and she recalled seeing it at Court a time or two. As noble as he

claimed to be, but of no important family . . . and about the same
age she was.

"Is it locked?" he asked.

"Not yet," the war wizard told him. "Its locking awaits the revela-
tion of your name."

The man in black broke his dramatic pose long enough to spin to
face her. "Lady Wizard," he said, striking another pose, "I am Lord
Rhallogant Caladanter!"

"Well met," Tsantress replied. She made her own little show of
locking—and bolting—the door, then leaned back against it, folded
her arms across her chest, and asked, "So you wish to speak to me
regarding a matter of utmost delicacy?"

The handsome young lord looked both ways again, even in
her small, dim antechamber, then sank his head low between his
shoulders and murmured in a deep voice, eyes darting this way
and that as if he could see watching eyes appearing in every corner,
"*I* have overheard some disturbing things about a few Wizards of
War—Vangerdahast and Laspeera, in particular—who have been
meeting in secret with some Sembians and Zhentarim. I fear for the
realm, but I know not where to turn."

Tsantress stiffened, her face going pale. She was an ambitious,
capable young war wizard and had been *very* careful to watch and
learn much, for fear of putting a foot wrong as she sought to ascend
ever higher in the Royal Magician's regard. A few of the folk she had
seen Vangerdahast meeting with had troubled her deeply. So *this,*
now . . .

"Come," she whispered as she crossed the antechamber into her
study, taking him by the sleeve. She was pleased to see that although
he trembled with excitement, he showed no triumphant grin of
lechery or brightening opportunism. "Sit with me, and tell me all
you have seen and heard. *All.*"

As she'd suspected, it wasn't much. Yet it was more than enough
to make her shiver. She regarded the Royal Palace in a new way:
as a brooding fortress of suspicions, every shadow something that
peered and listened. "Den of traitors, den of thieves," she murmured,

remembering the old Suzailan song deriding the Court.

"Lord Caladanter, I thank you," she said then, putting a firm hand on his knee and staring deep into his eyes. Under her palm, he seemed as excited as a puppy, his eyes glowing as he stared into hers—but again, there was no hint of the seducer.

"Your very life is in danger," she said, telling him what she knew he wanted to hear—and knowing it was all too true. "If you breathe one word to anyone about speaking to me and anything that even hints at what you've just told me, someone—possibly several someones—*will* kill you."

She paused a moment to let that sink in and watched his excitement slide slowly into fear. Not as swift-witted as he'd first seemed, this one. Madwits, yes, but a *slow* madwits, to boot.

"You must not be seen leaving my rooms," she said. "Will you submit to a spell, if I cast a translocation upon you?"

He started to nod eagerly then frowned. "A—oh. To whisk me in an instant from here to . . . somewhere else?"

Tsantress nodded. "To one of the gates where the Royal Gardens lets out onto the Promenade. Whence you can easily stroll home."

"P-please!" he stammered.

She rose, gesturing that he should, too—and the moment he did, touched him with a ring she had already awakened. In its silent flash, he vanished without another word.

"No touching farewells, young lord," she murmured, more to hear her own voice than for any other reason. She didn't want to wallow in how deeply this news had troubled her, didn't want to—

Hold! No one had seen him depart, yes. But had anyone seen him *arrive?*

Tsantress marched across the room and flung the door wide to do her own sharp look up and down the passage.

She found herself meeting the startled gaze of a doorjack in the usual livery, standing formally outside the door across the passage and a few strides down.

It was a man she'd never seen before, and it was an odd door to stand upon ceremony—because it led onto a landing of an internal staircase, not into a state room or anyone's chambers.

At her scrutiny, the doorjack's expression turned cold. He was almost glaring at her as he slowly turned, opened the door, and stepped through it.

Tsantress saw a slice of landing and stair through its frame, just as she'd expected—but she also saw something more.

The doorjack had turned his head to stare at her as he strode out of sight, and just before he passed from view, his unfamiliar face *slid* into the features of someone else.

Vangerdahast.

Chapter 9
THE LOST PALACE

Yet though I live so long, I pray you lords
thrust your blades deep into me,
to make sure I breathe no more
if ever I begin to become
the sort of king who forgets his own name,
knows not lifelong friends nor foes,
and loses even palaces in the fogs of his failing mind.

The character King
Brighthawk Godsummer
In the play The Fall of Three Kings
by Ornrabbar Helikan, merchant of Athkatla
First performed in the Year of the Weeping Moon

The door closed behind Vangerdahast. Tsantress stared at it, her mind racing. Her entire world whirled away in an instant . . . what to do? What should she *do*?

She looked up and down the passage out of sheer habit, seeing no one, then heard the faintest of sounds in the room behind her—or thought she did—and whirled around.

Nothing. Her antechamber was dark and still, with no grimly smiling Royal Magician or anyone else standing there. Tsantress closed the door again, strode swiftly across the room to snatch up a wedge of cheese for later consumption and took down her dagger in its thigh-sheath from its usual place on the wall. Drawing in a deep breath, she used her teleport ring again.

It was the only way out, given the wards in place over the vast Royal Court and the Royal Palace beyond that would foil any translocation cast by someone not wearing such a ring—and she had to get out.

To find time to think, if nothing else.

Wherefore she found herself standing on a ledge high on the Thunder Peaks, lashed by rain. She stared bleakly out over fog-shrouded eastern Cormyr for a few moments, called on the ring again, and teleported to where she was *really* bound for. An extra "jump" should foil any tracing magic Old Thunderspells used to follow her. She hoped.

The ledge went away in the usual instant of falling endlessly through bright blue mists, and then there was solid stone under her boots again, and familiar dank gloom surrounded her amid smells of earth and old bear dung.

She was home. Or rather, she was back in a side-fissure of a wilderland cave that she'd long ago cast a spell upon to keep a bear or anything else from settling into it and lairing. The cave was nigh the Moonsea Ride near Tilverton, clear out of Cormyr, where she'd spent days and nights practicing her spell-casting when she'd been younger.

"Tluin," she whispered, taking a step to where she could perch one foot on an upthrusting rock and more easily buckle her dagger about her thigh.

She was gone from Cormyr, gone from the life she had known that had made her feel so happy, so important, so . . . needed.

Now what?

A lantern was unhooded, and the Knights of Myth Drannor found themselves staring down a littered stone cellar at four men. The foremost of whom was Lord Maniol Crownsilver.

Behind the noble lord were three unfamiliar men in robes, arranged in a stony-faced line. All were glaring at the Knights.

One robed man held the lantern high; the other two had their hands outstretched toward each other, and the air was flickering and pulsing between those reaching fingers—little flowerings of blue radiance that grew, winked out, then flashed into existence again, more strongly.

Three wizards. By the style of their sashes and rune-adorned jerkins, Sembian wizards-for-hire.

"Jhess," Florin muttered. "What magic's that?"

"A portal, I think," Jhessail murmured back as they saw the lantern set down carefully on the floor—and the flickerings form a pulsing blue-white upright oval of glowing air as tall as a man.

Belatedly, Florin bowed his head and said respectfully, "Well met, Lord Crownsilver."

The noble took a slow step closer to the Knights and swept them with a withering glare. There was no trace about him of the quavering, broken shell of a man they remembered seeing last. Crownsilver seemed alert, purposeful, and even—when one saw the fire in his eyes—frenzied.

"Slayers of my wife and daughter," he said, "taste my revenge! For Narantha! *For Jalassa, damn you!*"

The three Sembian mages snatched wands out of their rune-adorned jerkins and grinned in cruel triumph as they aimed—and unleashed.

The Knights shouted, sprinting desperately this way or that, but ravening wandfire roared down the cellar in a blinding white flood that drove a million tiny lances into bare skin even as it hurled and tumbled the Knights hard into the unyielding stone wall behind them.

Very hard. Faerûn started to go watery and whirl away from more than one Knight, with the searing magic still roaring on and on.

Amid a splintering groan of riven support posts, the ceiling above started to collapse—and Florin, Pennae, and Islif, still struggling to move and to see, beheld the little tracer-gem Pennae had stolen bursting forth from its concealment beneath her tattered leathers. It spun and spat strange purple flames and sparks as the roaring white wandfire tore at it, then it surged down the cellar toward Lord Crownsilver.

Only to explode in its own burst of blinding white light, a blast that—laced with Pennae's shriek and startled shouts from the Sembians—drove its own burning rays into everyone. . . .

Aumrune Trantor stopped midstep, teetering awkwardly with one foot raised—and then brought it down, lurched against a passage wall, and stayed there, leaning like a drunkard.

Old Ghost had found something.

Something in Aumrune's mind made him seethe with excitement

and glee—so bright and fierce that Horaundoon, sharing that mind with him, cowered.

Aumrune's pet project, kept secret from all except Manshoon and Hesperdan, who seemed to approve of it, was adding magics to an ancient, flying magic sword: Armaukran, the Sword That Never Sleeps. Aumrune had already infused the blade with new powers to make it obey him.

Surging in bright exultation, Old Ghost uncovered the way into the sword from Aumrune's mind.

The body of Aumrune Trantor thrust itself away from the wall so briskly it almost fell. It hurried off down that gloomy, deserted passage in Zhentil Keep, headed for where a certain hidden sword awaited.

This was going to be good. *Very* good.

Two flights down a deserted staircase in the Royal Court, while passing his forty-third faded tapestry, Vangerdahast stopped and murmured, "Far enough. Best alter things before we run into the *real* Vangerdahast."

The features more than a thousand courtiers and servants knew and feared rippled and flowed, melting down off a quite different face as the hargaunt sought the chin of Telgarth Boarblade, and points below.

As he held open the front of his doorjack's jerkin to let the hargaunt flow down out of sight, Telgarth Boarblade smiled. Lord Rhallogant Caladanter was a buffoon of the most childish sort, aye, but he must have done well enough in telling War Wizard Ironchylde the tale Boarblade had so carefully concocted. She'd been white with fright and seeing foes in every shadow. Well delivered, indeed.

Still wearing his satisfied smile, the doorjack who was not a doorjack went down the stairs at a more dignified pace, and out through a door three floors down.

Only after he had heard the familiar slight scrape of that door closing did the old doorjack—who'd been watching Boarblade's transformation from behind one of the faded tapestries that lined the staircase walls—dare to breathe again.

Myarlin Handaerback was trembling and purple from lack of air and indignation. As he thrust aside the tapestry and started his own ascent in the gloom, he muttered, "There's more confounded *creeping* as goes on in this place! Not like in the old days, when it was all pretty lasses seeking their suitors or the suitors chasing after them. First adventurers and now men with oozing things that disguise their faces! Now we're getting the riff raff, to be sure!"

The little tower room was thick with dust from the many yellowing, rolled maps, deeds, and contracts that choked its storage shelves—but not a single speck of it marred the sword that lay gleaming on the trestle table that filled the center of the room.

Aumrune carefully locked, latched, bolted, and then barred the lone door behind him. Old Ghost made him edge past the table and do something he never did: Undog and swing aside the inner shutter that covered the window and its bars, unlatch and take down those bars, and undog the window itself.

Horaundoon paid little attention. Horaundoon, crouched in one corner of Aumrune's mind, had all his attention bent on the magnificent sword that lay on the table.

It was a long blade, nigh as long as some men stood tall, about two thirds of it a slender blade of bright silver and the last third a large hilt neatly wrapped in black silver, with sleekly curved double quillons and a cabochon-cut blue gem for a pommel, smooth and rounded and glowing with a faint light of magic.

Gods, it was beautiful. The Sword That Never Sleeps, crafted by that rarest of creatures, if the tales could be believed: a smith of the elves!

Not that Old Ghost could tell, after all the enchantments that had been cast, recast, broken, and overlaid upon the sharp steel. Certainly its curves suggested elven stylings, and the oldest surviving enchantments felt like elf work.

Armaukran was the name of someone it had slain, whose life-force had been infused into the sword through dark spells. It had been forged for a purpose—but that purpose was lost, at least to Old Ghost and Horaundoon.

What remained clear and delighted Old Ghost very much was that seven enchantments remained rooted in the blade that shared a purpose: binding souls, spirits, or sentiences into the blade.

Horaundoon wallowed in the intricacies and elegances of all the castings upon the blade. Their sweepingly shaped, subtly reinforced incantations, the balanced flows of Weave-work . . . even the lesser, simpler magics added by Aumrune Trantor, grafted on recently, were but plainer outer garments draped over great beauty beneath. He ached to do such work, to so ride the Weave that he could craft such beauty. . . .

Lost in lust, he never saw his peril.

Old Ghost found the words of magic he needed in those seven binding enchantments, gathered himself—then spoke them, clearly and crisply, plucking the forces they unleashed as deftly as any master harpist and using them to *thrust* a helpless Horaundoon into the Sword That Never Sleeps. Down into the brightness the younger, lesser spirit so hungered for, down into the cold, thrilling embrace of bindings that tightened and anchored themselves upon him in a dozen ways, then a score of ways—bindings that burned when Old Ghost bent his will upon them.

The splendid sword rose into the air to float silently above the table.

"Yes," Old Ghost murmured through Aumrune Trantor's lips, his thoughts blazing loudly into Horaundoon through the sword's bindings, "you are mine now. Mine to bid, to command as surely as if my hands were firm around this hilt. Yet chafe not, Horaundoon. This is a task you'll thoroughly enjoy."

Aumrune Trantor opened the window and the outer shutters beyond, letting in the sun and a cool breeze that was scudding past all the towers of Zhentil Keep.

"Go," Old Ghost commanded. "Go and kill Zhentarim. I shall

be with you, watching. Try to take them alone, where others will not see you. Go and seek Zhents to slay. Not Manshoon, mind. Not yet. And not Hesperdan, for both of them can probably destroy Armaukran with ease. Which leaves you, O Hungry Slayer of Zhentarim, just about every other member of the Brotherhood you care to fell."

The Sword That Never Sleeps rose from the table and slid forward through the air, point first, as sleek as any arrow.

Out the window it went, banking and plunging hastily down out of sight, seeking concealing shadows.

A part of his awareness plunging down with it, Old Ghost smiled inside Aumrune Trantor and made the Zhent mage reach out and close the shutters and then the window.

It was time and past time to begin remaking the Zhentarim into something worthy in fair Faerûn.

Florin blinked.

Aye. He was Florin.

Florin Falconhand . . . and he lay on his back on cool, hard stone.

It was too smooth to be anything but a floor, and there was nothing but darkness above him.

Or so it seemed. Things were coming back gradually. They'd been in that cellar, facing Lord Crownsilver. Then the blast . . .

Wherever he now was, it wasn't the cellar. This place was larger and a lot less dank. Dusty, even—

Florin sneezed. Hard and uncontrollably and several times, bouncing his shoulders off the unyielding stone beneath him.

Someone groaned from floor level nearby. Off to his left.

Florin tried to move his hands. He couldn't seem to feel them, but they were there . . . and whole. When he thrust one up in front of his face and wriggled his fingers, they responded normally enough. He thrust two of them into his nose to quell further sneezes, and he tried to roll over onto his elbow and sit up.

Done, as easily as usual. Aside from aches all over—the back of his head and his left arm and shoulder in particular—it seemed he was unhurt, with his fellow Knights lying sprawled and motionless around him. Or almost motionless. Yonder, someone was moving and groaning. Doust, from the sound.

Florin tried to peer in all directions, seeking Lord Crownsilver, Sembian wizards, slavering monsters, or . . . well, anyone approaching.

He saw nothing like that. In the darkness, he couldn't really see much at all. He dug in his pouch for the little glowstone Vangerdahast had given him—had given all the Knights, and weren't they very likely to bear enchantments that would let the Royal Magician trace their whereabouts at will? He set it down and sent it skittering across the floor.

Well, now. This "elsewhere" they'd all somehow landed in seemed to be a deserted room somewhere very grand. "Very grand" as in very high ceilings and large rooms, with walls covered in unpainted wooden panels with carved frames, borders, fluted half pillars, and heavily ornate scrollwork supporting . . . well, curlicues. All cut out of the same dark wood.

As grand as some of the rooms he'd seen in the Royal Palace in Suzail. The room might be underground, but it didn't seem as damp as, say, that cellar. Nor did it smell of earth. Dust lay everywhere, like a thick, furry blanket, but the only bits of rubble he could see were small, fresh chips and flecks of stone around and under the Knights. That looked as if the Knights had brought it along with them.

Someone else groaned loudly. Semoor.

Florin stood up, wincing—one of his shins wasn't any too happy with its present condition, it seemed—and staggered around the fallen Knights, looking for wounds and anything missing. He winced when he saw the crossbow quarrel through Islif's arm.

Doust silently joined him. "If you slice it off here," the priest said, pointing, "and slide it out, I'll have a healing spell ready before she loses too much blood."

"How much has she lost already?" Florin asked.

"More than enough," Islif whispered, startling them both, "but I'll live. Do it." Her eyes were still closed, and she lay sprawled as if unconscious.

Florin used his dagger to saw through the shaft of the quarrel, then left Doust to his work. He went around to examine the rest of the Knights.

Everyone was accounted for. It appeared, looking over the litter of weapons lying strewn around them, that everything they'd been wearing or carrying had made the journey with them, too. Plus all the stone shards he'd noticed.

Made the journey, more or less, he amended his judgment. Pennae now seemed to be wearing as much soot as leathers.

Was she—? When he laid a fingertip gingerly on one bared, scraped shoulder, her eyes snapped open, and she uncoiled like a whirlwind to clutch at his hand.

"Easy, lass," Florin said. " 'Tis just me."

She turned her head until she could fix him with one sparkling eye and said, "You're never *just* you, big ranger man."

Semoor started to chuckle—until the dust made him choke. Evidently his eyes had been open, too, and the glowstone he had out had given him light enough to see the expression on Florin's face.

The ranger cleared his throat loudly and told Pennae, "I, ah, have to check on the others. Ah, right now." He hastily turned away.

Pennae rolled onto her side, wincing, and then made it up to a sitting position.

"Naed, but I *hurt*." Jhessail gasped, flinching, as Florin helped her sit up. "Where by the Nine crackling Hells are we?"

Florin shrugged. "I have no idea."

"Neither do I," Pennae said, struggling to her feet and clutching at her hip and then at her knee, ere limping a few tentative steps away, "but I know how we got here."

"Enlighten us," Doust told her.

"That tracer gem explosion awakened a portal behind us—a portal that must have been there for a long time but was hidden. I saw just a glimpse of it, as I was being flung back at it. It must have snatched all of us—and this litter of stones and suchlike, too—out of the cellar as the place collapsed."

"So Lord Crownsilver's pet wizards blew him and themselves up?" Semoor asked. *"That's* rich!"

Pennae shook her head. "They'd just spun their own portal, remember? It would do the same thing to them, taking them wherever they'd set the portal to reach."

The Light of Lathander frowned. "So they could be somewhere nearby."

"Yes," she replied. "Glowstones out, everyone. I think we're in some sort of palace."

"I think so, too," Florin murmured from where he'd stooped to recover the glowstone he'd sent journeying across the floor. "And I see an archway yonder and a closed door over *that* way."

"Let's leave closed doors closed, for now," Jhessail said, wincing and rubbing one of her elbows.

"Agreed," Florin said, looking around at everyone. "Any grievous wounds? Can everyone walk?"

"Being as we seem to keep losing our horses . . ." Jhessail replied with a frown, "I seem to be getting steadily better at walking."

Everyone pulled out their glowstones, and the light in the room grew with them. Semoor got a good look at Pennae, and he leered appreciatively.

"Like 'em?" she asked calmly and without waiting for a reply added, "Can't have 'em!"

"I'm making like a good Cormyrean, successful and wealthy and settled in Suzail," the priest replied innocently. "I'm window-shopping."

Doust and Jhessail snorted in amusement, and even Pennae grinned.

She shook her head and waved a finger in mock warning. "That tongue of yours, lad . . ."

"Yes?" Semoor asked brightly, hope shining in his eyes.

"Never mind. We've a palace to explore, or hadn't you noticed, lost in your unholy fixation on my charms?"

Semoor looked aggrieved, though his eyes were dancing. "Madam, you wound me! 'Unholy' how? Lathander warmly embraces new beginnings, and I perceive an opportunity to warmly embrace—"

"My left hand, crushing your codpiece and all it contains, if you don't *leave off,* Bright Morninglord of Lust!" Pennae snapped. "Now belt up! *Some* of us have work to do that just might keep the rest of us *alive.* And spare me whatever clever little jest you were trying to think up about how this could be another 'new beginning,' too."

Above them both, Florin was standing by the archway, glow-stone raised, peering into the darkness and ignoring their dispute. Without looking back, he waved his hand to get their attention. "Kick some of the stones we brought with us together into a little heap to mark this room for later. We'll have to start exploring or just die of thirst—and I *don't* think we should split up or leave anyone behind. For any reason."

Semoor obediently applied his boots to sliding most of the stones together, then looked up. "Done. Let's go exploring. I'm getting hungry."

"Would that be a holy hunger?" Islif teased.

"One of mine," the priest replied, drawing smoothly back out of Pennae's reach. "One of mine."

He strode to join Florin. "Come. None of us is getting any younger."

The little, out-of-the-way room in the Royal Palace of Suzail where Vangerdahast was closeted with his most trusted Wizard of War had no name, and the Royal Magician liked it that way. He'd have been even happier if it hadn't ever appeared on any floor plans of the Palace, even though he'd done his level best for years now to track down and seize every last formal or hand-drawn charting of anything architectural about the most royal of buildings in Suzail.

Vangerdahast enjoyed having and knowing secrets, liked having hideaways where no one would be able to track him down and disturb him, and especially valued being able to occasionally take off his boots, fart, belch, scratch himself, and genuinely *relax* in the company of someone who wasn't offended by such behavior.

That the "someone" was a beautiful woman whom he trusted and regarded as a friend made her company that much more precious. Despite the facts that they were both—aside from his boots—fully clad and likely to remain so, and they were discussing grave business of the realm.

Specifically, the most pressing problems the Wizards of War needed to deal with.

"Then there's the matter of the Hidden Princess," he said heavily across the little table where they sat crouching, murmuring almost nose to nose.

"That never seems to go away," Laspeera said, nodding. "What now, specifically?"

"Some of the elder Illances have gotten it into their heads that I'm up to something."

Laspeera grinned. "And are you?"

"*Hardly*, Lasp," he growled. "They think I've got her spellbound and stashed in a bedchamber somewhere and visit her every tenday or so for a night of wildly trying to sire a secret branch of the Obarskyrs to hold in reserve in case—"

He stiffened suddenly, lifted his head so abruptly they almost bumped noses together, and started cursing softly.

Laspeera raised an eyebrow in silent query.

"The Lost Palace," the Royal Magician said. "Someone's triggered one of my alarm spells. They're inside, somehow."

Laspeera stood, went to a wall carving, did something to it with her fingers, and swung it forward from the wall as if it were a door. Its hollowed-out back sported a rack of sheathed wands. Deftly she started taking down sheaths and hooking them onto her belt.

"*Nay*, Lasp," Vangerdahast said. "This is my folly and my battle."

"Lord Vangerdahast," she replied, "you can't be everywhere, and if the realm loses you on *this* sort of backchamber—"

"No! Take off those wands and sit *down!*" Vangerdahast roared, slamming down a fist on the table and startling her with his sudden fury. "There are good reasons I alone should go there! Not the least of which being that all the defenses are keyed to me, and anyone else will have to battle them every few steps, not just our unknown intruder!"

Laspeera nodded and handed him wands.

Vangerdahast took them, crooked a finger to whisk another two particular wands across empty air from the panel into his hands, whirled away to the door, and hurried out.

He was out and down the passage beyond like a storm wind, his robes billowing out behind him, and didn't notice Wizard of War Lorbryn Deltalon step out of a doorway in his wake. Deltalon grimly watched him go.

The Knights found themselves cautiously exploring room after dark, thick-with-dust room. A seemingly endless labyrinth of deserted, interlinked chambers, all of them ornately paneled with soaring ceilings lost in the darkness beyond the reach of their glowstones. A palace.

Perhaps an underground palace. They could find no sign of a window or sunlight or any way out—nor any sign of other life. The air smelled stale and long unmoving, the dust lay like an undisturbed blanket everywhere, and the only light, aside from their glowstones, came from the faint glows of old, decaying preservative magics on the magnificent wood paneling all around them.

A hallway larger and longer than most brought them to a crossway of similar grandeur—and across it, only a few strides along a stub end of passage, a huge wooden door. As wide as Florin's shoulders three times over and more than twice as tall, it was carved with an oval badge of a unicorn's head thrusting forth to the dexter from between two curving trees: an oak and a maple.

"Esparin," Jhessail said. "This was a palace of Esparin—probably *the* palace of Esparin."

Semoor, who was staring hard at the carved device, frowned

without looking away from it. "I didn't know you knew olden-days heraldry."

"You've never asked me what I know," Jhessail replied softly. Something in her voice made him look at her sharply.

"The Lost Palace of Esparin," Doust murmured from behind them. "There was something about this place. Something I read . . . that I should remember. Some interesting peril or other . . ."

Something half-skeletal shuffled into view around the corner where the crossway met the stub end of the passage.

It peered at them with eyes that were twin points of cold light in a face that was half falling off the skull beneath. It looked like what was left of a man, in what was left of once-grand robes.

"Oh, Tymora. Liches," Doust whispered, as cold fear fell on all of the Knights like a heavy cloak, washing over them and leaving them trembling uncontrollably. "I remember now! Th-th-this is where Vangerdahast's predecessors b-b-bound all the wizards who went mad!"

The lich took a slow step forward, raising its hands. As the Knights of Myth Drannor tried to curse and scatter, magic rings on those bony fingers winked into life.

Chapter 10
TASKS, TRAVELS, AND LIFE-ALTERING CHOICES

Tasks are given to us all
Travels embraced or forced upon us
All our daily choices alter our lives
And shape also those of others
So we must master tasks, travels, and choices
Or lack precious time enough
For love, friendship, and laughter

Saying of the Church of Lliira

The duskwood tree was old, large, and had been lightning-scarred long ago, leaving its loftier reaches with a sort of natural seat where its trunk split into three. Anyone sitting in that juncture could readily lean his back against the eastward trunk, prop one booted foot against the rising northwestern trunk, and stare between it and the southern trunk to enjoy a good view southwest over Cormyr. Even as the thick canopy of leaves above gave him full shelter from the wind, weather, and all but the closest prying eyes.

A lone man sat in that lookout seat now, a heavy sack beside him, enjoying the view.

The Immerflow was *just* visible far off to the left, a glimmering silver ribbon in the sunlight with the unbroken dark green horizon of the Hullack Forest beyond. Rolling emerald hills rose to a few gentle peaks in the distance ahead, and the higher, broken Stonelands—all torturous cliffs and crags cloaked with scrub woods—thrust up to the right, with the Moonsea Ride arising over a succession of hillcrests between the peaks and the Stonelands to run right past the tree. Two distant dust clouds were moving along the road, but otherwise it seemed deserted.

That suited Torm fine, just now. He needed time to sit and think, and the bulging sack of stolen coins, gems, and small valuables sharing his perch was a large part of why he was pondering where to go and what to do next.

Things were getting rather hot for him in the Forest Kingdom, but he'd found he vastly preferred it, for all its laws and ever-nosy war wizards, to noisy, crowded Sembia, where hired spying and alarm and warding spells were becoming all too common, and rivals and foes both too numerous to count.

Abruptly he became aware that something was floating in midair right in front of him. Something that certainly hadn't been there—two arms-lengths away from his nose, blocking his view of the gentle peaks—a moment ago.

It was a curved pipe of a style favored by older and whiskered men or backcountry farmers. A thin wisp of smoke was arising from its bowl, as if someone invisible, who could somehow recline leisurely on empty air about sixty feet off the ground, was enjoying a relaxed smoke.

Torm was so astonished by this sudden apparition that he almost fell out of the tree, but he knew full well that he was staring at magic, and that magic in Cormyr meant war wizards, and—

He snatched out a dagger.

Only to find his hand pinned against the tree trunk by a stone-strong force.

"Oh, *stop* that," a man's voice drawled at him, apparently issuing from the pipe. "As I see it, ye now have a choice, young Torm. One of those life-altering ones. Ye can accept the task I'm about to offer ye, or I'll dump ye into the hands of the war wizards—specifically, into a cell in the little prison they maintain in the Royal Court in Suzail. I'm feeling rather patient at the moment, so I'll give ye the space of six full breaths to decide which fate ye wish to embrace."

"What *sort* of task?" Torm asked suspiciously.

"Stealing something."

Torm brightened.

"Traitors, you cannot escape the vengeance of Cormyr!" The lich's voice seemed hollow and distant. Tiny blue bolts of lightning leaped and spat from its rings, arcing back and forth—and suddenly twisted up into a writhing, crackling lance that stabbed at the Knights . . . only to become a flood of white blossoms that showered petals in all directions as they tumbled to the floor.

"No Witch Lord shall depart this place alive!" the lich said. "You have wrought your last craven foulness and foolishly strayed within my reach at last! Die! *Die!*"

The magic that roared forth at the Knights this time was a rose red flame that made hitherto-invisible preservative enchantments on the great carved door flare up a vivid blue—a spitting tongue of fire that became a hissing rain of—

"*Cider?*" Islif exclaimed. "That's cider I smell!"

The lich flung out a hand to point at Islif's nose and stalked forward, right at her. "You, Pretender Prince, are the very root and branch of evil that we have for so long striven to winnow out of fair Cormyr! I know you and decry you, false knight! You no more have Obarskyr blood than I do! Why, I'd not be surprised if you were even a woman, behind your posturings and oversized codpieces!"

"Strangely enough," Islif said wryly, as the lich-fear faded suddenly from all the Knights, "neither would I."

That pointing fingertip was only inches from her nose. She resisted the impulse to chop it with her sword and instead ducked away.

"Come!" Islif urged her fellow Knights—as the fear surged back over her in a wave that made her heart lurch, and the need to *run* rose in her mindlessly. She sprinted along the wall and took the cross passage. "Let's get away from this thing. We don't have the spells to stand and fight it if its charms suddenly turn effective!"

"R-r-right behind you!" Doust panted as he and Semoor stumbled over each other in their clawing terror to be the first to follow her. In their wake, teeth chattering, Florin slashed aside the lich's arm as the creature turned to follow them. His strike sent it tottering away across the passage.

"Filth of Sembia!" it said, pointing now at the wall. "You fail to deceive me with your clever disguise of aping polished wood! I shall hunt you down and destroy you utterly! *Hah!*"

The magic that roared out from it this time looked like a darting swarm of tiny white hummingbirds that burst into tinkling, flashing dust before they could reach the wall the lich was now angrily confronting.

Fear surging and ebbing in them like roiling nausea, the Knights fled, following Islif around the corner and down the cross passage.

"This is . . . *not* good," Pennae snapped, wiping sweat from her face. "I know it's the lich-magic making me afraid, but I feel just as scared as if there were a good reason to be! We've *got* to find a way out of this place. That mad lich back there won't menace the wall forever!"

"I'm thinking the way out might be on the other side of that door," Semoor said. "Care to lead the charge?"

"Sabruin," Pennae cursed him. "Tluining well do it yourself, Saer Holy Smarttongue."

"Ah, *no,* I think not," he said. "Getting blown apart with a spell isn't the sort of new beginning Lathander intends his priests to seek."

The thief gave him a contemptuous look. "So priests of the Morninglord justify becoming adventurers how, exactly?"

"Not *now,* you two," Florin said. "We've got—ohh!"

His voice rose in helpless fear even as a bolt of fire snarled past his ear to claw at the paneled wall high over his shoulder. Protective magics arose from it like rainbow-hued flames to ward off the fire-bolt, even as the Knights cursed and backed away from this new peril: a second lich, taller and clad in robes less decayed than the first one.

It strode toward them as purposefully and lithely as any vigorous living foe, wearing no rings but waving some sort of scepter that clasped around its forearm like a bracer and sparkled in the wake of its firebolt-hurling.

"Intruders into the royal vaults can expect only one fate," it said, raising the scepter again, "and I shall swiftly visit that doom upon you!"

Fear ebbed from the Knights again, and Florin said, "Scatter!

Don't give it a good target! Give yourselves room to run without slamming into someone else!"

The lich laughed hollowly. "Scheming will avail you naught, foes of Cormyr! Prepare to *die!*"

"These fellows were waystop-inn actors in life, weren't they?" Semoor asked. *"Bad* ones."

"The first lich isn't blocking our way back," Islif said. "We still have time to get back across that passage crossing by the door and go the other way!"

"So *run!*" Semoor cried, spinning around and doing just that. A firebolt snarled past, so close to his shoulder that his right ear and cheek felt its heat. The firebolt wrestled again with flaring defensive magics, then fizzled out.

The Knights ran.

"Is this the being brave adventurers part?" Doust panted in the rear of the line. "Fleeing like children?"

"Who's fleeing?" Pennae called back. "Have you no appreciation for battlefield strategy? We're not retreating. We're strategically with-drawing to seek better ground!"

"Ah *hah,"* Doust said in open disbelief. "Better ground *where?"*

They pelted past the cross passage where the first lich was still loudly threatening the wall. They ran down a slight ramp or slope through another passage crossing to reach . . . a dead end.

"Doors, anyone?" Florin called, slowing. "No one digs out a passage to a dead end and then goes to the trouble of *paneling* the walls!"

" 'Digs'? How can we be sure we're underground?" Pennae said. "Holynoses, your glowstones! I need to get a good look at the walls, to see it—"

" 'Ware, all!" Doust shouted, fear making his voice high and wild again. "We're trapped!"

"Trapped?" Pennae asked.

The Knights whirled around again to stare at the priest and where he was pointing.

Out of that second cross passage had stepped a *third* lich, this one taller than the other two and wearing a gold circlet around its brow. It carried a black staff surmounted by a bulbous head, inset with gems and graven with glowing copper and silver runes. The lich did not seem to be calling forth any magic from the staff. Instead, it held the staff in the crook of one arm and raised both hands to cast a spell—hands whose skeletal fingers were adorned with many glowing rings.

"Naed," Semoor muttered. "Jhess, is there *anything* left that you can cast to get us out of this?"

"N-no," Jhessail replied from beside his elbow.

A moment later, Islif and Florin both drew in breath in loud, startled hisses.

As the other Knights looked at them and saw where they were staring and pointing, they realized why.

Standing among them were *two* Jhessail Silvertrees, not just one.

The cave was deserted. Tsantress sighed with relief as she reached its mouth and peered out into the forest. There was no sign of any lurking creature and no spoor suggesting anything had even come close to her little hidehold.

"Tsantress Ironchylde," she murmured as she stepped past the little teethlike knobs of stone jutting up through the tangled grasses that marked where she'd cast her wards. Saying her name would prevent her passage from ending the ward spell she'd cast seasons ago.

She needed to think—think hard and not stlarn her conclusions, because for once her life really *would* depend on that—and knew she did that best while wandering the woods near the cave, not crouching in its dark depths.

What should she do? Where should she go?

And, stlarn it, was there any way Vangerdahast could trace her?

Tsantress was a good six paces out into the tall grass, with birdsong starting to die away at her presence, when it struck her that she should probably pray to Azuth and Mystra for guidance—and an answer to that last question.

She returned to the cave and sought out its deepest, darkest back crevice and in the cool, damp darkness knelt down. Her knees knew the right spot, even if she could see nothing in the gloom. She cast a spell into the darkness in front of her. A small working, a light-kindling.

The altar she'd made swallowed the magic silently, giving her back a brief glow all around its edges. A very good sign. It was intact, still holy, and she was being heard.

Which meant she was still worthy of attention.

"Lord Azuth, Guide and Wise One," she prayed, "and Great and Most Holy Lady Mystra, Yourself the Greatest of Mysteries, hear me now, I plead. Unworthy I am, unworthy I remain, yet strive to know and obey you both better. Hear my prayer, as I seek to kiss the Weave."

She kissed her own fingertips, reached out into the darkness, and started to pray as she always had, as if addressing an affectionate mother who was somewhere very close by, just beyond her reach.

As a war wizard, Tsantress had been afraid from time to time and uneasy more times than she could count—but it had been a long time since she'd been as bewildered and at a loss as to what to do. She prayed from the heart, respectful and yet blunt, speaking candidly rather than resorting to the flowery phrases of praise so many Mystran and Azuthan clergy excelled at or even used exclusively before altars.

"Come what may, I remain your servant, Wise One and Mysterious Mother," she finished, "and I pray that your own time be bright until next we speak."

Letting her hands fall into her lap, she sat back, awaiting any sign that might come. She expected none, but it would have been the height of disrespect to *assume* no response would manifest and rush to rise and depart and go on with mundane things, as if the prayer had been rote duty and not something truly meant.

The altar remained dark, though she sat there for a breath longer than usual. Tsantress sighed, rose to her feet—and became aware that the faint light from behind her, the dim radiance from the forest outside that reached this deep into the cave, had just been blotted out.

"Well, well," came a cold and familiar voice from behind her. Light blossomed from a torch. "You're one of the war wizards who helped slay my Jalassa! *I* remember. Kill her!"

She turned swiftly. Lord Maniol Crownsilver was standing with his arms folded across his chest and a triumphant smile upon his face—and there were three robed wizards standing behind him. Sembian hirelings, by the looks of them.

The three looked reluctant. One of them leaned his head forward and said in the noble's ear, "Yon's an altar to Azuth and Mystra both. 'Twere—"

The noble whirled around as if they'd slapped him. "Who's *paying* you?" he spat. "Two deaf deities of magic? Or me? *Strike her down!*"

The harmless spell Tsantress had cast into the altar erupted back out of it, arcing over her head with an angry rumbling that was more felt than heard. It lashed out at the three mages, startling them with its flash of light. Behind them, an ornrion of the Purple Dragons rose up with a stout tree bough in his hands. Tsantress knew him and tried to keep astonishment at his appearance off her face to avoid alerting the wizards.

Crownsilver saw Dauntless, of course, but so incoherent were his first gabblings of outrage that he warned his three wizards not in the slightest.

Dauntless brought his bough sweeping down, braining one Sembian solidly. That mage toppled silently, out cold. By the time the wizard standing beside him saw his fellow fall and turned, mouth dropping open, to see its cause, Dauntless had his club ready to smash him across the face—and did so.

That mage collapsed into the third wizard, who was already springing back. The last Sembian lifted one hand like a claw, and blue bolts streaked from all his fingertips, lancing into the ornrion and sending him staggering back, grunting in pain.

Which gave Tsantress more than time enough to hurl herself

backward until she stumbled into the altar and sat down hard on it, and from that undignified perch unleashed blue bolts of her own.

True to what she'd been told, long ago, the altar she'd so recently made offering and prayer at doubled the strength of her spell, sending a swarm of bright blue missiles racing into the last Sembian mage.

The mage crumpled in silent senselessness, leaving Lord Maniol Crownsilver alone, facing Tsantress and Dauntless.

The noble paled—and darted past Dauntless, seeking to flee the cavern.

The ornrion pounced, dashing Crownsilver to the ground with one blow of his battered tree bough. The nobleman's head lolled loosely, and he joined his three hired wizards in the land of dreams.

Dauntless looked at Tsantress and gravely bowed his head to her. "Much as I dislike slaying lords of the realm," he growled, "this one has brought grief to many. Should I—?"

"No," Tsantress said. "That's a temptation always best avoided, I'm afraid. No matter how much I want to say yes."

They eyed each other in silence for the space of a long breath or two, ere she spoke again. "Ornrion, I've seen you before. Escorting the Princess Alusair, among other things. What brings you here, clear out of the realm?"

"The orders of Lord Vangerdahast. A task that—if the Knights of Myth Drannor don't seek to turn back into Cormyr—is done." Dauntless regarded her expressionlessly for another long moment ere adding, "So, Lady Wizard, command me."

"I am called Tsantress," she told him, gave him a half-smile, and added, "and I believe I will. Come. Let's see what these Knights of yours are up to."

Wizard of War Lorbryn Deltalon stopped. He liked the look of this little clearing—and he was more than close enough to the person he was seeking. From here, he could *just* smell the woodsmoke of the man's fire.

Taking the palm-sized, enspelled plaque from his belt pouch and tilting it on a handy rock so he could clearly see Laspeera's face and body from the waist up, he strode two paces north to a fallen tree trunk and set up a polished metal mirror angled in the same manner.

Stepping back to make sure he could see both at once, he murmured the incantation, bent his will, and watched himself slowly take on the likeness of the second most powerful war wizard of Cormyr.

He could mimic Laspeera's speech fairly well and her gestures and gait closely. That would have to be good enough.

Should be good enough to fool one war wizard-avoiding bully-blade, who was now encamped alone and brooding just over the next ridge.

Lorbryn collected mirror and plaque and returned them to their pouches. He took up the two clinking sacks he'd brought, smiled—Laspeera's wryly gentle smile—and vanished from the clearing, in the proverbial blink of a sailor's eye.

The feeling of being constantly *watched* while in Zhentil Keep was something one just had to get used to. Or go mad.

The wizard Targon got that feeling more acutely from time to time and supposed everyone else did, too, but it had long since ceased to bother him.

He was feeling it now. "Stlarn and blast all," he murmured, not feeling any real irritation. He'd undressed and sought his bed long before he'd really begun to feel tired. As usual. He still didn't feel tired now.

He would be sleeping alone—also as usual—but was sitting up against a small mountain of pillows, happily immersed in his spellbook. As was his wont of evenings, his favorite part of any day.

Targon never tired of the exciting waking dreams he could conjure up in his mind. He saw himself casting spells, *felt*—from memory—the magics flowing through him as he worked the magic and then unleashed it, imagined how altering this and adjusting that would affect a spell, and . . . saw himself hurling it at this foe and then at that, humbling them with a wave of his hand and giving them a superior smile as they gasped and groveled—and died.

Something small and metallic *pinged* off the bedchamber wall to his left. Startled, he looked up. That had sounded like a ring. He'd once dropped one of his on the tiles outside a spell-casting chamber, and it had sounded just like that. He leaned over, craning his neck to see if there was a ring on the floor right now—only to feel a weight on the bed right beside him.

He whirled, heart leaping in fright—and was astonished to see a face he knew bumping noses with him, a mouth finding his. It was Aumrune, one of the wizards under his command, stark naked and—*kissing him?*

Then something raced from Aumrune's tongue into his mind and revealed itself. Old Ghost was bright and terrible and so mighty that Targon's mind could not even begin to resist.

So Aumrune had not been a lover. Had not even been Aumrune anymore. Had—

And then Targon stopped being Targon and so stopped worrying about anything—thinking about anything—at all.

The body that had been Targon calmly closed his spellbook, pushed the limp body of Aumrune off the bed, and walked over it to thrust aside the curtain, go to the bedchamber door beyond, and restore the little warding spell Aumrune should not have been able to break—but Old Ghost could.

Door sealed again, "Targon" kicked the body of Aumrune well clear of the bed and cast a blasting spell at it, destroying the largely burned-out body he had just vacated. As he waited for the room to stop rocking and thundering, he reached for his robe. If anyone bothered to come and investigate the brief tumult, he would inform them he'd just been forced to "execute the traitor Aumrune."

He calmly stepped over the ashes and the few lumps of larger bone and went seeking the ring.

Things fallen and forgotten had a habit of being needed or useful later.

Right now, Old Ghost was ready for a lot of "later." With Horaundoon elsewhere and his own hunger for life-energy sated for now, Old Ghost intended to make this new host body last a long, long time.

Brorn Hallomond flinched and then grabbed for his dagger.

"You'll cut yourself with that, mind," the beautiful woman on the other side of his tiny fire said calmly. "Don't bother. I mean you no harm."

"So you say," Brorn snarled, letting his hand fall away from the dagger without unsheathing it. "Myself, I've not known war wizards to tell the truth overmuch."

"Ah, you know who I am. That'll save us some time." Laspeera sat down crosslegged, just as the bullyblade was sitting—only right across the fire from Brorn. She gave him a good look down her unlaced bodice as she did so and saw his eyes flicker.

"You're Laspeera," Brorn said bluntly. "The realm says you sleep with Vangerdahast and boss half the war wizards for him while his back is turned bossing the other half. You're here to taunt and kill me, right?"

"Wrong. I need you alive, unharmed, and able—and so does the Crown. The royal family specifically said they needed you to serve Cormyr. You will be well rewarded for it. *Not* to do something that you'll be betrayed or blamed for later. But a little spying on the man who is most responsible for the death of Lord Yellander."

"The *Crown* said that? King Azoun, himself?"

"Himself. Yes, Brorn Hallomond, this I swear. The king and queen both feel your loyalty was ill repaid by the fate of your master. They admire that loyalty and deem you a capable man they want working for the Dragon Throne, not against it. And not living as an outlaw, doing violence to every passing citizen of Cormyr who might yield a few coppers to you."

Laspeera plucked up one of the sacks she'd brought with her and tossed it over the fire to land just beside Brorn's right hand. It landed with the heavy clink of coins. "Open it."

Brorn eyed her, and then reached for it without taking his gaze from her. He dragged it into his lap, worked the knot open, and then held it out and dumped a little of its contents out onto the leaf mold beside him, at arm's length. Gold coins, every one. Bright golden lions of the realm.

"The other sack's full of the same," Laspeera said. "All good coins, none of them marked or enspelled. As good as anything in the king's own purse."

"Mine if I do what?" Brorn asked.

"Spy on Vangerdahast and any of his agents—war wizards who serve him more than they serve the king, plus his own thieves and spies—for me. Just watch them, mind. I am *not* asking you to try to fight or even reveal yourself to the Royal Magician. Just watch, then tell me of any treason you witness or suspect."

"And how will I tell you?"

"Whenever you see me. *I'll* find *you* from time to time, and I'll bring more gold with me."

"That's all?" Brorn asked.

Laspeera got up, pulled open her bodice to bare her front from waist to shoulders, and purred, "That's all for *now*."

Brorn swallowed, stared at what had been bared to his gaze for a good long time, then lifted his eyes to meet hers and said roughly, "I'll do it."

Laspeera's smile was warm with promise. "You won't regret it."

Making no move to cover herself, she added, "Please don't be surprised or offended if I—or all of the royal family—pretend not to know you, if you happen to see us, even in private. If we think Vangerdahast is spying on *us* at that moment, our acting thus may be all that protects your life. Remember always that you will be safest if he doesn't notice you at all."

She leaned forward over the fire.

"As for me, I've been watching you for a long time, and I like what I see." Then she blew him a kiss and added softly, "Take care of yourself, Brorn."

A moment later, she was gone. Vanished as if she'd never been there at all, leaving only the other sack of coins across the flickering flames from him.

After a moment, Brorn cursed, raced around the fire, and clawed that sack open. More golden lions and—he plucked up a few at random and eyed them very closely—aye, as good as any minting he'd ever seen.

"Tymora," he muttered, "I don't know *what* I did to gain your good graces, but—thank you. A thousand thank yous. I hope you won't be offended if I bury most of these, take a handful, and go and get myself a playpretty for a long night of proper rutting before I seek out one of your altars and make a proper offering."

Filling his pouch, he scooped coins back into the sacks, retied them, and sat back with a disbelieving shake of his head.

"Holy dancing dung-goblins," he told the fire in happy disbelief.

Tymora was merciful. The fire didn't answer back.

Chapter 11
DELIVERANCE FROM TUMULI AND FIRE

For to us all, when most afraid
Comes a pressing need for aid
Deliverance from tumult and fire
Challenges, or doom most dire;
Aid, mayhap, for a bold Harper bright
Or means to drive down a lich or a wight
Or wise words, hope, a smile or a kiss—
Answered need our greatest bliss

from the ballad
"Wept By Fireside At Twilight"
(Anonymous)
First prominent circa the Year of the Highmantle

Princess Alusair was rather proud of herself.

For months now she'd been trading dark, well-made, but plain gowns—of the sort one of her maids could *just* get away with wearing on special occasions outside the Royal Palace—for specific garments from among their "everydays." She'd built up quite a bundle of patched and worn smocks, aprons, breeches, jerkins, and hooded half-cloaks. These gains, bundled up together, were all hidden, stuffed under a loose tread-board on the private stairs down to the Princes' Stable. Though she and Tana, princesses both, now shared that little enclave in the sprawling Palace stables, it was still "the Princes' Stable" and probably always would be. Her sister rode only at regular times these days, so for the rest of the time the narrow, dark stair was Alusair's own.

Wherefore she now had suitable garments in which to depart the Palace by way of those same stables, without immediately being recognized as a princess. Which meant she was spared the racket of alarm gongs and horns and the humiliation of being pounced upon by well-meaning Highknights and Purple Dragons and war wizards and dragged before her royal father—or mother or both—for discipline.

Hmm. Discipline. Her shapely behind was still burning, but the spanking hadn't chastened her one whit. Gods above, but her mother could whack hard!

Alusair's rump burned a little more painfully at the mere recollection. Not to mention the homespun rasping over rawness wherever where her silken clout didn't cover her.

She was, she'd discovered, actually a little proud of her burning behind. Though it was hardly something she could show casually to passersby, she felt it gave her something in common with the scarred old retired Purple Dragons she'd been seeing for as long as she could remember—the veterans who showed off their war marks proudly on feast days.

She, too, had been wounded standing up for Cormyr.

The step, tugged a little sideways to free it from its pegs, came up readily enough. Out came the bundle, and she stripped on the stairs in excited haste, shoving her glossy nightgown in with the clothes she wasn't going to use. Tugging on breeches, a worn and stained jerkin, and a hooded half-cloak, Alusair replaced the step and scampered on down the stairs.

Not to the bottom, where she was sure to be seen by stablehands or one of the guards. No, she'd long ago noticed that her stair passed an open end of the hayloft. It took but a moment to reach up, swinging and kicking in midair to bring her legs up over the edge then around a riser. With that post securely wedged into the backs of her knees, she could twist and claw the rest of herself up to join them.

The loft was low, long, and straight, like an attic. Mice squeaked and scampered through the hay as she crawled swiftly along through it, but they didn't bother her. The length of the hayloft could take her right out of the royal stalls into the next part of the stables, above the horses of equerries, envoys, and senior courtiers, to a third area reserved for the mounts of visiting royalty and dignitaries. She knew none were visiting Suzail just now, which meant there'd be neither stablehands nor guards, and all would be in darkness. Right next to the sprawling Royal Gardens, which she knew like her own morning face in the mirror, leaving her with an easy way to slip out of the Palace and back in again later.

Guards patrolled the Royal Gardens, but Alusair knew where they'd be. Moreover, they were watching for undesirables trying to sneak *in,* not get out. So long as her mother forbade the lopping of boughs off the mrimmon trees to quell any wisp of a chance that there'd ever be a paucity of mrimmon jelly on the royal cheese platters, there'd be several easy ways over the garden walls for a fairly light and agile princess who didn't mind undignified acrobatics.

Two strides away from the still-bouncing bough in her wake, Alusair was the very image of a weary, head-down underservant, trudging home late and in much need of a crust and a tankard of warm soup.

"Not a bad actor, our little spitfire princess," Wizard of War Baerent Orninspur said to his fellow mage.

Nodding, Wizard of War Mrask Tallowthond replied, "Almost as if she's done this a time or two before."

They indulged in a shared chuckle and fell into step behind the princess, keeping to the shadows on the harbor side of the Promenade—the side they were almost certain Alusair would soon be seeking.

Both wizards were tall, thin, young men who would not have looked out of place in armor, but Baerent was the one with the flashy good looks that caught feminine eyes wherever he went. Less handsome Mrask, lacking such easy charm, took refuge behind a moustache and a sharp tongue.

"Least she *entertains* us on these little jaunts," Baerent said. "Where d'you think she's bound for, this time? Another night of drinking and flirting?"

Mrask shook his head. "Too purposeful, and too much restless haste in her chambers, earlier. She's bound on some secret little mission or other and excited about it." He jerked his head. "There she goes now."

The weary little servant had crossed the broad Promenade, dodging lamplit coaches and the ever-numerous throngs of citizenry walking with handcarts and sling-satchels and lit pipes, to reach the mouth of a side street.

The two war wizards walked faster, trying to get closer to see where she went ere the corner between them hid her going through a door, ducking down an alley, or sprinting up a stair to some upstair abode.

Tiny locks of her hair rode in their belt pouches, so they could use tracing magic if they had to, but Obarskyrs tended to go strolling weighed down with magical gewgaws. If Alusair felt their trace, her revealing behavior would change—even before things started getting unpleasant for Mrask Tallowthond and Baerent Orninspur.

As it happened, Mrask got to the corner a stride ahead of Baerent. He was in time to fling out a hand to keep his colleague back out of sight. "The spitfire gets adventurous! She's headed into the Touch!"

"The *Moontouch?*" Baerent stood thunderstruck and could not resist the temptation to step around Mrask's hand and reach a spot where he could see for himself.

He had training enough to step back before dropping his jaw and staring disbelievingly at the side of Mrask's head. Mrask hadn't looked away from the princess since reaching the corner and wasn't about to do so now.

There was no way either mage could be mistaken. One of Suzail's finer pleasure-houses, Daransa's Moontouch was situated above several haughty shops that sold gowns, gloves, hats, and lace adornments to women who could afford ruinous overcharging. There were two public ways into the Touch, both outside stairs that led nowhere else. The princess was on a landing at the top of the more public stair right now, speaking with a mountainous door guard—and no doubt having a hard time convincing him that she should be allowed past.

Just what a Princess of Cormyr could be seeking in luxuriously furnished rooms where highcoin lasses lived and worked was something neither war wizard wanted to speculate about. Not when it was their task to ascertain for certain what she was up to and report back same to the Royal Magician of Cormyr.

"She's going in," Mrask said. "Do we—?"

"No," Baerent said. "She's not a dullard, and she knows my face. She won't think two war wizards just happened to want to slake their lusts at the very time she's visiting the Touch. We won't just learn nothing; we might well get our faces scratched half off and that door guard set upon us."

"Just for a start," Mrask agreed. "More importantly, she'll know we were set to watch over her, our usefulness in doing so would be ended—and Old Vangey will *not* be pleased."

"Tluin," Baerent agreed thoughtfully as he stepped behind Mrask to cast a scrying spell so as to watch and listen to the princess.

"Done," he said a moment later. "Your turn."

They traded places, Baerent now watching the closed door of the Moontouch and the impassive door guard standing against it with arms folded, staring down at all the folk of Suzail hurrying past.

Mrask worked the same scrying spell Baerent had, nodded to show his readiness, and the two war wizards found a little stretch of building wall to lean against and start their spying.

Only to stiffen in astonishment. Their spells had been cast perfectly and were working well—but something was stopping them, right at the closed door of the Moontouch.

Not one but *two* war wizard scryings, utterly blocked.

Doust Sulwood liked to be calm and quiet, so these surges of lich-fear were unsettling him more than a little. Yet he was neither stupid nor distracted, and he wasted no time in staring sternly into the eyes of the nearest Jhessail, who was moving her fingers in the swift gestures of a spell. Doust unleashed a command with all the holy power of Tymora he could muster: "Fall!"

Pennae's dagger was already in her hand. She thrust it under the curve of the same Jhessail's bodice, so the wizard's fall would plunge her right onto it. Fingers still spellweaving and eyes wild, Jhessail crumpled, crying, *"No!"*

Pennae whipped her blade away as swiftly as any racing lightning bolt. The helpless mage crashed to the floor unbloodied. In the same motion, Pennae whirled to menace the other Jhessail in the same way. Semoor was already shouting the same command.

The second Jhessail swept the dagger aside with her forearm, giving Pennae a crooked smile, then sagged at her knees, as if starting to fall.

"*Not* fooled," Islif said from right behind her, clamping iron-hard fingers on both of the mage's elbows and yanking them back to touch each other—as she brought one knee firmly up into the wizard's back. "Jhess couldn't withstand that holy magic, so you're not Jhess!"

Lifting the false Jhessail by the elbows and using her knee to pivot her captive, Islif swung the now-struggling wizard in front of her like a shield.

"Behind me, everyone!" she said, her eyes hard as she watched the lich grandly babble the last words of an incantation.

The impostor in her grasp tried to hiss out an incantation, but Florin was ready. His belt flask was in his hand, and whenever her lips opened, he squirted water into her mouth, hard, drowning her words in helpless choking coughs.

Then, in a flood of crawling emerald fire, the lich's spell washed over them all.

Alusair found herself in a warm, richly paneled parlor lined with scarlet draperies, over which hung tapestries depicting vivid scenes of lovemaking—scenes so well limned that they seemed almost lifelike.

She blushed, despite her firm resolve to the contrary earlier, and took refuge in the warm brown eyes of the ivory-hued woman who rose to greet her. As finely gowned as any noblewoman at a formal Court dinner, the tall apparition of striking beauty smiled in genuine welcome, reaching forward to take Alusair's hands—with fingers as soft as warm silk—as if she were a long-lost friend. The gesture made the unlaced front of her gown fall open right down to the girdle that encircled her hips, but she seemed unaware that this had occurred.

"Lady," she said warmly, "your arrival brings much pleasure! Pray, take your ease! I am Daransa, and this is my house. What is your will?"

It was obvious that Daransa hadn't recognized her as the Princess Alusair but merely thought her to be some young wisp of a commoner. It was just as obvious that she was genuinely pleased to see her unexpected and unfamiliar guest.

"I, uh, I—" Alusair began, stumbling under that friendly gaze.

Daransa had kept hold of her hands, and she gently drew Alusair to her breast, urging her to a handy couch and murmuring, "Yet I am overbold. Tea, perhaps? Warm broth? Speak at your leisure, dear. I don't mean to press you."

Alusair halted that gentle steering once her knee was against the edge of the couch and her nose almost touching Daransa's bosom. She lifted her chin and blurted out what she'd come to say.

"Your kindness is much appreciated, Lady Daransa, but I am here only to deliver a message for you to pass on with all urgency: 'Three pearls have been lost, but one is now found.' "

The eyes staring into hers flickered, and Daransa gravely repeated the message in a low whisper. Accustomed to the subtle signals of Court converse, the princess could tell by Daransa's eyes that she now knew who Alusair was.

Breathing in the delicately spicy scent that clung to Daransa's curves, Alusair added, "So that you know I mean no deception, hear me: Harper Dalonder Ree gave me those words and told me that if ever I wanted to call on him, they could be said to you here. He'll know where to find me. So far as I know, I shall be found in the usual places. As much as possible, I'll keep to my chambers until I hear from him."

Daransa knelt, keeping hold of Alusair's fingertips only long enough to kiss them, and rose to whisper, "Highness, this shall be done—and know that you are always welcome in my house."

Alusair gave her a real smile. "You have certainly made me feel so. My thanks."

Bowing her head and assuming once more the bent-over posture of a weary servant, she turned to the door. It opened in front of her, seemingly by itself, to reveal the guard beyond. He neither bowed nor made any flourish of ushering her out but bent near to mutter, "Please know that inwardly I am on my knees to you, Highness."

Alusair gave him a sidelong grin, ducked her head, and went back down the stairs into the bustle of the city.

She headed straight back the way she'd come, placing speed before stealth, and spotted Baerent Orninspur's handsome features right away—despite his swift movement to turn his back on her and converse with his friend, whom she now recognized as *another* war wizard.

"Fair evening, you filthy spies," she greeted them cheerfully as she swept past, giving the dumbfounded pair a sweet smile.

Green flames seared and tore like a thundering waterfall of heavy, battering fire that burned as it smashed into Knights and swept them away.

Florin was hurled away in that raging flood, and Islif after him, her grip on the false Jhessail lost.

Slammed hard into the paneled walls, winded and heaped atop each other, the Knights gasped amid sudden relief, as rainbow-hued protective magics surged up out of the wood to drive back the emerald flames a foot or so from their noses.

The flames slowly died away, leaving the lich with the staff standing in triumph as it surveyed the twisted bodies heaped along the back wall of the dead end.

It didn't seem to notice the man standing right in front of it, alone in the open space its spell had cleared—the seemingly unharmed man the false Jhessail had turned into.

Tall, slender, and darkly handsome, wearing stylish black boots, breeches, tunic, and half-cloak, the man regarded the Knights of Myth Drannor with a half smile.

Semoor gaped up at him. "And who in the Nine Hells are *you?*"

"Ah, adventurers," the man sneered. "Always *so* eloquent."

"Get after her," Baerent said. "Be her shadow; stick to her like tight new hose, no matter how much she spits and snarls. See where she goes and who she speaks to."

Barely waiting for Mrask's nod, Baerent trotted across the street and bounded up the Moontouch stairs.

The guard was waiting for him, sword already drawn.

"I'm a war wizard," Baerent said. "Stand aside!"

"No," the guard replied. "Vangey and I have an agreement on this, and I'll *not*—"

Baerent cast the spell he had ready, shrugged, and strode past the now-motionless guard, who would not be a statue for long. But long enough.

Flinging wide the door of the Touch, he stepped into the parlor where Daransa stood by the tea table. "Goodwoman," said Baerent, "I speak with the full authority of the Crown, and I must ask you—"

"Ah, Wizard of War Baerent Orninspur!" a new voice interrupted. A door behind Daransa's little desk opened, and a tall, shapely, silver-haired woman strode into the room.

Baerent blinked. How could someone recognize him before they even saw him? His amulet would prevent scrying or warn him of more powerful mag—

Oh. Spyholes. Of course.

"Tea?" Daransa offered, nothing but pleasant welcome on her face.

Baerent looked from one woman to the other and decided bluster was no longer his best option. "I regret the abruptness of my intrusion," he said, "and I intend no harm to any in this place. I merely—"

"Burst in here," Dove interrupted, "after your scrying spell failed—and that of your companion Mrask. Then you thought to bully Daransa into revealing why Princess Alusair was here. What she said, and what she did, too. My, but Vangey is suspicious these days!"

"But I—" Baerent sputtered, then took a deep breath, waved his hand in a calming gesture directed more at himself than anyone else, and asked, "Lady, forgive me, but who are you? I have my suspicions, but—"

"All war wizards do, which is the root of our trouble here," the silver-haired woman replied with a pleasant smile, coming closer. "As I see it, you are here on duty, bound to uncover the private and personal business of a princess, and to that you have now added the little task of trying to learn how a few elegant professional playpretties can block your magics—and to do a little bullying to drench them in fear, so you can forbid them from ever trying to do so again, and hope to be obeyed. Have I stated truth?"

Baerent blinked again. "Lady, you can hardly expect me to discuss such matters with . . . with—"

"Someone whose name you don't even know? Yet I *do* expect you to confirm truth and to speak openly and fully when dealing with someone who just might be one of those you are supposed to serve. You *serve* the citizens of Cormyr, remember? Lording it over them is your own embellishment. Or Vangerdahast's. Speaking of which, you are not to say *one word* about any of this to him. Beginning with my name, which is Dove."

Baerent blinked once more. "Ah, *the* Dove?" Without awaiting a reply, he rushed on into more dangerous words. "I could hardly fail to notice that you just gave me an order—or tried to. Lady Dove, you must appreciate that I cannot accept orders from anyone but—"

Dove waved away the rest of his words. "Call it a suggestion, then," she said with a gentle smile, strolling still closer. "I am *suggesting* that if you forget about all that has happened since you saw the princess cross the Promenade, and depart this house right now without trying to seek any answers or give any commands in the Moontouch now or ever again, I will probably see my way clear to letting you keep your life."

"My *life?*"

"Yes. *If* you just go back to yon Royal Palace right now and refrain from ever bothering Daransa or any of her ladies again. *And* refrain from saying anything about this to Vangerdahast."

Baerent stared at her. He suddenly believed that this strikingly beautiful woman was one of the fabled Chosen of Mystra and the "highly dangerous," active-in-Cormyr Harper all war wizards were often warned about. But more than that, he believed she could—and would—do just what she was promising. To him.

"B-but, Lady," he managed to protest, "the Royal Magician! He looks into our minds and sees our memories! Even if I say nothing, he'll know of your, ah, demands."

Dove's gentle smile widened. "Yes, he will, won't he? Perhaps he'll even recognize them for the clear warning they are and take heed. For once."

Eyes steady on his, she then gave a gentle toss of her head that was clearly a directive to him to seek the door behind him and depart.

Baerent hastened to obey, discovering something else as he passed the still-motionless guard and stumbled back down the stair. He was shivering in fear.

Wizard of War Lorbryn Deltalon stood on the familiar high ledge, looking out over the forest. He shook his head.

"Well, well," he told the wind. "It seems I make a livelier Laspeera than I'd ever thought to be—certainly more flirtatious than she's ever likely to be. I think."

Well, well, indeed. Yet it had worked, and that was the main thing.

He shook his head again, smiling ruefully. "Whew."

He hadn't had occasion to teleport here often in recent seasons, but this crag in the forest often served the war wizards as a lookout. He wasn't all that far from the bullyblade he'd just left. He should really be getting back to Suzail, but . . . he'd always liked this spot.

It was probably his favorite place in all Faerûn for just standing alone, thinking.

Lorbryn used it that way now, as his true form slowly melted back.

He was doing the right thing.

At long last, he was working for the best outcome for Cormyr.

Both the Knights of Myth Drannor and the band of Purple Dragons led by the ornrion Dauntless were Vangerdahast's agents, he felt certain—and Vangey had sent them out here, along the Ride, to accomplish *something*.

Just what, he didn't know yet, but Brorn just might help him find out.

The bullyblade wasn't stupid. He might want to bury those coins swiftly to avoid being found with something Lorbryn could claim had been stolen. Yet he'd need a few coins in his purse right now, just to live on.

Six coins on top of each sack had tracer spells cast on them that would enable Lorbryn to know their whereabouts at will.

He smiled into the breeze as he readied himself to teleport back to the Royal Palace.

So *this* was how Vangerdahast felt, sitting like a spider at the center of an ever-expanding web of plots and little schemes.

Lorbryn's smile widened.

Wincing, Florin struggled to his knees. His skin raged with fire blisters of the like he'd not felt since his days at the forge back in Espar, and his body ached as if he'd been punched hard, all over, for most of a day.

His sword was lost somewhere under Jhessail—the *real* Jhessail, he reminded himself dazedly—and a half-empty water flask didn't seem that formidable a weapon to use on either a lich or someone who could shrug off that humbling spell.

The lich stood smiling down at the Knights, as the darkly handsome man was doing now. Florin caught sight of a ring on the man's finger, and he tried to fix the device on it—an M with a flaring left leg and a right leg that curled right around to form a ring—in his memory for later.

If there *was* a later.

"So much for my little jaunts here to explore and plunder this place," the man drawled, still regarding the Knights with a sneer. "I believe I've found almost everything, as it happens. Enjoy your deaths."

He was suddenly not there.

The groaning, feebly crawling Knights faced the lich across a bare and empty expanse of floor.

The lich shuffled forward, grounding its staff from time to time in unhurried ease, to peer at the results of its spell. Faint rattling and rasping sounds arose as it hummed a merry tune—or tried to—and came forward, the rings on its bony fingers winking with bright and quickening glows.

Florin tried to rise, but he couldn't. He collapsed beside Islif. Wisps of smoke rose from her limbs. Jhessail lay sprawled and silent under Semoor's legs, but Pennae seemed to have been shielded from the green flames by the tumbling bodies of the two priests, and she was now rising unharmed from behind them, trying to tug them to their feet.

"*Up*, holynoses!" she said. "Our time to save everyone's behinds!"

Semoor laughed, a little wildly. "You want us to defeat *that?*"

"No, I want you to die trying!" Pennae snarled. "Look at it this way: Lord Manshoon has gone, so you've just got *one* mad, gone-beyond-dead archwizard to deal with, not two of them!"

"M-*Manshoon?*" Doust stammered. "As in Zhentil Keep?"

"Yes. Saw him once across a crowded street and remembered that voice and those looks. Now think of some spells!"

"Before you ask," Semoor told her, "no, we don't know how to teleport like Manshoon did."

"Well then," Pennae said, "we won't be able to get out of this place *that* way."

Florin and Islif were struggling to rise again, and behind them, Jhessail—reeling about unsteadily in a real daze—was on her feet.

Pennae gave them all a tight smile, whisked her dagger behind her back, and strolled forward to meet the lich.

"I don't suppose," she asked, "you could direct us poor lost travelers out of this palace, Lord?"

In reply, the lich threw back its skull-head and cackled, then pointed with a finger that flared with ruby radiance as the ring on it unleashed its power. Florin shrank down into something brown and hairy and snorting.

Or rather, snoring. A fat, hairy boar, or boar piglet, or whatever young boars were called. Pennae knew she should have been trying to leap at the lich or at least get past it and try to flee, but she couldn't help staring.

Florin had a long snout and was lying contentedly on the floor, loudly asleep. He was about the size of a small hunting dog that had somehow swallowed a handkeg of ale whole.

As Pennae stared, Islif fought her way to her feet . . . only to shrink right down again, sprouting a snout and long, brown hair and snores of her own.

"Dung and tluining doom!" Pennae whispered, realizing her peril. She whirled to run just as the ruby glow flared again.

Then she was trying to run but was somehow *heavy* and wet and weak and collapsing into helpless sliding softness, too, and the world went dim. Her attempts to shriek came out as squalling, snorting squalling that . . . that . . . that sent all Faerûn and its cackling liches away.

The lich tapped its staff on the floor in a way that seemed somehow satisfied, then shuffled forward again.

Straight for Jhessail. It reached out a long and skeletal arm toward her. "My lady," it said, "it has been so long. It seems years since I felt your warm and yielding eagerness, your ardent mouth upon mine. Come to me now! Come."

The red-haired mage backed away in horror.

Silent in their own terror, hardly daring to move, Doust and Semoor exchanged helpless glances.

Jhessail's shoulders met the wall. She had nowhere left to go.

The lich advanced.

Chapter 12
THE FIRE ANSWERS BACK

As they go through lives so bitter
There are those who faith do lack
Worship they may soon deem fitter
When altar-fire answers back

Old folk saying of the Sword Coast

Two priests of Bane conversed in the temple courtyard in Zhentil Keep.

"Done so soon? They haven't much backbone, these priestesses of Sune! All that warm and all-conquering love a poor shield against true pain, eh?"

"Done, hah! The whip broke!" The Tyrant-har of Bane held up his ruined lash for inspection. What should have been its upper third dangled uselessly, hanging by the merest thread. "A bare backside did that! Someone's been selling us shoddy work, to be sure!"

His superior frowned. "You only brought one lash?"

"Far from it. I broke the other three earlier, one by one—and I'm not the strongest arm among us, by a long bowshot! These new 'holier lashes' are naed, utter naed, I tell you!"

The Watchful Hand of Bane nodded. "We'll have to find out who made them, track them down, and exalt them with a fittingly slow and painful death for the greater glory of Bane." He shook his head. "Work, work . . . never ends, does it? Why, just last—"

No one customarily crossed that temple courtyard in Zhentil Keep except clergy of Bane, so neither of the priests was in the habit of paying much attention to movements around them there.

They never saw the long, gleaming blade racing through the air, all by itself and point-first like an arrow. Speeding out of the shadows, it sliced open their throats so deeply that their heads wobbled on their shoulders before their bodies toppled.

By then, the flying sword Armaukran was far across the square and climbing, trailing a thin ribbon of blood through the twilight, as Horaundoon hurried to find more Zhentarim to slaughter.

Arrogant priests were easy prey. What was puzzling him was how he was going to manage the slaying of an eye tyrant. Or thirty.

The wall was cold, hard, and smooth behind her shoulder blades. Jhessail drew in a deep breath and closed her eyes, then cast one of the few spells she had left, carefully saying the Weave-words—gibberish, they would seem to most hearers—then the rhyme: "So now let all beholding gazes upon me see, not one Jhessail, but rather three!"

She passed her hands, held vertically, back and forth in front of her so the forming mirror images would appear to shift through each other, and which Jhessail was the real one wouldn't be glaringly obvious to the lich.

Sidestepping back and forth to enhance the confusion, she willed the two false images to move to her right, then raised her hands to sketch out the elaborate gestures of . . . a counterfeit, no spell at all. A false magic she hoped might give the lich pause for a moment, as three identical Jhessails worked an impressive-looking magic it couldn't recognize.

Instead, it grinned, brown-gray flesh crumbling away from its skull and falling past its jaws as it did so. "Ah, up to your old tricks! How I love being overwhelmed by your caresses! Come to me, Mara! Come to your Elmariel now!"

Not waiting for her to obey, it shuffled forward, right past Doust and Semoor. On either side of it but a few paces away, the two priests stood frowning at each other, at a loss as to what to do.

The lich steadily closed the gap between itself and the three anxiously spellweaving Jhessails.

Doust shrugged and soundlessly mouthed the word "Breakbone!"

Semoor shrugged back "why not?" agreement, and they both worked breakbone spells; magics probably far too feeble to affect a lich whose bones were animated and protected by its own magic, but what else was left to them?

Doust gave the lich a hard-eyed glare and sent his spell at its head, while Semoor aimed for its raised hand, aglow with all those rings.

They saw the brief, silent radiances of their spells striking those targets, glows that flared and died away again, having done nothing at all. The lich went right on ignoring them.

It also went right on shuffling forward and was now barely more than an arm's length from Jhessail. Her nonsense-chanting mouth was trembling on the verge of a scream.

Semoor took two swift steps and snatched up the snoring, hairy thing Florin had become, taking hold of it high on the legs, where they joined the body.

It was *heavy*—Watching Gods Above, it was heavy!—but he could . . . could . . .

Semoor staggered for a moment under the boar's weight, saw Doust staring at him with mouth agape, and started to run.

Semoor was bent over backward under the weight of the boar, making of his arms and chest a sloping shelf on which the snoring beast bounced as the priest rushed forward. Semoor prayed its hairy bulk would serve as a shield against any spells the lich might cast.

He was almost at the wall—where Jhessail was staring in horror at the lich, as its arms reached hungrily for her—when he caught up to the lich, planted his right foot, and used the staggering momentum he'd built up to swing around to face the lich and heave the hairy, snoring bulk in his arms right at the lich's hands.

The boar fell through them to the floor, crashing solidly down and awakening with an aggrieved and startled snort. In his wake he left tumbling pieces of bone. Magic rings bounced in all directions. Two splintered, broken-off pairs of forearm bones clattered to the floor.

The glittering points of light that served the lich for eyes blazed up into flames of fury. It roared in anger and turned to confront Semoor.

The Light of Lathander shrank back, just as terrified as Jhessail.

Doust's piglet, the sleeping Islif, hurled with all the grunting might the Jewel of Tymora could muster, smashed right into—and through—what was left of the lich's face. The falling boar took the head off the lich's shoulders. The skull struck the floor and exploded into bony, spraying shards. The reeling body was now topped by cracked, chipped shoulderblades and collar bones. As the two priests stared, one arm fell off.

Doust and Semoor looked at each other, shrugged a little more happily this time, and sprinted past what was left of the lich to pluck up the last piglet.

"Up, Pennae," Semoor said, as they clawed the piglet up to their collective knees, staggered, and hefted it higher. "You make a most fetching boarlet—or whatever these beasts are properly called!"

Trotting together this time, the two priests took careful aim at the lurching remnants of the lich, got the boar to almost the height of the skeleton's ribcage—and gave a little heave before letting go.

The third piglet crashed right through the lich, smashing the corpse's pelvis and legs to ruin.

With triumphant yells the two priests sprang in, beating at those bony shards with their maces, pulverizing bones down to grit and dust.

"Holy water!" Semoor snapped, plucking at one of the precious belt vials he and Doust had been given by the Royal Court in the wake of the now-infamous reception for the lady envoy of Silverymoon.

He and Doust kicked what was left of the bones together, mashing the few larger pieces down to grit with a few last mace-blows, then sprinkled their mace-heads and the heap of riven shards with holy water.

Smoke gouted up with loud hissings, as if they were dashing water on a fire. In the wake of those sounds, the heaped bone remnants glowed momentarily. A faint, eerie half-moan and half-sigh . . . and the bone grit melted away to nothing but a dark patch on the stone floor.

Doust knelt and plucked up the cobweblike, collapsing rag that had been the lich's robes. Crouching together, he and Semoor peered at it, watching its row of buttons slowly fall through the disintegrating fabric, one by one, to shatter as they struck the floor. The dyed bone domes bore alternating engravings: the dragon encircled by nine stars and then a circle of chain, which was the old sigil of the Wizards of War, and the old crossed hunting horns badge of a noble family Doust couldn't quite recall.

"Emmarask," Jhessail said over their shoulders, her voice still thin and panting. "That was once an Emmarask."

"And a war wizard," Semoor said grimly. "Good to know what fate they can look forward to, eh?"

"I *wasn't* thinking of becoming a war wizard," Jhessail said.

"I wasn't thinking they'd accept you," he retorted. "Now, O great mage, about all these other liches and our friends the snorting boars—"

"Yes?" Islif asked from above them. "I've been called worse, mind, yet even a farm lass prefers not to be mistaken for—"

Jhessail and the two priests looked up, as the last of the cloth crumbled away from between Doust's fingers. Florin, Islif, and Pennae smiled down at them, back in their proper shapes.

"Always thought you were a real *pig,* underneath," Semoor greeted Florin with a grin.

"Careful," Pennae said. "Any priest fool-tongued enough to make any jests about sows or anything of the sort is going to regret it—as the toe of my boot makes reply to *that!*"

Semoor looked at Doust, who raised a warning finger and said over it with a smile, "Hail, fellow destroyer of liches!"

The Light of Lathander grinned. "Aye, wait'll they hear about *that* at a temple! Real fire-at-the-altar deeds—and ours!"

"Ahem," Jhessail tremulously reminded them both, "forget not one thing: We have to find a way out of here, somehow, and get to a temple, first."

"Indeed," a familiar male voice said from out of the darkness.

+ + ✦ + +

The younger Princess Obarskyr of Cormyr had made it back to her chambers without anyone in the stables or Palace seeing her in her commoner's garb, but she *had* been missed, and neither her maids nor the old, scarred war wizard nor yet the younger but no-less-scarred Purple Dragon guard commander had been all that pleased with her.

In the end, Alusair had planted her hands on her hips, faced them all across the receiving room of her chambers, and said, "You all seem to forget that I'm a *child*. Well, children—even princesses, and yes, even in *civilized* Cormyr—get to play and have adventures, and I was busy doing those things."

"You," her senior maid said, "stopped being a child about seven days after you were born."

"And whose fault is *that?*" Alusair said, finding herself on the verge of tears and made even angrier by that humiliation. "I can't even squat on a *chamber pot* without being spied upon! All the Watching Gods *damn* you all, can't I even—"

She caught herself on the very precipice of blurting out what she'd been out doing, but by then the Purple Dragon ornrion, bless him, had growled, "I've heard enough. Leave the royal miss alone, all of you. Damn *me* if I'd not feel the same way, were I standing in her boots. Er, slippers."

He turned for the door, windmilling his arms so as to sweep all the rest of them along with him, and added, "Now let's get out of here and leave her some peace. I'm sure you'll all take the opportunity to report her or scold her yourselves over the next day or so, anyhail, so—"

The war wizard protested something in an angry whisper as they shouldered through the door together, but the guard commander didn't bother to whisper his response. "I see that as *your* problem. Get Old Thunderspells to cast some sort of waist-down chastity spell on her if that's what you're so worried over."

Then, blessedly, Alusair was all alone, except for the glaring senior maid and two chambermaids who'd carefully kept silent and out of sight in the inner rooms.

Alusair curtly dismissed old Tsashaeree two words into the tirade she was starting, then rang the bell that would bring in the two Purple Dragon door guards to escort her out. They came grinning, one of them giving her a wink, and Alusair was careful not to let Tsashaeree see her winking back. She didn't want to give anyone the idea that she needed Dragons at her elbows day and night.

Alusair went in through the rooms to submit to the deft and deferential attentions of the chambermaids. They seemed in awe of her, for once, but this night that gave her no pleasure. She was too restless, too apprehensive that there would be consequences, and all for nothing. The Harper might have forgotten his promise or be half Faerûn away from hearing her entreaty—or lying wounded or even dead somewhere, never to answer any summons again.

Lying in her bed in the dark, that same restlessness kept its hold over her, and she tossed and turned for what seemed like an eternity.

She must have fallen asleep in the end—because she certainly came awake when a male whisper asked softly into her ear, "You wanted me, Highness?"

The wizard Targon stood alone on the high balcony of a tower in Zhentil Keep, glaring out into the night. It wasn't something Targon often did, but then there was no one near to see him doing it and think his behavior strange.

Old Ghost made his new host body smile wryly. 'Twasn't all that surprising, this lack of spying Zhentarim, given just how many Horaundoon had slaughtered before word had properly spread to bring down any official wariness.

Right now, it was taking all Old Ghost's will to reach across the distance between them and tug the unwilling flying sword back from even more happy slayings. Armaukran was a thirsty blade, and Horaundoon, it seemed, *really* hated a lot of Zhentarim.

Wherefore it was time—and more than time—for them to talk.

The warding spell Targon had cast around himself was ready to turn aside Armaukran's piercing point and deadly edge if the blade somehow outpaced his ability to govern Horaundoon's will, but Old Ghost really didn't think Horaundoon would be that stupid.

The sword came streaking out of the night with a flourish, arrowing point-first but then sweeping up, twisting in the air, and coming to an abrupt but silent stop in the air just out of reach of Targon, vertical with hilt uppermost.

"Well met," Old Ghost said.

"I'm finding I enjoy removing unworthy elements from the Brotherhood," was the response. "I hunger to eliminate more."

"I'll return you to that delight soon enough," Old Ghost told the sword. "How many have you slain? And who, specifically?"

"Fourscore and a few," Horaundoon replied. "Harkult and old Gesker and some magelings who were fawning over them, paltry wizards I knew not. No one else I can put a name to, but many, many priests of Bane, mostly underpriests because I could catch them alone and unseen—oh, and one little spy."

Targon lifted one eyebrow in silent query, and the sword explained, "A beholderkin the size of my fist or a little smaller. A little floating eyeball that was hovering by the shoulder of a wizard who got away."

Old Ghost made his host body nod. "He wasn't the only one to escape you. Your work is causing tumult in the Brotherhood, with every Zhent suspicious of his fellows and many of the senior wizards conducting their own 'investigations' into who's behind the slayings."

"Dozens of futile inquiries, yes. One Brother suspecting all his fellows of meaning him murderous ill is hardly unusual, but the elder Zhentarim have started giving orders and handing me an increasing problem. They are retreating inside warded and spell-guarded fortresses and sending their greenest magelings and most lowly acolytes out to do Zhent business. It is slowing and crippling Brotherhood work but leaving me with few targets worth slaughtering. More than that, Manshoon seems to have gone missing. Many senior Zhentarim have tried to contact him and met with only silence."

Old Ghost shrugged. What mattered it, if Horaundoon knew this? He shared something that had for years been his host body's greatest fear and secret, one that Targon knew would someday bring about his death, very soon after the moment Manshoon discovered he knew it. "That silence is almost certainly real. Manshoon is probably off on one of his little magic-gathering forays."

"Gaining new magic is certainly a good way to remain atop the Brotherhood, yes," Horaundoon agreed. "What forays, exactly?"

Old Ghost discovered with some amusement that Targon's fingers were drumming idly on the stone balcony rail. So this body retained some will of its own, after all. He must take care to remember that.

"From the days before there was a Black Brotherhood," he explained, "Manshoon had the habit of venturing alone around Faerûn, usually in disguise, to ah . . . explore. It's how he first met the eye tyrants, I believe. Translocation spells and old portals are handy things."

"Go places, find those with magic you want, kill them, return home with the loot."

"Not a new strategy for any of us," Old Ghost agreed. "Long, long ago there was a kingdom in the north of what is now—nominally— Cormyr. Occupying most of the Stonelands and a little of the land along the Ride north of the Hullack."

"Esparin."

"Esparin. And kingdoms often have palaces. Now, not quite so long ago, Cormyr had a king named Duar, who had to fight for his throne against a conspiracy that ruled most of Cormyr for a time."

"Executing or exiling the nobles who conspired against him," Horaundoon replied. "I have been told about the reign of Duar Obarskyr. Civil strife means wizards killed and magic hastily hidden."

"Indeed. So we have the Lost Palace of Esparin, which has

remained lost because it lies hidden underground—somewhere under the Stonelands. We also have one particular noble family out of the dozen-some who were exiled for their deeds against King Duar. The Staghearts, now extinct. Which means the Crown owns the old, ruined Stagheart mansion but is unaware that it is linked by portals to the palace. More than that, Vangerdahast and his war wizards are unaware of these portals, too, or they and the Obarskyrs would never have let the place fall into ruin and be swallowed by Cormyr's ever-vigorous forests."

"So Manshoon knows this way into the Lost Palace?"

Targon nodded. "For years, Manshoon has been *occasionally* slipping into the Lost Palace of Esparin to explore, and he has plundered it of many magic items and old spellbooks."

"So if I were to get into this Lost Palace . . ."

"No," Old Ghost said. "Put out of your mind thoughts of becoming mightier than me by picking up magics that lie waiting in those halls. You'll find your own doom instead. The Palace has . . . complications."

"That you're going to keep from me, aren't you?" Horaundoon asked, more thoughtfully than bitterly.

"No," Old Ghost said, "but they certainly exist and close that particular door to both of us. Wherefore I'd prefer to discuss what you *should* do first and only then chat about, ah, romantic fancies."

"Very well. So Manshoon is in hiding and so are all the other most powerful Zhents, leaving me only worthless magelings to kill. While the beholders and the Bane priests and the most senior wizards all try to find or craft magics to find and destroy me."

"Well put. So we must make that tumult of yours shake them right out of doing so by making it much greater. I believe the best way to flush the most powerful out into the open is to hand the Brotherhood either a real crisis or a real opportunity. A war with Cormyr, perhaps . . ."

Old Ghost could feel Horaundoon's mind swirl with incredulous, eager delight. "Which you're going to cause *how?*"

"Through your *strict* obedience to my orders," Old Ghost said. "I am sending you to find and slay any of the Knights of Myth Drannor and to seize the Pendant of Ashaba. You will then bring it back here, by means of its chain looped about your blade, so Zhentil Keep can openly lay claim to Shadowdale. I—that is, this body I inhabit—can handle that."

"While I—?"

"You will already have slipped back into Cormyr to do a little more butchery."

"Specific butchery."

"Indeed. You will slay the spies Vangerdahast sent after the Knights. You will also kill Myrmeen Lhal, in Arabel, then anyone the war wizards and the Dragon Throne send to look into her demise and the disappearances of the pendant, the Knights, and their spies. Cormyr will thus be weakened and infuriated at the same time as the most ambitious Zhents seek to take advantage of this weakness."

"You again."

"Targon again, suggesting and advising and 'discovering' where it will do the most good. I'll see to it that Brotherhood military strength in Shadowdale is built up and commanded by someone recklessly ambitious—we have a lot of Zhentilar like that—and goad them into taking Tilverton and Halfhap and threatening Arabel. The Zhentilar are to do battle with Purple Dragons wherever they see them. That will soon bring Cormyr riding this way with fire and sword—and *that,* if conquering Tilver's Gap hasn't done it already, will inevitably draw the rest of the Brotherhood into the conflict."

Horaundoon's mind had darkened, eagerness giving way to apprehension. "But what if Cormyr is too strong and shatters the Brotherhood, menacing Zhentil Keep itself?"

Old Ghost's satisfaction could be felt even more strongly than Targon's face could express. "As to that," he said, "we need never fear Cormyr's strength. The Lost Palace is bulging with mad liches, all of them deranged but very powerful spell-slayers. All we need do is work the Unbinding that frees them all, and it will thrust them through an old portal right into the heart of the Royal Palace in

Suzail—dooming that city. Its citizens will die horribly, twisted or blasted by ruthless magic, before the liches start to roam."

"And we'll then stop these rampaging liches how?"

"It matters not if they wreak havoc in other lands. In fact, we would do well to goad or steer some of them into dealing much death in Thay. If they do turn on us, who is better equipped than the Brotherhood to destroy them?"

"A Zhentarim empire . . . Thay brought low . . ." Horaundoon's thrilled mind was bright with eager, growing hunger.

"Once the elder wizards of the Brotherhood are out of their fortresses and active, we can select victims at will."

"Manshoon and the most debauched wizards."

"When they are eliminated, Fzoul and the beholders are certain to seek command of the Zhentarim. When *that* bloodbath is done, one side or both will be gone, leaving just the hardened survivors and the weakest of magelings."

"Whom we can control."

Targon nodded. "Whereupon the Brotherhood will be back on the path to greatness—an empire—at last. Which we safeguard, watching and continuing to prune away anyone who reveals himself as the same sort of power-hungry fool that Manshoon has become."

The brightness in Horaundoon's mind suddenly clouded over with fear again. "What about Hesperdan?"

Old Ghost made his host body shrug. "He's always been a mystery, that one—and far more powerful than he has any right to be. Yet even if he steps forward to seize all, he has never seemed as reckless as Manshoon. Yes, Hesperdan just might be the greatest tyrant mage Faerûn has ever known."

Princess Alusair's heart was pounding so thunderously, she thought it might awaken the maids dozing in the outer robing room. She rolled over in a flash and by the faint, familiar glow of her moonstone bracelet on her bedside table could *just* see that there was a dark figure in bed beside her. A man-sized figure.

"Who are you?" she whispered, clutching the silken sheets up to her chin. She was suddenly very aware that the nearest knife was hidden behind a panel inside one of the four soaring bedposts *on the far side of the intruder*—and that all she was wearing was a black ribbon choker around her neck.

"Dalonder Ree, Harper, here in answer to your summons," he said.

Alusair let out a great sigh of relief then said, "I need you to help me!"

Dalonder gazed at the young princess, briefly marveling at the way her eyes almost blazed with excitement and anger. "Help you *how*, Princess?" he whispered.

"Vangerdahast sent away my personal champion, an ornrion everyone calls Dauntless, though his real name—"

"I know him. You want him brought back here?"

"Yes!"

"And what's to stop Vangerdahast from just sending him away somewhere worse?"

"I . . . don't know."

Dalonder plucked something from a belt pouch, deftly captured a royal hand in the darkness, and pressed the item into her palm.

"What—?"

" 'Tis just a black leather button. Nothing magical. If someone takes it from you, find another. Think about how you can protect Dauntless if he does return here. When you've thought of something, drop this out your window into the garden bed below—and I'll come back, probably in this manner. Until then, be aware that Harpers are already watching over Dauntless and the Knights of Myth Drannor."

"The Knights?"

"Yes. Your ornrion was sent to see them out of the realm. Old Thunderspells neglected to tell you that, I see. He neglects rather too much, these days."

Whatever Alusair was going to say vanished when the man in bed with her deftly captured her other hand, dropped a gentle kiss into her palm—and was gone through the bed curtains, leaving her alone with her heart pounding hard again.

After a long, tense time of listening to nothing, Alusair relaxed, rolled onto her back, and smiled into the darkness.

She was caught up in Palace intrigue at last. Men slipping into her bed in the proverbial cat-hours of the night. *Her* bed.

She *mattered*.

Chapter 13
Drowning and dismembering curses

So, laughing man, hear you now my curse:
If you speak not truth, plain and fair,
If this deed does not victory prepare,
May you be drowned, dismembered, and worse.

The character Talanassa the Fishwife
In the play Karnoth's Homecoming
by Chanathra Jestryl, Lady Bard of Yhaunn
First performed in the Year of the Bloodbird

The war wizard who was no war wizard at all scuttled quietly along a back passage in one of the dustier wings of the sprawling Royal Court, looking thoughtful. His identity was counterfeit, but his "thinking hard" mien was all too real.

Boarblade had spent some time practicing the real Torst Khalaeto's scuttling gait, the pitch of the timid war wizard's voice, and Khalaeto's favorite phrases, because he needed to fool quite a few people. Not so much nobles, who were apt to be uncaring, barely noticing anything that wasn't all about *them*, but folk who knew Khalaeto. War wizards and courtiers he might well meet in these very halls and chambers.

Thankfully, this dangerous little imposture seemed about done. A few drinks with Torst in Khalaeto's favorite tavern and the skill of the hargaunt had given Boarblade a perfect copy of the face of timid, bespectacled War Wizard Torst Khalaeto, and fate—in the form of a land ownership dispute between two old families of Immersea—had promptly taken the real Khalaeto off into some of the dustiest chambers of Crown records for some days. When Boarblade thought of war wizards, he never pictured anything like a hesitant, peering-at-life, fussy old clerk, but . . . well, as the old saying put it, the gods daily taught a noticing man something new.

Khalaeto with his recording scroll, scrollboard, and little collection of quills had been the perfect questioner to leave nobility unsuspicious. He went to several of the noble families in whose sons the Lady Narantha Crownsilver had planted mindworms, to ask them just which war wizard had later visited them.

Their answers had all been the same: either Royal Magician Vangerdahast or Wizard of War Lorbryn Deltalon.

Telgarth Boarblade may have been many things, but fool was not one of them. Wherefore he knew better than to try to speak with Vangerdahast. Yet there might well be a way to, ah, *worm* the secrets out of the lesser war wizard of using mindworms to control those nobles.

So he'd gone seeking Lorbryn Deltalon, only to discover that the man seemed to have gone absent from the Palace.

What was making Boarblade so worried was the "why" of that disappearance and its implications. He quickened his scuttling pace, wanting to be out of this disguise—and the Royal Court, too—as quickly as possible.

Without coming face to false face with the wizard Vangerdahast.

Wizard of War Maraertha Dalewood knew very well that Royal Magician Vangerdahast keenly scrutinized every word of the house wizards' reports. Even so, he was in the habit of oh-so-casually asking anyone bringing him such a report if there was anything of "importance" his attention should be drawn to. She also knew that Old Thunderspells asked such questions far more as a test of her and the other report-runners than out of any concern over missing a fact, hint, or nuance.

Wherefore—as someone young, quiet, and fairly plain of looks, but ambitious—she'd taken care to pay close attention to the reports coming in from noble houses across the realm, to be ready for Vangey's questions.

She took care to keep the slightest hint of triumph or pride out of her voice, "I *believe* so, Lord Vangerdahast, though I fully understand I may merely be unaware of orders you've given to others. I have noticed a pattern in the reports. Many house wizards say War Wizard Torst Khalaeto visited the noble households, unheralded, to ask if their heirs had recently been visited by a war wizard. He further inquired as to the identity of the visitor."

Vangerdahast looked up at her sharply and frowned. "And do the reports mention what answer they gave?"

Maraertha's heart started to thud. Unless Old Thunderspells was a better actor than she gave him credit for, this *was* important.

"Every one," she said carefully, "stresses that Khalaeto was told the truth. That the visitor had been either yourself or Wizard of War Lorbryn Deltalon."

"Good, good," Vangerdahast replied almost absently, rising and striding for the door. "Leave the reports there on my desk, lass—and say nothing of this to anyone. If anyone should ask you about this, remember well for me who they are."

"Yes, Lord," Maraertha said to his dwindling back.

The Royal Magician raised his hand in a curt wave of acknowledgment ere he vanished down the passage outside.

Very carefully, squaring the papers just so, she set the reports on his desk, taking great care not to so much as glance at anything else on it.

Lord Manshoon of Zhentil Keep smiled to himself, out of long habit taking care that no trace of his mood reached his face.

These Knights might ably serve his current purposes.

He dare not work the Unbinding himself. Certain parts of the ritual would be fatal to those performing them, so he needed several capable persons, working together, who would press on with the Unbinding even after more than one of them died rather than abandoning it out of fear or grief.

In short, he needed adventurers. Adventurers such as these, eager to serve Cormyr and take pride in doing so, despite the apparent disapproval and suspicions of Royal Magician Vangerdahast and the usual generous supply of malicious, noble rabble.

That in turn would make the irony all the more delicious, when the Unbinding freed all the mad liches in the Lost Palace and poured them in a murderous, capering flood into the heart of the Royal Palace in Suzail, dooming most in that city to the proverbial "horrible magical deaths." Working the Unbinding would be seen as an act of treachery few would forget, even centuries hence. A fitting reward for zealous loyalty to the Purple Dragon, and a warning to all meddlesome adventurers.

Yes, my simple dupes. You will serve Cormyr *very* well.

Vangerdahast strode through the Royal Court, his robes billowing behind him. Where *was* Deltalon, anyhail, and why was Khalaeto—*Khalaeto,* who never concerned himself with anything that wasn't a document—seeking him?

His spell-summons to Lorbryn Deltalon, whose mind he read lightly but often these last few seasons, and whose loyalty he'd never once suspected, were met with only silence. Torst Khalaeto, however, responded instantly, from near at hand in another wing of the Royal Court.

Vangerdahast stopped, ignoring several impassive doorjacks standing stiffly at attention at their posts. He bore down into Khalaeto's mind more harshly than was his wont.

He found honest bewilderment and blossoming apprehension—not for Torst himself, because the timid mage truly knew of nothing wrong, evil, or disloyal on his own part, but for some unknown calamity facing the realm. Vangerdahast also found a turmoil of facts and mental "must check this, then that" notes about a certain lost, centuries-old, Crown-to-commoner-family property agreement.

Mindspeaking to Khalaeto with an apology for the intrusion, and even adding warm thanks for the assistance, Vangerdahast ended his magic and stood shaking his head.

That visitor to the nobles had *not* been Khalaeto but someone wearing his shape. Which meant it could be every last damned shapeshifter or spellhurler in Faerûn. That left Deltalon as his only lead in trying to find out what was going on.

"Suspicions aroused," Vangerdahast muttered, then gave the nearest doorjack a baleful "You listening to someone?" glare and strode away, heading he knew not where.

He had to find Lorbryn Deltalon and get a good long look into his mind. Was this something small and pranksome or *another* conspiracy within the ranks of his war wizards?

"Lady," Telsword Bareskar of the Palace Guard asked unhappily, as he peered cautiously into the gloom of the ruined mansion, "what is—er, *was* this place?"

"Once it was part of the country mansion of the Staghearts, who were stripped of their nobility and exiled long ago," Highknight Lady Ismra Targrael replied. "This was their hunting lodge. The mansion proper stood yonder, where all those trees are now. Duar had it razed. They knew the right way to handle things in those days. Mercy is the besetting weakness of kings."

"Uh, yes, Lady Tar—"

"My *name*," the Highknight reminded him icily, the point of her sword at his throat, "is *not* to be used."

"S-s-sorry, Lady, uh, Sir, uh . . ." Telsword Bareskar was a long way from the Royal Palace of Suzail and less than happy about being so. He liked shifts of mundane boredom, filled with simple, clear-cut rules and a lack of any need to think. To say nothing of being relatively free of danger, not—

"Yes, take the stair down," Targrael said in his ear, "and as a special favor to me, *try* not to sound as if you're a charger in full barding, stumbling down steps in the dark."

"Y-yes," Bareskar replied, starting down the stair with his sword held out in front of him, feeling his way along an unseen railing and fervently wishing he had a lantern.

He'd gone down six steps into what smelled and felt like a damp stone cellar when Targrael said from behind him, "Stop. There's no one here. They've gone. So back up and out around the back. We'll have to do what I was hoping to avoid. Look behind every stlarned tree in the forest."

When Bareskar got to the top of the stairs again, Targrael was standing and staring thoughtfully down at the great hole in the floor that presumably opened into the cellar from which he'd just come up. Without looking at him, she pointed with her sword at the square of light where there had once been a pair of back doors, and Bareskar obediently went where he was directed, peering cautiously out into the forest and seeing nothing but trees, trees, gloom, and more trees.

He stepped outside, looking right and left, and on an impulse chose the left and stalked along the back wall so as to peer around—

"Now!" someone commanded from the forest to his right, and that was the last thing Telsword Bareskar ever heard.

The circling hawk didn't even have time to blink, let alone squawk or shriek in alarm.

The sword, faster than any arrow, was simply there one moment—and gone the next, streaking through the air, point-first and glittering. South and west, from Zhentil Keep to a spot in the forest just north off the Moonsea Ride, where of old the Stagheart banner had flapped.

Just as the hawk was flapping now, dazed in the wake of that streaking blade.

Lord Crownsilver rolled his eyes. "Yes, I ordered you to blast him! No, I did *not* order you to destroy that corner of the building!"

"What does it matter?" The three Sembian mages-for-hire were conscious again but none too happy. Their healing potions had done their work, but such quaffs were expensive and not easily replaced out here in this wilderland. "It's a ruin."

"It matters because this land swarms with nosy war wizards, and they can hardly help but notice a spellblasted *building!* Nor can any other Knights who might be lurking all around us!"

The Sembian who'd hurled the spell shrugged. "You think they'll dare do anything after—"

The knife that spun through the air to sprout in his throat forever prevented him from finishing his question.

It was the shocked noble who muttered, "That?"

The other two wizards turned in the direction the blade had come from and hurled their best spells. "Time to fell some firewood," one of them snarled, watching full-sized trees hurtle and tumble.

"Never liked forests," the other agreed, watching a racing wave of crackling flame die away into the blackened distance.

Lord Crownsilver blinked in awe and then winced. All that good, coin-worthy timber . . .

Manshoon was certain his spellwork was perfect. It wouldn't be his looks that might betray him.

His acting would have to be perfect, too. Not that he was worried.

By Bane and by Symgharyl's waiting, willing body, this was going to be *fun.*

Targrael's lip curled. Idiot wizards. They'd not last long at home in Sembia if they blasted buildings like that. Even if that fool Crownsilver had mistaken Bareskar for one of the Knights, the thing to do would have been to enthrall him and so lure the rest of the adventurers within reach, not blast and burn everything in sight.

As it was, she was safely behind the Stagheart ruin, short one knife—for now—and itching to exact a higher price for Bareskar's death. Surely he was worth at least three foolheaded Sembian wizards.

Woodsmoke drifted past her face. She would have to set about stalking them with a little care, given that these madwits could fell generous stands of trees in an instant, but if Beshaba didn't best Tymora in the next few breaths, she had no doubt she could slay the two surviving wizards. Leaving her with one noble lord to cow into doing whatever she wanted him to do.

For the good of Cormyr, of course.

"Back inside," Lord Crownsilver said. "Being as your fellow left a *little* of the place standing!"

The two surviving Sembians exchanged glances. Crownsilver's irritation was overwhelming his usual caution, it seemed.

The lord strode back into the ruined hunting lodge. "They obviously got out somehow. Or one of them did. We must look properly down their end of the cellar, this time, to see how many of them are lying dead there. Then come back up, when all the fire's died, and see how many you cooked yonder. I like to know how many enemies are after me."

The Sembians traded glances again. They needed no words to make it clear to each other that they both thought their employer was mad, gone well beyond reason in his hunger to slay Knights of Myth Drannor—all Knights of Myth Drannor, everywhere!—but . . .

The mages traded elaborate shrugs. He was paying . . .

They followed the seething nobleman, not even bothering to look back.

So they never saw the black leather-clad Highknight retrieve her knife from the throat of the wizard she'd slain, wipe it clean on his robes, and close in behind them.

They tramped down the stairs, preceded by complaints about the lack of a mage to cast any magical light where it was needed—

Only to come to an abrupt halt, in common astonishment, to gaze upon Crownsilver's complaints suddenly answered.

An upright oval of glowing air, a portal if they'd ever seen one, appeared in the dark cellar of the ruin. Right at the spot where, in the wake of their wandfire, when that end of the cellar ceiling had come down, the Knights of Myth Drannor had been standing.

"Vangerdahast!" Jhessail spat.

All of the Knights stared.

The bearded, paunchy old mage in robes stood alone where the passages met. Facing them, he wore an expression they were used to seeing, too—grimly haughty distaste or displeasure as he regarded them. He shook his head and said, "I might have known."

"What is this place?" Semoor said. "And what in all the Nine Hells are *you* doing here?"

"Kindly speak more quietly, Wolftooth," the Royal Magician replied sourly. "Unless you have some means of besting liches that I lack. We're standing in the Lost Palace of Esparin, and I am here because I was trapped here by a Zhent impostor who means ill for the realm. Whereas you are here because, I suppose, you are adventurers who will do anything other than depart the realm of Cormyr as you were ordered to do."

Pennae gave him a cold look. "So we're somewhere in Cormyr?"

Ignoring her, Vangerdahast asked, "So how *did* you get here?"

"So we're somewhere in Cormyr?" Islif echoed Pennae.

"Somewhere underground, near Cormyr. Probably north of the realm proper." The wizard turned to cast glances down passages in all directions and then strode toward the Knights. He put his back to a wall. "My turn, I believe. Again, how did you reach this place?"

"Magic!" Pennae said. "Not ours. Something done by Lord Crownsilver or rather his three hired, wand-waving, Sembian mages. In the woods just north off the Ride east of Halfhap, in an old roofless ruin behind a caravan camp. A place I'm sure you can name."

"No doubt," Vangerdahast said. "So—"

"That was not," the thief snapped, "merely an observation. I can tell all too well by your temper and your hesitancy that you're going to ask for our aid, Vangey, so pray do us the little courtesy of telling us what we want to know."

The Royal Magician's bushy eyebrows rose in unison, and he looked straight at Florin. "Haven't learned the cost of overly smart tongues yet? Adventurers usually have quite enough trouble without needlessly borrowing more."

Florin regarded Vangerdahast calmly. "I don't recall our charter saying anything at all about obeying the Royal Magician of Cormyr—nor the Court Wizard, or for that matter any war wizard. I thank you for the advice. In return, here's some for you: Politely answer the lady. You'll live longer that way."

"Growing fangs, Falconhand? Tell me, O Wise Advisor, is this a wise time to do so?" The Royal Magician sighed, moved his hand as if to wave his own words away with the back of it, and said, "Forgive me, Knights. I . . . am under some strain at the moment. I very much need to get myself out of here in some haste. Alive, too, and as you see me now, not turned into a bird or boot or some such. I do indeed find myself in need of your assistance just now."

"Does your neediness extend to an appropriate reward?" Pennae said.

"And of what, specifically?" Semoor added.

Vangerdahast smiled wryly, just for an instant. "Ennoblement for you all. Which would mean titles, a small gift of Crown funds, and the removal of any requirement upon you to depart the realm. Moreover, if you do continue to Shadowdale and settle there, I can promise much funding, military aid, and war wizard assistance— under your authority—in securing and transforming the dale into what you want it to be. We can even make it part of Cormyr. Ah, only if that's what *you* want, of course."

Pennae crooked an eyebrow. "My, you *are* desperate, aren't you?"

Jhessail frowned. "What assistance do you have in mind?"

"And how do we know you *are* Vangerdahast," Pennae added, "and not a mad lich playing a little game with us?"

The wizard sighed and waved a hand at Doust and Semoor. "Are there not holy men among you? Simple magics on their part will reveal my undeath—or would, if I happened to be undead. Now, as for aiding me, I need you to do something the spells laid upon me here prevent me from doing myself, of course. It's called the Unbinding, and—I'll not lie to you—there *is* danger in it."

"As in fatal danger," Pennae said. "Care to be more specific?"

Vangerdahast gave her a dark look. "If you work arcane spells, they can twist into quite different magics and be unleashed without warning to harm yourself and others. This occurs only in the wake of your working a particular unbinding, in the long sequence that makes up the ritual."

"So this Unbinding is a series of little steps?" Pennae asked. "Destructive ones, I presume?"

"Yes, and I must warn you that powerful enchanted items on your persons can be affected just as powerful spells can. Minor magics of either sort should do no harm, though their presence may give you something of a headache."

The Royal Magician pointed along the wall across from the one he was leaning against. "There are many carved panels among the wood sheathing of these walls. Some are actually thin, worked stone, painted and treated to look like wood. At my direction, you Knights must shatter a particular stone panel, and then go and do the same thing to whichever nearby panel winks with sudden light when you shatter the first. The Unbinding is simply a series of such breakings."

"Which will do what?" Islif and Florin asked, in perfect unison.

"Deliver all of us from this place. The liches will fall apart. The bindings are all that is keeping them from doing so right now. You'll know the Unbinding has worked because now-sleeping portals hidden all over this palace will awaken and reach out to suck us through, snatching us all to one place: the robing room behind the Throne Chamber in the Royal Palace in Suzail."

"And then?" Semoor asked. "We'll be blasted down by some waiting guard of war wizards?"

"No, but I'd take it kindly if you fought at my side as I seek out the false Vangerdahast. We'll have to move swiftly and— regrettably—deal with any war wizards we meet who try to stop us, because the impostor will undoubtedly seek to reach the royal family, probably to slay one of them and take that shape or to try to hold them hostage in return for his own safe escape."

Vangerdahast fell silent then and turned his head to give all of them the closest thing to a beseeching look that any of the Knights had ever seen on his usually imperious face.

The Knights stared at him, then eyed each other.

There were several unhappy sighs before Florin said slowly, "We must confer and decide *together*."

"Aye," Pennae agreed. "Let's talk."

Targrael sank down onto the stairs, melting against them. She dared not count on these three dolts being such utter fools as never to look back her way.

After all, they might well turn back from the portal right now, and—

"One of you in front of me and one behind," Lord Crownsilver said. "Come! The longer we give them to get ahead of us . . ."

Warily, one of the Sembians walked up to and through the portal, vanishing in a silent instant. Breathing something that might have been a prayer or a curse, the nobleman followed. The second Sembian peered for a moment at the rubble behind the portal, where beams and the ceiling had crashed down in a now-frozen torrent of sagging collapse, sighed loudly, and strode after them.

Still flattened on the stairs, Highknight Ismra Targrael waited in cautious silence for some time ere she rose in smooth, catlike silence and stalked to the portal. Turning smoothly in a complete rotation to look everywhere behind her, she stepped into its embrace, drawn sword first.

In silence it swallowed her, and that silence stretched for several long breaths before something else moved in the darkened cellar, rising from behind a particularly large heap of rubble.

It was a man—a man known to a diminishing number of living Cormyreans as Brorn Hallomond, personal bodyguard in the service of the Lord Prester Yellander, and more widely termed a lord's "bullyblade"—and he hefted his sword in his hand as he stared at the portal he'd just seen four people pass through.

Would it be the folly of a reckless fool to go after them? Or his road to riches enough to settle down somewhere safe in the Forest Kingdom and live like a lord the rest of his days?

A short way down the passage, beyond the moot, a door opened, and a lich clad in robes of rich purple strode out, clutching a rod that winked with magical lights up and down its dark length.

"Aha!" it cried. *"More* thieves! Come to despoil the royal vaults of fair Cormyr! Can't turn my back and lose myself in a spell for half a candle without another scurrying infestation of you creeping in behind me to—"

Running out of words, it growled in rage and charged forward, waving the staff.

Vangerdahast calmly worked a swift and intricate spell, a casting unlike any Jhessail had ever seen before—and a strange red mist appeared, swept along the passage, snatched the lich off its feet, and bundled it back through the door, rod and all. The mists melted fingerbones, robes, and the feet off the lich as it struggled.

Then the mists slammed the door and roiled in front of it, sealing it off.

"That much," the Royal Magician turned and told the Knights a little sadly, "I can still do." He seemed on the verge of saying more, then hesitated before adding, "I quite understand and respect your need to take some time over deciding to aid me or not. I have waited decades for certain things to befall Cormyr, worked for years to bring many of those things about. I have mastered waiting. I shall withdraw yonder"—he pointed down the passage, a little way beyond the door where his spell was raging—"and let you debate without my interference."

Pennae nodded and held up a hand to silence the rest of the Knights as they watched Vangerdahast walk away. "Doust," she said softly, "watch him as if you're a hungry hawk. Speak if you see him do anything that might be spellcasting."

"Understood," Doust said.

"We're lost here, and these liches seem real enough to me," Islif said without waiting for anyone else to speak. "Which means we'll die, sooner or later, if one comes blundering up to us like the one we just saw—whether he staged that or not. We may need him as much as he needs us."

Florin nodded. "Yet before we plunge into talking tactics—"

"Arguing tactics," Pennae interrupted with a grin, never turning her head from watching Vangerdahast.

"Arguing tactics," Florin granted, "I think we must decide how far we can trust Vangerdahast. Is he speaking truth to us now?"

Doust shrugged and pointed at Semoor. "If I pray—if either or both of us priests prays properly—we can be granted the power to know falsehoods when uttered. We can do this and put specific questions to Vangey—questions we should frame carefully. The spells have strict limits, but we will *know* if this tale of Unbinding and an impostor and our ennoblement is truth."

"Let's do that," Islif said.

"Agreed," Pennae said, "but remember this: Vangey will be standing listening to everything we say. Let's decide some things, quickly, while we have this much privacy."

Manshoon had half-turned away from the Knights, feigning what he fancied might be the dignity—or perhaps pomposity would be a better word—of Vangerdahast. They were walking slowly toward him now, all of them, so he turned back to face them.

Florin walked at their fore, face stern. "Very well, Lord Vangerdahast," he said formally, stopping a few paces away. "We'll do it. And may the curses of all the gods of Faerûn drown and dismember you if you've deceived us."

"You probably got it all," Dauntless said. "One can't tell from the smoke. That's apt to go on for some time. Yet I'm not expecting the forest to flare up around us." He shrugged. "We'll have Dragon patrols here, regardless. The smoke'll do that much."

"I didn't want to use any magic," Tsantress said grimly, "but . . ." She shook her head in exasperation and went back to staring through the thicket in which they were crouching at the roofless ruin that half the population of eastern Cormyr seemed to have vanished inside, now.

Watching Gods Above, it can't be that *big inside. If they weren't falling down some pit or other, they must be heaped up like . . . like . . .*

"Oh, gods," she whispered, "are they all dead, d'you think?"

"Now, lady wizard, thinking always gets us Purple Dragons in trouble—as the Royal Magician is all too fond of reminding us," Dauntless said. "If you're asking me if I'm anxious to draw sword and step in there, the answer is no. Not at this time."

Tsantress grinned at his mimicry of one of Alaphondar's favorite Court phrases. She stiffened and tapped a warning finger across her lips. When Dauntless stared a silent question at her, she used that same finger to point through the brush in another direction. She crouched down even lower.

Another man had come into view, walking warily and holding a wand out before him as if it were a sword. He seemed unfamiliar with the terrain and almost to be *feeling*—no, sensing—his way forward.

"What's *Lorbryn* doing here?" Tsantress breathed, more to herself than Dauntless. "What's going on? Is Vangerdahast sending watchers to watch his watchers?"

Chapter 14
INTO OUR LAPS

Forward, my bold, brave Dragons
Swords out, all, and check the maps
A plentitude of beauties and flagons
Seek, all to end up in our laps!

The character Great King of Cormyr
In the play Riding the Purple Dragon
by Alimontur of Westgate
First performed (and banned in Cormyr)
in the Year of the Wandering Wyrm

Growling to himself, the Royal Magician of Cormyr cast the scrying spell a second time, then sat back to gaze upon the glossy black marble tabletop and wait.

Again, nothing.

He shook his head. With all of these augmentations and a perfect casting, the magic should have yielded *some* indications. Even if Deltalon was on another plane or dead, the Weave echo should have come back to Vangerdahast to tell him the magic had sought but failed.

Yet it became clear that no echo was coming. Nothing. As if the spell were racing away across infinite distances, seeking, forever seeking, and not finding. . . .

Vangerdahast grunted. This looked darker and darker.

He heaved himself to his feet and started to stride from the room, then stopped, settled down in his chair again, and cast a much simpler magic.

Not seeking Deltalon, this time, but on impulse, checking on Taltar Dahauntul through the ornrion's belt and boots. He murmured the added incantation that would also let him see through the Dragon's eyes. That would give Dauntless a raging headache, but, hah, to quote words he'd used far too often down the years, we must all make these little sacrifices in the service of Cormyr.

The air over the table whirled silently, then coalesced into a scene.

He was now seeing what Dauntless was gazing at . . . and he was peering through a thick tangle of saplings, clinging vines, and forest brush at—Lorbryn Deltalon!

Vangerdahast blinked, drew breath to swear, and abruptly the view over the table changed as the distant Dauntless turned his head. He was now looking at Wizard of War Tsantress Ironchylde, who was evidently crouching in a forest thicket somewhere, right beside the ornrion.

Dauntless turned his head again to watch Deltalon stalk cautiously across a clearing of sorts, wand in hand, up to the missing door of—

Vangerdahast stood bolt upright, upending his stool with a clatter, and roared the most furious curses he knew at the ceiling.

The scene above the table calmly continued to unfold, no matter how hard and often the Royal Magician glared at it.

"All gods stlarn it all!"

He ran out of verbal filth to spew and shook his head, aghast at where the two war wizards and that pain-in-the-sitter ornrion were: the only open way into the Lost Palace.

Vangerdahast called on the power of his rings and bellowed, "Laspeera!"

Through a surging red mist of pain and a gasp, both supplied by his most trusted Wizard of War half the Palace away, he saw the astonished faces of the novice war wizards she'd been instructing.

She was wincing and clutching at her head, but Vangey wasted no time on apologies or niceties. Brutally ramming what he was seeing over the table into her mind, he snarled, "Do *you* know anything about this?"

"No, Van—Lord Vangerdahast," Laspeera groaned, fingers clawing at her temples and face pinched in pain. "I don't. At all."

The students staring at her clearly heard the Royal Magician's answering roar, spilling out of her ears. "*To me!* Right now! *Hurry!* The safety of the realm hangs on this!"

Laspeera slumped over with a gasp as the raging wizard left her mind, then she straighted and gave her young war wizards a lopsided smile.

"He's always like this," she explained. "One gets used to it."

She turned and dashed out the door.

"What is this place?" one of the Sembians asked, peering at the dark passages ahead.

"I was hoping *you* could tell *me* that," Lord Maniol Crownsilver snapped. "You're the wizards here."

"Hold!" The other Sembian's voice was tight with fear. "What's that?"

He was pointing ahead into the dark mouth of a side passage, where something half-seen was moving.

Out into their passage it came, walking as slowly as an elderly, unsteady noble, and wearing the ragged remnants of what had once been splendid garments of shimmerweave and musterdelvys. Its head was half flesh and lank hair and half bare bone, and its eyes were two glittering motes of light. It was smiling.

"A lich, I'm thinking," the first Sembian said quietly, his hands already busy at his belt.

"So, my tutor," the undead asked them, "what is it to be this time? Are we calling up fiends? Or hurling fire into flagons?"

The Sembians looked sidelong at each other. "Neither," the second Sembian said. "No magic this day."

"No? But I've practiced so long! Watch!" Bony fingers sketched briefly in empty air, rose-hued motes of light started to trail from fingertips, and a sudden flare of rose-purple light snarled out in Lord Crownsilver's direction.

"Do something!" the noble shouted, cowering back. "I'm paying you to *do something!*"

Even as his voice rose in wild fear, the crawling, stabbing rose-purple radiance struck something half-seen and emerald-hued that seemed to be emanating from the first Sembian's belt. The purple light was deflected to strike at the passage wall, where rainbow-hued radiances flared into being and wrestled with it.

"Oooh!" The lich clapped its hands together, staring at where its magic was striking the emerald-hued warding. "Pretty! *Very* pretty! And have you *more* delights to share with me, dusky sorceress?"

Lord Crownsilver and the two Sembians exchanged glances then looked back at the lich. It had turned its back on them and was strolling away down the passage now, flouncing along as if dancing or skipping, and crooning, "Pretty . . . oh, so pretty . . ."

"Look," the second Sembian said, pointing past the wandering lich at something leaning out to look at them from another passage mouth. "There's another one."

"Azuth's flaming spittle," the first mage cursed.

The two Sembians looked at each other, nodded in accord, and turned away from the liches.

"Here, now!" Lord Crownsilver snapped, plucking at the sleeve of the first Sembian. "What're you playing at? I'm paying you to—"

The Sembian thrust his face forward at his patron so aggressively that the shorter noble flinched back, and the wizard snapped, "Lord, those are *liches*. Mad liches. Not all the gold and gems in Cormyr will keep me here now."

"Aye," the other Sembian said. "Dead men spend no riches. And we'll all be dead men—or worse—very swiftly if we tarry here longer. Why, I—"

His fellow mage-for-hire gurgled loudly.

The Sembian had torn his sleeve from Crownsilver's grasp, taken two swift strides back down the passage—and run right onto the sword that a grimly smiling woman in black leathers was holding ready, right at the level of his throat.

Her free hand snatched the warding token from the wizard's belt and held it up to ward off any magic the other Sembian might hurl.

Thus defended, Highknight Lady Ismra Targrael watched the man choke and strangle on her steel. Her smile never changed as he sagged, gurgling his way down to the passage floor with his staring eyes fixed on her.

Letting go of her sword as the dying Sembian took it to the floor and as Lord Crownsilver stared at her, aghast and paling, she plucked a dagger from her belt, danced sideways, and threw it deftly.

The noble couldn't turn his head fast enough to follow its flashing flight, but he saw well enough where that journey ended.

Wearing the dagger hilt-deep in his left eye, the second Sembian mage toppled, tiny lightnings spitting and swirling vainly around the blade as feeble defensive magics sought to deal with it . . . and failed.

Targrael didn't even bother to watch him fall. She was busy tugging her sword free.

Lord Crownsilver stared down at the two bodies on the passage floor in front of him. Then he looked up at the woman who'd killed them. Who was still smiling.

"Well, little traitor noble," she purred, stalking forward, twirling her sword. "It seems it's now just you and me."

Manshoon smiled. He'd been ready to foil the priests' truth-sensing magics—feeble things, really—but he'd been spared the trouble. They were so *eager* to save Faerûn, these Knights. Naive fools.

If every land had a dozen such bands, he could conquer the entire Realms in a season.

There had been a time when Vangerdahast had come here often, when the treasures stored here had been everyday needs and comforts, armor of sorts against his fears. Yet it had been a long time since he'd burst in here in any hurry, seeking . . . seeking . . .

Snarling like an angry wolf, Vangerdahast raged around the room, snatching up wands here, rods there, and—and—and belts of potions over there! Amulets—best have some of them, too.

He dropped them in a great heap onto the table and whirled away to face the nearest wardrobe. Snatching it open, he glared at a suit of gleaming magical elven armor inside. He peered past it in a vain search for something more useful, then savagely slammed the doors on the armor again, turning away with a heartfelt growl.

Which was when he caught sight of a man in worn leathers watching him from the doorway. A man whose name he didn't know, but whom he vaguely recalled seeing around the Palace once or twice before.

This in itself irritated Vangey. *No one* should visit the Palace more than once without the Royal Magician knowing who they were and why they were there.

"Who—?"

"Dalonder Ree, Harper," the man said softly, "here to help. You look very much like a Royal Magician of Cormyr who needs it. And if the Royal Magician doesn't, the Court Wizard of Cormyr seems in even worse need of aid."

"I need nothing of the sort!" Vangey snapped.

Laspeera ducked past the Harper into the room and said breathlessly, "I've never heard you this upset before! What d'you need me for?"

Vangerdahast stared helplessly into the Harper's carefully expressionless gaze for a moment, then threw up his hands in surrender and snapped at his most loyal war wizard, "Strap on all of this you can carry, and come with me! Some madwits may be about to work the Unbinding and empty the Lost Palace onto our laps!"

Laspeera blinked, cursed in a crisp and very unladylike manner, and started grabbing at the magic items Vangey had dumped on the table. So did the Harper.

"Not *you!*" Vangey snarled at him. "Don't you have something else to meddle in?"

"Nothing nearly as important as this!" Ree said.

"Well, you *could* stay right here, keep your hands off all magic, and go running around rounding up Wizards of War and sending them after us! If we all go down, it really won't matter how few are left here to defend the throne! Oh, and you could warn the royal fam—"

"As it happens, wizard," Princess Alusair said crisply from the doorway, "I can and will take care of that. This valiant Harper *will* be accompanying you, if he desires. I can't give him a royal command, but I *can* so command you—and I should have started doing so *years* ago, I'm thinking."

Vangey started to say something, anger rising in him like a great tide, but the younger princess of the realm raised her voice in superb mimicry of his own, roaring right over him, "Now stop arguing with everyone you see and *get going!*"

"This one should do, to begin the Unbinding," Vangerdahast said slowly, stopping at a panel. As the Knights gathered around him, Islif couldn't help but look back the way they'd come, and Jhessail and the priests spun around to face outward, faces tight with fear.

The *smell* was following them. A faint, sickly rotting scent, overlaid by mildew, that was wafting from the six or so liches now shuffling after them.

Gods, if just one of them decided to hurl a spell . . .

"Florin?" the Royal Magician asked gravely.

The ranger nodded, drew in a deep breath, and swung the mace he'd borrowed from Doust.

The panel shattered under his solid swing, its magical disguise of stained and polished wood disintegrating in brief little puffs and swirls of blue-green radiance.

Vangerdahast told them, "Look up and down this passage, everyone! *Quickly!*"

"There!" Pennae said, right on the heels of his words, pointing.

"Hasten," the Royal Magician said, shouldering through the Knights in the direction of the distant glowing panel. "Hurry! We must mark the right one!"

He strode straight toward the liches, snapping over his shoulder, "Come! They won't hurt you. They *want* to be freed, to find rest at last!"

A gruesome gallery of undead was still gathering, appearing out of dark side passages and through doorways, but they parted and gave way even before the empty air glowed blue-green around Vangerdahast and forced the liches back.

The Knights hurried in his wake, trying not to look too closely at the shuffling crowd that was now watching them—and that closed in behind them to follow down the passage.

The liches were in many states of decay, from floating, glowing disembodied skulls wearing crowns to rotting women who'd lost limbs, in ragged wisps of crumbling gowns. Some were even carrying their heads under their arms.

The blue-green wardings seemed to hold back liches in one direction and quell real terror in the other, but none of the Knights was really calm. On three sides, as they walked, the silently drifting and shuffling crowd was almost close enough to touch, and the liches looked so macabre that it was like walking through a nightmare that wouldn't end.

"I think I have to relieve myself," Semoor said.

Behind him, Jhessail winced. "I *wish* you hadn't said that."

"I—wait! Don't kill me!" Lord Crownsilver babbled, backing away. "I'm rich! I can pay you well! Rubies, gold, even king's tears! I—"

"Talk too much," the Highknight told him, a certain fire in her eyes. "I don't want gold, puling little man."

"Land, then! Land—a little keep, all your own? Or a tallhouse in Suzail—*two* tallhouses!"

Step by step, the nobleman was giving ground, and step by step, Targrael was stalking him, leisurely, stretching like a cat. "Oooh, a little castle," she drawled. "Now you tempt me, Maniol."

"I do?" Lord Crownsilver brightened, gabbling wildly. "Th-that's good, isn't it? Wha-wha-what can I do to tempt you more?"

"Die," the Highknight told him calmly and stretched out to her full sleek length. Her lunge sent her blade through Maniol Crownsilver's hand and into his throat.

"Almost leisurely," she said. "Not the hardest noble death I've dealt down the years, to be sure."

He stared at her, jaw open in disbelief, blood welling up in his mouth, so Targrael blew him a kiss and said with a sneer, "The gods be with you, little failure of a man. Fare you well in the Hells."

By the last word, he was probably beyond hearing, his stare now fixed. Targrael straightened, pulling her sword back, and let him fall.

He fell heavily, as wet and solid as an oversized pumpkin dropped on a cobbled street—and as messily. Blood splashed long fingers in all directions. Targrael took a swift step back, eyes narrowing as she saw golden, glowing smoke rise from that gore—for all the Realms as if the man's blood were a flow of molten fire in a forge.

Then she retreated farther, casting swift glances behind herself and bringing her sword up to slash the air in a menacing circle around her.

Liches were drifting and striding toward those flames from all directions, their eyes glowing the same golden hue.

"Keep back," she warned them, paling as they gave her gap-toothed grins and closed in.

"I am the Highknight Lady Ismra Targrael. In the name of the Dragon Throne I serve, I command, you begone!"

The Highknight brandished the warding token she'd plucked from one of the Sembians she'd slain, but bony hands struck it aside as many other bony hands tightened like chillingly cold claws around her arms.

She hadn't even time to struggle ere bony fingers throttled her. Almost leisurely.

Bellowing wordless rage into the Princess Alusair's face to make her shrink back out of his way, the Royal Magician of Cormyr rushed out of his armory and along the passage, seeking the nearest spellcasting chamber.

Dalonder Ree was right behind him. "If I find Dauntless, I'll send him back to you!" he said to the princess as he raced past.

Laspeera, trailing belts and wand sheaths and a sculpted hand festooned with glowing rings, panted behind them both. Some six running strides down the passage, she slowed, whirled, and told Alusair, "Get Tathanter Doarmund or Alaphondar to assemble all Wizards of War they swiftly can to teleport a dozen Dragons to me. They know how to key on me!"

"Purple Dragons?" Alusair cried. "Not more war wizards?"

Laspeera was already running on down the passage. Without turning her head she called back, "We'll be needing someone with common sense!"

The third panel spilled the familiar blue-green radiance as it shattered.

"There!" Pennae cried as she espied the next panel.

Doust staggered, almost falling. His stagger took him into Jhessail and almost bore her to the ground. She struggled to keep them both upright, planting herself until Islif reached out a long arm, took the priest by the shoulder, and hauled him upright.

He reeled, knees briefly as limp as greens steaming in a kitchen. "Numbed me, that one did," he muttered. Looking at Jhessail, he added, "Keep back from the panels. I think doing this'll kill any mage outright." He gave Vangerdahast's back a suspicious glare, then clung to Islif for support as all of the Knights hurried down the passage to the fourth panel.

"How many of these panels will we have to break?" Islif called to the Royal Magician.

Ahead, they saw his shoulders lift in a shrug. "I know not. More than a dozen. We tried to trace the magics once, and I saw ten-and-three nodes before the trying overwhelmed me."

Pennae lifted an eyebrow. "Overwhelmed you?"

"Struck me senseless," Vangey replied curtly, giving Florin a nod.

The ranger set his teeth, swung the mace, and dashed another panel to glowing ruin.

"A glow!" Semoor called from behind them. "Through that doorway!"

They all turned to see his pointing arm, and Florin reeled just as Doust had done.

"Help him, someone!" Vangerdahast snapped, heading for the glowing door. "Pennae, run ahead. We need to see which panel in yon room is the right one, before it fades!"

As they hastened, the Royal Magician muttered some sort of incantation.

"That's the second time you've done that, right after Florin struck a panel," Islif said suspiciously. "Just *what* magic are you working?"

"I'm gathering the wardings before they collapse, to shield us all with them. Against the liches and against any wild magics breaking a node might release."

"What wardings?" Semoor asked, as they entered the room, finding it cold and bare.

"The ancient spells that protect the walls, floors, ceilings, and all against magic unleashed by the liches here," Vangerdahast explained, hastening over to the panel Pennae was standing beside. It was no longer glowing.

"They'll be lost if I don't gather them," the Royal Magician said. "Do you *want* to be torn apart by a lich?"

A lich near Semoor's elbow chuckled coldly, and he shrank back from it, shuddering. "Why are all these liches here, anyhail?"

"Bound here by the Royal Magicians before him," Doust said. "Wizards who went mad, that is. They did not come here as liches. I think this place makes them liches."

Vangerdahast turned, gave them the grimmest of smiles, and said gently, "And *I* think you're right about that. And before any of you ask, no, I haven't bound anyone here."

"No need," Semoor said, stepping quickly behind Islif. "You just take all the mad mages and make them war wizards."

"*Thank* you, Light of Lathander," Vangerdahast replied sarcastically. "Your observations are *so* helpful, in our present situation. Boosts the morale of your fellow Knights to no end."

Florin started forward, but the Royal Magician flung out an arm to bar his way. Vangerdahast nodded when Islif plucked the mace from the ranger's grasp from behind.

"Enough heroics for you," Vangerdahast said and looked at Islif. "Will you break this one, Lady Knight?"

She nodded, stepping forward, and Vangerdahast looked at the other Knights. "Face outward, everyone," he said. "Pennae and . . . you, Wolftooth, go back to the door and watch for glows. I'll thrust out the wards to keep liches away from you."

Pennae started for the door, but Semoor didn't move. He was frowning at Doust.

"What're you staring at, Clumsum?"

"That," Doust said quietly, pointing across the room into its darkest corner. His finger was leveled at the largest floating, disembodied skull among the liches. It grinned at them, eyes twinkling. Around its brows was a slender-spired crown, still silver-hued in places but mostly black and in a few spots green with age.

"So that was a king, or prince, or something," Semoor said slowly, giving Vangerdahast a look. "Is this some dark state secret?"

The wizard shook his head, putting out his hand again to keep Islif from striking the panel.

But Doust spoke again. "No, not the crown. Look above the spires."

The Knights peered. It was hard to see the crown's spires and the space above them clearly in the gloom, but from the door Pennae said, "The end spire doesn't have a gem on top. The gemstone is floating in the air above the spire. So, Doust?"

"It wasn't there at all—the gem, that is—before we entered this room," Doust said. "I happened to look right at that skull with the crown."

"You're sure you haven't mistaken it for another?" Florin asked.

"None of the other floating skulls are wearing crowns. Not even a circlet."

"I am haunted, truly haunted . . .," Semoor started to sing a well-known tavern song.

Islif gave his stomach a solid poke with the mace, and he stopped with a startled gasp.

"So we watch it to see if anything else happens," she said firmly. "Nothing else we can do, aye?"

"To the door, Wolftooth," Vangerdahast reminded Semoor. "Sulwood, why don't you keep a close eye on yon skull, now and henceforth?"

"I'll do that," Doust said, as Islif stepped forward to menace the panel with the mace again. This time the Royal Magician stepped back and nodded to her.

She swung, connecting with a crash, and the panel split apart in blue-green fire—and that glow spat out bright arcs of lightning, hurling Islif away and making all the Knights scream as the wardings flared up bright blue-green around them.

Briefly blinded, none of the Knights saw that neither the lightnings nor the blue-green glow touched Vangerdahast. He stood smiling in their midst.

"Now," Vangerdahast said, "the hard part of this Unbinding begins. Be strong, my Knights. For just a little longer."

Brorn Hallomond licked his lips, drew in a deep breath and let it out again, threw back his head to stare at the ceiling—and then shrugged, held his sword ready, and stepped boldly forward into the magical glow.

It swallowed him.

A moment later, a dark shape arose from where it had been crouching on the stairs. Lorbryn Deltalon didn't have a sword to brandish, but he held his wand like a weapon as he walked warily across the cellar to the waiting portal. He hesitated for a moment and then stepped through.

Two faces that had watched the war wizard's disappearance drew back from where they'd been peering down the stairwell. Their owners traded glances.

Wizard of War Tsantress Ironchylde and Ornrion Taltar

Dahauntul of the Purple Dragons exchanged a long look, then they shrugged in unison, drew wand and sword respectively, and started down the stairs to the portal.

The Unbinding had become a slow march of pain. Every time the Knights shattered a panel, lightnings shot throughout the wardings, searing everyone.

Grimly they plodded from room to room, the host of undead silently following. There were more than forty liches now, the lights of their eyes glittering hungrily. They pressed ever closer to the Knights as warding after warding fell away.

Whenever the Knights entered a room, another floating gem appeared out of nowhere—literally materializing out of the empty air—to join those already hanging above the spires of the largest floating skull's crown.

Thrice the Royal Magician tried to direct Jhessail or one of the priests to take a turn breaking a panel, until Florin and Islif had both told him to cease giving such orders. Their hair and faces scorched, the ranger and the fighter were taking turns swinging the mace now. They trudged along, bent and trembling between those ordeals.

The Knights could no longer see the glow of the next panel, but Vangerdahast seemed to know or be able to feel where they should strike next.

"Why aren't the lightnings harming you?" Jhessail asked the Royal Magician, as they trudged along yet another passage that looked very much like the rest.

"They are," Vangerdahast said. "I'm just far more used to agony than, say, your average band of Crown-chartered adventurers. I've been enduring pain for years."

Jhessail gave him a look that was dark with disbelief.

He stared back, twisting his face momentarily into a manic, gleeful smile—and then letting that smile fall right back off his face to leave it looking grim and old.

"This door," he said, not bothering to look at it. "The next panel is in here, to the left. I can sense it."

"Can you sense what I'm thinking now?" Semoor rasped.

"Yes," Vangerdahast replied. "Two things occupy your mind. One is your bladder, and the other is treasonous, so I'd advise you to start thinking of Lathander instead. The Unbinding will certainly bring about a new beginning."

Semoor groaned. "Will we be alive to see it?"

Chapter 15
SWORDS AMONG THE WALKING DEAD

Nothing worse could be than raw butchery
The stink, the screams, the blood so red
But that was before I first made war
With swords among the walking dead

From the ballad
"No Grave So Warm"
by Bendilus the Bold Bard of Berdusk
Published in the Year of the Shattered Oak

The sixteenth panel fell in shards, and lightning flooded forth, a blue-white tide that dashed all the Knights to the floor.

Only the Royal Magician stood unmoved. He waited patiently as any statue amid the feeble groaning at his feet.

It was some time before anyone could rise. Pennae managed it first, crawling grimly to where the two priests lay heaped upon each other. She clawed her way up that heap until she could sit on it. Sliding her feet out to the floor, she shoved at the entangled priests behind her, thrusting herself upright to stand unsteadily. Taking a few trembling steps, she reached down, almost falling on her face, to haul Jhessail to her feet.

The two of them clung together, leaning breast to breast for support. When they found the strength to break apart again and stand free, most of the other Knights had made it at least as far as their knees.

Islif was the first to manage normal strides—and when she did, lightning crackled in the air before her at her every step. The air seemed thicker, as if she were wading in stiffening mud or trying to bathe in some of her aunt's hardloaf dough.

Not far away from her, Florin bit back a curse.

"You, too?" Islif asked. "When you walk . . . the air seems thick?"

The ranger nodded and gave Vangerdahast a long look.

The Royal Magician spread his hands, looking—or trying to look—innocent. "I can guess what's befalling you, but a guess is all 'twill be. No one's ever made it this far in the Unbinding before."

"You fail to surprise me," Jhessail said from beside his elbow. "Point us to the next room, Vangey. Let's just take care of the next panel, and only then concern ourselves with the one after that. I find I lack the energy for doing anything else."

"Har hur stlarning hardy har har," Semoor said to that, struggling to his feet. "Tymora, walk with me!"

"If She does, see if you can get Her to break the panels for us," Pennae said, watching Vangerdahast's arm rise to point out the door.

The portal swallowed Tsantress and Dauntless without a sound, and the cellar fell silent and deserted.

For about half a breath.

Then magical light flooded it, making it as bright as any royal court lit by tiers upon tiers of hanging candles, thanks to a wave of the Royal Magician's hand.

Vangerdahast hastened down the stairs, Laspeera and Dalonder Ree at his shoulders. He watched the portal flicker as his conjured radiance swirled around it. He sighed at the sight of that silent, magical skirmish and told Laspeera, "I'm not waiting for any Purple Dragons. If whoever it is manages that Unbinding . . ."

She nodded, and he stalked forward. Dalonder Ree hastened after him, throwing out a long arm to bar Laspeera's way to the portal.

The look she gave him was a silent question, and in response he pointed back up the stairs out of the cellar, then at her, clearly intimating she should tarry for the Dragons Tathanter should be sending.

Slowly Laspeera nodded, and Ree strode after Vangerdahast.

Who had turned, just before the portal, to see Laspeera nod to Ree and then hang back. He drew in a deep breath and roared, "Has *all* Cormyr fallen out of the habit of obeying me? Hrast it, the realm *is* doomed!"

"Belt up and get in there and save it," Ree said, giving the wizard a firm shove into the portal.

Still glaring, Vangey vanished.

Ree shot Laspeera a smile and plunged through the portal himself, muttering, "Well, we all have to die *some*where."

"Gods!" Islif swore, head bent with the effort of trudging forward. "Now I know why no one ever managed this Unbinding before!"

Pennae cast a dark look at Vangerdahast, walking slowly but unharmed behind them. She gasped and said, "No Royal Magician ever had a large enough band of stone-headed pain-lovers before, I'd guess."

"Did I mention I *really* need to piss?" Semoor groaned.

"Not now, holynose!" Pennae told him. "This is *lightning* around us, remember?"

For all of the Knights, it seemed harder and harder to move, as if the air had turned to sucking mud. Their strides were slow and labored, and the Lost Palace had gone very quiet around them. Even their strained breathing seemed hushed.

Jhessail kept stumbling, and Florin kept clawing her up again. Struggling, with Vangerdahast standing unbowed in their midst, the Knights of Myth Drannor fought their way along a long, high passage.

Far ahead, facing them at the end of the passage, stood a tall door graven with a unicorn's head amid trees.

As they came closer, the door started to glow, its graven lines flaring a deep blue. As they got nearer still, those glowing channels started to pulse and spit little blue lightnings.

This was Rhallogant Caladanter's favorite room in all Suzail. Which was a good thing, being as it was a room in his own house. Reclining on his favorite lounge, he sipped another tallglass of wine—his seventh, or was it eighth?—and wondered where Boarblade had gotten to.

The door opened. Rhallogant looked up to see which servant was daring to disturb his solitude, and then his jaw dropped. He was staring at—himself!

As he gaped, the other Rhallogant pushed past the lounge and strode toward the door to his bedchamber.

"Here, now!" Rhallogant protested to the intruder's back, waving his tallglass. "Who d'you think you are?"

His double stopped, turned, and gave him a crooked smile. The face wearing that smile changed. He saw Telgarth Boarblade and something more. Something humplike was receding down the front of Boarblade's jerkin. Ah. Some sort of mask he'd tugged off. Must be.

"Good disguise, hmm?"

Rhallogant nodded, flustered at being so bewildered. "Certainly, certainly. 'Tis indeed. So, what's afoot?"

Boarblade's smile widened to near smugness. "Much tumult. We'll be going to the Palace later this night with an urgent need to speak to some war wizards."

"About?"

"About something secret."

Boarblade went to Rhallogant's spirits cabinet as if it were his own, carelessly swinging open the doors and taking forth a tall, slender decanter the master of House Caladanter couldn't remember ever having seen before.

As it caught the light, he saw it was more than half full of a purplish translucent liquid. As he watched, Boarblade unstoppered it and calmly set about dipping the blades of all the daggers he was carrying in it, one after another, setting them on the tallboard to dry. He seemed to be wearing a *lot* of daggers, some of them hidden in rather surprising places.

"What're you—?" Rhallogant started to ask, then he hastily waved his hand to banish his question. "No, no. *Don't* tell me. I don't want to know. I want to live."

Boarblade looked up with an almost fond smile. "Very wise of you. And you will, if you do exactly as I say."

"Poison," Rhallogant muttered.

"What a good thing I didn't catch that," Boarblade said. "The results, if I had, might well have been fatal. Some war wizards are going to catch some of this soon, and we'll see how they fare, hmm?"

Rhallogant suddenly felt very cold. He found himself shivering and decided—reaching for the second decanter of his best rubyfire—he needed another glass of wine to warm himself up.

Watching the noble trying unsteadily to refill his tallglass, Boarblade's cold smile grew wider.

Laspeera climbed up out of the cellar, out of the ruin, and into the forest. If she was fated to die after she followed Vangey through that portal, she wanted to smell a fresh breeze and see forest leaves one last time.

Three steps away from the opening that had once held a door, a dozen Purple Dragons suddenly appeared all around Laspeera. The trodden turf was empty of all but leaves one moment—and full of grim, fully armored soldiery the next.

Warriors who were all staring at her expectantly.

Laspeera met the eyes of most of them, trying to look as calmly imperious as Vangey always did, then turned, pointed at the doorway, and said, "Through there! Down the stairs and step right through the glow. Save Cormyr, and obey Vangerdahast. As usual."

That earned her their grim grins—grins that widened when they saw her turn to hurry in and lead them down the stairs rather than stopping to watch them go on into the unknown without her.

Barely finished nodding and smiling pleasantly to the armory door guards as he passed by, Lord Elvarr Spurbright looked ahead of himself once more and blinked in surprise.

Yes, 'twas the Princess Alusair hurrying toward him along the passage, striding along as sternly as any angry Highknight. What was she now, all of thirteen summers?

As she approached and their gazes met, her eyes fairly scorched him. Oh, she had the fiery side of the Obarskyr temperament! Flame where her mother, the queen, was ice.

Almost jovially he sketched a deep bow and asked her if he might be of service.

"Yes," she snapped, startling the lord. Her next words took him past blinking into dumbfounded staring. "Find a sword and that preening son of yours—and anyone else you can think of who's handy and knows how to die for Cormyr—and get to the Hall of the Unicorn as quick as you can! There you'll find Wizard of War Tathanter Doarmund and the Royal Sage Alaphondar. Tathanter will send you to where you're needed. I understand there's a portal you must step through, in a ruins."

Lord Spurbright gaped at her. "Die for Cormyr? Doing what?"

"The same cause of death that awaits most Dragons," she told him tersely over her shoulder as she continued on, "obeying Lord Vangerdahast."

"While you will be doing what, exactly?"

"Deciding where and how I can best defend the king, my father," she said, as she stopped before the doors of the armory and waved at the door guards to get out of her way.

Spurbright blinked again at her back as she plunged through those hastily opened doors.

Then he turned and started to trot along the passage. Torsard should be in one of the forehalls by now, enjoying a goblet or two before departing the Palace for the Spurbright city tallhouse.

"With me," Laspeera commanded, and she plunged through the portal.

The six Purple Dragons right behind her never slowed, charging into its glow after her.

The others were still hastening down the stairs, in such a hurry to follow that the flying blade that came lancing down the stairs behind them struck thrice in swift succession before the last three Dragons even knew it was there.

Its third victim fell forward after the sword banked, whirled, and thrust its gleaming length in his open helm and through his throat—to thrust into the Dragon who'd just reached the bottom of the steps below him.

Both men slammed to the ground to the accompaniment of a startled shout from the Dragon underneath. That made the two Dragons hastening for the portal whirl, their own swords flashing out of their scabbards.

They were in time to see a sword that flew like an arrow, with no warrior's arm guiding it, sliding at them out of the darkness. They were not in time to parry well enough to save their lives.

The flying sword whirled away from them and buried itself deep into the mouth of the Dragon fallen at the foot of the stairs, who'd just shed his dead comrade and had struggled to his feet.

The sword drew back, dripping dark blood, and hung in the air for a moment, as if studying the portal.

The glow of that magical door seemed to brighten as the Sword That Never Sleeps drifted slowly nearer, point-first.

Then it shot forward, racing into the waiting glow.

The portal flickered, snarled as angry lightnings burst out of it and raced up and down its length in wild spirals—and then the portal collapsed in a flood of drifting sparks that swiftly scattered and faded, leaving only darkness to cloak the sprawled dead Dragons.

"Welcome to the Lost Palace of Esparin," Vangerdahast said grimly to the Harper behind him as they sprinted through dark, empty chamber after dark, empty chamber.

Dalonder Ree was wise enough to keep his mouth shut and let the wizard lead him. The Royal Magician, it seemed, needed almost all of his breath just to keep up his whirlwind pace.

"Graul," he muttered at last, as they came out into a room where someone had recently smashed one of the wall panels, "feel that? They're almost done! We've got to . . ."

The two men plunged through the door at the other end of the room, out into a passage, and rushed along that passage until they rounded a corner. The two found themselves looking at the rear of a mass of undead who were filling the hallway, crowded together and moving slowly along the passage away from Vangey and Ree.

With all their wands, long flowing robes, and gem-winking crowns, the undead looked to be liches. All of their attention was bent on something beyond them that neither the wizard nor the Harper could see through the press of dark-robed, skeletal bodies.

Yet there was something else for Vangerdahast and Dalonder to gaze upon, or rather four somethings—and they were much closer than the liches. About three paces away, in fact.

Four living persons they knew.

One was facing their way, cowering on his knees. It was Brorn Hallomond, longtime bullyblade of the Lord Yellander, and he was staring fearfully up at the other three, who stood in an arc facing him, menacing him with two wands and a sword. Neither Vangerdahast nor Dalonder Ree needed those three to turn around to know who they were: the War Wizards Lorbryn Deltalon and Tsantress Ironchylde and the ornrion most widely known as Dauntless.

Vangerdahast calmly drew wands from his belt. Brorn saw that movement, stared past the three foes facing him at the Royal Magician of Cormyr and the Harper, and cursed, "Stlarning gods above, take me now! Tluining *Vangerdahast!* Stlarning well spare me being turned into frogs and gasping fish and being fried alive!"

His shout made even the rearmost liches turn to see who he was staring at—whereupon Vangerdahast spellburned undead with his wands. He snapped at Ree, "Use those things if you know how, or you'll die right here and now!"

The Harper nodded and awakened the wands in both his fists, sending bright bursts of magic arcing down the passage. Aiming the wands carefully, he set about blasting liches as hard and as fast as he knew how.

Lorbryn and Tsantress hurled themselves to the floor to get clear of all the wandfire and started crawling to reach Vangey and Ree.

On hands and knees the bullyblade scuttled in the other direction, seeking escape through a side door down the passage.

Dauntless ducked wandfire and in a low crouch charged through and under more wandfire and the fell magical beams now stabbing back at the war wizards from the liches. He soon caught up to Brorn.

The bullyblade turned to slash at Dauntless, but the ornrion backhanded Brorn's blade out of the way with one hand, knocked him cold with one swing of his other fist—and fell flat atop the bullyblade as ravening magical fire sizzled past too close for comfort.

The passage and the very air in it was starting to shake, as lich after lich cast spells that struck and wrestled with the wandfire in a blinding, billowing chaos that flashed and roiled, building to hide all sight of the liches from Vangerdahast's view.

Then Lorbryn was past the Royal Magician and plucking wands from him, and Tsantress was similarly plundering what Dalonder Ree was wearing but not using. Crouching against the walls of the passage, the two war wizards added to the wandfire, driving back the crawling chaos of magic until they could see liches again—including liches blown apart into dust and shards as wandfire smashed into them.

Liches started to fly, turn wraithlike, or just wink out, teleporting away as the unleashed wand fury tore into their ranks.

"Scatter, everyone!" Vangerdahast said. "Get a solid wall at your back!"

He hurled down a spent, crumbling wand and snatched out another. A moment later, Ree cursed and did the same, shaking his hand at the pain of scorched fingertips. His spent wand rolled away along the passage floor, smoldering.

Tsantress shrieked a warning as a lich suddenly leered at her elbow, green magical flames roaring up to shroud its bones as it tried to embrace her. The fire of four wands promptly met inside the lich and sent its upper body into oblivion. Tsantress was able to kick its flaming, stumbling legs away until they crashed to the passage floor.

Behind the wand wielders, Laspeera and a handful of scared-looking Purple Dragons came rushing down the passage, weapons out.

Even as Tsantress called a greeting to them, she saw a sword appear, gleaming in the air behind them. It darted at them like an arrow loosed from a bow.

It ran through one startled Dragon from behind, up under the tail of his codpiece and into his vitals. He shrieked, clawing the air in agony, and collapsed.

"Get against a wall! In pairs!" the Royal Magician bellowed, aiming the wands in his hands so the beams of snarling magic streaming from them met in midair right where a lich had just appeared. The lich burst in the blinding white explosion that followed, but more were appearing down the passage behind the Dragons, teleporting in from the group Vangey and Ree had been ravaging with wandfire.

Cackling wildly, a skull flew past everyone, eyesockets streaming flames, attacking no one but mad with glee at all the destruction. The flying sword struck again, darting as nimbly as any humming-bird in a palace garden, and Purple Dragons hacked at it frantically. Wandfire spat in all directions. Deltalon shouted for another wand as one he was using darkened and burst into dust in his hand. Ree flung one to him, sending it cartwheeling through the roiling air. Liches cast spells up and down the passage, and the palace's defensive magics flared up in scores of places.

In all of this, Vangerdahast glanced back at the liches he'd first scorched with wandfire and through their thinned ranks caught sight of the Knights of Myth Drannor—and in their midst, another Royal Magician of Cormyr. A perfect likeness of himself, who smiled at him in cold triumph through the chaos of magic now storming around the passage.

Staring into the eyes of his impostor, Vangerdahast snarled in wordless rage. Rage that was all too likely to be futile.

"I wasn't much liking the look of this," Semoor said, waving at the tall door at the end of the passage. It was graven with a glowing blue badge of Esparin, "But for the love of Lathander, let's get to it and through it! *Now!*"

A long, slender sword streaked out of the spell battle, flying by itself with its point first. It glistened with fresh, wet blood, raced as fast as any arrow—and was headed right for Vangerdahast!

The Royal Magician's hands were already moving, shaping intricate gestures in feverish haste. A bare instant before the sword would have thrust into him, he vanished, reappearing well down the passage amid all the milling liches and swirling spells.

The sword plunged through the spot where the wizard had been standing, then soared up and around in a loop to come racing at Florin's face.

The ranger set his teeth and struck it aside with his own blade, striking as hard as he could and sending the flying sword singing and clanging along the floor until it bounded up at Doust.

The priest ducked away from it, cursing, and all the Knights pounced on the sword, hacking at it furiously until it sprang up out of their midst, struck the ceiling with a clang, and—

Arrowed right back down again, plunging into—and through— Semoor's armored breast.

Vangerdahast saw the sword streak down the passage at the impostor, but he then lost all sight of that end of the passage. Knights, flying blade, his false double, and all disappeared in a huge explosion as a lich snatched the fell magic out of several other liches, destroying them in an instant, and twisted that freed, writhing magic into a withering wall of harrowfire.

Vangerdahast had seen such a doom only once before in his life, but he knew what had to be done. He hurled the wand in his left hand into the heart of that advancing wall of flames, then unleashed the full fury of the wand in his right hand at the tumbling wood he'd thrown, murmuring an incantation that would dissolve the controlling magics of that wand.

The wand flared, turning the harrowfire into flames of a different sort. They blazed up into a blinding white wall of flame that sucked half a dozen screaming liches into it. Vangerdahast sealed off the rest of the passage for the few breaths the fire would last before it burnt itself out.

Grimly, hoping he wasn't dooming loyal war wizards he could no longer see, Vangerdahast thrust at those flames with his mind, forcing them back and through as many liches as he could get, before the fire faded away.

White fire blazed briefly around the wound in Semoor's chest as the minor spells on his armor failed. Screaming, the Light of Lathander arched over backward, writhing in agony.

From down the passage, the fierce-eyed Vangerdahast shouted a spell. Jhessail understood enough of the incantation to know the wizard sought to disintegrate the sword.

Caught in the sudden eerie glow of that magic, the sword standing up out of Semoor's breast rang like a bell, then shivered—and spat out something dark and smokelike. It billowed up into a huge, evil face with white flames for eyes, a face that jeered at the Knights as it grew a hand to clutch at the sword.

Vangerdahast's spell faded from around the sword, and the towering, leering thing plucked the blade out of Semoor.

The stricken priest crashed to the passage floor. White fire leaked from his chest, and blood spewed from his mouth. His fellow Knights, shouting in fear and rage, all hacked and hewed at the flying sword, the sheer fury of their blows striking sparks from it as the smokelike wraith looming over them tugged at it, fighting to hold and wield the blade even as they tried to strike it down and shatter it.

They prevailed, dashing it out of the great wraith's grasp. The smokelike thing drew back, freeing the flying sword to stab and dart at the Knights assailing it.

The adventurers sprang and ducked and hammered at the sword in a frantic, gasping dance that kept them all alive until Vangerdahast shouted another spell. From down the passage the spell came, gathering wardings from the passage walls all around.

The magic howled down the passage and closed in around the sword in a tightening, crackling fist that crushed the wraith-thing back down into smoke that streamed back into the blade.

The flying sword sprang high and went streaking back down the passage, with the wardings clawing at it angrily.

The Knights found themselves staring over Semoor's body and the scattered bones of liches at the distant Vangerdahast, who was standing down the passage with the wardings now streaming back to him and building up in a crackling cloak. Beyond him, the sword vanished through a bright wall of flame that hadn't been there before, that now hid the rest of the passage behind its bright raging.

"Get through that door!" the Royal Magician shouted to the Knights. "Stop to defend yourself against liches when you must, but *get through that door!*"

"But—Semoor!" Jhessail wept.

"Leave him!" Vangerdahast roared.

"No!" Doust, Islif, and Florin shouted, all reaching for their lifeless friend.

"I'll take him," Doust told the other two. "You do the fighting!"

He lifted Semoor in his arms, staggered, and promptly fell under the weight.

Islif reached out an arm and said, *"We'll* take him, we two!"

"Do it," Florin snarled, springing past them to meet oncoming liches with furious swings of his sword.

Pennae led the rush in the other direction. The blue glows in the graven badge of Esparin were flaring and flickering wildly now, and the air seemed to thicken and thin in successive waves, shoving them back when it was thick but letting them struggle forward between its moments of thickness.

"Hurry!" Florin called from behind his companions. "Can't . . . hold them!"

Jhessail shrieked as a lich's bony fingertips tore across her ribs and breast, trailing magical flames. She kicked it frantically, sending it staggering back—and hurled herself forward into it in a wild dive, punching with her fists. Fell flames roared up all around her, bathing her, clawing at her face, and setting her hair to sizzling . . . then she hit the floor hard, amid breaking, scattering bones, and the flames were gone. A lich cackled from somewhere above her, and suddenly a strong hand took her by the ankle and pulled.

"Sorry," she heard Florin gasp. " 'Ware your eyes, Jhess!"

She was being dragged swiftly over bony shards, back toward the door.

"Won't open!" she heard Pennae shout. "No lock, but I can't get this tluining thing *open!*"

Then Pennae sobbed as if in sudden pain, and Doust cried, "What?"

"Burned my fingers," the thief gasped, sounding much closer now, as Florin's dragging went on. "This door is . . . is . . ."

"Magical, yes," Islif panted. "Doust, leave Semoor. We need you to fight these *liches!*"

Florin let go; Jhessail opened her eyes, tried to struggle to her knees—and screamed at what she saw. A dozen liches or more had gathered in a sort of wall across the passage. They advanced on the Knights. The glowing, pulsing door was only a pace or two away behind their backs, and the liches were thrusting forward, seeking to overwhelm the swinging swords of Florin and Islif, bear them down under weight and numbers, and tear them apart. Spells seemed to have become useless in the waves rushing out from the door, spell after spell fading vainly from the fingertips of the liches casting them. But liches were working magics on themselves, too, making their fingerbones into long, raking claws, and those spells seemed to be holding.

"Endless!" Doust panted, joining Islif and Florin with his mace.

Pennae mewed in pain and flung herself at the door again, braving its magical fires to feel for any catch or lock or opening her eyes might have missed. "These stlarning liches are endless!"

"Pretend you're hewing firewood back in Espar!" Islif gasped. "Take it all down, and we can go in and lounge by the fire!"

"Oh, *gods,* I wish you hadn't said that!" Pennae snarled from right behind them.

The door exploded.

Chapter 16
ORDERS, STRICT AND OTHERWISE

Much of the troubles, in my or any ordered life come about as the sometimes-deadly results of orders, strict and otherwise, that are flagrantly disobeyed or that never should have been given in the first place.

Miyurs Carthult, Merchant of Calaunt
The Coins I Made: A Merchant's Tale
Published in the Year of the Smoky Moon

The world was all bright flame and silence—the brief and troubled silence of the temporarily deafened. The passage spun around Jhessail as she was hurled far down it, tumbling helplessly through the air with her fellow Knights around her. Vangerdahast and many liches were swept along as helplessly as storm-whipped autumn leaves in front of her.

Bones bounced and broke apart, skeletons scattering as they struck the unyielding passage floor, and Jhessail just had time to realize that she was racing to experience the very same bone-shattering fate before she slammed hard into something very solid that wore armor. Something that groaned at her arrival, even as it wrapped arms around her and skidded along the passage floor under the force of her landing, leaving a silently sprawled bullyblade in its wake.

It was Dauntless. She'd landed in the arms of the ornrion who'd murderously stalked the Knights for so long—and what was he doing *here,* anyhail?—and he was now staring at her in open-mouthed startlement, as sounds slowly came back to her. Jhessail dazedly started to think she was still alive, after all.

Someone else, huddled on the floor right by her outflung left foot, moved, heaving himself upright. It was Vangerdahast. Magic swirled around him as he staggered, and he seemed for a moment to be someone taller, leaner, and darker of garb.

Then he was the familiar paunchy, glowering Royal Magician of

Cormyr again, muttering out a spell entirely unfamiliar to her as he shot suspicious glances all around—in particular at the bright wall of flames that cloaked one side of the passage, well beyond him.

Liches watched Vangerdahast from the distance, down the passage beyond those flames, but no one struck at him or hurled magic his way.

Vangey finished growling out his spell and stepped back, spreading his hands in a sort of grim triumph.

Whereupon the empty air right in front of him split apart in a dark, roiling rift, as if slashed open by an unseen giant's blade. The rift was taller than a man and rapidly drew wider, roiling darkness churning half-seen within it.

As it grew, Jhessail, Dauntless, and everyone else felt a sudden, terrible *tugging*, a plucking at their flesh and clothing and even the breath in their lungs that sought to drag them to the rift. As they stared at this new danger, Vangerdahast calmly stepped into it.

At his heels there was a flash of light—and the rift and its inexorable pull were gone, as abruptly as they had come into being. Jhessail blinked. Now that the passage was empty of Royal Magicians of Cormyr, she noticed something that had been hidden from her behind his arm-waving bulk.

The flying sword was back.

It arrowed toward the rift, racing fast to try to reach it.

With the rift gone, the sword—Gods Above, but it was a splendid thing, large and long and sleek!—flashed vainly through the empty air where the rift had been and sped on, not slowing in the slightest.

Jhessail found she could turn her head in the ornrion's cradling grasp to follow its speeding flight. That magnificent sword went right on down the rest of the passage to plunge through the dark opening where the door that had blown her away had been.

Or try to, that is. As it entered the empty doorway, the darkness there vanished in a burst of light as another glowing, upright oval— tluin, was there no end to portals lurking everywhere?—flashed into being.

Jhessail clearly saw the portal swallow the scudding sword. The blade winked out rather than piercing through the glow.

The glow that now hung, silent and bright, waiting in the air.

Laspeera, Lorbryn, and the Harper were aiming their failing wands with care and precision. They had their backs to the wall of flame as they took down lich after lich. Vangerdahast trusted their skill enough to risk leaving off blasting for a moment to snatch a look or two behind him.

The harrowfire he'd twisted into lich-melting flames was fading and dying, just as he'd expected. Yet for no reason he could fathom, those flames were melting away from the far side of the passage toward the near wall, revealing more and more of the bone-filled passage as they did so.

"A graveyard of liches," he murmured, more to himself than anyone else, looking at all the strewn, crumbling bones.

The sword had gone streaking down the passage to its end, and he could see no sign of it now. Nor the false Vangerdahast, either.

He suspected the terrific blast had been the enchantments on the door at the end of the passage exploding. And he'd been right. Yonder was the gaping doorway where the door had been, and here, strewn before him, were the bodies of the Knights, fallen where they'd been flung. Some were moaning. Falconhand and the farm lass, Lurelake, were even moving, struggling to rise.

Enough. They had to be stopped. *Now.*

"Dauntless!" he snapped at the ornrion sitting dazedly on the floor with one of the adventurers—the little lass, of course; soldiers never miss a chance, do they?—in his lap. "Stop the Knights! Stop them smashing wall panels, if you have to kill every last one of them!"

He saw Dauntless turn his head and look at the Knight in his arms—Jhessail, that was her name—and saw her look right back at him, their noses almost touching. Their faces wore looks that were more bewildered than anything else.

Together the mage and the ornrion looked at the Knights around them. Doust was sprawled senseless, Pennae a ragged and broken thing, Semoor sprawled and looking just as dead as the thief, and Florin and Islif were wincing in pain as they fought to rise.

Jhessail turned her eyes to Vangerdahast. "Consider us stopped," she said to him, her voice a hoarse, husky ruin—and she slumped unconscious in the ornrion's arms.

"*Listen* to me," Rhallogant Caladanter told the Royal Palace door guard. "I'm noble, damn it."

He waved a reproving hand at the man and discovered it was trembling. In fact, he was shaking all over. Shaking with fear.

Boarblade, however, seemed as calm as ever as he leaned close to the guard's mustache and said, "You'll understand that my lord is quite upset. Over a *magical* matter, if you take my meaning. A matter that might be very important to the safety of all Cormyr. Which is why we need to speak to a senior war wizard. Urgently. We may well be mistaken—I very much hope we are—but as loyal Cormyreans, we dare not take that chance. If you are one, *you* dare not take that chance."

The guard stared at them, as expressionless as ever, then said, "Wait here." Stepping away from his closed door, he went a little way along the wall to where a faint magical glow shone, like the light of an invisible lantern, and said into it, "Young nobleman and his manservant, upset and wanting to see a senior Wizard of War. Both armed, but I see no ready magic."

Rhallogant couldn't hear any reply, but the guard nodded, muttered, "Hear and obey," came back to the door, and rapped on it sharply in a particular rhythm with the hilt of his dagger.

"I'll take your stand," said a voice from the gloom within, as the guard led Rhallogant and Boarblade inside. The guard nodded, not slowing, and marched to a passage crossing. He turned and snapped, "This way, please."

They followed the guard down a passage, then around a corner and along another passage, ere the impassive Purple Dragon stopped at a plain, closed door and flung it open, waving at his two guests to pass him and enter.

They did so, finding themselves in a large room whose walls were hidden behind tapestries. A great, six-candle lantern was hanging from a chain above a large and littered-with-parchments desk, behind which a rather weary-looking war wizard in dusty red robes sat alone, making notes with a bedraggled quill pen.

"I'd view that as a tactic rather than an irenicon," he was murmuring to a book he was consulting, paying no attention at all to the door opening and the two visitors entering the room.

As the guard drew the door closed again, staying on the far side of it and leaving the two visitors alone in the room with the mage, the wizard made a last note, unhurriedly set aside his book, and looked up at them, his expression neutral but somehow unimpressed.

"Tathanter Doarmund's my name," he said rather grimly. "Yours? And your business?"

"Lord," Boarblade asked respectfully, leaning forward, "are you a *senior* war wizard?"

"I believe I have two questions outstanding," Doarmund replied.

"Of course," Boarblade said with a smile—plucking a dagger from its sheath behind his back and hurling it at the seated mage as he straightened up.

It struck an unseen ward and clanged aside, harmlessly. Boarblade muttered a swift spell as he turned back to the door, but halfway through the incantation he fell silent and motionless, still as a statue.

Something small bulged under his jerkin as it drew together, then struggled out of the garment under Boarblade's chin, thrusting out into midair in a strange, amorphous blob that lacked eyes, mouth, and even limbs, yet was obviously alive. In the act of sprouting protrusions, it stopped to hang frozen in midair.

"A hargaunt," a voice said from behind one of the tapestries. "Quite harmless until that spell wears off, I assure you."

The speaker stepped out from behind the tapestry with half-a-dozen war wizards in his wake.

It was Alaphondar, Sage Most Learned of the Royal Court, wearing robes of rich maroon glimmerweave and an irritated expression. He pointed at the dagger on the floor.

"There's poison on that blade," he told the wizards behind him. "He'll have more. Be careful."

He bent his dark and knowing eyes upon the cowering Rhallogant. "Lord Calandanter, why don't you come with me to where we can sit down while you tell us everything you know about your friend here?"

"Y-y-yes," Rhallogant managed to stammer. "Why don't I?"

Vangerdahast handed out replacement wands to the three standing with him, and the last of the wall of flames died away entirely behind them.

"There goes the shield at our backs," Laspeera said. "Should we—"

Whatever she was going to ask was drowned out forever as the liches far down the passage hurled powerful spells. Their magics crashed into the unleashed wandfire and wrestled with it, creating a roiling, growing conflagration that surged back toward the four living Cormyreans.

"This is what I feared would happen," the Royal Magician said. "The more we fight, the more their wandering wits sharpen with anger, and they remember how to work spells and clutch at a purpose for doing so."

"Aye," Dalonder Ree agreed wryly. "Destroying us."

"Indeed," Vangerdahast said, watching spell after spell batter the whirling magical chaos, driving it nearer. Some spells were managing to win past the struggle, too, despite the wards he'd devised that reached out to draw in all manner of magics. Even as a sudden jet of flame scorched the stones not far from Laspeera's ankles, an errant magical whirlwind slammed into the ceiling, shredded the protective magics there, and sent a fall of stone down to crash and tumble just behind Lorbryn Deltalon.

Hastily he thrust his own wands into his belt and set about casting another ward spell. The weavewall Elminster had taught him years ago was designed to draw in all manner of magics, like water sucked down a drain in a spinning whorl, but if it went on too long without discharging its snared effects into a creature and took in too many spells, it might well collapse, spilling wild magic everywhere—or explode, destroying them all anyhail.

The new weavewall melted into the old one, flaring momentarily and taming the snarling magics down into a more circular, solid, and smooth doom that drove closer and closer to the Harper and the three war wizards.

Nearer . . .

Now a few paces nearer . . .

Vangerdahast watched grimly as their fate became obvious.

The roiling weavewall drew closer still.

When it touched someone, all the spells it had drawn into itself would rush back out of it into that creature. This one was so large that it would slay in an instant, leaving most of its fell magics to leak out in all directions—and probably slay every other creature left in the passage.

Laspeera and Deltalon were both white with fear now, and Vangerdahast judged that the tight-lipped Harper knew what was coming, too.

"Ree, Deltalon—spread out so you can keep your wands on my weavewall," he ordered, drawing forth the most powerful rod he had from its sheath and twisting it to awaken its magics.

"No, Vangey," Laspeera said softly. "No."

"*Yes,*" he said, striding forward until the roiling weavewall was right in front of him, and raising the black rod as the colorless gems up and down its length flashed excitedly.

"Royal Magician Vangerdahast," Laspeera said, "I believe what you're now about to do is a mistake, and—"

"Laspeera, *belt up!*" Vangerdahast roared at her. "Open a portal—*don't* use that one where the door was—and get everyone out! Including Ree and Deltalon! *Everyone!*"

"Lord Vanger—" she tried to protest.

But he raised his voice in a furious bellow, "Obey me! May the one true Purple Dragon damn you! Just stlarning well *obey me!*"

Then he said something to the rod and stepped forward into the roiling weavewall. The rod flashed in the heart of that blinding chaos—and the weavewall became a roaring torrent of magic that swept down the passage, shredding liches as it went.

Watching skeletons crumble, small fragments of bone hurtle in all directions, and skulls bounce and shatter, Dalonder Ree and Lorbryn Deltalon both swore softly, the fire of their wands steady and sure.

Shaking her head and turning away so they would not see her tears, Laspeera set about obeying Vangerdahast the Royal Magician.

Wizard of War Gheldaert was never in the best of tempers—even when he awakened from slumber at his own pace. Roused frantically from his bed by several perturbed younger war wizards, he was decidedly not in the best of tempers now.

Glaring around the room full of anxious young faces, he said, "And why should I care that a barn burned down outside Wheloon? Why should I even be *told* that a barn burned down anywhere? Why should any of you waste your time and tongue-wagging over such trifles? Are you not war wizards? And being so, have you nothing *better* to do?"

"Gheldaert, this wasn't just any fire!" Rhindin said. "The barn burst like a spell blast and hurled out bolts of lightning in all directions—and balls of green flame that flew everywhere, too!"

"So someone was spellhurling and made a mistake, or two mages decided to hold their little private duel in a barn! I presume you've spent a few spells trying to find out, yes? As the standing orders that Old Thunderspells never tires of reminding us all about insist be done? Or are you telling me all this because someone forgot to do so—or cast the spells but blew himself up, leaving only smoking boots behind? Or just went missing?"

"We're telling you this, Irvgal Gheldaert," came a cold voice from the door, "because the investigator of the fire that destroyed Indarr Andemar's barn wrote his name in the duty book, added the title of a report on his investigation, and then stopped writing, leaving the rest of the page blank. And the name he wrote was Gheldaert Howndroe. *You* wouldn't know anything about that, would you?"

Gheldaert gaped at the person standing in the doorway. "Q-Queen Filfaeril?"

"Ah, war wizards always penetrate my best disguises," the woman in the doorway, who wore no disguise at all—and clearly nothing much at all beneath her clinging silken nightgown—replied in a voice that dripped with acid. "Wherefore I'll expect a full report on this in the morning. Not until then, mind. I have a little private duel of my own to attend to right now. In the Royal Bedchamber."

"Y-yes, Great Queen," Gheldaert managed to reply. "I, uh, I—"

"And while you're at it, Irvgal," the Dragon Queen added over her shoulder, as she turned and strode barefoot out of the room, "you've been following up on that shapeshifting matter in Shadowdale—Craunor Askelo's report, remember?—for some months now. Are you not a war wizard? And being so, have you nothing *better* to do?"

Gheldaert swallowed, not knowing what to say, then tried to say something. What came out was a heartfelt "Tluin."

He froze, aghast. Gods! He had just said a very impolite word to the Queen of Cormyr.

"Indeed," she replied from down the passage. "That's exactly what I'll be doing. How perceptive of you. With such keen-witted Wizards of War serving us so diligently, there's hope for the realm yet."

Then she added something that sent him staggering to the floor in sudden relief.

She chuckled.

It was as dry and gleefully dirty a chuckle as he'd ever heard.

Dalonder Ree blinked, shook himself, and blinked again. He was standing out of doors on well-trampled ground amid trees. Somewhere. Where *was* he?

Oh.

The Harper was standing in the camp hollow between the road and the Stagheart ruin, in the bright moonlight of a calm, warm night.

In just the same manner as he was blinking and staring around Lorbryn, Tsantress, and two of the Knights of Myth Drannor—the ranger Florin and the fighting-lass Islif, both looking more than a little dazed—were staring around at the hollow, at each other, and down at themselves.

Those glances down showed them the Wizard of War Laspeera lying face-up and senseless on the trampled turf between them, clutching the broken and smoking ends of wands in both her hands.

Farther away, strewn all around them, lay the crumpled bodies of the ornrion Dauntless, the bullyblade Brorn Hallomond, and the rest of the Knights.

"How—?" Florin asked hoarsely.

"The wizard Laspeera," Ree told him. "Obeying the Royal Magician to get us all here, out of the Lost Palace. While he remained behind to fight alone against—"

He stopped speaking and whirled, raising his wands, as behind him arose a faint chiming as of faerie bells, and the air glowed a sudden, vivid blue-white.

Then the glow was gone, and a dozen or so men who had not been there before were standing where it had been. They blinked around at the hollow. Each held a sword in his hand. Most were Purple Dragons in armor, but standing with them in Court-fashionable finery were the noble Lords Spurbright, father and son, looking stern.

"Well met," Tsantress greeted them in a dry voice, raising and aiming her own wands at them. "How come you here, Lords, and on what purpose bent?"

"To defend Cormyr by aiding the wizard Vangerdahast in his

time of need," the elder Lord Spurbright replied. "We were sent here by the Princess—"

One of the Dragons behind him shrieked, flung his arms wide, and toppled forward. A glowing blade was just sliding back out of his backside, glistening with his blood.

" 'Ware!" Dalonder Ree cried, firing his wands at the blade. "Guard yourselves!"

Tsantress blasted it, too, as the Dragons and nobles hastily scattered, cursing. Deltalon scrambled to where he could blast it clearly.

The sword darted here and there, thrusting at legs and hands and then springing up to stab at Purple Dragon faces.

"Get it!" Ree snarled. "These wands must be good for something! *Blast it to shards!*"

Lorbryn and Tsantress joined him in blasting the sword, striking it repeatedly as the Dragons and nobles flung themselves down, scrambled and rolled aside, and clawed their ways back to where wandfire could give them some protection from the flying blade.

Flying raggedly, the sword finally veered off behind trees and fled, disappearing back into the forest under the lash of their blasts.

Silence fell, broken only by the hisses of pain from some of the lacerated Dragons. Ree looked at the wounded men, then down at all the silent bodies. The last place he looked was up at Lorbryn and Tsantress to ask, "And now . . . what?"

As the Spurbrights came silently up beside them, the two war wizards shrugged.

Tsantress frowned as a thought struck her. Wagging a finger, she said, "Turn Laspeera over. She'll have some healing potions on her. She always does."

Gingerly, Ree lifted the war wizard's limp torso and turned her over. Bending over him, Lorbryn Deltalon plucked some metal vials from loops along the back of Laspeera's belt.

The Harper frowned. "I'm wearing a whole sash of those, I think. Took them off Vangey's table."

He slapped his hip, and a hitherto-invisible baldric melted back into visibility and solidity.

Tsantress peered at the row of metal vials ranged down that baldric. She nodded and smiled at what she saw, then pointed at the stricken and the bodies all around.

"Start pouring them down throats. Don't choke someone you're healing, mind, or they'll haunt you."

Remembering the liches crowding in closer back in the passage, Ree shivered.

In a spell-sealed chamber in a certain tower of Zhentil Keep, the Brotherhood wizard Targon peered into a scrying sphere at a moonlit hollow that now held nary a flying sword at all.

Old Ghost knew a magic that Targon had never known, which would have enabled him to force the crystal ball to trace and watch the sword's flight on through the forest—but he couldn't be bothered.

Shrugging, he turned away. "Horaundoon, Horaundoon!" he told the empty air disgustedly, as he flung the door-bar aside and threw open the doors into the moonlit chamber beyond. "No *discipline*. Slaughtering just anyone merely gets you blasted. I gave you *orders*. Idiot."

The same moonlight that fell upon the exasperated Zhentarim mage Targon fell also upon a high room in a ruined, window-less tower that soared up out of the leafy canopy of a wooded wilderness.

It touched the boots of the wizard Hesperdan as he stood with his arms folded across his chest, watching a floating, glowing, spell-spun scene in midair. The disgusted Targon was turning away from that distant scrying sphere and striding to the door.

Hesperdan smiled. "And so, Arlonder 'Old Ghost' Darmeth," he murmured, "you begin to know how it feels to have reckless, know-better-than-thou underlings disobey your every order, intimation, warning, and suggestion. Get used to it, in the time you have left. It shall not be nearly as long as you think it will be."

The archwizard strolled about the ruined room, the glowing scene moving with him to stay right in front of his gaze.

"Winnowing the Zhentarim of the unworthy is going to take even longer than I expected," he said to himself. He often talked to himself, for he had discovered long ago that a certain Hesperdan was by far his most patient audience. "Moreover, shifting Fzoul to the fore so I can use Manshoon for my own purposes is going to take some seasons on top of that. 'Tis a very good thing I'm a patient man."

He stood thinking for a moment and almost absently corrected himself in a voice so soft even he could barely hear it. "Well, 'patient,' at least."

Princess Alusair gave the two men her best glare. "I thought I gave you strict orders . . .," she began menacingly, nettled by their almost-grins and well aware that she looked ridiculous in a full suit of very ill-fitting armor that had been her father's when he was young.

Yet she stood her ground, her gauntleted hands clutching her drawn sword's quillons. She kept it grounded point-first on the floor, her feet planted wide behind it, grimly defending the doors to her parents' bedchamber.

"The definition of an idiot," Tathanter Doarmund replied tartly, "is someone who obeys your orders. Your Highness."

"Truly, Cormyr is full of idiots," the sage Alaphondar added, his voice all I'm-merely-making-an-observation innocence.

"Hrast you, take me *seriously!*" Alusair snapped at them both. "If you wake my parents—!"

"Oh, we're awake," growled the King of Cormyr from just behind her.

Alusair whirled, astonished she'd never heard the door open.

"So, little lioness," Azoun asked his younger daughter, crooking one darkly splendid eyebrow, "have you a clever explanation for this?

Can't your mother and I enjoy a little time together to bounce on the royal pillows without—"

His jaw dropped open in astonishment, and he stared over Alusair's shoulder down the passage.

Everyone turned.

Vangerdahast was limping slowly up the passage toward them. His face was gray, one of his arms looked like it had been melted away just below the elbow, and bare ribs showed through seared flesh on the other side of his burnt-bare torso.

"The mad liches are bound again," he rasped, "but there are far fewer of them, I fear."

"The . . . the mad liches?" Alusair asked, hefting her sword—and feeling herself blush hotly as she saw that the blade was trembling.

"Crown secret," Vangey said. "That you're too young to know yet."

"Oh?" she flared. "And when will I be old enough?"

"Around highsun tomorrow," he mumbled—and collapsed on his face at her feet.

Chapter 17

ANOTHER CROWN SECRET, OR SEVEN

So I let them take my horses tall
My chest of coins, wagons eleven
My best boots, sword, and all
For no thief can find or measure
My greatest carried treasure
In my head, crown secrets seven.

Dasshara Lornyl,
Lady Merchant of Neverwinter
"The Trader's Song"
First performed in the Year of Thunder

He had done the right thing, cutting his losses and getting out.

The right thing, he reminded himself, seeking the cool, calculating calm he prized so much.

Hotheads doom themselves. Hot rage burns the rager. Be as the patient ice and stone, biding in silence until the right moment of thunderous fall.

The trite sayings brought just about as much comfort as he'd expected them to, and Manshoon kept right on striding along the dark passages of Zhentil Keep, knowing he should feel relief if he let himself feel anything at all. Still he burned with fury.

"Black, black temper," he murmured the words of a currently popular ditty, seeking to divert himself. And failing.

He *was* in a black temper. He'd done a masterful job of impersonating Vangerdahast. He'd brought the Unbinding to the proverbial brink of being complete. He'd brought about the destruction of many of the liches he'd had to work so hard to escape or pacify on his earlier visits to the Lost Palace. And he'd caused many potential foes—those adventurers, a few Harpers, some war wizards, perhaps even Vangerdahast himself—to be wounded, weakened, or even slain.

Yet he could find no pleasure or satisfaction or even just some scrap of comfort in any of that.

He was furious at those who'd brought him so close to death and more furious at himself for being afraid to return to the Lost Palace to destroy them all.

"Blackfire," he snarled. "Talar and blackfire!"

Mild oaths, but he seldom cursed at all—and almost never aloud. Commanders had no need to curse, and that was the image he'd chosen to armor himself in—especially among all of these sly, murderously ambitious Brothers in his Zhentarim.

Murderous, yes. That's what it was time to be, now. For the greater glory of Bane and the greater exaltation of a certain Manshoon, too. He knew now what he had to do.

Accordingly, he took the side way out of the next grand chamber, turning in the echoing darkness to head for a certain vault.

It was not a short journey. Keeping his face impassive, he strode past guardpost after guardpost, crisply answering challenge after challenge.

Ahead, beyond yet more guarded doors, was a table. It stood alone in a dark room, four straight legs and a smooth top upon which rested an open-ended wooden cradle. On that cradle lay the greatest magical treasure he'd managed to craft thus far: a Staff of Doom.

Not quite a match for the doomstaves of old yet. In fact, something of a one-joke jester's act. Aside from allowing a wielder to fall slowly from a cliff or high place, and altering light in a small area about itself, it could do just one thing: emit death tyrants. That is, its globular ends, upon command, became portals that spat out an undead beholder each from a stasis-space he'd filled with four-and-ten undead beholders thus far.

He'd been saving this secret for a pressing need, in hopes that such a need would come *after* he had mastered ways of augmenting the staff with other battle powers.

Yet death comes for those who wait too long for their needs to seem pressing.

He could—should—use it *now*.

He'd whisk himself back to the Lost Palace, plant the staff in a suitable spot, trigger it to unleash two death tyrants to destroy all life and unlife in the place, and depart. A few tendays later, upon his return, the death tyrants should be the only sentiences left. He'd command them back into the staff for later use and plunder the place at leisure. Or leave them drifting around to do battle with Vangerdahast or any war wizards who came blundering along while he was stripping the Lost Palace of all the magic he wanted.

He had passed the last human guards long ago, and the monsters held in stasis—except for the venomous spider that waited in the vault itself. He had passed the last pair of sword-wielding automatons, too, and he was just stepping through the opening his murmurings had made in the spell-confined curtain of crawling, flesh-eating ooze. Which left only his own wards: shimmering curtains of interlaced magical spells that could be destroyed by a sufficiently powerful onslaught of magic but couldn't be restored exactly as he'd left them by anyone except him.

In front of him, they glimmered untouched. Of course.

He walked on, parting each one as he reached it and letting it seal again behind him. Carelessness kills more mages than anything else, and being careless among the Brotherhood was like dancing blind-folded and naked in a pit of angry, hungry vipers.

The last ward parted at his word and gesture, and he strode into the vault, speaking the words that would keep the spider frozen above him.

He stopped, gasping in disbelief.

The cradle on the table was empty.

He shot glances all around the room, even as he strode over to the cradle. "Whiteblood!" he whispered slowly, aghast.

The staff—*his* work, his unfinished masterpiece—was gone.

Manshoon raced around the table, knowing his search was futile. He could already see every corner of the vault and the floor behind the table. He looked up, seeing only the soft, steady glow of the radiance spell he'd cast long ago to give him light in this place. The ceiling, just like the floor and the walls, was bare. He went to his knees and peered at the underside of the table, even though the staff was far too long to be hidden there. Nothing, of course.

Rage rising in him, Manshoon of the Zhentarim cast a tracing spell on the cradle, in hopes that some too-small-to-see dust mote or fragment had crumbled off the staff and been left behind there that he could use to try to trace the vanished staff. If the magic did its utmost, he'd be able to identify who'd taken it and where.

His spell flared, wild hope leaping in him as it found *something* and began to work.

The spell died, leaving Manshoon staring at something small and white lying in the cradle, that hadn't been been there—or visible there, at least—before. It was . . .

A tiny stone carving of a human left hand, in a fist but with its forefinger pointing straight out or up. Smooth-carved of some white stone.

A tiny holy symbol of Azuth.

Manshoon *really* cursed this time, his face going as white as bleached bone.

He drew back from the little carving as if burned—and then warily approached it again to stare at it intently. His rage slowly left him, and he wrapped himself in cold calm.

Traveling back through all the guardposts, he consoled himself with a sudden thought.

Manshoon of the Zhentarim. He had become important enough for gods to notice.

"An agreement, Friend Procurer, is an agreement," the plump, ragged-robed priest of Tymora said with dignity, "and I took care that this one would be a bond before the gods—or at least the gods that most govern us both. Tymora answered my prayers with holy visions both vivid and specific. Did ye not assure me that Mask did the same for ye?"

"Y-yes," Torm said reluctantly, hefting the staff in his hands. " 'Tis just that I . . . I've never stolen anything quite this powerful or well-guarded before. I . . ." He waved one hand to indicate the strength of his struggle for the right words, his usual wit failing him, then burst out, "My hands don't want to let it go out of their grasp.

I hunger to hold it, to stroke it—not like a woman, mind, but yes, *stroke* it—often. Whenever I feel the need. Something inside me doesn't want to let it out of my presence, lest I never get the chance to hold it again. Haularake, this seems fool-headed, even when I'm just saying it to you, but . . . 'tis so, I tell you!"

Rathan nodded sympathetically. "We consecrated holy ones feel the same way when we first touch holy altars and relics of our gods. We cannot bear to be parted from them. 'Tis why some temple altars are surrounded of nights by sleeping priests with their hand or cheek or some part of their skin pressed against the holy stone. They end up heaped in a great snoring ring around an altar!"

"*That* must hamper morning devotions a trifle," the young thief said, folding his arms around the staff as if it were an overlarge child he was holding tenderly to his breast. "I—no, I *can't* do this!"

"And failing to do it, stand foresworn before three gods?" Rathan reminded him. "Saer Torm, are ye already, in thy green count of seasons, *that* tired of living?"

"You're not much older!"

"I," the priest of Tymora replied with as much dignity as any old, slow, and wise high priest, "am not the one contemplating breaking a holy bond. My age enters not into this. I have never claimed to be grayer in years then ye, nor wiser. I merely believe that a bond is a bond—and even a thief to whom lying and bond-breaking is everyday ease should hold that a bond is a bond when the very god of thieves hath been a part of the bond in question. In short, staff-stealer: break this agreement, and ye're tluined."

Torm sighed gustily, looked down at the staff in his arms, then glanced around the forest glade they were sitting in. "I *know* that," he said in a voice raw with anguish, kicking his heels against the great rock he was sitting on. "What, precisely, was the agreement again?"

"So ye can slither all over it like a snake seeking a hole to slide through?" Rathan asked in amused tones. "Very well. I'm a priest. I have every last waking moment left in my life to talk over holy matters. Except when actually praying, of course. I *trust* that doesn't goad ye into seeking to end my life, here and now."

"Don't tempt me," Torm muttered. "Let me hear the deal."

Rathan smiled and leaned forward on his rock to stab one stubby finger at the thief. "*Ye* were to steal the staff and put the token of Azuth that I gave ye in its place. Ye would thereby be protected from all harm by the spells and vigilance of the Unseen One, god of spellcasters, while ye did the theft. After, I am to put the staff on this altar of Azuth"—the priest swung around on his rock to point down the glade at the circular, flat-topped stone that lay in the leaf-littered moss and dirt at the far end of the clearing—"and the Unseen One will then magically claim it and leave a reward in its place. We split that offering evenly—*evenly*, thief—and ye give thy half to Mask, whilst I lay mine upon an altar of Tymora."

Torm nodded a trifle wearily. "I rise in Mask's measuring thanks to my daring theft of something truly powerful, and you earn a smile from Lady Luck for chancing this crazed scheme and persuading me to have a hand in it."

"*Precisely,*" Rathan agreed heartily. "Tymora be praised."

"And Mask be tickled pink or some such favorable hue," Torm replied sourly—and thrust one end of the staff out to touch Rathan's chest, bowing his head and closing his eyes. "Take it!"

Carefully, almost reverently, the priest closed both hands around the staff and tugged ever so gently.

Flinging back his head to sigh loudly enough to stir an echo in the nearest trees of Hullack Forest, Torm let go.

"There, now," Rathan said soothingly. "That wasn't—"

"*Don't say it!*" Torm shouted, springing up from his rock to yell in the priest's face. "Yes, it *was* stlarning hard. Thank you *very* much for not asking nor even suggesting I think along such lines! Grrr!"

He strode around the rocks, drawing his needle blade and slashing the air with it so furiously, it hissed and whistled as it cut nothing at all.

He stopped, sighed again, resheathed his thin sword, and sat down on the rocks again as if nothing had happened.

"Right," he said calmly. "*That's* done. Your turn, I believe."

Rathan nodded, his attention—as it had been from the moment the thief's sword had slid back into its sheath—on the staff in his hands. He wasn't stroking it as Torm had been, but he was studying it, hefting it in his hands as if to try to *feel* the magic it contained.

"Tymora look down!" he gasped. "Such arrogance! He even *labeled* it!"

"Staff of Doom," Torm intoned grandly. "Made by Manshoon, mightiest of Zhentarim." He chuckled. "Modest, isn't he?"

"Hmm. Mayhap he feared it would get mixed up with the staff of another Zhent at some Brotherhood gathering or other," the priest of Tymora said. "We must grant that possibility."

"We can grant the possibility that the tree he cut this from grew this limb with those words graven in it by the hands of the gods," Torm replied sarcastically, "and he merely found it and was seized by inspiration, but forgive me if I refrain from betting on such a likelihood, hey?"

Rathan raised his head and gave the thief a severe look. "Thy faith is less than strong."

"My faith in *myself* is strong," Torm countered. "The gods, I'm not so sure about. Especially the fanciful versions of gods some priests try to hand me. Some priests, note. Not you, stout champion of Tymora."

Rathan looked up again. "*Stout* champion?"

"Ah, you were listening." Torm grinned. "Purely an accidental slip of the tongue, I assure you."

"Thy assurances," the priest told him dryly, "are as strong as thy faith."

He stood up, the staff in his hands, and gave Torm a long, steady look.

"Do it," the thief said quietly after a time. "I won't jump you or try to snatch it."

Rathan nodded, turned slowly, and then solemnly strode the length of the glade, the staff held out before him horizontally.

Torm trailed after him, well to one side, watching the staff and the altar in turn, half expecting either or both of them to burst into something loud and bright and different.

Nothing happened, and no one sprang into view behind the altar.

When he reached that massive, plain disk of stone, the priest of Tymora stopped, held out the staff, and announced calmly, "Rathan Thentraver am I, and unworthy, a priest of Tymora. To holy Azuth this we give, Saer Torm and myself."

Leaning forward, he carefully laid the staff down on the altar, stepped back, bowed deeply, and stepped back further.

The staff stayed motionless on the altar. Silence fell. Nothing happened.

After several long breaths had dragged by, Torm sighed. "Well, that was a bit of a—"

The altar glowed, a bright white fist of dancing motes rising from the bare dark stone around the staff and gathering together in a sphere a foot or so above the altar.

As Torm and Rathan stared, the sphere grew to shield size, then as large as the boulders they'd been sitting on at the far end of the glade, a blinding white light that made the thief hastily back away. "If that explodes—!"

Rathan stood his ground.

The light streamed down to cover the altar, dripping down its sides like white candle wax, hiding the staff entirely. Then, very suddenly, it went from white to a deep, rich blue . . . and started to fade.

The staff was gone, but there was something in its place. A heap—no, two heaps, accompanied by a whiff of pipesmoke.

The blue radiance ebbed even more, and two small heaps of gems could be seen sitting side by side on the altar, each covered with a leather pouch from which protruded a neat quartet of cylindrical metal vials.

"Healing potions?" Torm breathed as the last of the glow faded away.

"Mayhap," Rathan muttered, his gaze never leaving the altar.

One of the two pouches was labeled "TORM" and the other

"Rathan." Both had small, folded scraps of parchment thrust into them.

Torm and Rathan broke off staring at the altar long enough to stare at each other in astonishment. Then they both shrugged, stepped forward, took up their parchments, and read them.

"Well, holy man?"

"Rathan," the priest read aloud, "go ye to Shadowdale. Once there, use any pretext to become a trusted Knight of Myth Drannor."

Then he made a surprised sound. The parchment melted away to dust in his fingers. He looked quickly at the thief.

"Torm," Torm read out rather hastily, "go ye to Shadowdale. Once there, use any pretext to become a trusted Knight of Myth Drannor." His parchment, too, promptly fell to dust.

They stared at each other. Again.

Rathan finally found his voice, rather feebly. "Trusted? *Us?*"

Torm grinned. "Got anything to drink? I find myself in need of something like that just now. Rather a *lot* of it, too."

Standing alone in a room of the Royal Palace in Suzail, the War Wizard Laspeera carefully finished casting a spell.

There was a momentary twinkling of sound and light around the hargaunt, where it was floating motionless in midair, and Laspeera stared at it in grim silence for the space of a long breath.

Nothing happened. The hargaunt was securely held in stasis.

Stepping back out of the chamber without taking her eyes off the amorphous blob, Laspeera used a wand to seal the door. Then she drew a second wand from its sheath on her hip and cast a second seal atop the first.

Standing in the passage beside her were three people who had watched all she had done: Princess Alusair, King Azoun, and Queen Filfaeril. They all turned away together and started down the deserted, door-lined passage.

"And so we gain another crown secret," Azoun murmured. "Quite a collection, now."

"Indeed," Laspeera said, falling into step behind the royals.

"I believe I heard you think—but not *quite* say—the words, 'And that's counting just those we let you non-Wizards of War know about,' if I'm not mistaken," the queen said.

Laspeera halted in midstride, just for a moment, then repeated politely, "Indeed," and walked on.

"Is knowing when the Royal Magician is going to be his usual snarling self again one of them?" the king asked.

"For the moment," Laspeera replied gently, "yes. I'm afraid so."

They all jumped, then—and Alusair let out a little shriek—as from the dark doorway they were passing, the wizard Vangerdahast thrust his head out and snapped, "Snarl!"

Then he favored them with a grin of the sort generally termed "sheepish."

Queen Filfaeril rolled her eyes. "I keep forgetting Elminster trained you."

Slowly, dimly, Highknight Lady Ismra Targrael became aware of herself again. Her limbs tangled, she was lying on her back on something hard and smooth. Cold, damp stone, underground. A place that seemed not familiar but seen before . . . recently.

She tried to disentangle her arms and legs. Her body felt heavy and somehow profoundly *numb*. There was a faint smell rising from it. An unpleasant smell.

She moved again, trying to sit up. Her limbs were heavy—very heavy—and unresponsive. She was dead, wasn't she?

It was dark around her, with walls of dark, paneled wood rising up beyond the reach of what she could see in the dimness. She was still in the Lost Palace.

So this must be undeath.

Something moved closer to her. Something she could feel—power, a cold energy—before she could see it. Something that became a man standing over her.

Looming over her and looking down at her with eyes that were coldly twinkling lights in dark sockets, out of a face that was mere flesh wrapped loose around a skull. A lich.

Then there was another. A third, and fourth, a ring of skeletal faces above her, staring coldly down. Targrael recognized one of them as the lich that had killed her.

"Rise," that lich commanded. "And dance. Can you learn to love us?"

Lying on the floor among the gathering, Targrael looked around at all the cold, glittering eyes, skulls, and rotting flesh and murmured, "I . . . I don't think so."

"Well," another lich observed coldly, "your flesh still has beauty—for a time, at least. Long enough for you to learn."

Skeletal arms reached down. Targrael discovered her newly heavy self could not move nearly fast enough to evade them.

With astonishing strength they plucked her body upright.

"Learn to embrace madness," the lich who'd murdered her said, and he leaned in to kiss her.

Targrael tried to scream but found herself mute.

His hand on his sword hilt, Dauntless glared at the Knights of Myth Drannor. "I am the Royal Champion of Princess Alusair," he said, "and stand here—still!—under the clear and explicit orders of the Royal Magician, Vangerdahast. I am to see that you depart the realm, tarrying nowhere and working no treason."

"We intend none," Florin replied a little wearily. "Tell Lord Vangerdahast that when you see him."

"And tell him this, too," Islif added. " 'Tis never too late to learn to trust folk of Cormyr. Even adventurers."

"I will deliver your messages," Dauntless said. Then a smile that was as sudden as it was unexpected split the ornrion's face. "Though I believe it might be decades too late for that particular wizard to learn anything."

At his elbow, the War Wizard Tsantress rolled her eyes. "I'd hate to have heard that, because I just might agree with it—and then what sort of trouble would I be in?"

"*I* still can't believe he's alive," Lorbryn Deltalon put in from behind them both.

"Believe it," Laspeera said wearily. Then she stepped forward, astonished Florin by embracing him, and over his shoulder announced, "You are good folk, you Knights. But get you on to Shadowdale with your pendant, before anything *else* happens."

The Knights muttered various forms of agreement, turned with waves and smiles, and went out to the Moonsea Ride to walk east.

Dauntless promptly strode to where he could watch them go. Laspeera grinned and shook her head at that, then turned and carefully conjured a portal in the center of the clearing.

When the glow of that magical door was bright and steady, she ushered the Harper and her fellow war wizards toward it. They obeyed, filing through the glow and journeying back to Suzail in a single step.

"Ornrion," she called.

Dauntless turned his head, saw the portal and her beckoning gesture, gave the dwindling figures of the Knights one last, long look, then obediently started toward the waiting glow.

He was still a pace away from it when something slid silently out of the trees at the far end of the clearing.

The flying sword, point-first, gliding low beneath the leaves.

"Get through!" Laspeera snapped at the ornrion. "No, *don't* stop and turn—*go!*"

Dauntless ran, and Laspeera ducked aside from the portal and hastily started to close it.

The flying sword streaked at the portal's waning glow.

Laspeera frowned as a sudden thought struck her. She whipped two wands from her belt and unleashed them with care at the flickering, shrinking edges of the portal.

It guttered, rippled wildly, and suddenly shot up into the air, the sword slicing air just beneath it, then arcing around to speed at it again.

The rippling glow dodged again, the sword *almost* plunging

through it. The radiance seemed for just a moment to collapse into a wildly agitated helix . . . then became bright and hard again, but smaller and humming loudly.

The sword shot toward it again.

Laspeera willed the doorway onto its edge and to rise, and again the sword just missed it. By then, her former portal had raced to hover before her like a shield.

The sword was getting faster. It darted at the shield, plunged into it as silently as if the shield were mere empty air . . . and slowed to a snail's pace in midair, hanging almost motionless as it worked its way through the glowing barrier.

Its point was glittering a mere arm's length from Laspeera's breast.

She stepped aside leisurely, resheathed her wands, and got the strongest spell she knew ready, mouth going dry.

Either she had just made the biggest—and quite likely the last—mistake of her life, or . . .

The sword emerged from the shield, still gliding so slowly it seemed almost frozen. It had acquired a strange glow of its own, a pulsing purple-white sheen that raced up its length to its elegantly curled quillons, then back down.

"Yes!" an exulting voice erupted from it. *"Yessss!"*

The Sword That Never Sleeps turned and streaked off northeast, faster than it had ever sped before.

Chapter 18
NO REALM CAN CONFINE ME

Sick of working? Want to be free?
Of lack of coins, of the drudge's load?
I'm an adventurer a-wandering
New forays ever pondering
No realm can confine me;
I'm for the open road.

Zaunskur Morlcastle, Bard of Starmantle
"The Song of the Open Road"
First published in the Year of the Starfall

So we almost got killed—again—and lost all our horses and gear. Is this the sort of adventure we can look forward to?" Semoor said. He winced as his feet pained him more and more with each step. The blisters weren't something he was looking forward to lancing. "How long before we're walking along naked and starving, waiting for the first hungry beast or knife-waving outlaw to happen along and put us out of our misery?"

"Think of it as an unending sequence of new beginnings, Wolftooth dearest," Pennae said, "and the Morninglord will provide. Or is your faith as weak as your backbone?"

"Hey *hoy!*" Semoor snapped, giving her a glare. "Do I question your profession, *thief?*"

Pennae shrugged. "I care not if you do, Saer Yapping Tongue. Some folk open their mouths and spew out mere noise that the rest of us soon cease heeding—and I fear you're one of those folk. I expect that at your funeral, your complaints and whinings and not-so-clever remarks are going to rise from your grave without pause until the gravediggers shovel enough earth on top of you that we finally won't have to hear it all any longer."

"Here, now," Jhessail said. "*Enough.* Some band of adventurers we'll be, if we start clawing at each other like brawling tavern drunkards!"

"I begin to have a new appreciation for the nightly entertainment on offer in Espar," Pennae said, "and while I agree with you to a point, Jhess, I think 'tis time and *past* time we aired some things. Before I strangle Saer Semoor with his own sharp, forked tongue."

Doust reached a quelling hand to his longtime friend's arm at about the time Islif clapped a hand over the crimson, fiery-eyed Lathanderite's mouth.

"Before you respond to Pennae, Stoop," she said in his ear gently, "I'd like you to do one thing for me. Pretend that several senior priests of the Morninglord are standing right here listening to all you say. Please?"

She withdrew her hand. Semoor shot her a simmering look and the words, "Thank you, Islif."

Then he turned to regard Pennae and said, "I am what I am. If there's something about me you think really must be changed, you'll have to convince me. Not that I think insults will move me much. Would they change *you?*"

"Oh, shrewdly said," Doust murmured.

Florin nodded. "Your words, Semoor, ring true enough in my ears. Pennae?"

The thief regarded Florin thoughtfully, then nodded, turned, and went to Semoor—and kissed him.

He tried to lean and turn his face away from her, stiffly, but she was far more agile than he and could caress and kiss very skillfully when she wanted to. In mere moments he was groaning under her tongue and embracing her fiercely.

Jhessail rolled her eyes skyward. "And of course there's always *that* way to solve every little dispute, too. Not being a jack, I haven't what fills a codpiece to be led around by, but it seems to work for them. Every time."

"Lead me around by my codpiece, lass?" Doust asked her hopefully, waving a hand. " 'Tis just down here!"

Islif decided it was her turn to indulge in some eye-rolling. *"How* far is it to Shadowdale?" she asked Florin, in world-weary tones.

"Don't ask me!" he jested. "I'm but a simple backwoods ranger!"

"Who walks with kings and beds noble lasses as calmly as some of us change our jerkins," Pennae teased him, coming up for air.

"If I pick another fight with you," Semoor asked her hopefully, not releasing her from his embrace, "will you make peace with me like this again? About the time we make camp and decide on sleeping arrangements for the night, say?"

"Speaking of which," Islif said, "we're walking through wild country, and we'd better decide how to camp and keep ourselves alive before we fall asleep and anything small with jaws has its way with us. Even a weasel or a groundcat can take your throat out with ease if you're just lying on the ground snoring."

"So we'll be standing watch every night? Oh, *gods,*" Semoor snarled, "why is the world so stlarning *unfair?*"

It was Florin who stopped walking this time, to spin around and fix Semoor with a stern look. "I don't know why. Perhaps the gods do. What I do know is that we're adventurers and that, yes, the world *isn't* fair. Making it fair is *our* job. Yours, mine, all of us."

Silence fell after he finished speaking those words, and in its cloak the Knights walked on, one by one nodding and murmuring agreement in their various ways.

Lost in thought, the wizard Targon turned from a high balcony in Zhentil Keep and strolled across the gloomy and deserted chamber into which the balcony opened. He had no particular quarrel with most of the Zhentarim wizards of lesser rank—they were ruthless graspers-after-power, to be sure, but who of the Brotherhood was not?—but the five or six mages he did want brought down were difficult targets. To avoid being exposed to the entire Brotherhood as a peril to all, he would have to move *very* carefully against whichever one of them he chose to slay first.

That meant he still had to learn a lot more about their alliances with beholders and Bane priests and the gods alone knew who else, so as to—

He staggered, arched over backward, and stood trembling, suddenly transfixed by the sword Armaukran.

It had come racing out of the sky and swooping through the archway from the balcony so swiftly that the light ward spell he was using hadn't even had time to chime. Now the agony was so white-hot, he could barely frame coherent thoughts.

He should have been able to sense the sword approaching.

What had happened to it?

Grimly, Old Ghost felt for the sword's enchantments with his will, red mists of pain rising to flood his mind with the looming threat of oblivion . . .

"Die!" Horaundoon snarled, his hatred a deafening bellow crashing through Old Ghost's thoughts. "I've been changed and need never fear you again, cruel schemer!"

The Zhentarim staggered blindly across the room with the blade through him, as two minds wrestled amid gathering darkness inside his head—a darkness that smiled and drew in around Horaundoon with tightening talons.

From somewhere near at hand, he heard Old Ghost ask silkily, "Oh? Need you not?"

Then the darkness struck, bursting into crimson fury as sentience flooded into and overwhelmed sentience.

This time, Old Ghost made sure of his foe, rending a howling Horaundoon ruthlessly and utterly.

When the mind thunder had fallen quiet again, and he stood alone in the dripping ruins of Targon's mind and dying body, he knew only the sword was vessel enough to trust in and inhabit.

He looked and felt, coiling through threads of enchantment and long-disused powers . . . finding excitement again, after so long . . .

There is much room in this blade. Room for a dozen minds or more, if I can command that many at once. Company for centuries, to warm me with their fancies and memories and hatreds—until I tire of them and subsume or destroy them.

The dying Targon slumped down, and the sword drew back out of him and flew away, out from the balcony in a great soaring arc, heading for Shadowdale.

One less fool to trammel me. On to find others.

As the humming, blue-silver blade flashed through the air, Old Ghost wondered idly if it was smiling as smugly as he was inside it.

Not that there was any hurry. There would be plenty of time to subvert adventurers when the Knights of Myth Drannor finally arrived in Shadowdale.

Brorn Hallomond found the old casket he was looking for. It would take the strength of an owlbear to drag aside the stone lid and maul him. Here he could sleep and heal.

Gods, he wished he'd been able to steal another healing vial.

Huh. As to that, he wished he'd been able to steal himself a castle full of servants and fine food and a title to go with it, too.

Perhaps *next* time.

He hammered the sliding stone catch with the pommel of his dagger, gasping with the pain each blow brought him. He hauled up the hinged lid with a howl of pain and more or less fell in on top of the brittle, shrouded corpse inside.

It crackled into riven boneshards and dust under him, and he clutched himself to lessen the inevitable agony of coughing and sneezing that followed. When at last that was done, Brorn clawed the lid back down, rolled to the crack in the stone so he could breathe, and lay still, waiting for weariness to overcome pain and let him sleep.

Thank whatever gods had smiled upon him. When that war wizard lass—Santress, or whatever her name was—discovered her little token missing, it would probably be about then that she'd remember that a certain bullyblade had vanished from the hollow where all the healing was going on, too.

Hopefully she wouldn't be mule-headed enough to come back here looking for him.

Though most war wizards were just that, stlarn it.

He felt for the dagger at his belt, so he could be ready if she did haul back the lid. Hah. A dagger against her wands. And probably those of half-a-dozen more oh-so-brave Wizards of War.

Still, 'twas the best he could do. He was only Lord Yellander's bullyblade, not Lord Yellander.

Yet.

"Night fog, and we're getting into rising rocks," Florin muttered. "I don't like the looks of this."

"Rocks at least are a solid shield at our backs," Islif said. "I've yet to find a tree, however large, that I dared trust as much."

"We must stand watch," Pennae said from ahead of them all, "and find some shelter we can defend. Even if we have to butcher some bear or other and take his cave."

"Adventure," Jhessail said in an acidic voice that struggled along the edge of a yawn.

"Up there," Doust said, pointing a little way up a slope of loose stones on their left that turned into a cliff face farther up. "That overhang. If we sleep up there, nothing that doesn't have wings can get to us without making a *lot* of noise."

"Rolling rocks aplenty down to the Ride under their feet, or claws, or slithery belly," Pennae agreed. "Well spotted, Luck of Tymora."

"Lathander smiles upon us too!" Semoor said.

"I've heard far better bed-me lines," the thief told him almost kindly. "Now, the swifter you get yourself up there and bedded down, the sooner you can be praying to the Morninglord to keep us alive to see his next glorious morning—and the faster we'll all get some sleep."

Semoor sighed, beckoned Doust, and started climbing.

"Sleep fully clad, boots and all," Islif put in, watching Semoor leading Doust gingerly up the slippery slope of sliding, tumbling stones. Then she looked at Florin and grinned. "Guess camp's been decided, valiant leader."

"I'm *not* our leader," Florin said wearily.

"Oh, yes, you are," Jhessail told him quietly. "You just happen to lead some adventurers afflicted with the minds of jesters that succeed in bursting out and conquering their wits from time to time." She started up the slope, unbound red hair swirling around her shoulders.

A little way up she stopped, looked back at him over one shoulder, and asked, "Tuck me in, valiant leader?"

Florin hoped she was teasing.

"Their names were Harreth and Yorlin," the young Wizard of War said to Vangerdahast as they stood gazing at the two corpses in the dungeon cell. "We've learned that much. Worked for the traitor Lord Yellander. I know not how Harreth got down here or how he thought he'd free Yorlin, but whatever he did failed and killed them both."

The Royal Magician sighed. "A reasonable enough conclusion, lad—but wrong. Yorlin may be hanging in yon spell chains now, but he wasn't the prisoner I put in here nor the prisoner who was in here yestereve, when last I scryed the deep cells. There's a man missing from this cell, a war wizard traitor, and 'twouldn't be a daring wager to say he was freed through the actions of these two and rewarded them for it by slaying them." His mouth crooked into a smile of sorts. "Come to think of it, 'twas a reward, indeed."

The young war wizard blinked. "It was?"

"However he killed them, they enjoyed swifter and less painful deaths than I'd have given them for loosing Onsler Ruldroun upon the realm again."

"Father!" Torsard Spurbright's shout was shrill with genuine excitement. His sire hastened to hide the little note from Silverymoon he'd been re-reading, by using it to mark his place in the thick tome—a history of the life of Baerauble of Cormyr—he was currently reading. He closed the book just in time, as the younger Lord Spurbright burst into the room.

"Have you heard the news? A war wizard traitor's escaped from the dungeons under the Royal Court—the deep cells!"

Lord Elvarr Spurbright lifted both of his bushy eyebrows. "The deep cells?"

"Yes! Rude Rune or suchlike, he's called! He's been hanging down there in spell chains because there's something precious in his mind, so Old Thunderspells can't just kill him. Have you ever heard the like?"

The elder Lord Spurbright nodded slowly. "I have, as it happens. Whence came this news? And had it any *warning* attached to it?"

Torsard waved a dismissive hand. "Oh, the usual, 'Mind under your beds—he's everywhere! Everywhere!' clap-cackle!"

"Cackle that was first uttered by whom?" Elvarr asked again patiently.

His son blinked. "Oh. Ah, the Princess Alusair, they're saying."

Lord Elvarr Spurbright winced, then chuckled. "Oho. Dearest Vangerdahast isn't going to be pleased by *that.*"

"My old friend Yellander repaid me well. Those dolts didn't know who I was, but they certainly knew where I was and what they had to bring to me. They even brought along his written instructions, to make certain they did everything *just* right."

"And?"

"And I killed them, of course. Using the spell I'd been thirsting so long to use again—the spell, by the way, that means you dare not try to betray me—I drank their lives. Which is why I'm grinning like this. The life-energy of three men is raging in me like a flame!"

Telgarth Boarblade kept his face carefully expressionless. He had wondered why a man he remembered as a cold-eyed, veteran war wizard was babbling like a gloating maniac. So he hadn't been rescued by a complete madwits, after all—just someone *mostly* mad-witted.

So, does taking a threefold life need three fatal blade thrusts? Something to ponder . . .

Onsler Ruldroun babbled on. "The beauty of it is, Vangerdahast can't lay the smallest spell on me! No realm can confine me, and no—"

"What's that?" Boarblade snapped to shut off this flow of insanity. He cocked his head and turned as if he'd heard something.

The war wizard or, Boarblade supposed, ex-war wizard—what did they officially do to war wizard traitors, anyhail, besides execute them?—fell blessedly silent. His eyes narrowed, and he thrust his head forward to listen intently.

Then he waved his hand in a swift spell.

After a moment, he nodded, scooped something from a belt pouch, and handed it to Boarblade. It was a small, ordinary-looking stone.

"Well done, Boarblade. You repay my freeing of you already. Throw that at the man you'll find skulking outside. Hit him with it, but throw it slowly, mind. Underhanded, like a little girl swinging her arm back and forth to throw something as high as she can."

Boarblade nodded, not asking for an explanation, but the bright-eyed wizard gave him one anyway.

"I need time to speak the awakening word, whilst the stone is in the air—to turn it deadly to the next living thing it touches."

"There's only the one person outside?" Boarblade asked quietly, wondering what innocent he'd doomed by his ruse—but not caring much—as he hefted the stone in his hand. "I can't mistake my target?"

"Just the one man. Throw *slowly,* remember."

Boarblade nodded and went out. Well, he'd worked for worse masters.

As the two princesses settled themselves in the chairs to which the Royal Magician had waved them, Vangerdahast himself closed and bolted the door, took up a wand from a sidetable close to it, and cast a careful spell that made the walls, floor, and ceiling all glow a deep, rich blue.

There arose a short-lived singing sound, and as it died away, so did the radiance, leaving everything looking as it had before.

"The strongest warding I know," the wizard explained as he strode back to join them. "As I promised you, this meeting will be *private.*"

Princess Tanalasta's gaze was cool, and her question politely calm. "So, Lord Vangerdahast, do our royal parents know it is taking place?"

Alusair looked around the small, simply furnished parlor. She didn't recall ever having been in the room before, despite spending some years delighting in crawling, darting, and worming her way into everywhere in the Royal Palace. How had she never noticed that door at the back of the Horndragons' Chamber before?

Stlarning *magic.*

Tanalasta grew tired of waiting for a reply that evidently wasn't forthcoming.

"Yes, before you ask," Tanalasta said into the deepening silence, "we *are* wondering why you, ah, 'invited' us here. We are also expecting some answers when we ask things, Vangey. Being of royal blood and speaking to a courtier and all."

The Royal Magician settled himself in the chair facing the two princesses, surprised them both with a friendly little grin, and said, "Sorry, Tana. Deeper apologies if informality is going to offend you—either of you. A great part of my life has been spent watching over you and trying to shape you, however fumblingly and harshly, and I all too often think of you as something akin to granddaughters. I'm hoping, in the years ahead, we can even become friends."

"He wants something," Alusair told her sister.

"Well of *course* he wants something," Tanalasta said. "Everyone we ever see or meet always does. However, I quite take your point—this wizard never bothers to be polite to anyone except Mother and Father unless he wants something he can't force or command out of them."

She turned her gaze back to the Royal Magician. "However, being as we are speaking in private, I don't care in the slightest if you call me Tana, Vangey." She glanced at her sister again. "Loos?"

Alusair shrugged. "He can call me anything he wants. If he gets too rude, I'll switch from 'Vangey' to 'Thunderpot.' Now can we get on with this?"

"Yes." Vangerdahast sighed with just a hint of weariness. "Why don't we?"

"Buried, and the manure pile heaped back over the grave," Boarblade reported, deciding not to use any extra words. Not when his babbling master could supply far more than would ever be needed.

"Good," Ruldroun said. "Close the door."

When Boarblade turned back, the former war wizard was standing silently in the far corner of the room with two wands in his hands, both of them trained on Boarblade.

The long runner-rug that had been lying on the floor between the door and that back corner had been twitched aside to reveal a sequence of chalked circles, like a row of stepping stones, each touching its fellows, between where he was standing and where his new master was regarding him from. The dangers were very clear.

"So, Telgarth Boarblade," Ruldroun said quietly, "the time has come for a little truth on your part. You are a mage of some small ability, yes?"

"Yes."

"You have been a Zhentarim for years."

"I have."

"You have not mentioned this to me."

"You've never asked nor intimated a desire to know about my past."

"Your past? Are you now intimating that you are no longer a Zhent? And will not work with them again?"

Boarblade nodded. "Yes. When you snatched me out of my imprisonment and offered me service with you, I accepted, and that ended all previous allegiances. If you should ever order me to feign loyal membership in the Brotherhood, I will do so—but even before being taken by the war wizards, I had decided that the Zhentarim were fast becoming a den of vipers who all hunted for themselves, exhibiting only enough obedience to avoid being counted among the hunted. A Cormyr stripped of cohesive war wizards would be a benefit to all, so I continued with my assigned task, but I had already begun to work on a means of faking my own death and disappearing. My judgment of the Brotherhood has not changed."

"You still seek a Cormyr where bickering factions of nobles rise to dominance, and the Obarskyrs lose the iron control their Wizards of War grant them?"

"I believe that would be better for all than the Cormyr we stand in now. I now seek nothing but what you want me to seek."

"Well said. Spells laid upon your mind prevent me from prying into it or affecting your feelings and views. Banish them."

Boarblade sighed. "I cannot. They were laid upon me by Zhentarim far more powerful than either of us. I cannot even begin to touch them. If you or another broke them, doing so would not only drive me mad, it would instantly alert senior Zhents as to what had happened and precisely where I was. It would also make me their tool to work through. I hardly think it likely you would want to face the spells of Lord Manshoon coming out of a body he doesn't mind risking in the slightest."

Ruldroun's eyes flickered. "That would not be my preferred choice of situations, no. So I must trust you—yet I cannot trust you."

Boarblade shrugged. "Consider. Every man in all Faerûn who is not a priest or wizard of power has to trust others without seeing into their minds—and many of them manage to do so. Sometimes that trust is justified and even rewarded. I intend to justify and reward your trust. Blood oath, if you prefer?"

Ruldroun could not hide his surprise. "That's the very spell I was going to insist upon. Better and better. Telgarth Boarblade, I could get to like you."

"And I, you, my lord. Even after the killings and betrayals start."

"I confess myself delighted with your candor, Vangey," Princess Tanalasta said. "I would go so far as to say I doubt very much if anyone in Cormyr right now is having as blunt and candid a converse about matters of the realm and loyalty and other weighty concerns."

"See me as pleased, too," Alusair agreed, "yet annoyed that you've never seen fit to treat us as this close to equals before."

Vangerdahast sighed. "Forgive me, Highnesses, but before now, you frankly weren't ready for this. Oh, I've no doubt you *thought* yourselves ready. Your royal father did, too, quite a bit younger than either of you are now. Yet he wasn't ready until he was almost a decade older than you, Tana. He was still putting his desires of the moment before his love for the realm."

"His desires of the moment?" Alusair said. "I'd say he does that still. A chambermaid here, a passing merchant's wife there, a—"

"Loos!" Tana snapped. "That'll do!"

"Hoy! I thought we were being blunt and candid," the younger princess replied. "Or are you still trying to set limits, the way Vangey here is?"

"Highness," the wizard said reprovingly, holding up a hand to signal Tanalasta not to make angry reply, "as I've told you, I am not—"

"Oh, but you are," Alusair retorted. "You control every conversation you ever have, Vangey. Even when answering direct orders or queries from the king and queen. By what you say and don't say—and what you refuse or oh-so-gravely warn must not be discussed—you set limits. You set limits for nigh everything in the realm. 'Tis one of the things you *do*. Someone has to do it, I suppose, though why you, I've never found a good answer for. My mother the queen would be far better at it, and even Alaphondar. I—"

"Loos, please, enough," Tanalasta interrupted. "I agree with all you're saying, but I find it beside the point, unless we're somehow going to murder this man sitting facing us. Decrying what he does and is simply wastes all our time. I want to hear rather more blunt truth from him, in case we never have such a chance as this again." She leaned forward in her chair and said to Vangerdahast, "So tell us a story, wizard. About why the Knights of Myth Drannor were sent away and what's been happening with them, and as much as you see fit to reveal about the conspiracy within the Wizards of War—and what *you* were just up to in the Lost Palace."

"Very well," Vangerdahast agreed. "Where to begin?"

"We can begin with my expressing, as politely as I can," Alusair said, "what my elder sister is too well-bred and polite to say: how *damned* angry we both are, wizard, that we didn't even *know* the Lost Palace was anything more than a legend! You call *this* preparing us to guide—or in her case, rule—the realm?"

The Royal Magician sighed. "I suppose you'll explode if I say you weren't yet ready to be told such things?"

"Yes," Alusair told him sweetly. "And all over you, too."

Vangerdahast didn't—quite—smile. "Then, being by far the wisest man in all Cormyr, I'll not say that."

Despite her best attempts not to, Princess Tanalasta snorted.

Chapter 19
DRAWN DAGGERS HAUNTING ME

In dark corners of the room I see you
Eyes like drawn daggers haunting me
Cold so cold my breast you pass through
Hunting me, hunting me endlessly
Why did you kill yourself and leave me?
Dark self-slaying can never be right
Hear me my love, I do so want thee
Come a-haunting, come chill me this night.

Jorn Tareth, Bard of Marsember
From the ballad "Haunting Me"
First performed in the Year of the Blade

The rapture that had made Onsler Ruldroun babble so excitedly was lessening. He was becoming more and more a watchful, close-mouthed, careful man.

His true self, presumably.

"There is one thing I would like to know, Lord," Boarblade said before Ruldroun became even more taciturn. "You impersonated the wizard Gheldaert Howndroe as fire investigator and wrote about that—or did *not* write about that, rather—in a war wizard duty book. Why? It has set war wizards to being suspicious of each other, and the royal family and certain high-ranking courtiers to watching closely the Wizards of War. Wouldn't it have been wiser to let matters stand as casually as they have always done, with no one's suspicions aroused about anything? Easier for you to work and with less risk of being noticed?"

"Easier is not a goal I strive for," Ruldroun replied, "and never has been. Inside the war wizards, I wanted Howndroe under suspicion so as to hamper his work. Outside their ranks, I wanted the wider realm to foster renewed suspicion that the Wizards of War are corrupt, and deadly conspiracies actively flourish within it, to this day. Wizards suspicious of their fellows are far more likely to hesitate in battle or not risk their own necks as much or even refuse to obey orders they disagree with. I need them that way, for my little scheme to work. And as the Lords Yellander and

Eldroon discovered, I will do almost anything to aid and further my scheme."

"I thought you were working for them."

"I was—skillfully enough that they thought so, when in truth they were doing my bidding, never realizing it. Time and again they ordered me to advance my own aims, thinking the plotting was theirs. Their deaths robbed me of many resources and of the convenience of having them to take the blame for whatever I did but hampered me no more than that. I am merely going to order you to do what they would have sent Brorn Hallomond and Eerikarr Steldurth to do. Get after these Knights, slaughter them without being seen by anyone, get their bodies hidden—or better, devoured or burned to ashes—and gain possession of the Pendant of Ashaba."

Boarblade nodded. "And when they disappear and the pendant of lordship with them? You think Vangerdahast isn't going to send someone to check on the Knights? You think the Harpers won't, with Storm Silverhand living right there? Nor the Witch of Shadowdale meddle?"

Ruldroun gestured with one of his wands as if it were a baton of the Court master-of-pages.

Five amorphous humps emerged out of the folds of the curled and twisted runner-rug and flowed a little way toward Boarblade before rearing up like the arms of eager recruits, foolishly volunteering.

Five hargaunts.

The wizard smiled. "Four men I yet hold will be going with you. You five will become the Knights of Myth Drannor—and I'll bestow memories in you all that will show Khelben Blackstaff working this impersonation."

Boarblade stroked his chin thoughtfully.

"That might work, at that," he said. "But there are six Knights, not five."

Ruldroun shrugged. "You choose which one dies."

"So this Lost Palace of Esparin has been used by Baerauble, Amedahast, Thanderahast, and all the rest for *centuries* to imprison every last war wizard or other mage in the kingdom who went mad?" Princess Tanalasta's incredulity had lifted her voice to a mere shred away from a shriek.

"Well, yes," Vangerdahast said. "As a preferred alternative to blasting them to death after we've battled them up and down the realm and scared all Cormyreans into fearing creeping madness afflicts every wizard in the process."

"And you've been sending loyal Cormyreans as well as passing opportunists off to unwittingly camp above this place for years, luring them with the promise of becoming Baron of the Stonelands?" Alusair said. "Before all the Watching Gods, wizard, you can sit here and say this and dare—*dare*—to sit in judgment of anyone else in all the realm?"

"Highnesses, Highnesses!" Vangerdahast said hastily. "Tana, Loos, *please!* This has been policy in Cormyr since its founding. There are mad elves in there, from the days when forests covered the land and your ancestors lived in cottages on the water's edge, clustered around log-wharves that had to be rebuilt after the clawings of the winter ice every spring!"

" 'And as all men have been dastardly villains before me,' " Tanalasta quoted the lines of a play, " 'I find I have no other option but to be dastardly in my turn—' "

"Lasses, please! 'Tis not like that at all!"

"So how then is it, wizard?" Alusair spat. "Convince us with your oh-so-clever tongue!" She drew back her sleeve to reveal a spell-warding amulet chained to it. "And kindly refrain from trying to spell-cozen my mind. This isn't the only shield against such tricks I'm wearing!"

"Princess! I would never—"

"No-ho? You stlarning well *invariably*, Thunderspells!"

The Royal Magician of Cormyr stared at her, face red with anger and embarrassment—a face that was now quivering. Then, suddenly, he burst out laughing, hiding his face in his hands, shaking his head, and finally throwing up his hands in surrender.

"Well," he said, when he could speak again, "you have me there. Dead guilty, as accused."

He looked from one simmering princess to the other, seeing no smiles. Triumph glittered in Alusair's eyes, while disappointment ruled Tanalasta.

Sighing, he looked down at his fingertips and told them, "I can see this is going to be a *long* talk among the three of us. Very well, put yourselves in my boots for a moment. You are newly in the post of Royal Magician, learn of this particular secret of the realm, and—do what? If you don't like binding mad undead spellcasters away in a 'lost' underground stronghold, what then do you do with them? No blustering, please. Try to make that decision calmly."

Silence fell.

Tanalasta pursed her lips. "Are they all mad? Forever?"

Vangerdahast spread his hands. "Who can know? There are scores of them, some of them so old their names have been forgotten, and we have no precise knowledge of their abilities. Some may be failing and diminishing, and some growing stronger. The realm lacks any secure place where we can take them, one at a time, to try to work with them—or on them."

Alusair asked quietly, "Are they all liches?"

"No, but the enchantments of the place seem to turn the living into undead, rather than allowing natural deaths. The imprisoned squabble constantly but rarely seem to destroy each other. There is some evidence that the Lost Palace restores or heals or however you want to term 'repairing damaged undead.' Some of them were foes of the realm in life, some loyal war wizards, some were traitors or noble dabblers who went too far—and some have Obarskyr blood, however illegitimate their births from the view of a herald considering inheritance."

Tanalasta's eyes narrowed. "And if they are all freed? Disaster?"

"Grudges pursued, for those who can still think coherently. The others would be like mad dogs, unleashed to wander. I almost lost my life not very long ago, rebinding them all."

Tanalasta shuddered. "You were reversing this Unbinding, then?"

"I was."

"How?" Alusair snapped.

"Forgive me, Princesses, but revealing to you the details of the spells would be both foolish—someone who caught you unawares with the right magic could compel you to speak of them—and unhelpful. Neither of you possesses the Art to work such magics."

"We are both aware of that, Vangey," Alusair said coldly. "What I was trying to ask was how you managed the rebinding, alone, after shooing Laspeera and everyone else out of the place. An important war wizard traitor, or so you have given us to believe, somehow escaped while you were busy in the Lost Palace. It is conceivable that in the future you might again be busy or dead when the need recurs. So consider telling us what you did vital to the security of the realm. As an Obarskyr, and therefore someone you are *supposed* to obey without question or reservation, I order you to tell me. Now."

Tanalasta gave her younger sister a pained look, but Alusair merely lofted her eyebrows and told her, "If I'm polite to the man, he glibly dances around telling us things we want to know and calmly maintains his 'I will decide what is good for you to know' superiority. That has to be wiped away, as of about six seasons ago. If I'm old enough to bear royal heirs or end up warming the Dragon Throne if calamity strikes our family, I'm old enough to be told such secrets." She aimed her chin back at the Royal Magician and added, "So tell us. Plainly and completely. And while you're at it, try to make me believe that Obarskyr king after king—and queen after queen, too—knew of this and approved of it down the years."

Vangerdahast sighed, looked down at his hands for a moment, then said, "Some of them never knew of it. The Royal Magicians always have, but—"

"My, my," Alusair said, her tone dripping with acid, "*such* deep and abiding loyalty to the Dragon Throne!"

Vangerdahast muttered a curse, drew in a deep breath, put a bright smile on his face, and said heartily, "*Well*, now, where to begin?"

"What's that?" Doust hissed, leaning forward to listen intently.

Florin held up a hand for silence and did the same thing. The faint rustling moved southeast through the brush below, before it was too far away to hear.

"Something small," the ranger said calmly. "Probably a rat. All that noise, the scuttling . . . nothing to worry over."

"Among our larger worries?"

"They're only worries if you let them be. Think of something else."

The priest sat staring out into the night for another long breath before asking almost reluctantly, "Such as . . . ?"

Florin gave his anxious friend a grin. "Women you haven't met yet, waiting in Shadowdale?"

"Florin! I'm a priest, stlarn it!"

"Doesn't Tymora regard holiness as boldly taking chances?"

"Well, yes, but—"

"So for once inexperience will serve you well. Blunder here, stumble there, please Lady Luck no end!"

"*Thank* you," Doust said. "I think." A long breath later, he added a chuckle.

"Hmm?" Florin asked.

"It shouldn't be too bad—the blundering, I mean. I'll just watch what Stoop says and does and do the opposite."

The ranger nodded but said gravely, "Tymora's going to be disappointed."

Doust gave him a gentle shove and chuckled again.

"No," Vangerdahast said, "that was no leak at all. I intended that the Princess Alusair be the one to warn all Cormyr of Ruldroun's escape and so alert folk to watch for him."

"To spare *you* having to announce a failure on the part of the Wizards of War," Tanalasta said.

"Not at all. In my judgment, citizens will be swifter to aid and please their youngest, most vulnerable princess than help the hated Royal Magician with his latest blunder. If Alusair cries warning, they'll see the problem as the kingdoms'—and so, theirs. If I do, they will growl that I should clean up my own problems. More importantly, it was time to begin to establish your sister's image and role in the eyes of the citizenry."

"Oh?" Tanalasta snapped. "And when do you start to establish *my* image and role?"

"Your image and role were set at your birth, because you are the heir. Alusair's is the one the Crown must establish—lest some foe establish it, where we have left silence."

"And *you*, wizard, are the Crown?"

"I am. Not the king, nor any challenge to him, but the Crown. I serve, defend, and maintain the Crown—the image the ruling Obarskyr dons, just like the literal circlet on his or her brow, every morning."

"And if I happen to believe differently?" Tanalasta asked very quietly, in the voice both her sister and the Royal Magician had learned meant trouble.

Vangerdahast leaned forward to meet her gaze directly and said, "To borrow a phrase from the Sage of Shadowdale, that's a bridge we'll burn when we're both standing on it. If I am still Royal Magician or Court Wizard when you ascend to rule this land, we will talk more of this."

"Talk!" Tanalasta spat. "Talk and more talk and change *nothing!*"

"Not so! The Royal Magician and the ruler of the realm must agree on who does what to helm Cormyr and where they are trying to take it. What the Crown is and how it works must always change until that agreement is reached."

"Point taken," Alusair said, and she held up a staying hand. "We could sit here arguing the future of the realm until it *is* the future of the realm. Let's get back to this Ruldroun and what's besetting us *now.*" She wagged a finger at Vangerdahast and added, "And don't forget to explain to us about the archwizard Ondel, and Sundraer the She-dragon, and this burning barn I've heard about."

Vangerdahast blinked at her, astonishment clear on his face.

"Oh, yes, Royal Magician," the younger princess said, "where you somehow neglect to mention things to me, certain Harpers who stop by the Palace from time to time tell me far more. They seem to have this odd notion that the royal family of Cormyr just might have the right—and the need—to be informed about matters of the realm, rather than being kept in the dark by courtiers. Who by doing so, wizards or not, are arguably guilty of a quaint little something called 'treason.' And before you bluster, bear in mind that I'm merely reporting their common notion. One that I happen to share."

"As do I," Tanalasta said.

Silence fell, and neither princess rushed to break it. They were too busy sitting in silent fascination, watching the Royal Magician wince—then blush a deep, rich scarlet.

Andaero Hardtower was not in a good mood. *Why* did the Brotherhood persist in allowing such dolts into their ranks?

And why did they all end up in his lap?

"Hearken," he said to the sullen mageling standing in front of him, "and hearken well. When you are given a specific and detailed order by a member of our Brotherhood who outranks you—"

The glowering mageling's face changed, eyes lighting up in interest that swiftly became alarm as they stared over Hardtower's shoulder, resentment giving way to astonishment.

Hardtower sighed, irritation flaring. "The oldest tricks not only don't fool us, young Galaeren, using them shames you—or should. Why, we—"

A merry chime sounded right behind Hardtower's back. It was the last thing he ever heard.

He had time to identify it as his own shielding warning him and to wonder what could possibly breach a five-layered magical shield so swiftly and quietly, before the Sword That Never Sleeps burst through him.

Vangerdahast sighed, steepled his fingers, and rested his chin on them.

"Deciding what to forget to tell us?" Alusair asked.

He gave her a pained look. "Onsler Ruldroun was a Wizard of War, yes. Stolid, strong in his Art but unambitious, and so not all that accomplished in the more powerful magics. Which was fine. I have an endless need for such mages, so long as their lack of ambition doesn't slide into sloth. He worked in the Royal Court, gleaning information from the many documents and reports that are sent there daily, and following up on interesting matters. Exciting, thus far?"

The two princesses gave him identical withering stares. "Say on, wizard," Tanalasta commanded.

Bowing his head in silent assent, Vangey did so. "Unbeknownst to the rest of us, a curious and ancient item of magic came into Ruldroun's possession, probably two seasons ago when he attended some family funerals in Marsember. It enabled him to cloak his innermost thoughts from all spells, even when mind-speaking to fellow war wizards. I believe he met the traitor lords Yellander—whom he had befriended years earlier—and Eldroon at one of those funerals and began working for them. He gave them some private Court and Wizard of War information. This was noticed, and he was imprisoned when we discovered we couldn't read his mind. In captivity, he remained uncooperative, until two agents of Lord Yellander found and acted upon written instructions Yellander'd left as to how to find and contact Ruldroun in an emergency, and telling them to take along certain items of magic. We believe Ruldroun earlier gave these to Yellander in a gesture of 'betray me not, and I'll not cross you' trust, but they served Ruldroun well when the agents reached his dungeon cell. He used them to get free, then killed the agents, leaving one of them in the chains that had prevented him from working spells. He then escaped. We assume he means us ill but are uncertain of both his whereabouts and his precise intentions regarding Cormyr."

"Why, if you have been so ruthlessly high-handed on other occasions, did you just imprison this traitor?" Tanalasta asked. "If you can quietly toss any madwits you please into the Lost Palace, why didn't you and Laspeera and anyone else just force your way into this Ruldroun's mind to learn what you had to know?"

The Royal Magician looked embarrassed. "We dared not. We had trusted him enough to let him be part of the warning magics laid upon *your* minds, when you were both infants."

"What? *What* warning magics?" Tanalasta cried.

Beside her, Alusair nodded grimly and shot her sister a triumphant "told you so" look.

"Shieldings that would prevent sudden magical attempts to invade your minds, drawing them instead into those of six Wizards of War—for each of you. This foiled most such attacks completely and warned us of their launching."

"Foiled?"

"Oh, yes. Many wizards—Zhentarim, wizards hired by Sembians seeking to gain future influence in Cormyr, a few independent spell-hurlers, and no fewer than twoscore mages hired by various noble families of the realm—tried to influence or read or control or just destroy your minds before either of you could walk."

"So is this Ruldroun still linked to my mind?" Alusair asked. "Or Tana's?"

"Tanalasta's, yes. Or so we believe. That mind-shielding item he gained prevents us from being certain."

"So this is another of your brilliant successes in judging loyalty," the younger princess said. "Like Applethorn and Margaster and—"

"Princess Alusair," Vangerdahast snapped back at her, "no wizard can or should—I can well imagine how you'd shriek at me if I tried!—mind-control even handfuls of Cormyreans. We are all served by many, many loyal Wizards of War. The few who go bad stand as *rare* examples of how power corrupts."

"I can think of many loyal Cormyreans who would name our Royal Magician among the ranks of the corrupt," Tanalasta said. "Tell me, what would you say to them?"

Vangerdahast sighed. "That I am not, and they have only to watch me to see that. Unless they don't want to see it. They may disagree with me as to what a loyal or honest courtier would do if in my boots, but few of them can properly appreciate what wizards do and face, let alone know all the secrets I do and the worries I have. If they knew just a little of what I hear and ponder and know, they might see me very differently."

"Fair enough," Tanalasta replied. "So tell us some of these secrets."

"Such as all about Ondel, and the She-dragon, and the barn," Alusair said.

Vangerdahast sighed again. "Very well. Ondel was a wizard of great power, a Sembian resident in Saerloon who was of interest to the Crown because he'd begun buying up farmland in Cormyr, near Marsember. Someone murdered him, probably an assassin or team of killers hired by a Sembian rival or perhaps someone in Westgate. We investigated but haven't learned who was to blame. We *suspected* that in his Cormyrean purchases he may have been acting for one of the exiled former noble families of Cormyr, but that's mere supposition on our part. He was cut apart, and pieces of him left all over Shadowdale—another place where he'd started buying land. Wizard of War Lorbryn Deltalon—who is *not* suspected of being any sort of traitor, by the way—did most of the looking into Ondel's death. None of you were told about this because we could learn nothing definite touching on the security or governance of Cormyr and because we delve into literally thousands of such matters every year. Would you *want* to sit through my filling your ears about odd murders of Sembian wizards, and half a hundred other things, for half a day, *every* day?"

"No, and I grant your point, Vangey. What about Sundraer the She-dragon?"

"Also a Sembian. Of interest to us because she was Ondel's lover, when in human form. She died some years back, but aside from some handfuls of valuables she shared with Ondel, no one ever found her hoard. It's been local legend in Saerloon for nigh a decade. The usual rumor after rumor about its great size and someone finding it. Well, we believe someone finally *did* find it—somewhere in the Thunder Peaks. Just where, when, who, and what they found . . . again, just guesses and rumors. Nothing to share with Obarskyrs who have real concerns about Cormyr to deal with. The Harpers take an interest in rumors and odd happenings just as we do, but I can't think why a princess of Cormyr would want to, unless nobles or courtiers or rising personages of this realm were directly involved."

Alusair nodded. "The barn fire?"

"Barns burn down all the time. If there are any suspicions about a barn fire in Cormyr, we investigate. This one was in our realm, and it spat out lightning bolts and green flames while burning. Therefore magic was involved, and we are investigating. If anything worth reporting comes to light, I'll certainly share it with you."

"See that you do, Royal Magician," Tanalasta said. "As you've no doubt gathered by now, Loos and I are both tired of being treated like brainless children."

Vangerdahast nodded, looking a little weary. "Have you heard enough for now?" he asked. "I'd think hearing all I hear and worrying about all I think about would soon darken your hearts and lives and make you rue being born an Obarskyr in Cormyr. Believe me, both of you: it has been my intent and my hard work to shield you both from as much of this as possible, so you can enjoy your lives before the heavy burdens begin—the burdens that, once taken up, will only be lifted from your shoulders by death."

"So is your heart darkened, Vangey?" Alusair asked, sounding almost gentle. "Do you have nightmares? What haunts you?"

The Royal Magician regarded her gravely and said quietly, "Dreams of drawn daggers haunt me. Picturing your royal mother weeping in grief haunts me. Seeing sorrow and disappointment in your father's eyes when he looks at me after I've been too slow to see peril and disaster has harmed any of his family. Those are among the foremost things that haunt me, but my collection of hauntings is not a small one." He rose from his chair. "Now, if you'll permit me the impertinence, what I've heard out of your mouths here in this room suggests to me that you've both become quite old enough to enjoy a stiff drink. I know I need one."

Doust yawned. Again. "Isn't it time to wake Jhess and Stoop?" he asked, fighting down yet another yawn.

"Yes," Florin said, leaning close to dig steel-hard fingers into Doust's ear and bring him instantly and very painfully wide awake, "but see that you do it *quietly*. And weapons out, all."

Doust blinked. "Why? Is there someone out there?"

"Someone. And a beast, too. They're watching us."

As he said these words, Florin rose, his drawn sword moving from across his knees to ready in his hand.

As it happened, he was just in time.

Chapter 20
TALONS IN THE NIGHT

Now dripping red where once so white
Fangs well fed flash not so bright
Yet no gentler now their thirsty bite
Fear always lurking talons in the night

Lharanla Tassalan, Wandering Bard
from the ballad "In The Night"
first heard circa the Year of the Grimoire

He had to leave.

Sooner or later a Wizard of War would discover some need to use a spell-shielded chamber and walk in on him. Yet he might never again have this much safe, quiet solitude in which to think.

And by Mystra, Azuth, and the Purple Dragon, he had to think.

Cormyr was a deathtrap for him, now and henceforth. Even if Vangerdahast should happen to drop dead before the next highsun—and he'd not be surprised in the slightest if the Royal Magician turned out to be one of those mages who has to be slain six or seven times before it worked—war wizards did not forget.

Not that Onsler Ruldroun had ever been bright lightning and gasps of awe as a war wizard. He had managed to steal a few spell scrolls down the years and retain a spellbook that should have been passed on to Old Thunderspells, but that still left him as "competent, but no more." He couldn't hope to challenge anyone but a fumbling lackspells and survive.

So he would have to be what he'd been before Yellander's gold had seduced him. *Very* careful. Until the bright empire could be founded, another mistake would mean death.

Which was why he'd dared to use the portals to take himself here after Boarblade was safe. He would have to disappear now and keep hidden, trailing along after Boarblade and the four. He'd keep close watch over their doings but stay unseen, using his spells to aid them only when he could do so undetected.

The four were on their way to join Boarblade already. Only the second man to whom he'd whispered had refused, and he'd managed to stuff that body down into the sewers. If he could manage it, those would be last individuals he would ever meet and have dealings with as Onsler Ruldroun.

Careful and cautious, that would be his way. From now on, he would work only through others, always hiding his true face.

As if it had heard his thought, his favorite hargaunt emerged at the top of the tapestry it had been hiding behind and flowed down the rich fabric toward him.

He reached out a hand to it, and it curled itself off the tapestry like a caterpillar to flow along his arm.

Ruldroun embraced it, kissing and then licking its wrinkled, purplish-brown warmth. It shifted in hue to match his skin and nuzzled him, emitting a purr he could feel more than hear.

His only friend, perhaps his only lover . . .

"Mother of my precious ones, I'll hide my real face using you," he murmured to it. "And when Shadowdale is ours, my beloved, you shall have the rewards I've promised, that you've been *so* patiently waiting for all these years. Your picks of the best humans to subvert and conquer: the strongest war wizard and Zhentarim agents who come skulking, the best Harper mages, perhaps even a Chosen of Mystra, if we dare that high. Persons of importance, who, when they return to the realms you desire to rule, can get you to rulers and those who choose rulers . . . and the *real* conquest of Faerûn can begin. Unnoticed by those who bluster and blow warhorns and gallop under banners."

He was humming happily to match its purrings now, as he tenderly stroked the shifting, caressingly moving bulk of the hargaunt.

"A hargaunt empire, where humans made docile reap rich harvests and burn out diseases and stand together against monstrous foes."

A sudden grin split Onsler Ruldroun's weary face, and he said to the silent room around him, "And Telgarth Boarblade wonders why I hold my tongue so tightly!"

Flowing from his cheek across his face, the hargaunt purred.

Belthonder prided himself on never uttering an excuse—and never needing to. Once he'd had to tell Vangerdahast, "Not yet," but the Royal Magician had known he was right and had smiled and nodded his approval.

Vangey knew who were his best Wizards of War.

And if Marim Belthonder was no longer as young and supple and devastatingly handsome as he'd once been, he was wiser, more artful in his persuasions, and just as tall. The women of Cormyr still smiled invitingly when he looked their way, which sometimes accomplished half his work for him.

Now, for instance. This path led to a glade where a certain nobleman's wife would be waiting for him, cloaked against the night cold but probably wearing nothing much beneath it save boots. The moment his seeking spell was done, to make sure she'd come alone and wasn't being followed by anyone suspicious, he would put on his very best smile and go to meet her.

Belthonder flexed his fingers before working the spell—precise and elegant, that was how all castings should be—and stepped away from the trunk of the sheltering shadowtop to give himself room.

The Sword That Never Sleeps promptly sliced through his throat and several of his fingertips as it raced past.

It looped and came racing back to bury itself quillons-deep in Belthonder's heart before the body had even begun to topple.

Then it twisted and flew backward, freeing itself from flesh and bone. Glistening with the best war wizard blood, the sword flew away, vanishing back into the night.

Armaukran's enchantments were peerless in some regards but merely adequate in others. Old Ghost was almost out of earshot before the noblewoman's screams began.

Drathar had no intention of playing the dead hero. So far as he knew, no Brotherhood superior was scrying him now. How he carried out the orders Hardtower had relayed to him was his business. Stop the Knights from reaching Shadowdale, kill as many as possible, and above all get the Pendant of Ashaba. Clear enough.

Yet there was no need to try for all three goals in one fray. That probably *would* get him killed, going up against a chartered band of adventurers. Killing one or two and wounding others so as to slow their travel would be solid work for this night.

So he could hang back and use his spells to watch. Or to whisk himself away if the need arose.

Let the dirlagraun—displacer beasts, most mages called them— take on the Knights of Myth Drannor and die in his place. The sword-sharp spell he'd cast on its claws had lengthened them into razor-keen, hooked talons as long as sabers, and the shielding spell he'd cast on the beast should hurl the first spell they sent at the dirlagraun right back where it had come from.

Perhaps—just perhaps—that would be enough. If not, there would be other nights before even Knights on fast horses could reach Shadowdale. And these Knights were walking.

And every night would hold another dirlagraun—or something far more interesting, if his spells could find and conquer it.

At them, my champion! He sent that burning thought and pulled out of its mind. There were two priests and a mageling up on that ledge.

Eagerly, barely needing his urging, the dirlagraun bounded up the scree, loose stones hissing and rolling under its paws—and pounced.

Omgryn cared not a whit if others got the praise. What mattered to him was that *he* knew—along with Belthonder, Vangerdahast, Laspeera, and even Queen Filfaeril and her lord husband, King Azoun himself—that he and Belthonder were the Royal Magician's best war wizards. The spellhurlers Vangey turned to when Cormyr stood in need, the two who could get the hardest tasks done—and do them well.

Which was why he was stepping out of a noble lord's hunting lodge at this darksome time of night, between two spell-frozen guard dogs, to pick his way around twoscore guards who were now snoring their ways through service to four different masters.

Behind them, those four masters sat slumped and silent, in no need of bodyguards nor any other sort of servant ever again.

They were the lord's second son, a Sembian trader, a merchant of Zhentil Keep, and a Dragon Cultist poisoner. All sitting dead around a table behind Omgryn, with the fire that would consume the poisons they'd been trading, their bodies, and the lodge, too, magically kindling among their unseeing faces.

Omgryn had to hurry. Deltalon and the others would be waiting, and it was risky to keep a portal open for long in this country, with that pulsing glow that drew wild beasts like nothing else. They—

The flying sword that swooped out of the night almost slashed Hendran Omgryn's head right off his shoulders. His head bobbled loosely, gore spraying in all directions from beneath it, as its jaw wagged up and down in a vain, dying frenzy that failed to frame the words Omgryn's darkening mind was so desperately trying to shout.

"The Sword That Never Sleeps!" he wanted to cry. "Beware! It's real! It's here in Cormyr! All Wizards of War, beware!"

All he could manage was a wet, energetic gurgling. Until the racing sword severed what was left of his neck and sent his head spinning off into the darkness. His body flopped down into brittle shrubs with a crash, and the head bounced twice, amid much smaller crashes, then rolled.

Almost to the boots of Lorbryn Deltalon, as he hastened forward in a crouch, a wand ready in his hand and two younger war wizards at his back.

"Is it—?" one of them gasped.

"It is," Deltalon said, backing away as the first flames started to lick up out of the lodge windows. "Back to Tsantress, and through the portal. I saw what did this."

He worked a shielding spell faster than the two younger war wizards had ever seen one cast before. *"Move!"*

They turned and ran. As he pelted along in their wake, hoping his shielding would fend off a long, deadly sword swooping point-first at his back out of the night, Deltalon wondered what he dared tell them.

Best discuss this with Vangerdahast first. Word of these slayings was spreading among the Wizards of War but was being kept as secret as possible from the general populace. Not that Cormyreans were fools. The whispers were flying about the realm already.

About as energetically as that deadly sword.

Deltalon shivered as the glow of the portal loomed up, the anxious face of Tsantress beside it.

"Get through, lass!" he panted. "Unless you'd prefer a brief new career as a pincushion!"

Then he launched himself into the air, hoping he could move faster than the sword.

"Tluin!" Semoor shouted in horror, really coming awake for the first time. Gleaming amber eyes were staring right at him as the fanged jaws beneath them opened wide. It was blue-black and six-legged, this beast, with two tentacles thrusting up into the air from its shoulders, long whip-like things that swirled overhead. It was large and sinuously graceful, like an emaciated panther, and—

It lunged at him.

He clenched his teeth and swung his mace—and a flaring-ended tentacle slapped out of the night to smash it away, arm and all, snatching him aside from those jaws and flinging him into Islif. They crashed and rolled into the scree.

Behind him, a spell-glow bloomed—and then flashed. Jhessail shrieked, Florin cursed, and Pennae shouted, *"No* spells, holynoses!"

Semoor devoted himself to frantic praying and even more frantic clawing his way back to his feet, so he could whirl around and watch—

Doust get raked with huge talons that tore away his breastplate with a shriek of metal that drowned out the Tymoran's own frightened cry. Then Doust was slammed to the ground by those two great tentacles that struck and struck and struck again.

Florin sprang in to cut at the tentacles, sword in one hand and dagger in the other, and the beast rounded on him with frightening speed. The ranger's blades seemed to hack at the monster yet slice only empty air, again and again.

" 'Tis a dirlagraun!" Islif shouted from nearby. She charged past Semoor, heading for the beast's rump. *"Wide* slashes, Florin! Swing wide!"

A tentacle came at her as the great catlike thing turned its head and snarled. Semoor stopped staring and ran forward. Anger was rising in him, red and warm, as he rushed along, a good four running strides behind Islif. Her slash drove the tentacle away behind her, letting her run right in and spring onto the thing's bony back—dagger first.

It was a small fang, but it bit deep. The dirlagraun roared and arched, bellowing its pain at the stars, and Florin hacked at its throat and forelegs.

Its roar became a wild shriek as it backed hastily away from the ranger, shaking a gory limb that bore a paw no longer—and Islif clung to its neck, drawing daggers from all over herself and driving them in as she went, hurrying to the head, thrust after thrust.

The displacer beast shuddered and thrashed under her in obvious pain, arching its tentacles up to flail at her as hard as it could, battering her.

It kicked at Florin with its talons and snapped at him, too. He ducked under its belly to slash at it from beneath; crouching between its legs, he could hardly miss.

Semoor reached the dirlagraun and struck aside its ratlike tail with his mace. Rushing to its nearest hind leg, he planted himself, took his mace in both hands, and swung.

Part way through it, his mace smashed into something hard that gave slightly as the dirlagraun squalled and hopped, its numbed rear leg threatening to buckle under it.

Semoor found himself tumbling face-first into the stones, dumped aside in the frantic thrashings of a beast that was simply trying to get away. The beast slid and flailed its way back down the scree slope. Riding it, Islif drove her dagger into one amber eye—and was flung off as the thing reared, bucked, shrieked, and tried to roll, all at once.

The dirlagraun landed heavily, rolled, and bounced to its feet, only to stagger sideways—with Florin racing along amid wildly spraying stones to stay with it, slashing again and again at its throat.

Stabbing tentacles finally sent him sprawling, but the dirlagraun behind them was doing no more fighting.

It was scrambling wildly away, dying and in pain.

Leaving Doust and Jhessail down and Pennae—where was Pennae?

As if in reply to Semoor's silent question, a man cursed somewhere out in the night, and Pennae called, "Like it? The next one'll find your heart!"

She grinned down at Semoor, a dagger glittering in her hand, and he decided it was a good time to faint. So he did.

To become the new Lord Yellander or at least get a farm or house or something that had been Yellander's from a grateful Crown, he'd have to present King Azoun—or Vangerdahast, more likely—with some great and loyal deed.

That wasn't going to be easy, and it had just become harder. Much harder.

For the four hundredth time, Brorn ran his fingers across his left cheek to feel the smooth, bare bone there. It was spreading. The eyebrow on that side was gone, and much of his forehead was bone, now, too. Tluin.

When he drew back his hand, he saw that it had begun to appear on his fingertips. They, too, were bone. For a moment he rubbed them frantically along the rough stone edge of the casket lid, where one of the cracks was, but that wore it off not in the slightest. Nor caused any pain. There was no bleeding.

He held his fingers up, the better to peer at them curiously. It wasn't that his flesh and skin were withering away. No, the bone was *growing over* him, cloaking his flesh with an outer armor. He could still move and flex his body, just as before, but there was a heaviness, a shell atop the left side of his face and the ends of all the fingers of his left hand now. It deadened sensation. He could feel things he touched or held, but at a little distance, as if through a gauntlet.

It was something amid the corpse leavings. It must have been. While he was healing, it had crept into him somehow.

And just might be stealing Brorn Hallomond from himself.

He cursed loud and long, standing there alone in the forest, then turned back to the casket and bitterly thanked the boneshards and dust therein.

For stealing his life from him, perhaps.

He strode away, hoping his clothes could hide his skeletal limbs when things got that far.

He doubted that war wizards would let him see the Royal Magician or anyone else when they saw a walking skeleton heading their way.

Alaphondar leaned forward across the table. The Royal Sage seemed as calm as ever, but the gentle, reassuring smile he put on his face made Rhallogant Caladanter, sitting on the other side of the table, shake in his manacles.

"Be at ease, Lord Caladanter," the sage said. "You've been *most* helpful thus far, and the Crown is pleased. Thus far. You are here today merely to answer another question, if you can."

He paused to give the young noble a chance to rush in and fill the silence, and the terrified Rhallogant Caladanter obliged. "I—I'll do anything! Ah, say anything! I will!"

"That'll be helpful," Dalonder Ree muttered sarcastically from where he stood lounging against one closed door out of the room.

The lady in battle leathers whom everyone addressed either as "Dove" or "Lady Dove" leaned against the other closed door.

"The . . . gentlesir in whose company you were found had some aims in life, some things he was striving to accomplish. Did he speak of them to you, at all? If he, say—to speak entirely in fanciful 'what ifs'—ran away from us, right now, where would he go, do you think?"

"I . . . I— Yes, he did, but I know not," Rhallogant babbled. "He . . . he . . . oh, let me think!"

"Please, be our guest," Ree murmured. "There's a first time for everything."

His fingertips burned briefly. A counterspell.

Drathar flung the dagger down, cursing.

Oh, 'twas a knife, and a good one. Useful enough and beautifully balanced for throwing. Plain, too; not traceable. Yet it held not one shred of a means of tracing her or working magic on her from afar. Of course.

Drathar threw back his head and went on cursing, loud and long, snapping out the words rather than shouting them. Beasts lurked in these wild woods, and he wasn't seeking to battle one just yet. Retrieving the knife—at least he knew it was clean, so they couldn't spell-trace *him* through it—he started walking along the game trail to keep his passage as quiet as possible.

It was too cold, before dawn, to sleep anyhail, even if he hadn't had a raw pain high in his chest, just in from his shoulder.

How had that *bitch* of a she-thief known he was there? He'd watched quietly from cover, not moving except to rise a little out of his crouch to see better, and not working any spells. How had she known?

Well, whatever the reason for that, she had, and this changed things. *She* had to be taken down, even before the spellhurlers and the ranger.

"The gauntlets," he told the darkness around him with an angry hiss, "are off."

He was half-expecting to hear an angry, answering hiss, but none came.

"Dead," Pennae said in grim satisfaction. "The displacer beast, I mean, not the man out there whose bidding it was doing. He got away. For now."

"So," Semoor grunted, feeling his ribs and wincing, "are we great heroes? Or do children in the Dales wrestle down displacer beasts?"

"It certainly looked fearsome enough," Doust said. "And I'm not going to be able to wear this armor again until we hammer it out."

Semoor grinned. "Give it here. I'd welcome something to batter flat, about now."

"No," Islif and Pennae said in unison, severely.

"You *want* to make enough noise to draw things to us for more than a day's travel all around?" the thief added. "Know how far that sort of sound carries?"

Semoor gave her a bright, idiotic grin. "Evidently not. Farther than your curses?"

"How's Jhess?" Florin asked. "I think she took the full force of whatever spell she sent at it. *Something* made the spell turn back on her."

"That would be the work of the wizard who was watching," Pennae told him, joining him as he peered down at Jhessail's sprawled, unconscious body. "Who I don't think is a war wizard."

"Doesn't seem like their style, no," Islif agreed. "So, what other foes do we have?" She shot Pennae a look. "Just how busy have you been, separating nobles from their coins?"

The thief shrugged. "No busier than we've all been, getting them separated from their heads by war wizards as they get caught doing treason, time and again. I doubt most of them care overmuch about us, if they think of us at all."

"Well." Semoor sighed. *"Someone* is thinking of us. Right attentively, too."

"Let's hope he's tasted enough battle for one night," Pennae said, looking at Doust's ribs. "This ledge and slope here is probably the best camp we'll find for defending in the dark against anyone who can't loose arrows at us."

She looked up at Semoor. "Heal your friend, here. Tymora shouldn't mind. He certainly took his chances."

"What about Jhess?"

"Let her lie in peace for now. At dawn, the two of you may need to be healing her. I didn't recognize the spell she tried to use—did either of you?"

The priests both shook their heads.

"Well, sit on either side of her and keep watching her. If she turns cold or doesn't rouse, start with the healings right away. Or we may be down one mage."

"Is she that bad?" Florin asked grimly, planting his sword and going to his knees beside the still, wan-faced Jhessail.

Pennae shrugged. "Don't know, not knowing the spell she tried. All we can do is wait and see."

"Why not cast the healings right now?"

"Because it's not morning yet, Florin," the thief said. "We don't know when we'll be attacked next. One of us may end up needing them more urgently than little Flamehair here."

Florin nodded and turned to face the night, where they could already hear beasts moving. The creatures were heading for where the corpse of the dirlagraun lay. To feed.

His left arm, leg, and the left side of him were all covered in bone now, and most of his face, too. His hair was falling out in great, dry, crumbling handfuls.

Brorn had shrugged off most of his clothing at first, for fear it would melt or rot away when the bone-change touched it.

Yet it was back on, now. His spreading, creeping covering of bone was affecting only his skin. Beneath it, he still felt like himself—strong, agile, alive, not a brittle, light, dead thing.

It hadn't covered his eyes. Yet. It had done something to them, though. He could see keenly in the night-gloom, walking among the trees as sure-footed as on a cloudy day.

And half of him, stlarn it, looked like a walking skeleton.

He dared not go out to the road, where folk could see him. He probably shouldn't let himself be seen as he was now, in Cormyr, at all. In the Dales, they were backwoods farmers, simpler folk. His appearance might terrify them, but they weren't of Cormyr, so he didn't care what they thought of him, so long as none of them got brave enough to start thrusting pitchforks or aiming crossbows his way.

What would happen to him when the bone covered him entirely? Would it start gnawing at his innards or growing across his eyes?

Was he doomed?

Not that there was a thing he could do to stop it.

Which meant he might as well keep on as if he was going to live, until the gods showed him otherwise.

So he was looking like a monster already and very soon would *be* a monster to most folk of Faerûn. Which meant the life of a lurking, forest-dwelling outlaw would be all he could hope for.

Well, the northern Dales were the best place he could think of to try to do that. All the vast forest to lurk in, good farms to plunder crops from . . .

There was nothing left for him in Cormyr, unless he could get the Pendant of Ashaba.

It would be useless to him in Shadowdale. No simple farmers would accept a walking skeleton as their ruling lord.

Yet if he could get it back to, say, Arabel and see the Lady Lord there, he could bargain with it and perhaps get a war wizard to banish this bone armor and turn him back the way he'd looked before.

To get the Pendant, of course, he'd have to kill some Knights of Myth Drannor. No great crime, that, in the eyes of the Cormyrean authorities. At least from what he'd seen and heard. That ornrion had looked to be itching to butcher some Knights himself.

Moreover, Brorn Hallomond had a sworn score to settle. Lord Yellander must be avenged.

Something shifted in his groin. Gods, it had covered him *there*.

Well, that was it. He was a monster.

Could he get work in Sembia in one of the festhalls? The Man of Bone, now onstage, dancing with the highcoin lasses?

Say, now . . .

No. Try for the lordship first. Noble lords in Cormyr were all far richer than dancers in clubs, and with coin enough he could buy all the lasses he wanted to dance with.

He *had* to have that Pendant.

Knights of Myth Drannor had to die.

Telgarth Boarblade leaned forward over the table, the better to murmur to the four conspirators Ruldroun had sent here. "See those men coming in now? Each of you get a good look at the face of one of them. Thorm, *that* one. Darratur, the tall one. Glays, the one with the mustache. Klarn, the balding one. I'll take the one with the beard. Go upstairs to pretend to look for rooms if you have to, or follow them into the jakes—just get a good look. *Don't* make them suspicious by staring. Try to seem bored, and look around idly, often, as if you always do. But fix their features in your memories. The moment you have, go out front, and we'll meet by the hitching rail."

"Why?" Klarn asked.

Boarblade decided there and then that Klarn would be the first of the four to die, if the need arose. He did *not* need someone questioning his every word.

"They are a Crown envoy and his bodyguards. We're going to wait until they're abed, use our hargaunts to adopt their faces, then firmly but urgently require the discreet use of our mounts—their horses; they'll be fast, first-rank beasts, believe me!—and ride on out of here."

Four faces stared intently at him. They were excited. Good.

"Trot until we're out of sight of this place," he added, "then walk until we find a stream. Rest the horses a bit, then walk them again, and start looking for a place off the road to camp. Come the warm hours after highsun on the morrow, if we do all that right, we can be galloping hard along the Ride."

He sat back and said firmly, "We've got us some Knights to catch, they've a long start, and I for one am not *walking* all the way to Shadowdale. Which is certainly how far we'll have to go if we try to catch up to them, just plodding along on foot. Anyone dispute that?"

No one did.

Chapter 21
ALONE I FACED THE DRAGON

And now you laugh and stamp your feet
And profanely bellow for more ale
And mock my limp, my burns, and scars
Weakness your valor makes hale
Well let me tell, sneering younglings
As 'gainst my feeble sloth you rail
There was a time when I was as you
Bold, foolish, young, and pale
Riding to tame the world entire
Though dreams 'gainst talons fail
Fell my friends and lovers all, one by one
Burned, gnawed, screamingly pierced-impaled
Gutted and bone-smashed, 'til in the end
Alone I faced the dragon and lived to tell the tale

Tameldra Anlath,
Lady Bard of Baldur's Gate
from the ballad "Alone I Faced The Dragon"
first performed circa the Year of the Sword and Stars

Drathar hadn't had magic to hurl for all that long.

Oh, he'd always known from the tinglings when he was near a spell being cast or when walking through the roiling aftermath of a spell battle that he'd had a touch of the Art. Yet he'd been a thief, and no more than a thief, before he'd found the Qaethur.

It had been the Qaethur, a worn and chipped gemstone carved into a shallow relief depiction of a human face, that barely filled his palm, that had whispered to him, opening up a door in his mind to the glory of the Weave. Unthinking and eternal, the Qaethur spoke the same things to everyone who touched it. He had been one of the lucky few.

He had Varandrar to thank for that. The senior Zhent in Arabel had sent him to do that slaying and robbery, had known the Qaethur was there for the taking, and had specifically mentioned it to Drathar. Varandrar had meant him to find it.

The bastard.

Now he had power few thieves could do more than dream of and the riches that power had let him wrest from others. Now he was truly someone worthy among the Zhentarim, not a mere tolerated lackey.

And now, he knew as much as many in the Brotherhood did and so knew something else: true fear.

His spells were too paltry and fresh-learned for him to battle any but the greenest wizard, Art against Art, and hope to live. Yet he had a talent for the spells that called and coerced beasts to his bidding.

Which is why the Knights of Myth Drannor were soon going to be facing a gray render.

"Soon" as in very shortly after it finished tearing apart the joints of the wyvern it had just slain, gnawed the last shreds of meat, and went looking for more to devour to fill up the yawning, gurgling emptiness in its belly.

Riding its mind as lightly and gingerly as possible, Drathar smiled tightly as the horrible rending and splintering of bone went on.

As the old Dale saying put it, his own mother wouldn't know him now.

The hargaunt was spread very thinly across his face—just enough to make him seem a pocked, wrinkled woman who looked nothing like a certain former war wizard. Most of its bulk was busy doing its best to thrust his chest out into a rather impressive, though sagging with age, bust.

The tattered and dirty dress he'd had to strangle the crone he now resembled to gain possession of—hargaunt-disguised as the ornrion Dauntless, he'd intended merely to rob her, but she'd persisted in screaming and trying to blind him with her clawing fingers and everything breakable she could snatch up and throw—was catching on thorns and twigs and the gods alone knew what else as he fought his way through the brush, but what of that?

Torn went with dirty, and dirty suited him. He didn't want to look well-to-do or beautiful enough to make anyone consider him worth waylaying.

Onsler Ruldroun was in a hurry to do a little waylaying of his own.

"Auril's kisses, but 'tis cold," Pennae murmured nigh Florin's ear, gently pushing aside the tip of his sword from where it had reached out to menace her as she approached. Hunched over and hugging herself for warmth, on the verge of shivering, she tried to thrust herself against his armpit. "There's always a chill before dawn, yes, but this is worse than I've tasted for a long time."

"And if a monster swoops swiftly in at me?" the ranger whispered. "What then?"

"Throw me at it, and use my screams to wake the others. Or use me as a shield."

Florin sighed, put his free arm around her, and started rocking the thief gently back and forth, shifting weight from one boot to another just as he was, to restore the rhythm he'd established before she'd risen from huddled sleep to join him.

It *was* cold, and he'd been feeling it.

"Alone I faced the dragon," he muttered to himself, barely above a whisper.

"And lived to tell the tale," she whispered back, her soft breath almost a tune. "And before you think of it, don't bother telling me to go back to sleep. I'm too chilled for slumber. In fact . . ."

Florin felt deft, iron-strong fingers sliding in under the waist of his breeches, reaching into the warmth—

He stepped away. "No. Not now."

Pennae moved back against his chest. "Flor, I'm not after . . . what you think I am. Right now, at least. I only wanted to get the tips of my fingers a little warmer, and there's always *just* enough room—"

"Indeed," the ranger growled into her ear in mock disapproval. Then he put his arm around her again and drew her gently back against him to settle into just where she'd been before.

"Who d'you reckon is still after us, now?" she whispered, sliding her fingers a little way back in under his breeches, then bringing them to a firm halt.

Florin shrugged. "Half the stlarning Realms, it seems," he murmured. "To say nothing of Those Who Harp and anyone else who may just be watching what befalls us, rather than hunting us down to do the befalling. I—"

He stiffened suddenly and thrust her away.

"What?" Pennae hissed, seeing his intent face and his rising sword. He was staring tensely out into the night, gaze hard upon something. Yet she hadn't heard a thing.

Trying to look down into the dark forest before them, she stiffened. That was just it.

She, too, couldn't hear a thing from in front of her. No little night noises, no gentle sighing of ghost-breeze-driven leaves.

Nothing at all.

She could hear those faint forest sounds coming from off to her right—and to the left, too, when she crouched and turned.

Yet straight ahead, noth—

Then she saw it. A movement in the trees, a thrusting that was mirrored by Florin's sword lifting sharply in response beside her.

Something large was approaching through the night-gloom. Something that was tearing aside trees and trampling down bushes and saplings in the heart of that eerie silence.

It was massive—a great, gray, neckless, hulk of stonelike hide and rippling muscle, reaching out with two huge black-taloned, manlike arms so long that they dragged knuckles through the brush whenever they weren't reaching up to claw aside a tree trunk. It was shouldering through a thick stand of trees to reach their ledge, lumbering along heavily, massive shoulders and that bony snout that thrust forward from between the shoulders rather than rising above them on any sort of neck.

Florin cursed softly, then told Pennae, "Wake the others now, in case its silence comes right up here onto the ledge with it. Not Jhess, but stand over her, ready to kick her awake or drag her aside if you have to."

The thief nodded, staring at black fangs jutting out of large, parted jaws, as the snout lifted to better peer in their direction. A line of three small, amber yellow eyes ran down each side of its bone-ridged head and beheld her with dull, hungry malice. Or was it merely hunger?

Drathar winced. The render's hunger was quickening, and that made its mind a flaring, roiling thing that threatened to draw him in. He didn't want to end up lost in that hunger-driven flood.

He was *too* good, mayhap, at this beast-coercing. Best to hang back farther. He'd intended to, anyhail, to keep well away from the thief's hurled daggers. The mindlink would tell him when it was feeding. There would be time enough when the real battle was over to skulk in closer and see how matters lay.

He'd cast silence on the creature to cloak its approach. That would have to be cleverness enough. Else he'd be striding along after it, bloodying his fingers on trees, presenting himself as ready meat for anything bold enough to get close to a feeding gray render.

Which would have to be something so bold, he wouldn't want to face it at the best of times.

"Tempus, Tymora, and doom," Islif muttered, managing to look angry and sleepy at the same time. "I don't like the chances of my sword being able to carve *that*. D'you think there are any loose shards of rock up atop this cliff you could climb up and shove down onto its head?"

Pennae shrugged. "I saw some deep clefts up there, with greenery doing the lush tumble down out of them. Whether I can get anything free in time is another thing. I'll take that battlehammer Semoor lugs with him but never wants to use and see what I can do—but mind, falling stone really doesn't care if it hits ugly monster or valiant Knight of Myth Drannor."

"Pennae," Islif replied, "We're too desperate to worry about that. Get climbing."

The thief nodded, turned away, and started up the weathered stone as if it were a well-lit ladder.

Islif wondered what Pennae would do if there were other forest prowlers waiting for her with bared and grinning fangs at the top of the cliff.

Then she wondered if the thief had already stolen the Pendant and, upon reaching the top of the cliff, would just sidle off through the trees, leaving the rest of them to a swift and bloody doom.

Then, joining Florin and a reelingly sleepy Doust and Semoor in a line along the ledge, she wondered if she'd have time to even know what was killing them, before it did.

What must be magical silence was ebbing as the hulking thing clawed its way up the gravel slope. She could hear faint clackings and rattlings as stones tumbled in a constant, growing flood.

Rolling over those sounds, she could hear something else—a deep, wet rumbling, like a dog growling deep in its throat. The thing was large—half again as tall as she was, its shoulders far broader than hers. Hairless and seemingly sexless, it stood upon squat, massive legs and had a stumpy little flap of a tail. There'd be a channel beneath that tail where it relieved itself. That and its pale, wet maw and the eyes—six of them—were the only vulnerable spots she could see.

Shaking her head, Islif wondered if she'd be able to reach any of them and if they really were weaknesses her blade could pierce.

At least she had time to ponder such things, as a little gravel showered and bounced down from above, marking Pennae's climb. This beast was digging into the loose stones below their ledge more than it was managing to climb them.

Yet there had to be solid rock or sturdy earth under all the rocks, pebbles, and gravel, if one went deep enough. It would only be a matter of time.

"Can we try to blind it, d'you think?" Florin asked. "Before it gets up here with us? Pennae?"

"She's gone," Islif said, not knowing if the thing could hear and understand them. "Up. So depend upon no cleverly thrown daggers to help us."

"Both of you *should* be able to reach the eyes with your blades, if standing right beside it," Semoor muttered. "If it doesn't stand up tall, that is, and all the shifting stone doesn't just slide you on past." It was obvious who "both of you" were meant to be.

"If we get down onto that loose stuff," Florin murmured, "can we get up here again?"

"Can we stand up to fight it at all?" Islif asked. "I'm not welcoming the thought of wallowing, scarce able to land a sword cut, and ending up sprawled flat in the scree, sliding helplessly down to its legs as it digs and churns, so it can reach out and break my back—or claw me up to dine—whenever it pleases."

"We could try to reach out and haul you back," Semoor suggested, eyeing those black-fanged jaws. The beast was clearly watching them, turning its head to regard each Knight in turn, and its rumbling was rising in tone and volume. It sounded angry.

Islif and Florin both shook their heads.

"That'll just mean you get hauled helplessly into the same doom as ours," Islif said.

Florin sighed and fixed both priests with stern looks. "No holy magic that can help now, at all?"

Doust and Semoor gave each other uneasy looks then shook their heads in unison. The ranger sighed then ducked down until he was half-kneeling—and sprang.

Off the ledge and forward, sword out. Those great, black-taloned arms swung up to claw at him but succeeded only in coming up under one of his boots and lofting him the extra bit he needed, not only to land on the beast's massive back just behind the eyes, but to turn in midair, so he came down facing the ledge and his fellow Knights.

Florin drove his sword sideways into the angle of the jaws. As he'd expected, the monster bit down hard on it, making it into a rock-solid handle for the next breath or two. Which was quite long enough for the ranger to use his other hand to snatch out a belt dagger and bury it hilt-deep in one of the beast's eyes.

It stiffened, then roared in pain and threw up its arms, rising out of its crouch. By then, Florin had yanked his dagger messily free of one eyesocket and plunged the steel into the next one.

The monster roared and reached up with one arm to claw him forward over its head and down into its waiting jaws—and Islif's sword slashed across its talons, severing or blunting them all and causing it to squall in astonished pain. It shook that hand wildly, seeking to banish the pain, which was more than long enough for the ranger riding it to plunge his dagger into the third eye on that side of the monster's head.

It stiffened again, then spasmed, wriggling wildly and uncontrollably beneath him. Florin clung to blade and dagger, fighting just to stay on its back—as Islif snarled to Semoor, "The big skillet, on edge, between its jaws!"

The priest blinked at her, then tore apart his pack and produced the pan. Islif snatched it, drove it in between those black teeth— and then lunged so deeply that her armored shoulder fetched up beside the skillet with a clang. Which meant her sword was arm-deep in the beast's maw but angled up into its massive shoulders and spine, piercing and now slicing and slashing viciously.

The monster reeled, flung up its arms to tear the swordswoman apart—and Doust and Semoor launched themselves from the ledge, maces smashing down on the monster's hands with all their weight backing the blows.

The monster staggered back, arms flailing, the rumbling now a bellow of raw agony, and Florin dared to drive his fingers into one gore-weeping eyesocket to gain a handhold to cling to. He let go his sword and used that hand to thrust the dagger into the first of the three eyes on the other side of the head.

The massive shoulders under Florin were shaking and spasming helplessly now, the arms flailing around in a wild thrashing.

"Get clear!" Pennae cried from above. "Flor, get *away* from it!"

Florin slashed open another eye, even as he kicked hard against the thing's back, and thrust himself free, toppling back into the night.

The thing tried to turn, to follow him and pounce, but it was lurching, its muscles rippling and shuddering uncontrollably. It had managed only a half-turn by the time Islif and the two priests had clawed themselves well apart from where it thrashed on the scree slope—and a long, wedge-shaped slab of rock came thundering down out of the night to smash the beast flat.

Broken and bewildered, all it could still do was scream. It did that, feebly, then fell silent and leaked gore out from under the now-shattered stone covering it.

"Well, now," Pennae's voice floated down to her fellow Knights, surprisingly calm and quiet. *"That* wasn't so hard, was it? Any other beasts you need taken care of?"

"Whoever sent this one?" Semoor said. "Four coins to get twelve that this hulk was brought or sent here to stand against us."

No one accepted his wager.

Which one of them had the Pendant? As he'd expected, his spell had found nothing, which meant he had to get closer to either spot it by chance—if one of them was foolish enough to wear it openly—or spell-see it at close range.

Drathar skulked closer, wincing as the render's rumblings rose into sharp shrieks. The night was dark, the Knights apparently had no lanterns lit.

Well, that just might seal their doom. They couldn't—

"Haaaa!" That deep, hoarse, triumphant roar out of the night had sounded right behind him!

Drathar hurled himself forward, right through a viciously sharp thornbush that was thankfully half-dead, and so collapsed with a crackle. Who—?

A morningstar crashed down right beside him, flaring momentarily into ruby radiance as it struck his feeble shielding spell.

Drathar rolled, becoming aware of a large, looming figure, a choking stink of unwashed, filthy flesh, and two tusked heads. A second morningstar whistled past his head to thud heavily into a treetrunk and rebound.

Drathar scrambled to his feet then ducked away, seeking to put several trees between himself and this . . . ettin?

Aye, it was a two-headed giant, and it was striding angrily around the trees, looking nothing like the stumbling dunderheads most bardic tales insisted ettin were. It looked to have just awakened, probably roused by the render's screams, and its every stride was faster and more purposeful as it rose to full alertness.

Which meant he had to act right now—or never.

Drathar planted his feet despite the wildly rising urge to flee, stared at the ettin lurching menacingly nearer, and carefully cast his last coercion spell. Whatever they'd managed to do to the gray render, the Knights of Myth Drannor had to be wounded and weary.

Which meant, against an ettin, they hadn't a chance.

"What *was* that magic?"

Boarblade was in no mood for Klarn's truculent questions just now. "Something the same man who contacted each of you gave me, to use once we were together, riding on an open road. I don't know its name. You saw what it did to the horses, and it's done now. So leave them—they're too exhausted to stray, and the hargaunt can smell them well enough to guide us back to them, after. Come!"

"Come where?"

"Into the woods, toward all that shrieking. Before we're too late. You to the fore with me. Glays, rearguard. All the shrieking may bring other things hunting. Thorm and Darratur, keep blades sheathed for now. I want none of us running onto each other's steel in the dark. Quick and quiet, quick and quiet."

"To do what, exactly?"

Glays was always calm and the only one Boarblade judged competent to obey orders and avoid utter dunderheadedness. So he answered the man.

"To go and see if this racket is linked to the Knights we're looking for. It sounds like a forest beast might just have done our work for us—and if it has we need to get to the bodies before it mauls their faces too badly and to find that Pendant before it's down some monster's gullet. If it hasn't, but the Knights are sore wounded or worn out, we watch and choose our best moment to rush them. They've got a wizard and some priests, remember? No better time and place to face down spells than the dark, in a thick forest, where they can't see who they're hurling magic at. *If,* that is, they've got any magic left!"

That set Klarn, Thorm, and Darratur all to nodding and chuckling. Boarblade used his drawn sword to wave Klarn forward, gave them all a grin, then turned away before they could see it fall right off his chin. Idiots.

In the doorway the Royal Magician of Cormyr came to an abrupt halt and blinked.

Sage Royal Alaphondar looked up from his uncomfortable, high-backed chair and sighed. There were more subtle ways of making it clear you were surprised—and disapprovingly so—to see someone in attendance at a secret meeting in the Queen's Retiring Room, but then Vangerdahast seldom saw any need to be all that subtle.

King Azoun and Queen Filfaeril were there, of course, crowns off on the table before them and arms around each other like lovers, as a clear signal that royal protocol was suspended for the nonce. Laspeera of the Wizards of War sat near them on a maid's ready chair.

The two whose presence seemed to discomfit Vangey were the War Wizard Lorbryn Deltalon and the man sitting quietly next to him in drab and well-worn trail leathers on the couch. It was the Harper Dalonder Ree, and he was giving the simmering wizard in the doorway a knowing smile and the words, "I'm sorry to announce that Dove can't be with us. She's off on one of her jaunts. Harper work."

"*What* Harper work?" Vangerdahast almost snarled, striding into the room and making for the comfortable armchair that had been left for him.

Ree shrugged. "What I know not, I cannot be made to say."

"Hah! You expect me to believe that?"

"*Yes,*" King Azoun said from where he sat, the word so sudden and steely that Vangerdahast blinked again, halted, and waited for more. Anticipated words that did not come.

After a breath or two, the Royal Magician continued to his seat and told the ceiling as he turned to sit, "Word came to me that the Dragon Queen had need of my presence at a moot, wherefore I am here. Do we await later arrivals, or—?"

"We do not, Vangey. Your grand entrance is unmarred." Filfaeril's tone was as dry as the sands of a desert. "If you're sitting comfortably enough, we can begin."

"I am. The purpose of this little conclave?"

"Thrust to the heart, thrust to the heart," Dalonder Ree murmured. The Royal Magician did not deign to look in his direction, but Laspeera and Filfaeril both gave him sly little smiles.

"It appears," the King of Cormyr said calmly, "that the Knights of Myth Drannor continue to be embroiled in some manner of violence in the wilderlands along the Moonsea Ride, beyond our present borders but in territory we customarily patrol and secure so that no menace may gather there for forays into our fair realm. The identities of their foes are a matter of some conjecture and dispute. I would hear your honest and informal counsel, everyone, on what we should now do about this."

"Nothing," Vangerdahast said, as Deltalon and the Harper started to speak. "They are adventurers, and they have departed the realm. Let them adventure and taste whatever fates the gods see fit to hand them. We cannot be forever reaching out our hands across Faerûn to meddle in the affairs of others."

"No, of course not," Dalonder Ree told the ceiling. "Only twice or thrice a day, when *we* want to—if we happen to be, say, a Royal Magician."

Two royal snorts of mirth quelled the icy rejoinder Vangerdahast had turned his head to deliver. He satisfied himself by ignoring the Harper's comment and said, "In this room we can only concern ourselves with Cormyrean interests and policies. As this is an informal discussion, let me express myself bluntly: I am very strongly of the opinion that no further aid of any sort should be rendered to the chartered adventurers known as the Knights of Myth Drannor. If they establish themselves in Shadowdale, as certain parties obviously intend that they do, we shall then extend the hand of diplomacy—"

"Envoys in the front door, spies through the back," Ree murmured.

"—*as usual,*" Vangerdahast said, giving the Harper a glare. "For one thing, I want to keep Wizards of War clear of that area just now for quite another reason."

Into the little silence that followed, Queen Filfaeril asked quietly, "And that reason would be?"

Vangerdahast looked at her a little beseechingly and murmured, "It touches on the royal family, and I would prefer not to speak openly in present company."

"That's difficult, Vangey," King Azoun said, "because *I* would very much prefer that you do."

The Royal Magician did not trouble to hide his shrug or his sigh. "Very well. There is peril to the Princess Tanalasta, owing to a magical link between her mind and a Wizard of War who has now become a renegade and a fugitive, whom I believe to currently be in the same area as the Knights."

"Ruldroun," Laspeera murmured.

Vangerdahast gave her a glare. "If we're laying bare every last secret of the realm for no good reason, aye. Ruldroun is the mage I speak of. I don't know of any connection at all between him and the Knights, but if we flood that stretch of forest with war wizards and spells get hurled . . . well, what happens to his mind could harm the princess, no matter what safeguards I weave around her here."

"I have no magic to speak of," the Harper said, "so I see no reason I shouldn't go to the aid of the Knights. I would even be so bold as to request war wizard aid in translocating me across the vastness of fair Cormyr so I can reach them in good time."

"I will furnish that," Deltalon spoke up, "and accompany you to assist and to bring back reliable report of what befalls."

"You will *not.*" Vangerdahast could put a ring of steel into his voice that echoed louder and more forcefully than even the "hear now my royal will" tone of King Azoun.

"He will," Queen Filfaeril said so softly and calmly that she seemed almost to be whispering. "Vangey, in this you are overruled."

The Royal Magician reeled in his chair as if he'd been slapped across the face. "You—you—"

"Dare?" the Dragon Queen inquired sweetly. "Of course. And please try my royal husband before you deem me foolish or standing alone in this."

With slow and obvious reluctance, Vangerdahast turned his head to look at the king, who smiled, nodded, and said, "The Harper is to be given all the assistance he deems necessary—*including* the service of Wizard of War Deltalon."

"I shall see to that," Laspeera said softly.

Vangerdahast's gaze snapped around to her—but he gave her no glare, only silence and several blinks of his eyes, as if some sort of facial tic were afflicting him.

"Very well," he said at last. "But hear me!" He gave the Harper a glare that might have melted a shield. "You're *not* taking an army of Purple Dragons!"

"Why would I," the Harper's face was all innocence, "when all I need is one Dragon? The man called Dauntless."

Slowly at first, then uproariously until his mirth expired in a fit of choking, the Royal Magician of Cormyr laughed.

Chapter 22

IF YOU SKULK OUT IN THE TREES THIS NIGHT

The moon is down, not shining bright
So lovers stay in, the beasts do prowl
If you skulk out in the trees this night
Be the one to pounce—not death-howl.

Fhannath Laree,
Lady Bard of Elturel
from the ballad "The Moon Is Down"
first performed circa the Year of the Shadowtop

Brorn had grown tired of looking down at himself.

He was entirely skeletal now, coated in bone that made his movements slower, his limbs heavy. Yet his joints were still supple enough, and thankfully he still had eyes and a tongue, his own insides—and what made him a man, too. And he felt . . . normal.

Hah. Normal.

He shook his head and plucked again at the tangle of belts, baldrics, and sheaths that were all he now wore. He'd long ago grown weary of his clothes falling off him with every step, breeches collapsing again and again around his ankles, and suddenly huge boots wobbling and even turning loosely on his bony feet, and he had finally abandoned them. He *was* thinner, everywhere, as if his flesh had melted away under the coating of bone.

So now Brorn Hallomond was, in truth, the Striding Skeleton. Whether this was really bone coating him or not—and it certainly looked like bone—it seemed something of a shield against the cold. He could no longer feel the gentle touch of the night breeze.

So was he dead? Did it matter?

The night was dark, with drifting clouds cloaking most of the stars and no Sêlune riding high, so he'd left the thick, tiring, confusing tangles of the forest to stalk along the Moonsea Ride.

Thus far alone and unmolested.

No honest traveler would still be out faring on a moonless night, outlaws would probably shrink back from a walking skeleton, and he could always duck into the trees if he saw anyone approaching.

So he strode along, trying to cover as much ground as he could without getting really tired. The Knights should be somewhere near, by now.

+ + ✦ + +

"Should I—"

"Remain still and silent? Yes. All else: No."

Laspeera's voice was brisker than she'd meant it to be, so she gave the ornrion a smile and added gently, "Keep your eyes open as the spell ends. You'll be plunged into a well-lit void, rich blue emptiness that it seems you're falling through, and then your feet will be on solid ground, somewhere at night in the forest—that 'somewhere' being wherever the Knights of Myth Drannor are. Speak and move and draw sword then, if you deem it needful, but not before. Please."

Dauntless nodded, a trifle unhappily and showing it on his face. He stood on a worn diamond mark painted on the floor at one end of the dark and cavernous undercellar of the Royal Court—deep under the flagstone garden yard that let into the Royal Gardens proper, if he'd correctly judged how far they'd walked—and there was another war wizard and another man standing on a diamond waiting to be transported across Cormyr in a winking instant, at the other end.

He knew them both. Lorbryn Deltalon and the Harper Dalonder Ree. They were watching him, the calm murmurs of relaxed converse passing between them, as they obviously waited for Laspeera to enspell him first.

Dauntless imagined Deltalon becoming just a trifle impatient and starting his spell as Laspeera was finishing hers—and the one teleport spell clawing at the other, flaring in an explosion that spattered all four of them in a thin drenching of gore over the walls of this spellcasting chamber, in the brief instant before those stones themselves shattered and heaved . . . and one end of the sprawling Court erupted into the night sky, towers toppling and scores of courtiers shrieking as they died.

Wincing, he shook his head, blinked, and found himself staring into the sympathetic face of the wizard Laspeera again. He felt shame, but it was swept away in a rush of gratitude at the caring he saw in her eyes. Small wonder that many Wizards of War called her Mother and revered her.

"Sorry," he muttered. "Pray pardon, Lady Laspeera. Silence, aye."

The smile she gave him lit up her face like a leaping brazier-flame, and Dauntless felt as if he were falling in love.

"Aye," she said and lifted her hands like a master server about to signal the servants under his command at a Palace feast.

She was going to cast the spell. The magic that would hurl him across the Forest Kingdom and beyond, out along the Ride into the wilderlands somewhere near Tilver's Gap, lands where Purple Dragons rode hard and often to keep outlaws and monsters and worse out of Cormyr proper. To see the Knights of Myth Drannor *not* dead, now, but safely past Tilverton and into the Dales.

Orders, as they said gravely in the service of the Purple Dragon, have changed.

Just where along the Ride he'd be in a breath or two, he didn't know, but there were a cluster of little glowing lights hanging in the air in the center of the room, a little higher than Laspeera's head, that told her where the Knights were. Each of those floating, subtly shifting glows represented one of the tracer-enchanted glowstones the Royal Magician Vangerdahast had given to the Knights of Myth Drannor.

Aye, orders might change, but some things never did. Rise up sun and go down moon, every last jack and lass in Cormyr danced to a tune, whether they knew it or not, and the piper was the wizard Vangerdahast.

Laspeera's hands finished tracing elaborate gestures in the air, her smile grew wider, and—

Smiling war wizard, chamber, and all were gone, and this particular Purple Dragon ornrion was falling endlessly through a deep blue void.

"Florin!" Pennae snapped, leaping down the last little stretch of cliff to land heels-first in the loose scree beside him, with a crash of shifting stones.

"I hear it," the ranger said. "Back up onto the ledge, everyone! Stoop, Clumsum, is there *anything* you can do for Jhess?"

"Pray?" Semoor said.

"Tluin!" Florin barked in amused exasperation. "Just tluin *off!*"

"Oh, bright Morninglord, aid me as I obey the esteemed and manly Florin Falconhand!" Semoor cried as he scrambled up onto the ledge. "Let the rosy hue of your approval bathe—"

"Semoor!" Islif and Florin roared in unison. *"Shut up!"*

"—even my decidedly less than devout, silence-loving companions—"

Doust reached the ledge, planted his mace on its stone with one hand, and swung his other arm up and around in a wild bid for balance.

Out of sheer luck, the hand on the end of that arm made abrupt contact with Semoor's mouth, and whatever else he'd been going to say was abruptly silenced.

Leaving everyone ample opportunity to hear the eager roar that was rising from two throats, as something twice as tall as Florin burst around and over the last few trees, branches splintering, and charged at the Knights.

It was a two-headed giant, all massive, corded muscles and hungry fury. Drool sluiced past the jutting tusks of its shovel mouths in a rain as it broke off its roaring run forward to bellow something.

"That's an ettin!" Semoor shouted. "Saw it in one of the Palace bestiaries!"

The ettin bellowed and flung wide its arms, both of them as long as Islif's body. Gigantic iron morningstars in its fists rattled out at full swing to crash against tree trunks.

"Why, *thank* you, Semoor!" Pennae said. "Whenever I want

to know what's trying to kill me, I can turn to you for its proper name!"

The ettin charged.

"Pennae, circle and hamstring, but only when you can get back and away fast!" Florin shouted. "Holynoses, pick up Jhess, and be ready to run along the ledge as fast as arrows! Islif and I will stand against it, but we can't shove it back!"

A morningstar crashed down as if to underscore his words, striking sparks from the stones as it *just* missed Islif—a result she managed to achieve by hurling herself face-first downslope into gravel.

Florin's sword rang like a bell, and his body trembled along with it, as the other morningstar glanced off it, whirling hard, and started to enwrap it in chain. Cursing, the ranger ducked down and let go of his blade, seeking to avoid being bound up helplessly against his own weapon.

"Where in the Nine stlarning Hells did it get two morningstars that size?" Semoor demanded of the night at large, waving his mace for balance as he and Doust struggled to loft the limp burden of Jhessail between them.

"Temple of Tempus?" Doust offered. "Tore them out of all those oversized weapons they like to hang above their gates?"

"While the war-priests did *what?* Sat and watched? Laid wagers?"

Doust shrugged. "Well, if it wasn't temple-theft, he killed someone and took them. A giant someone."

"Holynoses," Pennae's voice came out of the night from somewhere in the darkness at the bottom of the slope, "could you find something else to talk about, just now? Like what useful holy spells you can smite this thing with? I'd rather *not* be reminded of what those things can do!"

"Tymora!" Doust coughed, grimacing. "This thing stinks!"

"You *don't* say!" Islif shouted back, scrambling to her feet amid tumbling gravel and slashing out wildly at one huge, corded leg as she slid past onto firm footing.

The ettin roared and tried to club her with a morningstar, smashing thornbushes and saplings to tumbling splinters in her wake as Islif ducked around behind it—and ran full-tilt into Pennae.

Breast-to-breast they slammed together, the wind gasping out of both of them, and fell helplessly to the ground. Islif wrapped an arm around the thief and rolled desperately, trailing her sword behind her. Both she and Pennae had been slicing at the backs of the ettin's legs, but—

The ettin screamed—two raw, ear-numbing shrieks of agony— then stumbled, morningstars crashing down. Whereupon it suddenly became Florin's turn to dive for his life, face-first into gravel.

He did so, clawing and scrabbling to propel himself onward, riding the scree.

"Heroic, very heroic!" Semoor called from the ledge.

Florin called something back that was more profane than heroic.

He was still angrily doing so when his sword clanged and tumbled on stones somewhere far behind and above him, where the morningstar chain had flung it.

The ettin roared in pain, hopping awkwardly sideways—*through* a tree—and trying to turn and see what had hurt it so much.

Islif kept rolling with Pennae in her arms, whooping and fighting for breath, trying to get them both away behind too many trees for the two-headed giant to smash aside.

"Jhess!" Semoor said up on the ledge, shaking the shoulder he had hold of and trying to ignore the wildly lolling head atop it. "Wake up! Wake *up!* We need you to blast something!"

Florin reached the end of the gravel and slid into a thornbush. The ettin was headed away from him now, hitting out viciously behind itself with both morningstars. The ranger fought his way free and to his feet, snatching out his dagger and thinking just how useless it would be against this foe even as he did so. His sword was lost somewhere up on the scree yonder, with no moonlight to make it glint, and—

Right in front of him, not the reach of an arm from the point of his dagger, a vivid blue flash of light split the night-gloom.

Laspeera lowered her arms, looked over her shoulder at Lorbryn Deltalon, and nodded.

He returned her nod and began casting the same spell. Dalonder Ree stood like a calm statue until the blue flash claimed him, leaving the diamond on the floor empty and just the two war wizards in the chamber.

They looked at each other down the length of the room. By the faint glow of the shieldings Laspeera had raised around them when they'd first brought Dauntless and Dalonder into the spellcasting chamber, each could see that the other wasn't smiling.

"Well, that's done," Laspeera said. "Up to the scrying spheres to watch them."

Deltalon shook his head. "You watch. I'm going after them."

The second-most-powerful Wizard of War in all the land stared at him expressionlessly. Then, slowly and carefully, she drew a wand from her belt.

Deltalon took a step back, going tense. If she used it on him, there was little he dared do to try to counter the magic, standing here in the grip of her shielding.

Laspeera walked down the room toward him, face still expressionless.

Deltalon retreated another step, then stood his ground.

When she was close enough to touch him, Laspeera stopped, reversed the wand, and handed it to him, butt first. "Force spheres," she almost whispered. "To confine a foe or englobe and protect a friend. Nine of them. Come back alive, if you can."

She opened her arms to him.

Deltalon hugged her fiercely, overcome with gratitude and relief, the wand solid and comforting in his hand.

"And if I do not," he whispered into her ear as they rocked together in their shared embrace, "beware a possible Wizard of War traitor. The man I've seen binding the mindworm-touched nobles under his personal control: Vangerdahast, the Royal Magician of Cormyr."

Laspeera sighed against his neck, then whispered, "Thank you, Lorbryn. All good gods watch over you."

She kissed his neck, then drew smoothly back and away, leaving his skin tingling.

Deltalon swallowed, saluted her with the wand, thrust it through his belt, then carefully teleported himself away.

Laspeera stood gazing at the spot where he'd been standing for a long time, pondering things. Then she lifted her head and out of habit gazed all around the empty chamber.

It was indeed empty, looking precisely as it should. Biting her lip gently to keep a wry smile from climbing onto her face at what she knew she was about to discover, she lifted her hands and made the simple gesture that would banish her shielding spell. The new shielding was of her own devising, subtly different from the one Vangerdahast had taught her to use.

The shielding crackled and collapsed rather than fading—telling her that it had been under assault from a spell probe.

The smile found its way onto her face after all, though it was just as crooked as she'd thought it would be. It was his, of course.

So the second-most-powerful Wizard of War in the Forest Kingdom lifted her head and said softly to the empty air, "Fair evening, Lord Vangerdahast. Master."

Then she went to the door to throw its bolts and begin her ascent to the room of scrying spheres.

She knew she'd find a certain Royal Magician waiting there.

"*What* are they fighting?"

Klarn was, it seemed, one of those men who cannot abide not having his curiosity assuaged.

"We'll soon see," Boarblade said in tones intended as a clear and emphatic "Silence, dolt!" warning.

Klarn, it also seemed, was a man deaf to tonal warnings. "It sounds gods-murdering big! How in all these trees did they find it?"

"It found *them."*

"Huh?"

He left Klarn's astonished grunt unanswered and stalked ahead, crouching low and moving as quietly as possible.

Klarn came after him, thudding heavily through the forest like the oaf he was. Thorm and Darratur followed him like silent shadows. Boarblade couldn't see Glays bringing up the rear, but he had every confidence that the man was there, moving through the night as softly as a ghost.

Not that it seemed necessary any longer. Trees were being shattered, their rendings loud and violent, and the ettin was screaming. Nothing else could scream with two mouths like that, except a much larger two-headed giant, and Boarblade had seen nothing looming taller than the trees.

There was a lot of crashing and thrashing going on and men and women shouting. He skulked nearer, smiling openly now.

The smile went away in an instant when he saw the blue flash.

A man stood in front of him. He hadn't been there a moment ago. A man he knew. A man in armor who was snatching out his sword and throwing out his gauntleted hand to dash aside Florin's dagger.

The ranger stepped smoothly back, seeing the ettin peering their way and blinking. It wasn't too badly hurt to turn in a flash when it needed to, and both of its heads were thrust forward, low and menacing, in the direction of the now-vanished flash.

"Dauntless," Florin said, "look out behind you. We've got larger problems than each other."

"I'm a friend, not a foe!" the ornrion said, then risked a fleeting look back over his shoulder.

Dauntless, Florin, and the ettin were all in time to see the second flash.

Drathar frowned. Some sort of showy teleport spell. Bringing an individual here, not whisking anyone away. But who'd worked it?

Not that little flamehaired Knight, that was for sure and certain, unless Mystra or Azuth had arrived personally to work the spell for her.

Then came the second flash—and by its light the Zhent wizard saw something that took him far beyond frowning.

Telgarth Boarblade was coming toward him. He'd know that fluid, gliding walk anywhere, though his fellow Zhent—fellow rival, though just one of many—was using some sort of magic to disguise himself. There was at least one man with Boarblade, and likely more.

Drathar stepped hastily behind a tree, turned until his shoulders were against it, then worked a swift invisibility spell.

Thus hidden—as much as anyone could be hidden in a night full of flashing magic and roaring, tree-smashing ettins—he sat down against the tree trunk to keep quiet and watch what unfolded.

With the Knights of Myth Drannor, the ettin, Boarblade and his blades, and the Watching Gods alone knew who'd magically arrived all converging here, what unfolded promised to be good.

Or at least entertaining.

"Sorry," Islif panted, boosting Pennae to her feet.

The thief grinned. "Well, I'd rather be in your arms than embracing an ettin. Still have your blade?"

Islif waved it. Neither of them could see it in the dark, but they both heard the dull ring of its encounter with a sapling.

Pennae's grin widened. "I kept hold of mine, too. Let's both of us be after its hamstrings again. It's going for Florin, see?"

"Those flashes," Islif murmured. "Semoor? Doust? I can't believe it!"

"Nor I," Pennae agreed. "Looked like—"

She peered as a faint glow blossomed on one of the ettin's faces, and added, "*That's* Semoor's magic." Then she peered harder at what that radiance could let her see down in front of the ettin.

Frowning, she cursed.

"What?" Islif snapped as they both trotted forward.

"Tluining *Dauntless,* stlarn it!" Pennae spat. "Someone—Vangey the Royal Meddling Magician, for a wager!—must be watching us and has teleported him in here! Gods *stlarn* it!"

"Dauntless?" Islif gasped, astonished.

The ettin lurched forward in obvious pain, moving along the base of the gravel slope from left to right in front of them. Its discomfort was feeding a growing fury, and it was flailing the air with its morningstars as it sought to reach its foes: the ornrion Dauntless, Florin, and . . . that Harper from the Palace! Dalonder Ree, that was his name.

Pennae looked back over her shoulder, her fierce grin back. "Hamstring time! Both of us!"

She raced for the ettin so swiftly that Islif had to put her head down and sprint to catch up.

It was long past time for stealth. The ettin was cursing loudly and rending trees again—and Dauntless, at least, had decided to cling to tradition enough to snarl a war cry.

"For the Purple Dragon! Cormyr forever!"

Swords flashed, and morningstars swung—and struck. Smashed up and off his feet, Dauntless grunted in pain as the armor shielding his ribs crumpled and some of those ribs crumpled with it.

Dalonder Ree fended off the other morningstar with a precisely angled sword as he raced along under the ettin's swing. The ettin roared in triumph as he saw the ornrion's body go flying—and Pennae reached the ettin's far leg, leaving the nearer one for Islif, sprang as high as she could, and put all the strength in both of her shapely arms behind a keen slash of her dagger.

The blade bit into stinking flesh a moment before the Harper's sword sank into the ettin's crotch.

The two-headed giant stiffened, drew breath—and proved to every ear between Halfhap and Tilver's Gap that it *really* knew how to scream.

Islif reached its other leg, swinging her long sword as hard as she could.

The ettin screamed again, reeled, and toppled, felling several trees in its crash.

Dalonder Ree and Florin swarmed over its faces and necks, stabbing down into eyes and laying open throats.

The ettin convulsed with a wild, heaving violence that sent the men flying to join Dauntless in groaning, huddled heaps on the gravel slope. It fell silent and still.

"See?" Semoor observed from the ledge. "Lathander did that! All praise be unto the Morninglord!"

"Tempus *defend* me!" Islif snarled in exasperation, glaring up at the ledge.

"I wonder what the penance is for strangling a priest with his own tongue," Pennae said beside her. "I believe I've stolen just about enough to pay it, by now—and if not, I'd cheerfully enslave myself to the nearest orc-pandering festhall for a month or two to make up the difference!"

"Festhalls! That's it! *That's* how we'll make coin enough to do Lathander's great works for him!" Semoor called delightedly. "Pennae, I could kiss you!"

"And holynoses can fly, with about as much success," Pennae said under her breath. Then she brightened. "Unless I take you up atop yon cliff to start learning how, right now."

"Come!" Boarblade whispered fiercely, right in Klarn's face. "Tell all the others! We attack now, before they've settled themselves again! Swords out and *slay!*"

Klarn gaped at him, then turned and ran—blundering right into Darratur and receiving a firm shove that sent him aside into a tree.

The moment Boarblade saw Glay's face, he waved at them all to accompany him, turned back toward the Knights, drew his sword, and ran.

He could hear the four charging after him.

Good. Let them burst out to confront the Knights. He'd try to gut the ranger or the fighting lass as he ran past—and then keep right on running, past the fray and into the trees, to plunge back into hiding.

Where he'd hide and lurk, awaiting his best chance to find that Pendant.

If the four dolts he'd been saddled with butchered a good share of Knights, well and good. He'd have that much less work left.

Not that he was counting on it.

With Pennae and Islif helping him, Dauntless sat up, wincing.

"Are you *sure* you didn't bring this beast with you?" he growled, waving a hand at the sprawled, dead ettin. "Or let it loose from somewhere in your pryings and thievings?"

"Of *course* we did," Pennae snapped. "We have scores of pets like this one—and worse!—and as we cavort across Faerûn, we let them all loose to frolic through the trees and *try to kill us!* Gods above, how stupid can Purple Dragons *be?* You *do* know which end of a sword is which, I hope?"

"Oh, aye." Dauntless showed his teeth in a grin that wasn't pleasant at all. "I do know that—and so will your shapely backside in a breath or two, saucy lass!"

Pennae sneered. "Lick my sauce? Do my hair? Announce me to the queen?"

"Identify your head when I place it before her on a platter, more likely," Dauntless said. "With all the rest."

Pennae sighed loudly and gave the ornrion a shove that toppled him over, groaning in pain on his side in the gravel again.

"Pennae," Islif said reproachfully.

The thief shrugged. "My hand slipped," she said. "It does that. A lot."

"I've noticed," the ornrion said. "Lucky you are that my orders have changed."

"Oh?" Pennae said. "They've commanded you to be fair and reasonable, now? Is this is some special occasion?"

"When I can get up again," Dauntless said, "it certainly will be."

Boarblade raced along, heart pounding. It really didn't matter whether he had false Knights beside him—Ruldroun's four, or some of them, with their hargaunt disguises—or the real ones. Neither could be trusted, but perhaps the real ones would be the better companions in a fight.

Well, he was about to see, wasn't he?

The stump was more or less as he remembered it. A little damp, with wet dead leaves plastered to it because rain had fallen in this stretch of the forest several times over the last few days, but he cared nothing for the fate of this tattered, dirty crone's dress anyhail.

He settled himself on the stump, facing down the familiar little clearing so he'd see in an instant if any war wizard arrived. Nigh every last Wizard of War knew this lush little glade. It was one of the preferred "waystops" or "jump spots" for jaunts to Tilverton or the northeastern border wilds of the realm.

Hopefully, if one appeared, he'd not readily recognize Onsler Ruldroun behind the pocked and wrinkled crone's face the hargaunt had spun.

The scrying spell would be a little harder to explain away, but if he was given a chance to speak, Ruldroun knew enough of the catchphrases to seem to be one of Those Who Harp for a few breaths.

And a few breaths would be all he would need to triumph, teleport away, or die.

So he sat on his stump, looking down the glade—which coincidentally was also facing in the direction of the battling Knights, who were not all that far off through the forest—and watched the battle through his scrying eye.

All he needed was a little more patience against the surging excitement that rose again and again within him. It was the roiling energy of the three men he'd slain that was making him so restless, he knew, but he could master this now. Enough of the wild, feverish exhilaration was over and past. He was now always aware of what was really happening to him. When he kept away from exciting tastes and smells—good food—he could thrust aside the floods of emotion and tell himself calmly: You are awaiting the best time to step forward and seize the Pendant of Ashaba. Yes. The best time.

If Glays and the rest were dead by then . . . well, there were other men who could impersonate Knights and who would welcome the backlands life of Shadowdale.

Deltalon arrived a little farther from the glowstones than the Harper.

If you appeared right beside the Knights, you found yourself in the same peril that was afflicting them—and could well taste their own blades and spells before you had time to name yourself.

Which was the very reason he was bound for his favorite waystop glade in the heart of that part of the forest just north off the Moonsea Ride known as Hawkvale. No one dwelt there, and no eye that he knew had ever managed to discern a "vale" among all those tangled trees.

The clearing, not far from Tilverton, served the same purpose as his chosen destination. Appearing in the blink of an eye in the midst of a tavern or even just outside the walls of Tilverton warned everyone of your mastery of Art, no matter how skilled your acting to the contrary might be.

And despite what everyone remembered about the bad war wizards, *good* Wizards of War always tried to be deft and subtle.

"If you skulk out in the trees this night," the wizard Ruldroun half-murmured and half-sang. He stared at the glowing images of his conjured scrying dancing silently in midair before him. Boarblade was just beginning his charge.

Then he blinked. A man had appeared at the far end of the glade. A war wizard he knew! Lorbryn Deltalon, one of Vangerdahast's most trusted—

Onsler Ruldroun stood, his scrying forgotten, and whispered the strongest spell he knew.

He'd been saving that fire-gem for a long time, and it had cost him dearly, but what was that price against his very life?

The gem flashed and was gone—and the huge gout of flame blossomed from it and roared away down the clearing, fire that should sear flesh and bone alike, feeding on Art as well as mundane fuel.

Which should mean that if Deltalon was shielded in the usual ways against fire, he was doomed.

Yes, this was the place. Lush and damp and familiar. Dark now, in the depths of night, of course, but there was a spell-glow coming from the far end of the glade, and—

Lorbryn Deltalon had just time for one final thought as Faerûn exploded in blinding, white flame all around him:

So this is what it feels like to die.

Chapter 23
ALL THE NINE HELLS BREAK LOOSE

Oh, aye, I tell you I'll be there
When all the Nine Hells break loose
Wizards burn, heroes fall,
And the gods come tumbling after.

The character Ornbriar the Old Merchant
In the play Karnoth's Homecoming
by Chanathra Jestryl, Lady Bard of Yhaunn
First performed in the Year of the Bloodbird

The flames howled on, toppling trees and setting them aflame. Silhouetted against that bright raging stood all that was left of Lorbryn Deltalon.

A column of gray ash shaped like a wizard who'd turned his head in astonishment faced Ruldroun with one hand half-raised.

Then it slumped down and swirled away, gone forever.

Beyond it, the fire snarled.

Ruldroun hastened out of the glade on the far side from the fire, seeking—and finding—a tree with two trunks and a saddle between them large enough for him to stand in.

Leaning back against one trunk, eyes on the dying flames in the distance, he swiftly cast a spell many a Wizard of War had found useful when away from the cities of the realm.

The magic made his fingertips and ears tingle briefly as it took hold. Now, and for most of the time until dawn, he would be made aware of all minds approaching him, and their direction and distance.

It might well be imperative for the continued life of Onsler Ruldroun to see who—and what—the blaze lured near.

Fire roared into being off to his left, too suddenly and violently to be anything but a spell.

Brorn Hallomond smiled, held up his bone-coated hands to more clearly see how skeletal they looked, admired them in the dancing firelight for a moment, then turned off the road into the trees, heading for the blaze.

"From beyond the grave, I come for thee," he murmured the old saying and flexed his hands again.

Even if the fire-makers didn't happen to be the Knights of Myth Drannor, he certainly felt like killing someone.

"A gray render, too? You *have* been busy!"

The only answer Florin gave to Dalonder Ree was a shrug, but the Harper didn't have to look at the ranger's face to know his words had left Falconhand rather pleased.

He was just turning to begin a look all around, seeking any signs of other predators watching from the trees, when a great gout of flame blossomed out of nowhere with a roar, some way off in the forest, but racing toward them with frightening speed.

Off to Ree's left, Dauntless cursed at the sight, but even as he did the Harper could see the conflagration was small. It would die down long before getting anywhere near them.

Still, burning trees were toppling, sparks were wafting up into the night, and—*what was that?*

Dalonder whirled to his left, sword flashing up, and saw Florin and Dauntless doing the same.

Dark figures were racing at them, bursting out of the darkness, plunging out from between trees with swords and daggers flashing in their hands.

"*'Ware all!*" Dauntless roared. "We're under attack!"

By then, swords were clanging against swords in hasty parries, men were grunting as they tried to slash right through the swords and strength of foes, and someone was screaming as the tip of Dalonder Ree's sword slid through his hand, sending the dagger in it spinning away.

"Klarn!" the wounded man called desperately. "Klarn, *aid!*"

Steel clanged on steel. Dalonder Ree ducked one way and then hurled himself in another direction. The wounded man cried out in fear as his sword missed the dodging Harper entirely. Klarn didn't come—and the wounded man was falling, life-blood gurgling out of his opened throat.

Florin and Dauntless were hacking at three men, Klarn presumably one of them, and another had burst past the fray to come racing along the base of the gravel slope.

Pennae ran after him, dagger in hand. The *last* thing the Knights of Myth Drannor needed just now was a foe lurking in the night to fell them from behind, one by one.

It was a man, a little taller and stronger than she was but agile rather than hulking. There was something . . . *not right* about his head, as if something had shifted there, moving somehow since her first glimpse of him. A disguise slipping, perhaps.

The man came to a boulder among the scree. He dodged out and around it, which meant she had just enough time to—

Pennae threw the dagger in her hand, straight and hard. The man stiffened, arching back and grabbing at his shoulder; reflected firelight glinted off her little jutting fang there, just for a moment.

Pennae smiled a tight little smile and hurled her second dagger.

The man cried out as her dagger wobbled in the back of his upper left arm. Again he clutched at it. This time, her weapon fell out just before his clawing fingers got to it.

He ran on, stumbling, and Pennae bent at the full run and plucked up that second dagger, dark and wet with his blood.

By then, he was desperately climbing the cliff, stones bouncing down into her face with the clumsy haste of his climb.

Pennae's smile widened.

Drathar peered out through the trees at the battle and shook his head. Dark figures seemed to be leaping on all sides, firelight flashing back reflections on swords and daggers here, there, and fleetingly everywhere. He couldn't tell one combatant from another, stlarn it!

No—wait—there! *That* was Florin Falconhand, and the man beside him must be an ally, being as they'd both had chances to thrust steel into each other and hadn't. It was someone he'd seen before, someone—

"Sark it!" he said. "Blast them both!"

Invisibility be hrasted, he was going to hurl at least one foeblast!

There! He did the swift casting and flung out his arms in the usual triumphant flourish—and watched the night erupt in sudden green-gold flame, a burst embroidered by screaming bodies being flung into the air and away.

Heh-hah!

Right. Enough glee. Drathar crouched and went back to peering hard through the tangle of trees. In the eyeblinking aftermath of his spell, with the fire in the distant trees dying down, it was getting harder and harder to see. He doubted he'd slain Florin or the other man. His spell had struck just short, hurling them away rather than shattering them. Unless a helpful tree had done those shatterings for him when they'd been flung against it . . .

Not something he could trust in. He crouched, sinking into uncertainty again. Should he just blast away and so fell Boarblade and his men along with the Knights? Or save his spells to defend himself and leave Boarblade's men be, to help him do his work for him?

Would they help him? Or was he watching himself trade the Knights for new and stronger foes, who'd have the Pendant of Ashaba and be just as determined to defend it?

Drathar shook his head again. And some folk thought Zhentarim spent all their days preening and flogging slaves and spellhurling . . .

Holy Fist, when *was* the last time he'd flogged a slave?

In his fearful determination to get out of her reach, the man she'd wounded hadn't chosen an easy way up the cliff. Pennae knew the face she'd just climbed, and she was unhurt to boot. She swarmed up the weathered stones, tasting the iron tang of her foe's blood in her mouth as she bore the dagger between her clenched teeth. She was certain she'd passed him during her ascent, with quite some time to spare.

More than time enough to plant that dagger in the turf, pluck up two rocks of the right size from among the many strewn about atop the cliff, move to just the right spot, and wait.

Still and silent in the night, she hid in the darkness beyond the fading firelight splashing leaping reflections off the cliff face. The man never saw her until the first stone, flung full in his face, broke his jaw and left him stunned, just clinging to the weathered stone and fighting to try to think.

"B-Boarblade," he mumbled, after a moment, remembering his own name with some difficulty as he stared up into the merciless smile of the beautiful woman who'd crouched down to face him.

Then her second stone slammed into his nose, shattering it; the ruptured hargaunt hissed wildly in pain and erupted in oily, foul-smelling liquid all over his face—and Telgarth Boarblade lost his hold.

His despairing cry was very short. It wasn't a particularly tall cliff. But with nothing but very hard rocks awaiting him at the bottom, and his head reaching them first, it didn't have to be.

That cry ended abruptly. Pennae looked down at the sprawled, broken figure in smiling satisfaction.

Apprehension rose in her a moment later when she saw something dark and amorphous and leathery slither away from the man's face and *flow* away across the rocks, rippling and creeping.

Doust Sulwood darted into view, slithering down the scree slope from the ledge in some haste. He caught up to the eerie thing and battered it enthusiastically with his mace until it flapped wildly and stopped moving. Then he emptied an unlit lantern over it—and lit the dripping mess on fire.

Watching it sizzle wetly amid the flames, Pennae's smile returned.

* * ✦ * *

"Want to see who you're killing?" Semoor called from what sounded like the safety of the ledge.

Stlarning holynoses.

"Yes!" Dauntless bellowed back, seeing Florin staggering grimly back to join him. The Harper was struggling to stand somewhere farther off—which left a lone ornrion of the Purple Dragons, just now, to battle these mysterious men whose faces seemed to shift and even *melt* as they swung their blades.

One of them was down, sliced open by the Harper earlier, and another was fighting an unsteady battle to stand up. He'd been caught in the same spell-blast that had flung Florin and the Harper over yonder.

Which still left two—two who were clearly visible as Semoor's spell banished night, creating a sphere of bright sunlight.

Unfortunately, the two melt-faces were moving well apart so as to come at Dauntless from sharply opposing sides at the same time. Their swords, daggers, and teeth all gleamed. They wore identical merciless smiles.

"Gah," the Harper groaned from somewhere behind Dauntless. "This light! It's like fighting on a *stage* in some Sword Coast city theater!"

"We'll be . . . right with you," Florin gasped, reeling, from even closer at hand.

"Worry not," Dauntless called back over his shoulder. "There are *only* two, after all."

Florin lurched past him, swinging his sword for balance. One of the melting-faced men mistook the ranger's groggy state for clumsiness and went for an easy lunge to the vitals.

The man blinked as Florin was somehow—and quite suddenly—nowhere near the sword reaching for him. Rather, he was past the lunging man and aiming a cut at the back of an undefended knee on his way on to cross swords with the other melt-face.

That cut landed, and the knee's owner crashed to the ground, shoulders first. Winded, he was still struggling for breath when the sharpest knife Dauntless owned sliced through the shapeless thing on his face, which was rearing up like a snake—and slashed it right off his face.

Shorn of his nose, the man screamed. So did the shapeless thing on the ground beside him. Spurting gore and squalling, it had been severed into two pieces. Both of them reared up in energetic undulations, seeking to get away as swiftly as possible.

The Harper bent and deftly diced both into many small, wriggling fragments. "These should be burned," he said. "I've never seen them before, but I think I know what they are. Hrasted if I can remember the name, though. They shapechange."

"Ah," Dauntless said as he cut the fallen man's throat. In the same movement he turned to menace the last of the melting-faced men. "Useful to know. Can they change themselves into hard metal armor, or do swords still work on them?"

Florin was striking a series of ringing blows against the desperate parries of that last man, who was backing away as he saw that he now stood alone. His dazed and reeling fellow blade had just been slain by the Harper—who was now carefully butchering the hargaunt that he'd just sliced away from the dead face it was clinging to.

"Mercy!" the last melting-faced man cried suddenly. "I am Glays Tarnmantle and can offer twenty thousand golden lions of the realm in return for my life! I—"

The masklike, drooping thing on the man's face flowed with sudden urgency, streaming into his nose and mouth.

Glays struggled to shout something through its surging, but his nose was swelling up, stuffed full. His mouth was already distended into a grotesque, froglike shape, and as he shuddered and clawed at the shapeless thing, his face went slowly reddish-purple.

It was almost black by the time he staggered, then reeled, eyes bulging.

He fell headlong, crashing down to trampled forest turf. The sword clattered from his hand, and he lay still. The thing that had choked him flowed out onto the ground, dark and shapeless and menacing.

"Hooh," Dalonder Ree said, eyeing the corpse. "It seems

something was in a real hurry to collect that gold. We should burn that something."

"When we're done here," Florin said, pointing.

A large-boned skeleton was striding out of the night at them. It plucked up a fallen sword, hefted it, and then swung it with a flourish, still walking their way.

Dauntless sighed. "Some nights, you wonder *what* else the forest can spit up to entertain you."

Hefting his own sword, he strode to meet the skeleton.

In the chamber of scrying, everyone looked like a ghost.

Or so the saying went, established years ago by war wizards after their first experience of seeing the glow of over two dozen scrying spheres lighting all faces eerily from beneath.

As eerily ghostlike as any of them, Laspeera raised her eyes from some of those spheres to give her superior a rather grim look.

"So passes Lorbryn Deltalon," she said. "We have few enough left who are skilled at both Art and diplomacy *and* truly havens for our trust."

"Tell me what I *don't* know, lass," Vangerdahast said. "Reduced to sending Dauntless with a few enspelled trinkets in his pouches. That's us." He crooked an eyebrow at Laspeera's busy hands. "What're you doing?"

"Avenging Deltalon, if I can. It's worth a few scrying spheres to try to harm Onsler Ruldroun. I taught him so much. All wasted . . ."

"He's probably fled beyond our reach," the Royal Magician said. "Yet it's worth doing anyhail. At the very least, it'll stop him using the glade. Let him try to sleep up a tree."

Watching and listening to Laspeera's casting, Vangerdahast carefully began one of his own, deftly reaching his hands over and among hers with the familiarity of long practice at spell-weaving together.

When it was done, they both stepped back and thrust their wills at the other floating scrying spheres, seeking to force them away from the quartet that were flaring brightly and about to burst.

They weren't fast enough to save them all.

In the tinkling, ear-ringing aftermath, both mages rolled over from where they ended up—on the floor and driven against a wall. They looked at each other. Their upflung arms had saved their faces and throats from deadly shards of crystal, but they were bleeding from the usual countless tiny nicks and slices, and their garments now looked as if a dozen assassins had hacked at them with razor-sharp blades.

"Before you try to think of something clever to say about my new fashion look," Laspeera said, as she struggled to her feet and held out a hand to haul him up, "consider that you look worse. Much worse."

" 'Tis the paunch and the body hair," Vangerdahast said. "So now for the rest of our evening's entertainment: the intrepid Dauntless faring into the forest."

"As all the Nine Hells break loose," Laspeera said. She murmured the cantrip that would rid her hair of a thousand tiny shards of crystal.

Vangerdahast murmured something more substantial, and his hands were suddenly full of stark black robes. With a flourish he held the uppermost garment out to Laspeera.

She took it with a smile and asked, "Aren't you going to turn your back as I slip into this?"

"No," Vangerdahast told her, shrugging off his own tatters. "Why?"

He had always loved Laspeera's laugh.

The glade exploded.

Ruldroun didn't even have time to leap down out of the tree before its great trunks shattered above him, its boughs torn off and swept away in a crashing rain—and he was hurled along after them, his shielding buffeted, struck hard, slammed against other trees, and shattered.

He hit the ground in a tumbling chaos of snapping twigs, sliding wet leaves, mud, and bruised wizard.

"And so I taste the Royal Magician's little slap," he grunted. Pain flared in his left side. Broken ribs, probably. His shielding had done its work, but it was clear that it would be the act of an utter fool to tarry anywhere near the glade.

He'd best get to the Knights and skulk along after them. He could still conjure his best shielding and weave a lesser one as well, then combine the two—but he'd best do it only after he'd passed the clearing and gotten well clear of its other side.

Not that there was anything forcing the Knights to stay where they were. Ruldroun sighed, winced again at the pain that brought, turned to face the pattering of falling twigs that marked where the clearing had just enlarged itself, and started to run.

"I believe that particular tactic would be one I'd deem, in the words of Lord Piergeiron, 'less than wise,'" a warm, lyrical, woman's voice said. That would be Sharanralee.

"I'm not talking wise, look ye," Mirt the Moneylender rumbled. "I'm laying *all* the tactics I can think of before us, rather than sorting out just those I deem best or preferable beforehand. I've heard too many lords' deliberations—or Harper moots, come to that—to want to do otherwise."

"So," an amused, mature, man's voice asked in quiet amusement, "are we then as bad as Harpers, Mirt—or as good as Harpers?"

That would be the wizard Tarthus, straying from Piergeiron's shadow for once. The Open Lord of Waterdeep must be very well guarded by someone else just now.

The night was dark, the turret that held those three folk was widely deemed inaccessible to creatures who couldn't fly, and the wards around it would raise instant alarm upon the approach of any flying creatures.

It seemed those wards deemed hovering magical swords to be something other than creatures. Whereupon no alarm had been raised, and it was extremely unlikely that anyone would be out and peering up at the turret just to check up on the efficacy of those wards.

Besides, Old Ghost was making Armaukran float absolutely motionless, vertical, and quite close to the shutters of the window. The little conference was quite interesting.

It was folk such as these three whom he wanted to collect in the Sword That Never Sleeps. To know the workings of the Harpers, or the Lords of Waterdeep, or—

It was at that moment that a spell Old Ghost had cast a long time ago suddenly stirred, sending its brief and faint warning across half of Faerûn.

Battle spells had erupted in a certain clearing used by Cormyr's Wizards of War, a clearing he'd cast his watch spell upon—and now, scant breaths later, someone had cast a complex, manyspells shielding.

That caster had to be someone powerful, on important business bent.

Business—and a person—he was very much interested in knowing more about.

The long, slender sword silently drew away from the window, turned in the air until its point was aimed east, and raced silently away from the turret, as swiftly as if it had been loosed from the bow of a mighty archer.

Old Ghost had decided to get to that nameless forest clearing just as fast as the Sword That Never Sleeps could fly.

Tsantress was barefoot and in her nightgown, sitting upright on the edge of her bed—the bed she'd been tossing and turning in, mere moments ago.

No wonder, that, given the time, but her restless inability to sleep and the energetic propensity of certain unscrupulous merchants of Suzail to get up to things illicit the moment her back was turned had her renouncing all attempts to get back to sleep.

She ran her hands absently through her sleep-tangled hair and stared into her scrying sphere.

It glowed softly as it hung in the air in front of her nose, awakening into a view of Albaertus Tranth's private office, quite a few streets closer to the harbor than where she was sitting.

It seemed the good merchant—if that wasn't using the term too loosely—was also afflicted with sleeplessness just now. He was using his wakefulness to meet with someone cowled, masked, and gloved, who appeared to have fallen into the habit of knocking on back doors in Suzail in the dark wee hours with heavy sacks of gold coins in his hand.

The war wizard bent forward and peered closely. Tranth was unlocking a heavy metal coffer with a key that had been hanging around his neck, and—

Abruptly the scrying sphere flashed bright white, blinding her into a sharp gasp, and flung itself across the room.

Thankfully, it struck her row of cloaks and gowns, tearing them all off their pegs as it raced past to strike a heavy tapestry.

Tsantress rolled on her bed and then off its edge to land hard on her spread knees on the carpeted floor. She clawed at her flooding eyes and tried to crawl toward her door on her elbows. An inescapable conclusion reared up like a dark and inexorable foe in her mind: Vangerdahast was up to his tricks again.

No one else—save Laspeera, and *she* had more sense—would dare to cast a slaying spell through one of Vangey's precious scrying spheres, causing it to explode and shattering any other scryings going on at the same time. Certainly not anywhere near the Royal Court. Or the Palace, come to that.

Either the halls were going to be crowded with angry, wand-waving Wizards of War in the next few breaths, or the Royal Magician was to blame, and everything would remain still and tensely silent until morning.

Well, not this time. She could find and pull on her boots by feel, if her eyes didn't stop streaming, and probably find her way to the Palace, too.

She had to reach the Princess Alusair. That blinding flash had thrust a vision into her mind, fleeting and vivid and tluining alarming: Knights of Myth Drannor, fighting hard against some unknown foes in a deep, wild forest somewhere, with Dauntless—*Alusair's* champion, *that* Dauntless—fighting alongside them.

Now, the Royal Magician was . . . the Royal Magician. Very much a law unto himself, who said and did as he pleased and somehow seemed to escape consequences that would kill—not merely discomfit or career-shatter—others. She, Tsantress, was not the Royal Magician and would be before-all-the-gods damned if she behaved anything *like* the Royal tluining Magician.

She kept her word, once given. And she'd sworn to the Princess Alusair—an Obarskyr who just might end up on the Dragon Throne if bad things befell her family—that she'd inform the princess immediately if Vangerdahast ordered Ornrion Taltar Dahauntul into danger again.

Which meant the moment she had her boots on and had found and buckled her wand belt on over her nightgown, she was going to hurry to the tunnel that linked the Royal Court with the Royal Palace just as fast as she could stride.

Then, blindness or no blindness, royal slumber or no royal slumber, she was getting to the Princess Alusair just as fast as she could, spitting out the pass phrase that meant doom was coming down on Cormyr, so the guards barring her way at door after guarded door would be frightened as they hurried to fling open their doors for her.

Because if Dauntless died because of Vangerdahast's orders, and the Princess Alusair found out about it, doom *would* be coming down on Cormyr.

Chapter 24

ANGER A WIZARD, AND DIE

Aye, I have learned a thing or three
Thus far in a life well heaped in deceit
And treachery. There's keeping pacts
And knowing when to run
And this: Anger a wizard, and die.

The character Ornbriar the Old Merchant
In the play Karnoth's Homecoming
by Chanathra Jestryl, Lady Bard of Yhaunn
First performed in the Year of the Bloodbird

I've never seen a skeleton like that before!" the Harper said. "Keep back!"

"I've never seen a skeleton like that before, either," Dauntless said. "But never mind that. Look you past it at the creeping things!"

"Hargaunts," Dalonder Ree said, as he, Dauntless, and Florin backed away from Brorn and tried to peer past the sword-wielding skeleton. "They're called hargaunts."

"That's nice," Dauntless said. "It's always the height of urbane courtesy to know the name of what's trying to kill you."

Beyond the advancing skeleton, the hacked-apart pieces of hargaunts were flowing together like worms mindlessly converging on something dead and beginning to rise up into a vaguely humanlike figure.

"Saers!" Florin called to Dauntless and the Harper as he stepped to the left and waved at them to move to the right. He was motioning them to move so the three of them could strike at the skeleton from its front and from both of its sides, all at once. Ree and the ornrion nodded back and moved as the ranger had directed.

"Tluin," the skeleton said.

He felt much better with the shielding around him.

Two wardings and a lesser ironguard woven into the result, to turn back most magics and make him untouchable by the swords and daggers of Knights of Myth Drannor—or anyone else, unless those blades bore strong magics.

Yet there was room for something more. A simple deception for simple adventurers. He'd not face the Knights as Onsler Ruldroun or as some crone in a dirty dress—but as the ornrion Dauntless, in the shreds of a failed disguise, out here stalking them under Crown orders.

That, they'd believe in a trice. Letting him walk among them, rather than spending his days skulking out in forests, straining to get close enough without being noticed.

The hargaunt was already stirring approvingly, even before he really concentrated on the remembered face of the ornrion.

A few moments of creeping and flowing, and he'd be hurrying on again to the battle.

The Lion Room was warm and richly paneled, and the firesparkle in their goblets was good. They were almost past the sneering and elbowing each other stage, carried along on their own rising excitement into being fellow conspirators. And that was saying something, considering how fervently these young noble rivals had hated each other before this night.

Royal Sage Alaphondar knew how to defer to nobility. He knew their strengths and had praised them, saying nothing of their pride and pratfalls and indiscretions. Wherefore Lharak Huntcrown, Doront Rowanmantle, Beliard Emmarask, Cadeln Hawklin, Faerandor Crownsilver, Garen Truesilver, and Talask Dauntinghorn were all secretly thrilled to be sitting in this private chamber of the Royal Palace.

Youngbloods of most of the foremost titled families of the realm, they had all been recruited for some mysterious "special missions for the Crown." That meant something. Just being born into the families whose names they bore was enough to puff them up with their own importance when dealing with lesser folk. But every last one of them knew that they themselves had as yet done nothing to merit any personal respect. Or earn one thin coin of any minting.

It did not take more brains than those of the nearest dolt to suspect that if they performed these missions well, important Crown posts—and salaries, to boot—would be theirs. *That* would make their fathers sit up and take notice.

Wherefore they were now sitting, several-times-refilled goblets in hand, conferring with Alaphondar over a map-strewn table in the richly paneled Lion Room, as the doors opened and a few aging senior servants in splendid livery brought in a light repast. Platters of fried, breaded, and sugar-dusted soft-shelled crabs.

"That *bastard!*"

The hiss that came through the open doors in the wake of the steaming food was furious, unexpected, and feminine. Every head around the table snapped up in unison to regard the open doors.

In time to witness the Princess Alusair in her nightgown, striding furiously past the Lion Room without a glance and on down the passage, with a similarly garbed female war wizard half a step behind her.

With one accord, the young noblemen set down their goblets and reached for the hilts of ceremonial swords that no longer rode in their scabbards.

Then they sighed or cursed, recalling that they'd had to surrender their blades earlier. They boiled out into the passage in the wake of the princess to see what was afoot.

The forgotten Royal Sage smiled fondly at their backs and strode silently after them.

A dozen chambers and passages along, he murmured the brief incantation that silently restored seven courtsabers to as many rightful scabbards. It was interesting to watch just how many strides it took most of the youngbloods to notice the reappearance of their weapons. Truly, the Forest Kingdom stood not unguarded.

Alaphondar snorted at another thought. There would be trouble over this, but it would be well worth it to see Vangerdahast's face.

✦ ✦ ✦

Finally, his chance!

Drathar wasted not an instant on a triumphant smile. There'd be time enough for that later. He was too busy weaving the strongest foeblasting spell he had left.

One long, hissing incantation later, it was done.

And the Harper Dalonder Ree exploded, flattening his fellows as his shredded limbs were hurled everywhere.

Drathar's spell cut the walking skeleton in half, too, and collapsed the hargaunts back into scattered, blazing scraps.

And what of it?

Then Drathar smiled.

It was a grin that lasted a mere instant or two. The ranger and the ornrion were sturdier stuff—and had keener eyes—than he'd thought. They were up and charging at him already, with some of the other Knights—the young wench with the knife and one of the priests—in their wake.

Naed.

No matter how many years one spent mastering the Art, it all came down, again and again, to how fast you could run.

Hrast it.

Drathar ran, ducking under and past clawing branches, dodging around tree trunks that stood in his way like so many tall black statues, and whirling from time to time just long enough to catch sight of a pursuer. He sent a battlestrike spell back at them.

Those flaring blue bolts never missed, and it didn't take many of them to wound all but the strongest—or most foolishly determined—pursuer.

He was just starting to really gasp for breath and stumble because his feet were getting heavy, when he realized he'd managed it. The trees behind him were no longer filled with the crashings of angry, hurrying Knights of Myth Drannor.

Doust found them by the simple tactic of falling over them. Pennae broke off gasping for breath long enough to chuckle.

"Well met," she said, hauling on the priest's hair to lift his face out of the dirt. Doust spat out some twigs and crumbling old fern fronds and thanked her.

"I'm done," he added, unnecessarily.

"We all are," Florin said grimly, as they knelt together in the little hollow, panting hard.

"So he'll be out there," Pennae said, "lurking. Able to blast us at will, as he did to Ree. Hrast it, all he has to do is wait until we fall asleep!"

Florin nodded. "You're right," he said grimly when he'd found breath enough to speak. "We have to go after him. Doust, can you— can Tymora—give us light, yonder? If so, do it. Pennae, you and I are going wizard-hunting. You make noise, dodge about, and *don't* attack him."

"Oh?"

"Yes. That will be my task. I *liked* Dalonder Ree."

The Princess Alusair was good at storming. Many guards were quaking behind her by the time she'd traversed much of the Palace and the Royal Court to burst in on the Royal Magician in a certain little-known chamber.

He and Laspeera looked up, ready magic rising crackling into their hands.

"Don't even think of it, wizard!" the Princess said, as Tsantress and the seven young noblemen spread out behind her.

Vangerdahast stared past her at the sea of unfriendly noble faces. She watched him recognize each of them in one instant, then in the next put his best "aghast" expression across his face. "Who are *these?*"

"Cormyreans," Alusair told him. "The very citizens of Cormyr you are sworn to *serve*, Court Wizard. Remember?"

"Well, yes, as Court Wizard I am indeed, but as *Royal Magician* I cannot allow the security of the realm to be imperiled—"

That argument had always left her seething. Its goad was just what she needed right now. "True, Vangey, but in matters of precedence and formal authority, the Royal Magician takes orders from the Court Wizard, and the Court Wizard is obligated to take orders from *me*. Not just my father, King Azoun, or my mother or older sister, but from any Obarskyr. So, Court Wizard Vangerdahast, you just tell the Royal Magician to shut up for once and stop defying me and thereby practicing treason—and I'll overlook his open defiance of the Crown. *Once.*"

Vangerdahast stared at her, mouth opening and closing like that of a large platterfish in the royal fishponds, and said nothing. For once.

The Sword That Never Sleeps streaked through the night, its point cleaving mists and clear air alike. It was racing across Faerûn faster than any striking hawk, but it was a long way from Waterdeep to a certain spot in the wilderland forests that currently held the Knights of Myth Drannor.

Old Ghost bore down with his will until it hurt, to make the sword *really* move.

"Princess," Vangerdahast said, "this is none of your business, truly. Rather, it is a secret of the realm that none of these—"

"*I'll* decide what is, and what is not, a secret of the realm," Alusair said. "From this moment on, *everything* you and everyone else does in Cormyr is my business. *Especially* things you try to keep secret. So I'm going to be doing a lot of poking and prying and giving you orders. *Plenty* of orders. Wizard, get used to it!"

Among the grinning nobles, someone sniggered.

"None of that," Alusair said. "The man is doing his job—and it's one of the worst in all the kingdom. Even if he dwelt in a Cormyr entirely empty of snippy little princesses and haughty nobles. Now, Vangerdahast, tell me: Just why is my champion in the heart of a battle *outside* the realm?"

Vangerdahast stared at her again, his mouth once more opening and closing like that of a large platterfish in the royal fishponds, and said nothing. Again.

"They're not much," Semoor said, "but they should at least blunt a spell or two. One from Clumsum and one from me. You're as ready as we can make you. Go wizard hunting."

"My thanks," Florin replied. Clapping both of the priests on their shoulders, he rose and sought the night, Pennae at his side.

"I'm going after them," Semoor said. "Just down there, into that stand of trees, to keep watch. Any passing beast can't help but see us up here on this ledge. 'Tis like being on display in a Suzail shop window."

"Heh," Dauntless said, "now you know how lawkeepers feel when we go on patrol into the alleys of Marsember on foggy nights. Or the Stonelands, any time."

"Hey, what're you doing?" Doust asked. "What's that?"

"Very strong healing," the ornrion said, holding up the little steel vial he'd drawn from his belt. "Given to me by Laspeera, to treat any Knight who needed it." He waved the vial at Jhessail, slumped on the ledge beside him. "Like this one."

Doust looked at Semoor, who nodded reassurance, then looked back at Dauntless.

The ornrion had politely awaited their approval. He thrust two fingers onto the sides of Jhessail's face, opening her jaw—and upended the unstoppered vial into it.

Her tiny form spasmed under his knees, she coughed, and her eyes snapped open.

"What—whooo! What *was* that?" she asked, trying to slide out from under him. A large, hairy ornrion's hand was promptly planted on her bosom with a flat disregard for proprieties, pinning her down.

"Hoy, Orn—*Dauntless!*" she said. "Let me up!"

"To do what?"

"Go to wherever the fighting is, and—"

"No."

"My spells are needed, and—"

"No."

"Doust! Semoor! Anyone? Get him off me!"

Jhessail struggled, kicking and squirming and elbowing, but the ornrion had her overmatched in size, strength, weight, and position. He easily held her down.

Jhessail cursed, hurling words that would have astonished someone who was judging her by her size and looks.

"If you set out to be a hero, lass," Dauntless said through her profane fury, "you're setting out to die. Heroes are something bards create out of real folk who've struggled just to get through some danger or other. Anyone who stops in the heart of peril to think how he'll be regarded is stlarning likely to die a fool's death, right then and there. Now, the line between fool and hero is sometimes hard to see—so sane folk waste no time looking for it. They just do what they have to do or die trying."

"Ornrion," Jhessail spat at him, "your words are very interesting, and I both value them and await with pleasure an opportunity—if we both happen to live so long—to debate them with you, perhaps over goblets of something suitably delicious. But right now, my friends are in peril. So let me up, or so help you, I'll maim you with magic!"

"Fine thanks, that, for healing you," Dauntless told her sadly, as her vain attempts to jerk free dragged him this way and that along the ledge.

One of her frantic movements turned her enough to catch sight of a familiar face.

"Doust!" she called despairingly—and the priest of Tymora sighed, took hold of one of the ornrion's boots, and twisted, flipping Dauntless over.

In a flash Jhessail jerked free and was gone into the night in a tangle of tossed red hair and a last snarled curse.

Dauntless glared at Doust.

The priest had carefully positioned himself so as to block the ornrion's way off the ledge to pursue Jhessail. He smiled, folded his hands in prayer, and offered, "May the Lady of Luck be with you."

"You may need her more," the ornrion glowered, drawing back his fist to punch Doust in the face.

At that moment, a passable imitation of his own voice bellowed out of the night: "Ho, Knights of Myth Drannor! 'Tis Ornrion Taltar Dahauntul of the Purple Dragons, Dauntless to most, come to render you all aid in your time of need. Aye, I'm your friend now! Orders have changed!"

Doust, looking at Dauntless, lifted his eyebrows in a silent question.

Staring back at Doust, Dauntless snarled, "Caztul! Blood of the Lady! Arntarmar and Alavaerthus! Some tluining wizard or sneak-thief is pretending to be me! Gelkor! Talandor! Obey Vangerdahast for one hrasted breath, get plunged into a naeding murdering battle, and some motherless, harcrimmiting teskyre-head is witlessing-well using my name! We'll tluining well see about that! Let me at the bastard! Harcrimmitor!"

Doust grinned. "You want me to do all of that? At once? Shouldn't you be talking to Semoor?"

There it was again. A small, stealthy sound in the bushes very close by. To the right.

Drathar turned and blasted.

The momentary flare of his strike showed him he'd torn apart defenseless bushes—and the reason why. The thief-wench of the Knights was leaning out from behind a tree with a palm-sized stone in her hand. She'd obviously made those sounds by tossing stones into the bushes and was just as obviously intending to hurl the next one at him.

She was giving him a malicious grin right now and drawing back her arm for a throw.

As the glow died away, Drathar flung himself a few steps to the right and crouched down to avoid being hit. His next spell blasted the tree she'd been sheltering behind.

There was a brief crashing sound, as of thornbushes being crushed, nearby on his left, but he ignored it. She'd obviously thrown her stone there to divert him, rather than hurling it at him. What of it?

The riven shards of the tree burned fitfully in the wake of his spell. Drathar stood watching them, smirking in satisfaction.

Anger a wizard, and die.

An old, old saying, but perhaps thieves were too busy pilfering things to learn the wise lessons that kept most folk in Faerûn alive.

Bushes rustled again, very near, on his left. Drathar whirled, cursing, to hurl a swift battlestrike.

Florin's thrown sword took him in the face, and Florin was right behind it, punching hard and brutally, battering the breath right out of Drathar Haeromel's lungs even before Drathar hit the littered forest floor.

The Zhentarim took a hard punch in his throat and had no means left even to scream as the ranger's dagger plunged into his breast once, twice, and thrice.

Drathar had time to think that he was dying and to see a few stars through his welling tears.

Then the dagger came down again, and it all ended.

"So you sent my champion—*my* champion, Vangerdahast, one man out of an army of thousands you could have chosen from, to say nothing of all the Wizards of War under your personal command, who would seem to be far more useful in aiding the Knights against foes who are hurling *spells* at them! And now he bids fair to get slain while we watch, I helpless because I can do nothing to aid him but scream at you, and you helpless because you stlarning well *want* to be!"

Vangerdahast glowered at her, tight-lipped, but he made no reply.

"Well?" Alusair pressed him. "Are you going to do nothing? While we all watch? Very well, I *order* you to protect Ornrion Taltar Dahauntul of the Purple Dragons—to say nothing of my mother Queen Filfaeril's personal Knights! Do something! Work some magic! Or shall I just order all of these loyal, upstanding noble sirs to draw their swords and reward your treason fittingly?"

"Thereby dooming them all," the Royal Magician said. "I am not without defenses of my own, Highness. Pray think before you speak so rashly."

"Think before I speak? *Think* before I speak?" Alusair's voice rose like a trumpet. "I have seen barely more than a dozen winters, sirrah. I am a willful, spoiled brat—by your own description, don't think I haven't heard it—and I am an Obarskyr! Being born royal was not my choice, nor have I been much of a credit to my blood thus far, but I do know that one thing royalty do *not* have to do is think before they speak! They have Royal Magicians to do that for them—and speak for them behind their backs, all too often, too!"

Silence fell as Alusair panted to draw breath for the rest of her tirade. Into the gap burst a small, explosive sound that froze everyone in the chamber.

Laspeera, the demure and motherly second-most-powerful Wizard of War in the realm, was snorting in suppressed mirth.

"Hand me your sword," Pennae said. "It'll take me forever to saw his head off with this little dagger."

Florin winced. "You're going to decapitate him?"

"Just to make sure. He doesn't seem to have had any of those blast-the-countryside contingencies tied to his death, but perhaps he has a slow healing and will come after us after he's lain here long enough."

Florin winced again. "Someday soon I'll be wanting to hear more about when and where you heard of such things."

"Someday soon," she agreed. "If you tie me to the bed, you may even get some answers."

Florin was too busy blushing to reply as she rose, patted him on the arm, thrust his sword into his hand, and said, "Let's get back to the others. The Watching Gods alone know what trouble they'll have gotten into."

As they came out into the trampled and burned area in front of the cliff, Pennae said, "Well, well. Seems the gods guide my tongue."

Dauntless was charging across the corpse-strewn ground at . . . himself. Or rather, at someone else who wore the face of Dauntless and a ragged, dirty peasant's dress. Roaring, waving his sword wildly, Dauntless lumbered closer and closer to his foe.

After a shout of "I am the real Dauntless! Knights of Myth Drannor, strike down this impostor! Stop him!" the Dauntless in the dress seemed to realize his deception was hopeless. He raised his arms and started to cast a spell.

"Hrast, that's a stlarning strong war spell!" Pennae said as she and Florin sprinted forward. "Dauntless is doomed—or we are!"

The wizard wearing the face of Dauntless raised his voice to end his incantation—and noticed the running pair for the first time.

"Naed!" Pennae gasped, swerving to take herself wide and away from Florin.

The wizard hastened to finish the spell, eyes fixed on her.

Light bloomed around him as Doust cast the only thing he could think of to distract the foe.

Dauntless, running hard and fast, stumbled.

Florin ran faster, drawing back his sword for a desperate throw.

A long, slender sword raced out of the night, into the light, and plunged right through the wizard.

Black fire burst from the man's chest, some magic of the sword melting its way right through his body. Arms flung wide, incantation lost in an agonized scream, Onsler Ruldroun toppled, dying.

White fire boiled up from his limbs, setting afire something black and amorphous that had sprung off his face. Blazing, it fell beside Pennae, and she turned to pursue it, dagger out.

Fire raced out from the mage's boots, in a brush-crackling expanding ring that sent saplings sagging down and Florin swerving to snatch up Dauntless and haul him back and away. Just behind them, a running Jhessail was hurled back by a wind only she could feel.

The ground rumbled and shook, flinging everyone off their feet and sending the flying sword cartwheeling away through the night sky, trailing little flickering flames. Doust's modest little sphere of light expanded into a huge dome as bright as day, and at the heart of it the wizard's body, arms flung wide, hung motionless in the air, frozen in the instant before he would have struck the ground. The dead wizard burned.

"Now *these*," Pennae shouted, "are contingency spells!"

"Fury of Tempus!" Dauntless cried, his face gone from purple to pale. "Let's get *out* of here!"

"Oh?" Semoor shouted back. *"How?* Are we supposed to *fly?"*

Dauntless stared at him, then turned and pointed back at the cliff. "Everyone!" he bellowed as the ground shook again under them and the burning body of Ruldroun grew too bright to see, "Over there! Muster to me! Laspeera and Vangerdahast gave me magic!"

They all gathered around Dauntless.

He looked around at all of them, smiled tightly, held up what looked like a rune-covered tile shaped like a flat bar—and broke it.

The world quivered.

The cliff, burning wizard, and all the strewn bodies and scorched trees vanished.

They stood in an open area where stars aplenty glimmered through high, tattered gray clouds above them, and a narrower, more rutted road than the Moonsea Ride was under their boots. On either side of the road was deep forest, stretching as far as they could see.

A little way east, along the way—east if they'd judged the stars right—a mound of rocks rose up on the north side of the road, bare of trees. Otherwise, there was nothing that could be called a landmark anywhere in sight.

Semoor peered in every direction, straining to see as far as he could in the night gloom, then asked, "Where by the Morninglord's rosy behind are we now? And what fell wizards, monsters, and stlarning magic flying swords are sneaking up on us *this* time?"

Vangerdahast smiled upon the simmering Princess Alusair. He gestured airily.

"See? Just as we planned," he said, strolling over to stand on the far side of the scrying sphere that had just shown Dauntless and the Knights vanishing from the battle-ravaged forest.

He frowned and let disapproval creep into his voice. "If you're going to give orders, Highness, be very certain you know what's happening, what's been planned, and what you're blundering into the midst of. I always do."

Whereupon Cadeln Hawklin snarled, "So you walked in on me, when I was seducing Marissra Brassfeather, on *purpose?* You dung-eating *snake!*"

"Compliments, compliments," Laspeera said soothingly, her hand around Cadeln's sword wrist. Though the slender, ceremonial, Hawklin courtsaber was half out of its scabbard, that's where it stayed, no matter how furiously he glared and strained. Her grip was surprisingly strong.

"Now say nothing but pleasantries," the motherly Wizard of War added. "You'll only goad him into worse things. A lot of being a successful noble is something that's the same for succeeding as a commoner or a Wizard of War."

"Oh?" Lharak Huntcrown was unable to resist asking. "What's that?"

"Knowing when to keep your mouth shut and await a better time to settle scores," Laspeera replied.

"Every fell wizard, monster, and stlarning flying sword you just woke up, dolt of Lathander," Dauntless growled at Semoor. "Witless idiot."

"No, no, he has wits," Pennae said. "That's what's so tragic. Instead of using them, he carries them around in a bucket and hurls them at the rest of us."

"As is the way of holynoses," Semoor said with dignity, "despite the pointed lack of appreciation that—"

"Shut up, Semoor," Islif said. "Dauntless, have you any idea where we are?"

"Certainly," the Purple Dragon said. "In the Dalelands, past Tilverton and the Shadow Gap. This, under our boots, is the Northride. The road to Daggerdale joins it a half day's fast ride back that way, and yon rise is Bellowhar's Horn, a waymark where a drinkable spring rises. Caravans sometimes camped here, back before the goblinkin got so bad."

"Ah," Doust said. " 'Got so bad,' eh? *That's* reassuring."

"Keeping 'em down'll be your duty now, I'm thinking," Dauntless said. "Them and the Zhents. There's caravans as appears on this road, seemingly out of nowhere; they head for Cormyr but never come through Shadowdale. Or so our spies swear."

"Spies?"

"Spies. Shadowdale's an easy walk past the Horn. Fare you well, heroes."

The ornrion raised one hand in a salute as he stepped back.

"Huh," Semoor replied, "you didn't have to be sarcastic."

Dauntless stared right at him. "I'm not. If ever we meet again, be aware that I consider you friends. And good Knights of Cormyr. And true heroes that the bards'll sing about when they find out about you."

"Oh," Pennae said. "That changes something." She held out her hand to him.

There was something small, leather, and bulging in it.

The ornrion peered at it, blinked, and decided it was time for his eyes to bulge almost as much.

"My purse!" He stared at her. "Why, you stlarning little *minx* of a—" Then he chuckled, husky mirth that swiftly built into a loud guffaw.

Pennae strolled forward and dropped her purloined burden into his hand. It clinked when it landed.

"One doesn't steal from friends," she said. "Much."

And she leaned forward and kissed him. Very thoroughly.

The Sword That Never Sleeps scudded through the night, sharing the chill sky with a few tatters of cloud. Zhentil Keep wasn't far ahead, now.

Whom to collect?

Old Ghost pondered. Just because the sword that now held him could also hold a dozen or so others didn't mean he should make it do so.

He needed sentiences who knew useful things, who didn't raise his ire from mere contact, and whom he could control. Or did he?

There was no need to rush into this. Anyone the sword slew, whom he commanded its magics to subsume, would be drawn into the blade. Not their bodies but all else that made them who they were.

Bodies, they could regain later, if he helped them conquer the minds of beings wounded by Armaukran. They could shatter those minds and take over the bodies.

He could do that, too, and in the space of a few breaths become a king. Or a queen. Or even an adventurer. Preferably one less bumbling than, say, a Knight of Myth Drannor.

Old Ghost chuckled and flew on into the night.

Epilogue

Morning touched chilled skin and slowly brought cold, stiff Knights awake from wherever atop the boulder-strewn Horn they'd slumped to sleep the night before.

They yawned, stretched, scratched at itches, and winced at aching feet in worn boots, saying little to each other. The water in the spring was so cold that it numbed their mouths.

Before them, the road awaited, rising as it ran on through the trees. Around that little bend and over that hill, or the next one, was Shadowdale.

Florin peered around, collecting silent nods of readiness.

No one wanted to tarry over a roadside morningfeast of greens and ditchwater tea when there was an inn somewhere ahead. Semoor's stomach growled that message almost loudly enough to echo off the nearby trees. He winced amid a chorus of kindly, sympathizing chuckles.

Pennae strode to the fore, clapped Florin on the arm, and gave him her emphatic nod.

He nodded back, a slow smile stealing onto his face, and she set off at a steady pace, not hurrying. The Knights fell into line behind her.

"Oh, I've been walking all my days—" Semoor sang, but his mocking song ended abruptly when Doust drove an elbow into a gut, amid a general chorus of "Shut *up*, Semoor!"

No one, it seemed, felt much like talking yet.

That lasted until they reached the crest of the hill. Shadowdale wasn't stretched out before them on its far side but lay somewhere farther on. Of course. Out here, things were always farther off than they seemed.

Yet they knew that walking would lose the Forest Kingdom behind them, so they stopped and looked back at mountains and wild, rolling woods they didn't recognize, largely lost in morning mists.

"Farewell, Cormyr," Semoor said. His fellow Knights nodded silently. A few breaths later, he added, "Rest quiet, Narantha."

Florin flinched back as if someone had slapped him across the face, then stepped forward again, eyes suddenly glimmering. "Narantha," he murmured. "I'll never forget you."

"Farewell, Espar and all our kin," Doust said.

Pennae chuckled softly and waved cheerfully in the direction of the Forest Kingdom. "Gods smile on you, all you rampant young noble lordlings. I'll miss you—arrogance, heaps of coins, preening codpieces, and all."

She turned away, leaving Islif rolling her eyes. The tall warrior woman gazed back in the direction of Cormyr then said simply, "I *will* be back."

Jhessail sighed and turned away without a farewell. "Let's go on. I want to see Shadowdale."

Silently they started trudging along the road again. The red-haired mage walked along with her head bent, her eyes on the toes of her boots.

Florin stretched out a long arm that curled around her shoulders and gathered her against him. "Hey, Jhess," he said. "We've been through all this *together*. Remember that, lass."

And suddenly, out of nowhere, Jhessail discovered that she wanted to cry.

Here ends Book III of the tales of the Knights of Myth Drannor.

FORGOTTEN REALMS

Ed Greenwood Presents

Waterdeep

BLACKSTAFF TOWER
STEVEN SCHEND

MISTSHORE
JALEIGH JOHNSON

DOWNSHADOW
ERIK SCOTT DE BIE
APRIL 2009

CITY OF THE DEAD
ROSEMARY JONES
JUNE 2009

THE GOD CATCHER
ERIN M. EVANS
FEBRUARY 2010

CIRCLE OF SKULLS
JAMES P. DAVIS
JUNE 2010

Explore the City of Splendors through the eyes of authors
hand-picked by FORGOTTEN REALMS® world creator Ed Greenwood.

They engulf civilizations.
They thrive on the fallen.
They will cover all trace of your passing.

THE WILDS

THE FANGED CROWN
Jenna Helland

THE RESTLESS SHORE
James P. Davis
May 2009

THE EDGE OF CHAOS
Jak Koke
August 2009

WRATH OF THE BLUE LADY
Mel Odom
December 2009

FORGOTTEN REALMS

THOMAS M. REID

THE EMPYREAN ODYSSEY

What could bring a demon to the gates of heaven?

Book I
The Gossamer Plain

Book II
The Fractured Sky

Book III
The Crystal Mountain
July 2009

What could bring heaven to the depths of hell?

"Reid is proving himself to be one of the best up and coming authors in the FORGOTTEN REALMS universe."
—fantasy-fan.org

TRACY HICKMAN
Presents

The Anvil of Time

The Sellsword
Cam Banks

The Survivors
Dan Willis

Renegade Wizards
Lucien Soulban
March 2009

The Forest King
Paul B. Thompson
June 2009

The lost stories of Krynn's history are coming to light.